John Wilcox was born in Birmingham and worked as a journalist for some years before being lured into industry. In the mid-nineties he sold his company in order to devote himself to his first love, writing. He has published two works of non-fiction, PLAYING ON THE GREEN and MASTERS OF BATTLE; THE HORNS OF THE BUFFALO is his first work of fiction.

Also by John Wilcox

Playing on the Green
Masters of Battle
(Non-Fiction)

The Horns
of the Buffalo

John Wilcox

headline

First published in 2004
by HEADLINE BOOK PUBLISHING

First published in paperback in 2004
by HEADLINE BOOK PUBLISHING

9

ISBN 978-0-7553-0983-2

Typeset in Times by Avon DataSet Ltd,
Bidford-on-Avon, Warwickshire

Printed and bound in Great Britain by
Clays Ltd, St Ives plc

Headline's policy is to use papers that are natural, renewable and
recyclable products and made from wood grown in sustainable
forests. The logging and manufacturing processes are expected to
conform to the environmental regulations of the country of origin.

HEADLINE BOOK PUBLISHING
A division of Hodder Headline
338 Euston Road
London NW1 3BH

www.headline.co.uk
www.hodderheadline.com

For Betty

Acknowledgements

A first novel is very special and I owe a debt of gratitude to a small group of people who helped to bring it to publication.

My agent, Jane Conway-Gordon, believed in it, gave constant encouragement and helped me prepare it for presentation to Headline, where Marion Donaldson further fine-tuned it with gentle competence. The staff of London Library were patient, as ever, in assisting me to step back in time with, I hope, a fair degree of accuracy. In Cape Town, the large and happy family of publisher Alan Ramsay informed me on all things South African and, in particular, Alan's daughter Elize Ramsay guided this ignorant townie through the flora and fauna of the country. Lastly, I must thank my wife Betty, for not only trudging round old battlefields without complaint but also for proofreading so many pages and for knowing when to say, 'You've gone a bit too far here, I think . . .'

J.W.
Chilmark,
July 2003

Prologue

1865

He broke out of the woods at a gallop and pulled up on the edge of a large field. Quickly he studied the terrain ahead and then cantered cautiously across the meadow towards the house that lay at its corner. Reaching the cover of an ivy-covered wall that fringed a formal garden, he spurred again, head down, along its warm red length, until he gained the shelter of a coppice. It was there that he met the soldier.

The infantryman was young and clearly near to exhaustion. His Confederate grey hardly seemed a uniform, so tattered was it, and the rifle slung across his back had hooked upon branches that had torn away as he ran through the undergrowth. He scarcely had breath to speak.

'Thank God I've found you, Colonel. Message from General Lee, sir.'

'What?'

'The General says, sir, that the Yankees have captured the village ahead and that Grant is pourin' in men to hold the ford. Sir, you are to take your regiment and mount a 'mediate attack across the river an' move 'em all out.'

'Do they have cannon?'

'Yessir. Two batteries up on the top o' the hill by the post office.'

The rider's eyes narrowed as he weighed up his chances. If he made a frontal attack across the ford it would mean death for most of his command. From the hill the Northern guns could rake the crossing and the Yankees by now were probably entrenched in the gardens that flanked the main village road. Consequently they could add rifle fire to the cannonade from the hill. It would be a blood bath. But there was no other way across the river.

'Can General Lee give me any more men?'

'No, sir. General says you'll have to do it without reinforcements. He can't spare no men. But he says, sir, that he knows you can do it.'

'Does he now.' His thoughts ran ahead to consider the possibilities. Perhaps if he made a token attack at the ford, sufficient to keep the enemy occupied and draw his fire, he could take his main body of men across round Cooper's Hill, down through Long Eaton and . . .

'Simon. Simon. Where are you?'

The woman's voice came from the big house. Reluctantly he walked out of the coppice so that he could be seen.

'Yes, Mama. I'm here.'

'What are you doing?'

'Only playing, Mama.'

The boy bent down and pulled up his sock so that it met his knickerbockers and ran fingers through his hair. It was important not to be untidy.

'Please come here immediately.'

Simon Fonthill, ten years old, brevet colonel in General Lee's Army of Northern Virginia, obediently trotted across the lawn to where his mother stood at the French windows. She was tall and her dress of purple brocade brushed the ground. Her hair was pulled back into a severe bun and her eyes, which now gazed upon her son without any obvious sign of warmth, were of light blue. The mouth was wide and the overall impression was one of directness, self-possession and honesty. Unlike the rebel soldier in the coppice, it was clear that *she* was not to be commanded.

'I will not have you running around the grounds like a barbarian. What about your holiday composition?'

'I have finished it, Mama. And Papa said that I could go and play as it was a sunny day.'

Mrs Fonthill frowned slightly at the mention of her husband. The frown deepened as she saw the slight tear in the knicker-bockers where the hawthorn had done its best to slow the fast gallop through the wood.

'You have torn your trousers. Go immediately to your room, take them off and give them to Sarah to be mended. You will not be having tea today. But . . .' she called him back as he began to trudge indoors, 'your father wishes you to have dinner with us tonight. We have guests from the regiment coming. Ask Sarah to fill a bath for you and make sure that you wash yourself thoroughly.'

'Yes, Mama.'

The staircase was wide and balustraded sensuously in great curves. From one of these he had once single-handedly fought back a horde of Indian sepoy mutineers who had attempted to take the first floor in an attack from the kitchen. He climbed the stairs now, not as disconsolately as the loss of tea would normally have made him. To have dinner with his parents was rare, particularly if Papa was having fellow officers from the regiment. Then, immediately, he felt that familiar surge in his stomach, that moment of breathlessness as though his heart had dropped a couple of inches and the rest of his body was trying to adjust; a second or two of sheer panic. Fear took him as he faced the prospect. He was being put on show. His father was parading him before his colleagues. Why? Was it because he wanted them to inspect him and report back? Did Papa think that he would not be good enough to go into the regiment?

At the top of the stairs he paused. It was here that he had wrestled with the last mutineer and killed him by plunging a penknife into his armpit. Simon attempted to rationalise the prospect ahead – to weigh the pros and cons. It was a system he had worked out when first his heart had dropped those inches, some years ago. Was it *so* bad? Perhaps his father just felt that he was now old enough to begin to have dinner properly with them in the evening. Or – happy, warming thought – was Papa becoming rather proud of him and wanted to show him off?

He walked to his room more lightly. But the doubts returned as he sat on the edge of his hard bed. Mama suspected. She had tried, so obviously, to inject courage the first time she had taught him to jump his pony in the paddock: 'Dig in your heels and lift him, boy. Attack the jump. Go for it. No, no. The horse knows you're frightened, so he'll be frightened too. Simon, *don't be frightened.*'

His eyes filled with tears at the memory and he bent his head to hide them from Sarah as she bustled in.

'Come on, Master Simon,' she urged. 'Don't sit around mopin' like. Take them knickerbockers off and give 'un to me. They got to be mended. Get a move on. We've got to 'ave our bath yet. I've run it for you.'

4

Sarah was from Wiltshire and didn't much approve of living in Brecon, on the Welsh Borders, which she regarded as being on the edge of Celtic barbarity. But she liked her work. There was not too much to do with only Major and Mrs Fonthill in the house and their only child Simon when on holiday from school. And she was fond of Simon. She liked his shyness and his air of uncertainty. They allowed her to hustle and pretend to bully and be in command. Which, as a rather plump housemaid of twenty-two, she was rarely able to do with other folk.

She looked sympathetically at Simon. ' 'Ere, you ain't bin cryin', 'ave you?'

Simon straightened up. 'Of course not. Here, have the trousers. I must have my bath.'

He threw them on the bed and then discarded his shirt, under-vest, long drawers and woollen socks. He wound a huge towel round his thin body and walked along the landing to the new bathroom, whose plumbing was a source of much respect for Mrs Fonthill in the county. At the door, he whipped out a dagger from a fold in his burnous and plunged it into the breast of an Arab who lunged at him with a scimitar, before entering the steam-filled room.

It was hot, the water. Scalding hot, in fact. The bathroom was one of the first to be installed in the Borders and the temperature controls were erratic, to say the least. But it was a great luxury to have hot water piped right to the bath, without the fuss and inconvenience of bringing great saucepans of water from the copper in the scullery. Simon peered through the steam. More cold was needed, and he groped for the big handle with the C embossed on the hub. How much to pour? How to judge? Touch it, of course. He did so with his right forefinger. Excruciating.

The Pathan chief smiled at him from the corner of the room. 'If you don't tell us where your cavalry is camped,' he purred, 'then we will boil you very slowly. Your skin will peel.' He gestured to two of his tribesmen, who appeared through the steam. 'Never,' said Simon. 'Throw him in,' said the Pathan.

A test. A test of courage. To see if he had . . . what was it the games master called it? Yes, grit. That was it. He would put his hand into the bath water *before* he added the cold. And he would hold it there to prove to himself that he was brave, that he was good enough to be a soldier, like his father and grandfather. Then he could face the officers downstairs at dinner. Face them *knowing* he was all right.

Simon knelt by the side of the great curved bath and put his hand into the steam. The water looked black and the steam made his face perspire. At least, he *thought* it was the steam. He held his hand just above the surface and tentatively dipped a fingertip into the water, and held it there for a second. Aaargh! The pain was immediate and he snatched his hand away. The Pathan chief was grinning. 'No,' the boy cried. 'No. I can do it.' Again he put the hand into the steam and lowered it to the water. And there it stayed, an inch above the surface, shaking as he willed himself to immerse it.

Slowly he sank back, his hand wet from the steam but not from the water. He had failed the test. Thankfully the Pathan had disappeared. There was only the boy to contemplate his failure.

He was a coward, without question. He would never make a soldier. He groped for the cold tap as the tears mingled with sweat on his cheeks.

Later, after the bath had worked its gentle, reviving magic, the old rationality came to his help. The bath test had really been torture, hadn't it? And good, brave soldiers often succumbed under torture. This was well known. You could be brave and give in when tortured. He had overheard his father relate how sepoys had done terrible things to captured English officers during the Mutiny. His spirits lifted further as he thought of his father. In India, Papa had won the Queen's new medal for the bravest of the brave, the Victoria Cross. But he now refused to hunt, which meant that Mama rode out alone. Papa certainly could not be a coward, so it wasn't the jumps that frightened him, although he didn't like certain things. For instance, he hated thunder. Simon felt much better.

A murmur of voices from below indicated that the guests had arrived, and he tiptoed to the edge of the stairs to see. Beneath, the wide hall shone in the early evening spring sunlight. Indian rugs were scattered across the tiled floor, and the subcontinent's influence was further marked by the tiger head mounted on the wall. Under it, tall shoots of pampas grass emerged erect as sentinels from matching terracotta urns. Opposite, two aspidistras squatted stoutly in porcelain vases, resting on twin tables whose mahogany had been polished until it gleamed.

Mrs Fonthill was at the door welcoming her guests. She looked handsome rather than pretty in her dinner gown, the black velvet showing off well her white skin and the pearls at her throat. Anyone who did not know her better would say that she was gently flirting with the two captains of the second regiment of the 24th Foot who smiled stiffly before her.

'How very good of you to come,' she said. 'And how kind of the Colonel to spare you both from the depot. Who on earth will be left there to protect us from the Russians?'

The taller of the two took her hand and brushed it with his long moustaches. 'Covington, B Company, ma'am. Have no fear. I think the Rooskies are too busy planning to take India from us to attack us at home right now.'

The sally brought polite laughter from them all and Simon, looking down, marvelled at how handsome the officers looked in their white and scarlet mess jackets and extravagantly tight blue trousers looped under their insteps. Mrs Fonthill gave her hand to the other captain and then walked them along the hallway.

'It's a pleasant evening, so do come through to the conservatory,' she said. 'Sarah will bring you sherry or whisky and George will be with you in a moment. He's just gone to the wine cellar. Forgive me if I also leave you for just one minute. I need a word with Cook.'

They bowed as she turned away at the conservatory door. 'Oh.' She came back. 'I hope you don't mind, but our son will be joining us for dinner. I know it is slightly unusual – he's only ten – but George, er, wants to bring him along a little. He won't stay for coffee, of course.'

The officers bowed again and disappeared into the conservatory, followed by Sarah, blushing and anxious to please.

Simon crept quietly down the stairs, through the side door and out into the garden. He approached the conservatory treading softly, using all the training acquired during his years as a British spy on the North West Frontier, and was relieved to find a tall window open. The two Russian emissaries were speaking in low, guarded voices, but he could hear every word.

'Fine woman, that,' said the captain with the long moustaches.

His companion wore a monocle and ginger sideburns, which he had brushed forward in the approved style of the day. 'I should say.' He leaned forward conspiratorially. 'To be frank, can't quite see what she sees in a major on half-pay.'

'Yes, particularly one who's got a bit of a yeller streak.'

'Oh I say, that's goin' a bit far, ain't it? The feller did get a VC in the Mutiny.'

Covington tasted his sherry through the sieve of his moustaches. 'But weren't the circumstances a bit peculiar? I mean, he was knocked off his horse and, as far as I hear, flailed about him with his sabre like a madman in a blue funk. It was just a coincidence that his colonel was lyin' nearby and a section came back to get 'em both. Everyone thought at first he had gone back for the CO, but he confessed later that he'd been knocked down. They gave him the medal almost straight away. But there were second thoughts afterwards. Couldn't exactly take it off him, though, could they? Strange business.'

'Ah. Is this why he's known as Wobbly Fonthill?'

'Quite. And because he's given up 'untin'. They say he can't take the fences any more. But a damned nice chap for all that. Just not cut out to be a soldier, perhaps. Not really, well, gutsy enough – and the men sense it. That's why he's on half-pay, I suppose. They live on her money, I think. She's said to be quite ri—'

They were interrupted as Major Fonthill entered the room, apologetic and slightly flustered that his guests had arrived during his absence. Beneath the window outside, Simon lay down and silently buried his face in the long grass to hide the hot tears.

Chapter 1

1876

Simon Fonthill slowly drifted out of sleep and opened one eye and then the other. The whiteness was strong and dazzled him at first, so he closed his eyes again for a moment. Then, cautiously, he lifted his head from the pillow and looked around. He was alone in the room. He widened his gaze to take in the details. White, very white walls, unrelieved by pictures or any other form of decoration. One window with, in the distance, a glimpse of a green hill. Under the window a wooden table, with bowl and jug, white again, placed precisely on the table top. Another bed, empty, but the blankets severely squared above the three piled 'biscuit' mattresses. Beyond that a green painted wardrobe. Nothing else. He listened carefully. Not a sound.

He lowered his head back on to the pillow. The ache had gone now and so had that pervasive drowsiness that had slipped him in and out of sleep for . . . how long? He could not be sure. Blinking in the light – it must be midday or early afternoon – Simon looked on the table in vain for his timepiece. Perhaps it was in the wardrobe. He began to pull at the sheets and blankets which encased him, then thought better of it. Instead he called out.

'Hello. Hello. Anyone there?'

The words came out little stronger than conversational in level, but they echoed through the emptiness of the room. Almost immediately, however, Simon heard the clump of army boots approaching along a corridor and then an orderly came through the door. He was crisp in white jacket above blue patrol trousers, and when he spoke his voice was redolent of Welsh valley and chapel.

'Did you call, Mr Fonthill, sir? Good. You must be gettin' better.'

'Where exactly am I?'

'Hospital, sir. Depot hospital.'

'Is the regiment here?'

'Marched out yesterday and sailed this morning, sir. For the Cape of South Africa, see, to fight the black Kaffirs there.'

Simon raised a hand to his head. 'Ah yes. I remember now. So how long have I been here, then?'

The orderly sucked in his thick black moustache. 'Ohh, about three days, I think it is, sir. An' you lyin' there, 'ardly stirrin' so they didn't know what was wrong with you, see.' His voice rose gently at the end of each sentence, in that mellifluous Welsh intonation, as though every phrase conveyed soft indignation.

'Yes. Yes. I think I had better see the doctor, if you can find him.'

The orderly munched his moustache. 'I'll see if Surgeon Major Reynolds is about, sir.' He turned and crashed down the corridor.

Lying back on his pillow, Simon closed his eyes in reflection. So the regiment had sailed without him! Well, he supposed it was inevitable. It could hardly wait for a young subaltern to regain his health and composure. When he was fit, would they send him on to the Cape? A special posting? He turned his head impatiently. This begged the question, would the regiment value him enough to take that sort of trouble with a second lieutenant?

Unseeingly, his gaze wandered over the ceiling as he reviewed his brief career. Sandhurst Military College, graduation and then posting, some eleven months ago, to the 1st Battalion of the 24th Regiment of Foot, his father's old regiment, here at its depot at Brecon on the Welsh Borders. How had he performed? Well . . . he still couldn't sit a horse with confidence, but he had enjoyed his regimental duties: leading his platoon on exercises in the hills, picket duty, firing on the range, evenings in the mess, the relationship with the men – everything but the damned riding. Now this. A setback, of course. How would it look on his record? The thought lay heavily on him as he drifted off again into a light sleep.

He was wakened by a firm hand lifting his wrist and the strong odour of tobacco. He opened his eyes and looked into the iron visage of Surgeon Major Reynolds a few inches away: a heavily bearded face with hard blue eyes and hair that swept back from the brow in firmly set grey waves.

The doctor stood silently for a moment, one hand taking Simon's pulse, the other holding a watch. Eventually he transferred his gaze to Simon's face. 'Put your tongue out, boy.'

Simon did so, and half retched as a spatula rudely forced his tongue down. Then the doctor pulled down the lower lid of his right eye before the hand, rough to the skin, checked the temperature of his brow. Reynolds raised the spatula and held it before Simon's gaze. 'Follow this with your right eye as I move it,' he commanded. Simon did so without difficulty.

'Now the other eye.' The exercise was completed.

The doctor sat down on the edge of the bed. 'Well,' he said, ill-humouredly, his voice more distantly echoing the Welshness of the orderly, 'I'm damned if I know what's wrong with you. As far as I can see, you've been unconscious for three days with only a slight temperature to show for it.' He scowled down at Simon. 'Seemed like a slight fever. Ever been in the East?'

'No, sir.'

'Never had typhoid or typhus? No fits in your family – epilepsy?'

'Good lord, no, sir.'

'You've never turned yellow – been diabetic?'

'No, sir.'

'Can you sit up – swing your legs over the side of the bed?'

'I think so.' Simon broke the restrictions of the tucked-in blankets and put his legs over the side of the bed. With the back of a penknife Reynolds tapped just below the kneecap of both legs in turn. Reactively, Simon's feet swung.

'Reflexes are fully back, anyway,' murmured the doctor. 'I've been sticking pins in you over the last three days and you've hardly moved, although . . .' Reynolds spoke as though to himself, 'you did shift a *little*.' He looked at Simon. 'How do you feel now?'

'A bit weak. But all right, I think.'

'Good.' The Surgeon Major walked a few paces to the door and noticed the orderly standing quietly in the corner. 'Don't need you, soldier,' he said curtly. 'Get out of here.'

'Sir.' The orderly sprang to attention and marched out of the room. The doctor returned to the bed and pushed Simon back under the blankets.

'Now,' he said. 'Your parents have been very concerned about you, of course, and I promised your father that I would let them know as soon as you surfaced. Do you feel strong enough to see them?'

'Yes, sir.'

'Very well. I will send a telegram to Major Fonthill right away.' He looked down at his patient with a quick, puzzled frown. 'You sure, boy, that you've never been in the East? India? The Malay States?'

Simon shook his head. 'I've only been abroad twice. Both times to France.'

'Um. Strange. Feel like food?'

'Yes please, sir. In fact, I feel quite hungry.'

'Do you now?' One grey eyebrow was raised. 'I'm not surprised after three days. Right. I'll see to it.' He turned and strode to the door.

'Sir.' Simon elbowed himself into a half-sitting position. 'I'm sorry, but I don't really remember becoming ill. Could you tell me . . .' His voice trailed away.

Reynolds came back to the bed. His face bore no expression and his voice was cold. 'Very well. What *do* you remember?'

'Being in the mess when the Adjutant came in and called us to attention and told us something about being posted abroad without delay, and then . . . I'm sorry, but I don't remember anything else, except drifting in and out of sleep here. Sometimes I was half aware of people around me, but nothing else. It's very strange.'

The doctor's eyebrow rose again. 'You're damned right it's strange.'

Simon sensed a pejorative note in Reynolds's voice. There was no solicitude in his attitude. Simon felt himself colouring.

'What do you mean, sir?'

Reynolds was silent for a moment. 'Well, when the Adjutant announced the news that the 1st Battalion was being shipped in three days' time, to handle an emergency with the black tribesmen of the Cape, you suddenly collapsed and became unconscious. Try as I might, I could neither revive you nor diagnose your illness. No sign of diabetes or poisoning – just a slight temperature, although you did not toss or turn. You just lay there, dammit, breathing steadily.'

He scratched fingers through a pepper-and-salt beard. 'We asked your parents for help but they couldn't enlighten us from your past medical history. Apart from being what they called "a sensitive, rather imaginative boy",' he emphasised the phrase heavily, 'it seems you were fit enough, and certainly you've had no health problems while you've been with the battalion.' He turned and walked to the door once more. 'Now you've regained consciousness just after your regiment has embarked. One thing's for sure, then, laddie – they've gone off without you.' Then he was gone.

Simon sank back on to the pillow and heard the doctor's quick step recede down the wooden-floored corridor, like the tap of a side-drum.

He looked out at the hill framed in the window. Surgeon Major Reynolds had a reputation as a hard man. He had gained glory as a young surgeon at Inkerman in 1854 when he had carried out twenty-four amputations in the rain under heavy Russian fire. Mess gossip had it that his perception of bravery was based on his memories of that day and of how his patients had borne the knife. Since then, malingerers had always received short shrift from him. Simon turned restlessly to the wall. Did the doctor think that *he* was malingering now?

The thought made him indignant. Well, damn the man! He would prove him wrong. Was he ill now? Let's see. Slowly Simon raised first one leg and then the other, breaking loose the stern envelope of blanket and sheet that encased him. Nothing wrong there. He elbowed himself upright and cautiously pushed back the bedclothes and lowered one leg to the floor, then the other. For a moment he paused before transferring his weight and standing upright. This, he thought, is where I collapse again – but no, he could stand. Apart from that fuzzy feeling in the head, he felt quite fit and he easily retained his balance.

He was standing so, in his flannel nightgown, when the orderly entered, carrying a tray of porridge, tea and bread and butter.

'Oh, I think you'd be better back in bed, sir,' he said, his eyebrows raised solicitously. 'You bin out for a long time, look you, and you must get your strength back before you start marchin' about again. The doctor says you shouldn't eat anything too 'eavy to start with. Mind you,' he sniffed, 'eat *this* an' you won't be *able* to get out of the cot.'

Simon smiled and looked more closely at the po-faced orderly. He realised that the big moustache dressed the bright, lively countenance of a man not much older than himself – perhaps three or four years. Dark eyes and thick black hair revealed the Welshness and the upright bearing betrayed a few years' service, at least. The Welshman was short, about five inches shorter than Simon's five feet nine inches, but he was extremely thick-set and the powerful shoulders made him seem almost as wide as he was tall.

'What's your name?'

'Jenkins, sir, 352 Jenkins.'

'I don't want to know your damned number.'

'Beggin' your pardon, but you do, sir. See, there are seven Jenkinses in the depot holding company. We 'ave to use our last three to sort us out, look you.'

'Ah, yes.' Simon climbed back on to the hard bed and regarded the orderly with interest. Band boys or civilians usually did the medical orderly duties. What was this bright-eyed, obviously fit soldier doing in the depot hospital?

'Did you volunteer for this work? What's your regiment?'

Jenkins's face showed surprise at the question. 'The 24th, o' course, sir. Same as you. An' your battalion, too.'

Simon took a mouthful of porridge. Jenkins was right. It was awful. He grimaced. 'I don't remember seeing you before. What the devil are you doing here on hospital duty?'

For the first time the confident Jenkins looked slightly disconcerted. 'Ah well, sir. I got busted is the truth of it, see.' He pushed a rueful finger into his ear. 'I was a corporal but I had just a drink or two and lost me stripes. But it was me 'ittin' a colour sergeant which really did it, look you an' I've bin in detention in Aldershot for a year, until yesterday. The regiment was all packed up and it was too late to take me, so they've stuck me in 'ere. Nobody seems to know what to do with me, see.' The brown face broke into a grin.

Simon tried not to grin back but failed. Aldershot meant the army's new central detention centre, gaining fame already as 'the Glasshouse', because of its glass-fronted design. It was also feared as a hell-hole.

'Serves you right,' he said. 'Hit a senior NCO, did you? Lucky you weren't flogged.'

'Ah, no, sir. They stopped that six years ago, look you, except for offences committed on active service, an' then you can only get fifty lashes, and I weren't on active service, see, though it's true I was actively 'ittin' Colour Sergeant Cole.'

'That's enough – and don't lecture me on army law.' Simon tried another mouthful of the gruesome porridge. The orderly, quite unabashed by the rebuke, looked on interestedly. He showed no sign of wishing to leave. 'How do you know so much about Queen's Regulations anyhow?'

Private Jenkins's face lit up. 'I've bin studyin' for my certificate, see.'

Simon allowed himself to look puzzled. He had known about the reform of flogging, although not about the fifty lashes limit. There was more to this young soldier than met the eye. 'Certificate. What certificate?'

'It's the Army Certificate of Education, see,' said Jenkins proudly. 'It's not that I couldn't read, though . . .' his face screwed into a frown, 'sometimes I 'ad a bit of trouble with the big words, so I started about three years ago. I was doin' quite well till I was busted, like, but at the end of my time at Aldershot they let me 'ave a few books and a bit of candle to read by at night. There wasn't much time during the day, see.'

Simon smiled. 'I am sure there wasn't. Not in the Glasshouse. Bad, was it?'

The black eyes sparkled. 'Could 'ave bin worse, sir. Better than 'ome, anyhow.'

'All right. That will be all, Jenkins.'

'Sir.' The orderly crashed to attention, spun smartly – perhaps a little too ostentatiously – and marched to the door.

'I suppose,' Simon called after him, 'that we are both rather in the same boat now.'

'That's just what I was thinkin', sir,' said Jenkins, beaming.

And he strode purposefully down the corridor, the thump of his boots echoing back into the room.

The porridge, heavy as it was, made Simon realise how hungry he had been. He lay back on the bed and tried to order his thoughts once again. What now? He had never collapsed before. Would it happen again, whenever he was presented with something . . . disconcerting? Was it the old complaint of childhood which he thought he had overcome years ago? Or was there some recent event which had weakened him? No. Regimental life had been uneventful. True, he had taken a fall from his horse out on the Beacons a few weeks ago which had knocked him out temporarily. But, apart from a brief headache, there had been no bad after-effects. Far more uncomfortable had been the dinner party his parents had given at their house just outside Brecon for their old friends and neighbours the Griffiths. The visitors had brought their twenty-year-old daughter. Her manner had been restrained and somehow hostile. Perhaps she resented what might have seemed to be match-making by his mother. Perish the thought! But his mind was wandering, and after a few moments more of disjointed speculation, he slipped back into sleep.

A diffident knock on the door woke him. He knew the visitor's identity immediately and he smiled that, while others announced their arrival up that corridor like a battalion on the march, his father was able to arrive so quietly.

Major George Fonthill entered and stood at the door smiling at his son. His hair was now grey but it remained plentiful and he wore it long, so that it curled around his collar. His brown eyes were set widely apart and his mouth was full, giving his face an open, even ingenuous look. He wore a frock coat and carried a top hat. Only the erect posture betrayed an ex-soldier.

He approached the bed. 'My dear boy, I am so glad that you are feeling better.'

Simon struggled upright. 'Papa. How good of you to come.'

Rather self-consciously, the two shook hands. It was clear that they were father and son. Simon's brown eyes carried the same half-hidden look of uncertainty and his face had a similar open roundness, although the son had inherited his mother's firm mouth and squareness of jaw. The fact that father and son were both unfashionably clean-shaven marked further their resemblance.

'Mama is not with you?'

'No.' Major Fonthill smiled shyly, as though sharing a confidence. 'She is, of course, out riding, although the hunting season has finished, thank goodness. Reynolds's telegram came after she had left, so I pencilled her a note and came straight away. Had to take the dog cart. But never mind about that. How do you feel now?'

'Quite well, really. Still a bit weak and not exactly topping, but much better. In fact, I feel a bit of a fraud.'

They smiled at each other awkwardly. Simon looked hard into his father's face. Did he suspect him of . . . of deliberately avoiding the draft? It was not the sort of thing he would normally discuss with him. The few deeply felt matters that had arisen over the years had always lain unspoken between them. Simon decided to grasp the nettle: 'Father, what have they told you about my illness? About how it happened and all that?'

Major Fonthill frowned. 'Not much really. It all seemed rather peculiar. Reynolds at first thought you had contracted malaria or something like that, but you have never been to the tropics, and although I caught the thing out in India, I

21

understand that it is not hereditary. Anyway, it seems that you have not shown symptoms of high fever.'

The Major leaned forward in his chair. 'I am afraid that you have missed the show out in the Cape, because they immediately posted one of the subalterns from the 2nd Battalion to fill the gap. I am so sorry, my boy. It's very bad luck.' Then his face brightened. 'But the most important thing is that you seem to have got through the worst now and whatever it is that hit you has receded. I would say that you will be up and about soon. I expect that they will gazette you now to the 2nd, who are in Warwick but who are expected back here to do depot duty for a while.'

As he spoke, the Major's face reflected the meaning of the words, like the sun reappearing from behind a cloud. Simon thought – not for the first time – that his father would probably find it impossible to dissemble, even if his life depended upon it. He decided to test him.

'Are they gossiping about me here in the depot?' he asked in a low voice. 'Was there talk in the regiment before it embarked?'

Major Fonthill's smile disappeared but he held his son's gaze. 'Yes, I believe that some scuttlebutt nonsense was begun, but the senior officers soon stamped it out. You know what a mess can be like.'

Simon swallowed. 'Yes, but did they say that I was a coward and that I faked this illness to avoid being posted abroad and going on active service?'

The Major shifted slightly in his chair. 'I doubt it, and if they did, no one would really have believed it, you know. A bit of idle speculation, nothing more.' The older man's face lightened again. 'Anyway, by jove, it would have taken some consummate acting by you to carry the thing through for three days, eh? What?' He chortled. 'You always were a bit of a fantasist as a boy, but, really...'

Simon pushed himself further upright. 'Father, I cannot understand why I collapsed. I don't remember feeling ill at all before the Adjutant came into the room.' He hesitated for a moment. 'Could it have been that I was suddenly so frightened by the thought of having to fight the Kaffirs that I collapsed – in fear?'

In his straightforward way the Major considered the question. 'Never heard of such a thing in my time in the service,' he said. 'Cowardice is usually expressed in a different sort of way. Chaps sometimes get into a blue funk and, er, shout a bit. But I have never heard of someone actually folding up, so to speak, without a word.'

Slowly he turned his head and gazed out of the window. 'But then fear takes many different forms. I am sure that we are all afraid in our lives – probably many, many times.' His voice dropped a little. 'But soldiers are all so well trained that they rarely show it. Fear is a perfectly natural emotion and I think that it might be better, sometimes, if we recognised it occasionally, rather than, well, bottling it up. Perhaps we should face it openly and even, perhaps, give into it sometimes if we really must.' He looked round in sudden embarrassment. 'Not, that is, if we let the side down by doing so. That would be reprehensible. One must recognise one's responsibilities to one's fellows, of course.'

'Of course.' Simon nodded and carefully studied his father's features. Was he – could he have been – about to admit that he himself had been afraid in the past? Was this why he had given up hunting? Would it be offensive to ask? He and his father had

23

never discussed anything of a particularly profound nature. Their closeness had been intuitive and whatever empathy lay between them had never been acknowledged formally. It was difficult, now, to be personal. But Simon resolved to try. 'Papa,' he began.

Major Fonthill held out a hand and rose to his feet. 'I think we have talked enough for the moment, Simon. I have been warned not to tire you. But I shall be back with your mother as soon as we are allowed.' He proffered his hand. 'Goodbye, my boy.'

'Goodbye, Father.'

The next few days passed as slowly as they do only when boredom and inactivity predominate. Simon's strength returned quickly and both parents came to see him, observing a studied informality – although his mother, grey-haired now but as handsome as ever, could not contain herself for long.

'What made you ill, Simon?'

'I am sorry, Mama. No one seems to know.'

'Don't be silly, dear boy.' She smoothed the folds of her linen day dress with a controlled movement. 'The doctors surely must have some idea.'

Simon felt trapped on the bed, like a butterfly being dissected. 'I am sorry, Mother, but they don't. Surgeon Reynolds says that he could understand it if I had picked up some kind of malarial infection in the East, but as you know, I have never been there.' He laughed uneasily. 'Perhaps it was just a case of too much port in the mess.'

His mother arched an eyebrow. 'Don't be ridiculous. Men don't lie unconscious for several days because they have had too much port. I want to know—'

She was interrupted by a firm knock on the door. Jenkins entered and coughed apologetically.

'Sorry to interrupt, sir, but there's a message from Surgeon Major Reynolds.'

'Yes, Jenkins.'

'Just to say, sir, that he is anxious that your visitors don't stay too long and, er, make you excited, see.'

Major and Mrs Fonthill swung round in surprise. The Major examined the orderly, who returned his gaze with an air of huge innocence. 'But we've only just arrived, man.'

'Ah yes, sir. But Mr Fonthill's still under strict observance, er, observation, see. His temperature is very, sort of, delicate, isn't it.'

The Major shrugged his shoulders. 'Oh, very well. We shall be back on Friday, Simon. Perhaps you will feel better then.'

Simon struggled up. 'But I feel all right . . . Oh well, yes, of course. Thank you both for coming.'

His mother brushed his forehead with her lips and both parents took their leave, Mrs Fonthill completely ignoring Jenkins, who stood aside deferentially, coming to attention as the Major nodded to him.

As their footsteps sounded down that echoing corridor, Jenkins made to follow them.

'Oh no you don't, Jenkins.' Simon swung his feet to the floor. 'You were listening at the door, weren't you?'

The little Welshman drew himself up and seemed, in the process, to grow wider by the foot. 'Me, sir? No, never. I got something better to do than snoop at keyholes, Mr Fonthill sir.'

'Right, then. Fetch me Surgeon Major Reynolds.'

Jenkins looked stoically at the wall behind Simon's right ear. 'Can't do that, sir. 'E's gone 'untin'.'

Wearily, Simon climbed back on to the bed. 'No he hasn't. The hunting season is over. Get out of here, Jenkins, you confounded scoundrel.'

'Ah, very good, sir.'

Within seven days, Surgeon Major Reynolds's patience failed him and he gave up the quest for the cause of Simon's collapse. The subaltern was allowed to return home to complete his convalescence in the warm redbrick house on the Brecon hills. The spring weather was sunny and unseasonally dry. Simon began walking and then riding again in the Beacons, and Sarah continued to fuss over him, but no further mention was made of his illness. He was informed that he had been granted a month's leave and that the matter of his future was being considered by the Duke of Cambridge's staff at Horse Guards in London. Major Fonthill saw little of his son, his days taken up with the running of the small estate which surrounded the house. His mother, however, often took tea with him in the garden to rehearse on him her Whiggish attacks on the Disraeli government. The days passed slowly for Simon.

The invitation to dine at neighbours', then, was almost a relief. It was a return match for the occasion when the Griffith family had dined at the Fonthills', just before Simon's collapse. Brigadier Griffith had retired from the 24th Regiment at roughly the same time as Major Fonthill, although, unlike Fonthill, he had spent no time on half-pay. The two soldiers had served together in India and had established a comradeship there that had endured, despite Griffith's bluff lack of any intellectual interests and his inability to understand why his friend refused now to hunt. The chase and fly fishing in the nearby stony, gin-clear river dominated the lives of Brigadier and Mrs Griffith – that and the welfare of their only child, Alice.

The fact that both parents had single children, unusual for a time when families often numbered ten or more, also gave the Griffiths and the Fonthills a commonality. The matter was never discussed, of course, but it was apparent that both mothers had had particularly difficult confinements and that their husbands – again out of step with the times – had decided to make no further demands on them. Simon and Alice, however, had had no childhood friendship nor incipient romance. The Griffiths had only moved to the Borders three years ago and Alice had been away at school and Simon at Sandhurst or serving in the regiment for most of that time. Their first opportunity to talk, in fact, had occurred only six weeks before, at the Fonthills' dinner table. It had been a stilted affair and it was with mixed feelings, then, that Simon now contemplated the dinner engagement. It would be a chance to get out of the house, although he had no intention of dancing attendance on Alice Griffith all evening.

They rode the five miles to the Griffiths' home in an open carriage, so clement was the weather. Charlotte Fonthill sat bolt upright, tightly waisted in her favourite blue, with indigo pendant earrings framing her jaw line and gently swinging in rhythm to the rocking of the landau. Her husband and son, elegant in cutaway tails, faced her, leaning on their sticks, each lost in his thoughts. Far away a cuckoo celebrated the new summer, and to the left, flickering through the green brushwood, the River Wye gleamed below as it looped and twisted to accommodate the hill. The air was softened by new foliage that thrust forward everywhere. It was an evening of quiet gentleness and promise.

'Damn the Russians,' Mrs Fonthill suddenly exploded. 'They'll have India if we're not careful.'

Major Fonthill gave a sigh. 'I suggest, my dear, that we let the Government take care of India, just for tonight.'

Mrs Fonthill snorted but relapsed into silence and Simon and his father secretly exchanged half-smiles. Eventually they breasted a rise and Chilwood Manor appeared below them, nestling greyly against the green hill behind it. Brigadier Griffith welcomed them at the door and soon all was a bustle of greetings and divestment of coats and capes. Alice did not join her parents in the entrance hall but waited in the drawing room. As he entered, Simon saw a sturdy, fair-haired young woman, dressed in grey taffeta cut away at the shoulders to reveal a startlingly white décolletage. As far as he could tell, no cosmetics had been applied either to bosom or to the even-featured face, which was dominated by high cheekbones and steady eyes, as grey as the dress. Alice Griffith was not formally pretty – she was, perhaps, too strongly featured in that her jaw line was as firm as Simon's – but she was, Simon had to admit, looking attractive in the evening sunlight that filtered through the stone-framed windows.

'Good evening, Mr Fonthill,' said Alice, advancing, her hand extended, towards Simon. She saw before her a young man of medium height and slim build, with hair almost as fair as her own and with brown eyes set in an open, pleasant face. The eyes, however, did not hold hers and they quickly looked away as he took her white-gloved hand. 'I was so sorry,' she continued, 'to hear that you had been ill and I do hope that you are feeling better.'

Simon bowed low over her hand and then addressed the curtains behind her right shoulder. 'Thank you. I have recovered remarkably quickly and feel rather a charlatan now. I ought to be back with my regiment.'

The Brigadier bustled over. He had his daughter's directness of approach but towered over them both. 'Sorry to hear about all that, my boy,' he said, beckoning the footman to bring champagne. 'It must have been wretched to have missed the Cape boat.'

Simon fixed his gaze on the Brigadier's loosely knotted white tie. 'Oh, it was, sir. It was.'

'Any news of the Kaffir business?'

'Too early, sir. They may not even have landed yet.'

'Dashed bad luck for you. What exactly was the trouble?'

Simon looked desperately round the room. His father and mother were conversing with Mrs Griffith and the two other guests, the Reverend and Mrs Nathanial Harwood, before the elegant white fireplace. Glasses had just been filled so there was no rescue from the footman. He caught Alice's eye.

'Papa,' she said quickly, 'if I may say so, I do think it is rather unhelpful to ask a person about his illness when he is still trying to leave it behind him. I believe that we should talk to Mr Fonthill about other things. Even, if you must, the army.' And she gave them both a wide smile, revealing even white teeth.

Simon gave the girl a half-bow in acknowledgement and allowed himself a quick glance at her eyes. Was there just a hint of mischief behind that charming smile?

Dinner was grand by Brecon county standards. The Brigadier had inherited money and his farm tenants were adding to it quite acceptably. The rays of the late evening sun through the long window reflected in both the table silver and the rich mahogany. The leek soup was followed by poached halibut and then woodcock, served on great slabs of toasted bread soaked in brown gravy, which gave way, in turn, to a rack of Welsh lamb. The fare was rich and substantial, if not exactly elegantly served. Inevitably, Simon was placed next to Alice, but he contrived to spend most of his time talking to Mrs Harwood, on his left. Nevertheless, the table was small enough for them all to engage in general discussion which eventually, to Mrs Fonthill's delight, centred on the Russian threat to India.

Alice disconcerted the guests by cogently arguing – in the face of general opinion to the contrary around the table – against invading Afghanistan and so establishing a forward position in defence of India. Her articulate command of the military and political detail of the case clearly did not meet with the full approval of her parents who, Simon surmised, felt a little embarrassed at their daughter's domination of a debate more suitably conducted by men. It also surprised and rather daunted Simon, who remained silent, even when the argument – now rather one-sided – continued among the men after the ladies had retired to the drawing room.

Eventually the men rejoined the ladies and found Mrs Fonthill resisting bridge and arguing that good conversation was the best possible form of after-dinner entertainment. Avoiding direct disagreement, Mrs Griffith suggested that the company might first care to hear Alice play and sing. It was a clear attempt to reassure the guests that, despite her precocity, her daughter did possess more feminine accomplishments, and the gathering accepted the offer with polite acclamation. Simon noted that Alice showed no disinclination to perform and that she walked to the piano without hesitation.

She played with confidence but no obvious charm, accompanying herself in 'Where'er You Walk' and demonstrating a clear, strong voice without discernible vibrato. Her encore was a light piece from a current musical operetta. She sang it with style and a jauntiness which, once again, sat rather inappropriately on her young, provincial shoulders.

Leading the applause, which, Simon noted, was perhaps less than fulsome, Mrs Griffith rose to her feet. 'Charming, my dear,' she said. And then, with an almost desperate glance at the window, 'Now, why don't you show Simon the topiary before the light goes?'

Simon's heart sank and he looked with consternation at Alice. Again she surprised him. 'Of course, Mama,' she said and smiled at Simon. They left the room in an awkward silence.

The topiary was a monument to Mrs Griffith's determination and the skill and application of three gardeners. Silhouetted against the waning sun, green peacocks preened, lions crouched and pyramids pointed to the early stars.

Alice led him to the heart of it all and stopped. 'Well, what do you think of it?' she asked.

'Think of what?'

'The topiary.'

Simon looked about him in misery. 'It's . . . it's . . . very well done, isn't it?'

Alice scowled. 'No it isn't. I hate the bloody things.'

Simon's jaw dropped – as much at her intensity as her barrack-room language.

'Anyway,' she continued, 'I didn't want to show you this. I wanted to talk to you. I felt it was time we spoke.'

'Er, yes, of course.'

Alice stood quite close and gazed at him earnestly. She was flushing slightly and Simon felt that, in the fast-deepening twilight, she looked almost pretty.

'You know what's happening, don't you?' she demanded.

'Yes. Well, no. I . . . ah . . . am not quite sure that I do exactly.'

'Of course you do. They are trying to get us together.' Now she was frowning and she put her hand on his arm in emphasis. 'For some reason – and I suppose it is because our fathers are such good friends – our parents want us to get to know each other better so that . . .' she paused and blushed again, 'we will eventually fall in love and want to get married.'

Simon took a slightly alarmed half-step backwards. 'Ah. Yes. I see.'

Alice stamped her foot. 'Well, I hope you do. It is a terrible thing to do to two people. Why should I want to marry you one day just because my father served in the army with yours? It is intolerable. In any case, I don't wish to get married – probably ever. Do you?'

'Well, I don't know. Probably not. Not for a long time, anyway.'

'And you don't love me?'

'Er, well, as a matter of fact, I don't think I do. I'm terribly sorry.'

'Are you sure?'

'Yes . . . ah, that is, I think so. No. I am quite sure, thank you.'

'Good. How splendid.'

Despite her frown, the relief in Alice's face was luminous and they stood looking at each other, standing as close as lovers and gazing seriously into each other's eyes. It was Simon who first began to laugh, suddenly sensing not only the incongruity of the situation, but a great feeling of freedom, too. His laugh was infectious and Alice threw back her head and joined in.

Together they stood wheezing hilariously as the sun finally slipped beneath a Brecon peak and the topiary's shadows enclosed them.

'That's settled, then,' said Alice, taking a small lace-frilled handkerchief from her bag and wiping her eyes. 'I am so glad. This means that we can be friends – good friends, like our fathers. Doesn't it?'

Again that solemn, earnest look had settled on her face. Simon smiled at her. 'Of course it does,' he reassured. 'In fact, I would like that. Perhaps we can help each other.'

Four days after the Griffiths' dinner party, Simon received a telegram ordering him to report to Brecon Barracks in three days' time for, firstly, examination by Surgeon Major Reynolds and then interview with Lieutenant Colonel R. Covington, Commanding Officer of the 2nd Battalion, 24th Regiment of Foot.

'Covington,' mused Major Fonthill that evening at dinner. 'Yes. Never did know him very well, though I believe he was an ensign when I commanded a company. Strong fellow. Quite opinionated and not exactly subtle, I fear. But a stout enough soldier. Only just got command of the 2nd, I believe.' He turned to his wife. 'Didn't we have him to dinner, years ago?'

Mrs Fonthill looked vague. 'I'm afraid I can't remember, George. There were so many.'

'I believe that I remember him, Papa,' said Simon, looking ten years back to a small boy lying on the grass beneath a window. 'Big man with large moustaches?'

'That's the fellow. Not terribly bright, as I remember, but he's done well to get a command.'

For the appointment, Simon rode the ten miles to Brecon on his mother's best hunter. He felt the need to appear as soldierly as possible. Although the 24th was not a cavalry regiment – indeed, it was an infantry unit of some seniority, having been raised as long ago as 1689 – good horsemanship was a prime requirement for all officers. Throughout his short army career Simon had shown himself to be a good, even promising officer in most departments, distinguishing himself at languages, topography, military history, field tactics, fencing, marksmanship and mathematics at Sandhurst and displaying excellent man management as a platoon commander on appointment to the 1st Battalion. Equestrian skills, however, escaped him – to the continuing disgust of his mother and the mild amusement of his father. When he cantered between the stone pillars of the entrance to Brecon Barracks, then, he did so just a trifle gingerly.

The examination by Reynolds took little time. Without saying a word, the old doctor tapped his chest, recorded his temperature and repeated the eye and reflex exercises.

'Feel all right, then?' he asked eventually.

'Fine, sir.'

'Can you take up your duties again?'

'Yes, sir.'

The seamed face of Reynolds came within inches of Simon's. 'Yes, but do you want to – even if it means a posting abroad?'

'Of course, sir.'

The doctor looked at him expressionlessly for a moment, then turned and scribbled something on a white form.

'Here. I am passing you fit for duty. Don't you go collapsing again. Now go and see the Colonel.'

* * *

Shako helmet under his arm, left hand rigidly clasping his sword close to the blue line down his trousers, Simon stamped to attention before the grand mahogany desk behind which sat Lieutenant Colonel Covington. The Colonel took his time looking up and then examined the young officer languidly.

'At ease. You're Wobbly Fonthill's son, aren't you?'

'Sir? My father is Major George Fonthill VC, formerly of this regiment.'

'Yerse . . . Wobbly Fonthill. Yerse . . . I seem to remember dining at your house once. How is your father?'

'Very well, thank you, sir. He sends his regards to you.'

'Yerse, well. Please return them.' The Colonel stood up. The decade since he and Simon had last met had thickened his body, taking away a little of the elegance which had so distinguished the young captain. But the moustaches remained magnificent and the acquired bulk made him appear more formidable, less of a dandy and more a purposeful man of authority. The eyes were cold, however, and his tone remained languid and quite unfriendly. He walked slowly round Simon, a piece of paper in his hand.

'This means, I presume, that you are a gentleman's son?' He waved the paper.

'I don't, er, quite understand. But yes, of course, sir.'

'You don't understand and, well, neither do I. Why didn't you purchase your commission like a gentleman has always done?'

'Because, sir, as you may remember, the Cardwell Act abolished purchasing four years ago. I came in through Sandhurst after passing the army examination.'

'Ah yes, of course. You came in through school. I was forgetting.' The voice was soft and almost caressing. 'Had no trouble meeting your mess bills, I trust?'

For a moment, the direction of the Colonel's questions puzzled him. Then he understood. The Cardwell reform had raised a fear among serving officers that 'undesirable' lower-class officers would be afforded easy entry to the army, so lowering standards and even producing economic hardship among the new entrants. A second lieutenant's pay was only five shillings and threepence a day, which in some regiments hardly covered mess bills. Simon, however, received a personal allowance from his father to supplement his pay.

'Certainly not, sir.'

'Good. Good. Well, the army command at the Horse Guards want me to take you in the 2nd Battalion. I have to tell you that I'm damned reluctant to do so.'

'Sir?'

'You ought to be at the Cape with your own battalion, not here on depot duty.'

'I . . . I was ill, sir.'

'Were you now? Any complaint that I know of?'

'I am not aware of the nature of the illness, Colonel, but I believe it was some sort of fever. No doubt Surgeon Major Reynolds can enlighten you.'

'You know damn well that he can't.' The words came like a whiplash, directed at Simon from behind, a few inches from his right ear, all languid disinterest gone. 'I believe, Fonthill, that you are a malingerer and that you affected some kind of illness to avoid active service.'

The accusation struck Simon like a blow. The force of the words, their proximity – he felt a tiny particle of Covington's

36

saliva fall on his cheek – and precision, each syllable articulated with cutting care, made him flinch. His mind recoiled for a second and then indignation flooded in. He sprang to attention. 'That is quite untrue. I deny it and resent the insult. If you were my rank I would call you out – sir.'

'Well I'm not and you can't. Duelling is banned, as well you know.'

The Colonel walked casually back to his desk and sat down. He picked up a pen and idly tapped it on his fingernail. 'As I say, the powers-that-be have posted you to my battalion. You will have to serve with me if you want to stay in the 24th.' He leaned forward. 'The choice is yours. If you serve under me I shall drive you all the time. I shall see that no imputation of cowardice is levelled against you in the mess or anywhere else – that would spread unrest and I will not have any divergence away from our duty here. But you will have to prove yourself constantly. There will be no respite.

'Or, of course,' he sat back and balanced the chair on its back legs, one shining boot thrust on to the edge of the desk, 'you could apply for a transfer to another regiment. Or just resign your commission. As I say, the choice is yours. But you must make it now.'

Simon remained stiffly at attention, staring straight ahead. 'I need no time for consideration, sir. The 24th was the regiment of my father and of my grandfather. I wish to remain in it. I shall therefore serve under you.'

'Very well. Reynolds tells me that you seem to be fit. Report here tomorrow morning at six o'clock. You will be Officer of the Day. I shall inspect you personally before you go on duty. Good day.'

'Sir.' Simon wheeled and marched from the room, his mind

37

in such a turmoil that he had to be reminded by the Guard Sergeant to replace his shako before stepping out on to the parade ground. So the accusation had been made at last! In some ways it was a relief, in that it was better spoken than left to innuendo and gossip. Nevertheless, the shock was severe, like a hot iron pressed to the skin. He marched, erect, round the periphery of the parade square with no sense of direction or destination as his brain grappled with the situation. He had replied instinctively to the Colonel's challenge – and that was what it was, a deliberate provocation. Perhaps it would have been better to resign. Life with Covington was not going to be easy. But resignation would have been an admission of guilt, and he was never going to do that. In fact, he would do nothing to give that bastard pleasure . . .

'Mr Fonthill, sir.' His reverie was interrupted by a small, very thick-set soldier, dressed in blue patrols, who stepped into his path and offered a smart salute.

'Good to see you recovered, then, sir.' Simon frowned and concentrated on the dark brown face and wide moustache. The twinkle in the black eyes reminded him. 'Ah, Jenkins 352, isn't it?'

'The very same, sir. Glad to hear that you are joining the 2nd then.'

'How on earth did you know that?'

'Friend in the orderly room, see. I've been posted to the 2nd Battalion myself, so I'm out of the hospital now.'

'So I see. Well, good luck to you, Jenkins.'

Simon made to move on but the Welshman barred his way. 'Permission to make a request, sir,' he said, straightening his back and bristling to attention, so that his huge moustache made him look like an up-ended broom.

Simon looked at him quizzically. 'Request away, but I warn you, Jenkins, that I have no influence here.'

'No, sir. But you will be needin' a servant, isn't it? As an ex-NCO I don't fancy goin' back into the line. I'm lookin' for a change, see, and this would suit me perfectly, if you would 'ave me. And sir,' his black eyes looked directly into Simon's, 'from what I 'ear, you'll be needin' someone with a bit of experience like to look after you. And I *am* experienced and I *will* look after you.'

The two men regarded each other in silence for a moment. 'Thank you, Jenkins,' said Simon. 'You can be my servant. But I don't want a nanny, because I can look after myself in most things. Tell your colour sergeant that I have requested you.'

A smile split the brown face.

'But Jenkins . . .'

'Sir?'

'Don't hit him.'

'Oh no, sir. At least, not yet, sir.'

Private Jenkins saluted, rendered a perfect about-turn and marched away. Simon Fonthill watched him go, and somehow felt considerably better.

Chapter 2

1878

Jenkins entered the small room in the darkness, put down two mugs and fumbled to light a candle. He turned to the sleeping form on the wooden-framed bed and shook him. 'It's twenty before six, it's cold enough to freeze your armpits, here's your tea and I'm late wakin' you, so please 'urry.'

Simon sat up immediately and seized the tea mug. 'Why are you late?'

'Well, you're not the only one they're chasing, look you. Colour Sergeant gave me an hour in the cookhouse from half past four because they're very short of 'ands in there, or so 'e says.'

Simon dipped a shaving brush into the other mug and quickly lathered his face, barely covering it with soap before scraping it away with his cut-throat razor. 'Why did he pick on you? Didn't you do cookhouse duty last week?'

Jenkins's teeth flashed in the gloom. 'P'raps it's because I'm the prettiest.'

'Don't be so damned flippant.'

'What is flippant, then?'

'It's what you're being now.' Simon hurriedly wiped his face. 'Quick, hand me my boots.'

Jenkins crouched down and offered one gleaming riding boot and then pushed from the heel as Simon slipped his toes into it. 'No,' he said, looking up, 'what is flippant, then?'

'Oh, to hell with you and your certificate, 352. It means, er, trying superficially to be amusing. Quick, the other boot.'

'Well,' said Jenkins, performing the same service for the other foot, 'I don't know about bein' flippant, see, but you can talk, sir. They've made you do two picket duties already this week and now you're Orderly Officer again. Is the Colonel training you to be a field marshal, then?'

'Something like that, I think. But I am sorry that you seem to be getting more than your share. Where's my helmet?'

'No, it's not the helmet today, look you. The dress of the day for officers is the cap. I checked on it on the way 'ere an' just as well I did, 'cos it's been changed since last night.' He handed Simon the jaunty box-like blue cap, with its polished peak and big brass 24 on the front. 'Anyway, you once said that we were in the same boat. I expect they'll be postin' Colour Sergeant Cole to this battalion next, in which case, see, I'll 'ave to 'it 'im again. Ooh, sorry. I forgot.' Jenkins rushed after Simon as he strode through the door and down the corridor, buttoning his topcoat as he went. 'Here's a letter for you.'

Without glancing at it, Simon thrust the letter into his pocket and hurried towards the guardroom. The hour before dawn was piercingly cold and the January stars patterned the sky like sequins on a dark quilt. The big quadrangle of the parade ground glistened with frost as he made his way towards the yellow light of the guardroom. The sentry at the gate stiffened to attention and, with hardly a movement of his lips as Simon walked by, whispered, 'Colonel's inside, sir. Top button's undone.'

Dammit! Nearly caught. With a grateful nod to the sentry, Simon buttoned his greatcoat, settled the cap squarely on his head and entered the guardroom, calling firmly, 'Stand to the guard, Sergeant.'

The long wooden room was not, of course, brought to life by this command. The guard was already fallen in line, greatcoated and with Martini-Henry rifles shouldered. At the far end of the room stood Lieutenant Colonel Covington, greatcoat over his pyjamas, the trousers of which were tucked into riding boots. His bulldog, General Grant, was at his feet and a huge mug of cocoa was in his hand.

Simon sprang to attention and saluted. 'Good morning, sir.'

The Colonel took a sip of cocoa. 'You're late, Fonthill.'

'With respect, sir, I think not.'

'Really? Sergeant, tell me the time.'

'Sir.' The Sergeant smacked his boots into a left turn and marched to the large clock that was fixed to the wall of the guardroom by the door. There, he executed a perfect halt, made a right turn, studied the clock, swung in an about-turn, marched to the Colonel, crashed into a halt and in the great sing-song of Wales cried, 'Five fifty-nine exactly, Colonel sir.'

'Ah,' said Covington, pulling a large gold watch from his pocket and examining it with exaggerated care. 'My hunter must be a trifle in advance. Still, it does no harm to turn out the guard a little early. Carry on, Fonthill.'

'Very good, sir.'

The Colonel leisurely walked to the door, still sipping his cocoa, but his eye travelled over the young officer, taking in every detail of his dress and his bearing as Simon, in turn, inspected the guard. Covington turned as he opened the door. 'Oh, Fonthill.'

'Sir.'

'When you have finished your duties for the day, come and see me. I have some news for you. Now come along, General, there's a good dog.'

It was not until Simon had dismounted from his horse for a hurried meal two hours later that he remembered the letter in his pocket. Sitting close to the orderly room fire, he examined the envelope. It bore the familiar, precise hand of Alice Griffith and he opened it with a smile.

Dear Simon,

I have now been in this dreadful place for eighteen months and it seems Papa is about to be presented with a document that certifies that my education is now complete. You will not be surprised to hear that I don't feel at all educated – though neither do I feel un-educated, for that matter. Anyway, I am tired of the French and their ridiculous lessons in deportment and etiquette.

The good news is that I am about to come home and it would be most gratifying to see you again, if your duties at the depot can spare you, that is. I have been so pleased to receive your letters and to be allowed such a privileged insight into the life of an officer of the line on depot duty. Perhaps we can exchange boredom ratings on the respective teachings of table place settings for seventeen noble persons of various ranks and wheeling a company into line by fours from the left?

I am leaving tomorrow for home and, indeed, may well be there by the time you read this. If the gesture will not be misunderstood(!), I shall ask Papa to invite you and

Major and Mrs Fonthill to dinner soon, so that we can exchange experiences.

Please present my compliments to your mother and father.

Sincerely, your good friend,

Alice Griffith.

Simon's smile remained as he read the letter and then folded it and replaced it in his pocket. His correspondence with Alice had begun immediately after their tête-à-tête in the topiary two years before and had continued ever since – mainly, it must be admitted, at Alice's instigation. They had met only once in that time, when Alice had conducted a long and rather one-sided conversation on the problem of rural poverty in Wales. It would be good to see her again.

He stared into the bright coals. Life for the last twenty-two months had not been bad, despite Lieutenant Colonel Covington. Simon had rediscovered his joy in soldiering: the delicate interplay of relationships with the men, the elation of deploying his platoon on exercises, constant physical effort that had made his body lean and hard – even the cat-and-mouse games with the Colonel had their enjoyable side. Not once had he been caught, despite the laying of many traps by the CO. Once again Simon blessed the providence that had provided 352 Jenkins as his servant. Frequently, it was only the barrack-room caution and experience of the little Welshman that had saved him. The example of the cap was typical. Simon had been completely unaware of the last-minute change in the order of dress for the day. It would have been an awful solecism for the Orderly Officer to have appeared wearing the new Prussian-style helmet instead of the ordained field cap. It had obviously been another trap.

Immediately after the new guard had been mounted in the evening, Simon presented himself in the Colonel's office. There was no doubt about it, Covington was pleased. He oozed affability.

'Do take a chair, Fonthill,' and he gestured to the large leather button-back to the side of the desk.

'Thank you, sir. With respect, I prefer to stand. I am still on duty as Orderly Officer.'

'As you wish.' The Colonel smiled again, so that his eyes seemed almost to disappear between the bushy brows and the luxuriant moustaches. 'There's been no recurrence of your, ah, medical problem in the last year or so, eh?'

'No, sir. Not at all.'

'Capital. Capital. Just as well, then, because . . . Are you sure you wouldn't rather sit down?'

'No thank you, Colonel.'

The smile now was even more expansive. In fact, Covington's hirsute face positively beamed. 'Well, I've got a little job for you.' He stood up. Suddenly his manner changed completely. All affability gone, he rapped out the next sentence. 'You are being posted abroad to South Africa immediately on active service.'

Simon immediately felt the blood rise to his face and experienced a sudden shortage of breath. From childhood came that sudden lurch of the heart and, just for one second, a moment of dizziness. From aeons away came the Colonel's voice in mock solicitousness: 'Feel all right? Sure you don't want to sit down?'

Inconsequentially, Simon thought of Alice. Brave, stocky Alice, in her best dress, showing her wonderfully white skin, leaning forward and defiantly attacking the forward policy for Afghanistan. He recalled his father's description of Covington, 'Not exactly subtle, I fear.' Alice would have this bully for breakfast. And he smiled and felt better.

'No thank you, sir. Sounds good news. When can I go?'

Covington sat down again, a slightly puzzled look on his face. 'Not so fast. I have to tell you more about the job. Oh, sit down, dammit!'

Awkwardly, Simon gathered up his sword and perched on the edge of the armchair, while Covington picked up a document from his desk, which Simon could see carried the blue seal of the Horse Guards at its head. The Colonel arranged a rather incongruous pair of spectacles on his nose and silently re-read the letter.

Eventually he regarded Simon from over the spectacles. 'It seems you were quite a language scholar at Sandhurst, what?'

'Not quite a scholar, sir, but I did fairly well in the French and German examinations.'

'Hmm. Well, you did well enough to impress someone at the Horse Guards. Though what French and German has to do with the language of obscure African tribes I am dashed if I know.'

'Sir?'

'Look. The background is this. You will remember – yes, you *will* remember – that the 1st Battalion was posted to the Cape just under two years ago. Well, the brush with the Kaffirs did not quite materialise but it jolly well has now. In fact,' the Colonel's face took on an attitude of satisfied determination, 'I have reason to believe that the 2nd will soon be leaving to help out our brothers. But that doesn't concern you.'

He leaned across the desk. 'Ever heard of the Zulus?'

Simon frowned in concentration. 'Yes, I think so. Very warlike, aren't they? Strong chief called Sheeka, or something.'

'No. No. Shaka. Shaka. And he's bin dead for years. But you are correct in that the tribe is warlike, and Shaka did a fine job for a heathen in knockin' 'em into shape. They're up in the north somewhere and they've bin giving the Boers trouble for years. The Horse Guards think it won't be long before we have to be involved and they want a bit of, well, spadework done in the intelligence field up there.'

The Colonel removed his spectacles and leaned back. 'They seem to think that, because of your ability to pick up foreign lingos, you could be useful.' He smiled, the sarcasm coming back into his voice. 'They have asked me to reassure them that your horsemanship is good enough, because the work will mean long hours in the saddle. I am quite prepared to do so, if you feel . . . ah . . . strong enough to undertake the posting.'

Simon gulped. 'Thank you, sir. Yes, of course. I would like to go.'

'Very well. You will have four days' leave before embarking on the second of February. You may take your servant with you, if you believe he can serve well in the field, for there will be no boot cleaning to do out there by the look of it. Here are your immediate orders. You will be more fully informed of your task once you have landed in Cape Town.' He proffered the Horse Guards' documents.

'Oh, and Fonthill.'

'Sir?'

The Colonel smiled in his familiar languid fashion. 'Don't think we are parting company for ever. You remain gazetted to the 2nd Battalion. You are only seconded to the general staff in Cape Town for the time being, as a matter of convenience. And, as I say, I have every hope that I shall be seeing you very soon in the Cape myself.' He waved his dismissal.

Simon's main feeling as he left the Colonel's office was one of exhilaration that he had survived the shock of the confrontation. He had endured the last of Covington's tricks and he would now be free of him! There was no fear in his heart as he considered the task ahead – only puzzlement at his selection and at the vagueness of the commission. The question of how to stay in the saddle when pursued by spear-wielding savages would have to wait until he reached South Africa. Good horsemanship, eh? He would have to put glue on his breeches. His step lightened as he went to find Jenkins.

The little man took the news and the offer of accompanying his officer to South Africa with equanimity. 'Aye, sir,' he said, his smile stretching his moustache almost to his ears. 'I'll come. I'm thinkin' that you'll still be needin' me.'

'Certainly not. I can look after myself very well. But you should get out of this place.'

'That's true.' Jenkins rubbed his hands together slowly. 'An' you know what, sir. Colour Sergeant Cole is out there somewhere with the 1st Battalion. It would be perfect, look, to see him again.'

Simon sighed. 'Look, Jenkins. If you start drinking and hitting NCOs again, they'll put you away for life.'

Jenkins looked shocked. 'I wouldn't 'it 'im again. But I might 'ave a word or two, see.'

Simon hurriedly sent a telegram to his parents informing them of his imminent arrival, settled his mess bills and gathered together his kit. There was no tropical issue: his scarlet and blue serge was considered quite suitable for the sun and plains of South Africa, and the only concession to the change in climate was a cork sun helmet, a 'Wolseley topi', to complement his head gear. He set off home.

His welcome there was characteristically unemotional, but for all that, it was clear that Major and Mrs Fonthill were delighted, if just a little puzzled, at Simon's preferment. On his arrival, the Major hung on to his hand for a second or two longer than usual, and after the early questions, they accepted the imprecise nature of his orders with an equanimity born of many years of army service.

At luncheon his mother produced a gold-engraved invitation card. 'This is for us all,' she said, 'but as it will take place on the eve of your departure, it will be quite understood, my dear, if you choose not to go.'

'It's Griffith,' said his father, half apologetically. 'His daughter is out, so to speak, and he's so proud of her that he is throwing a ball for her at his house. Actually, she's a little old for it and it's short notice for everyone, but they are taking her to London and they want to launch her here first.'

'So Alice is being launched,' mused Simon. 'I'm not at all sure that she will like that.'

His mother smiled. 'Such a strange girl. At one time I rather approved of her, you know, but I can't help feeling that she's become rather too forward. It doesn't suit her even though she is twenty-two or so. However, we must go to support the Brigadier. Whether you come, Simon, is for you to decide.'

Simon was intrigued. Alice coming out! How would she handle it? 'Of course I shall go,' he said. 'I shall have to send my trunks on earlier, anyway, so there will be no problems with packing.'

The drive to Chilwood Manor was very different from that of two years before. Now the snow beat in blustering eddies against the hood of the coach and the wheels crunched along ruts in the frozen mud. Despite the rugs tucked tightly around them, the cold penetrated their limbs and made them shuffle and stamp their feet. The Major was concerned about Owen, their coachman, and every few minutes would lean out of the window, letting in flurries of snow, to enquire of the man's well-being.

The Manor, when they reached it, looked a picture. The Brigadier had installed great copper torches, topped with flaming twists of tar-treated rushes, at intervals along the front of the house, so that it was dramatically lit with a flickering glow that turned the snow to pink. Carriages thronged the drive and the auxiliary footmen, who Mrs Griffith had recruited from the nearby village, were hard put to handle the traffic and the mountains of cloaks deposited with them in the entrance hall.

Alice was standing at the foot of the stairs with her parents to receive their guests. To Simon, she seemed taller somehow, until he realised that she had lost that illusion of sturdiness which had probably only been puppy fat. In other ways she had not changed. Her white skin was made to seem even more translucent by the contrast with the dark blue gown and the two rows of pearls she wore, and although her face still seemed devoid of obvious cosmetics, her long hair had been taken up and elegantly arranged. To his amazement, she kissed Simon warmly on both cheeks when she received him.

'Sorry,' she said, her grey eyes twinkling at his discomfort, 'but I haven't yet shed these terrible Continental habits. But it is good to see you and I am so glad that you came.'

Her warmth and ingenuous charm embraced Major and Mrs Fonthill too and the evening was launched most felicitously, with the Brigadier almost bursting with pride at the confident bearing of his only child and Mrs Griffith clearly delighted that her arrangements – made at the last moment, as she told everyone – seemed to be 'coping'.

Later, Simon and Alice danced together, when his turn came on her card. It was a Viennese waltz, still considered rather daring, and Simon danced it none too well, his concentration not helped by the constant flow of questions from Alice about his career and future plans. It was the last dance before the interval – he had been shy about getting on to her card – and he led his companion to the punch bowl. As they sipped the wine cup, he realised that Alice was looking very, very pretty. It was not just the pleasing regularity of her features and the new slimness; it was the fact that tonight she seemed, well, virtually to be glowing. He made a sudden decision.

'Do you know what I would like to see now more than anything in the world?' he demanded.

'No, what?'

'The topiary.'

'Oh no! We would freeze out there.'

'Nonsense. We will borrow cloaks. I want to see what it looks like in the snow.'

She looked at him, only half smiling now, her head slightly to one side. Then, quickly, she nodded.

They slipped through a corridor into the servants' hall and picked up the first pair of cloaks they saw and, so muffled, opened a door into the garden. The peacocks, lions and pyramids were looking incongruous, carapaced with two inches of now rather soggy snow. It was slushy underfoot and not at all suitable for Alice's silver dancing sandals.

'Oh, I'm sorry,' said Simon. 'Perhaps this wasn't such a good idea after all.'

'Of course it is,' said Alice. 'You wanted to kiss me, didn't you? Well, please do so.' And she put her arms around Simon's neck and nuzzled her icy-cold nose under his ear.

Simon kissed her. Deciding he liked it, he did so again and Alice responded with if not passion, at least enthusiasm. Simon felt unaccustomed desire rise within him.

Eventually, Alice pulled away and looked up at him with an impish grin. 'Look,' said Simon, 'I think I love you.'

'No you don't,' she responded, without relaxing either the grip around his neck or the smile on her lips. 'Don't fall into the trap, Simon. Not long ago, in this very garden, you told me that you did not love me. We've only met once since then and nothing can possibly have happened to change your mind. It's just the atmosphere.'

Seeing the crestfallen look on Simon's face, she relented. 'But I have to tell you that I am unhappy that you are going away. I was so looking forward to getting to know you better.' She threw back her head and laughed. 'Your letters were very welcome but they weren't *too* revealing, you know.'

Alice unwound her arms. 'No, Simon. We are what we said we would be: good, very good friends. Maybe one day we shall mean more to each other. But I want you to know that what you said a moment ago does not mean that you are under a commitment to me. Nor does my kissing you mean that I am under a commitment to you.' She gave another quick smile. 'Though I did enjoy it.'

'How very kind of you to say so,' said Simon sulkily.

53

'Oh, don't be such a grouch. Here, let's do it again.' This time Alice kissed *him*, so warmly that he felt his ears tingle. He held her tighter and kissed her neck and shoulders. 'But I do love you,' he said desperately.

She gently thrust him away. 'You see,' she said. 'They've done it.'

'Who's done what?'

'Our parents. They've schemed all this.'

'I don't think so. I am not even sure that my mother approves of you these days.'

Alice threw back her head and laughed heartily, so that her breath rose in the air like a cloud of steam. 'I am not surprised to hear it and I think it's good news anyway.' Companionably, she sought Simon's arm under his cloak and began to steer him back to the house. 'We must get back,' she said. 'It's not that I don't like being here with you, nor am I worried about gossip. I don't care a fig about what people say, you know.' The old earnest look came back for a moment. 'But it is my party and I must put myself about a little. I know you will understand.'

Glumly, Simon nodded and they stepped carefully through the slushy snow back to the house.

The rest of the evening passed miserably for him as his new-found desire twisted into jealousy as Alice carried out her dance commitments with a succession of eligible and, it seemed to Simon, ever taller young men. His mother, too, fulfilled a full dance programme, elegantly sweeping around the floor with a mixture of old and young partners. Major Fonthill spent most of the evening sitting talking to old friends and comrades from the regiment, increasingly content with his cigars and brandies. Only once did he pass a comment to Simon, as the latter smiled

54

gloomily on his way to replenish his glass: 'Don't worry, my boy,' he said kindly, 'you won't be away all *that* long.'

Simon was allowed one more dance with Alice, which he managed to ruin by holding her too tightly and, twice, stepping on her foot. They exchanged hardly a word this time and Simon thought that Alice smiled too often at every couple as they swirled by. When the time came to say goodbye in the early hours, she did not kiss him, merely letting her hand rest in his perhaps a moment too long for propriety as he bowed over it.

'Will you write?' he hissed.

'Of course. I always have. Don't worry. Good night, Simon.'

The Major and his wife were noticeably mellow as they sat back in the coach, much warmer now as the indulgences of the evening combined with the milder air of the thaw. The Major's eyes positively twinkled as, his arm entwined with that of his wife, he addressed his son opposite. 'Jolly good evening I think, my boy. Wouldn't you agree?'

'Yes, Father. Quite pleasant.'

'You didn't dance much, dear,' said Mrs Fonthill. 'And you are not very good at it. Honestly, Simon, sometimes I despair of you. You can't ride and you can't dance. What *can* you do?'

'Ah, Mother,' sighed Simon. 'I wish I knew.'

The next morning Simon had just time to pen a quick message to Alice before Owen came to take him to the railway station.

My dear Alice,

You may think me no end of a fool but I do love you, whether or not our parents have manoeuvred me (at least) into this position – and I am convinced that they have not. However, I quite understand your feelings and I do not consider either of us, of course, to be engaged.

Nevertheless, I see no reason why we cannot remain good friends, as you wish, with me continuing to love you.

The thought of you will sustain me in Africa.

Yours most sincerely.

He read it through anxiously, decided that it sounded far too stilted, but sealed and dispatched it anyway. Time was running out and there were the goodbyes to be said.

Chapter 3

The cab rattled over the cobblestones of Southampton through dismal rain to the deep-water dockside, where Simon caught his first glimpse of the vessel that was to be his universe for the next few weeks. The SS *Devonia* seemed large enough, at least, for such a long voyage. She displaced some 8,000 tons and had been commissioned by the Horse Guards from the Anchor Line in Glasgow to transport a hotch-potch of military replacements to the Cape. She normally plied the North Atlantic route, carrying emigrants from Europe, mainly from Scotland and Ireland, to the New World, and she looked what she was: a workhorse. A succession of white deckhouses broke up and spoiled the clean lines of her iron hull. A surprisingly elegant clipper stern contrasted oddly with the bluff vertical bow and the single black funnel sat incongruously with three tall masts, square-rigged to take sail as both auxiliary power and stabilising influence.

Jenkins was already at work in the tiny cabin allocated to Simon, unpacking gear from the two trunks, one of which folded back to act as 'officer's table and desk on campaign'.

'Beg pardon, sir, but I'm not sure I'm goin' to like any of this,' said the little Welshman gloomily.

'Why, what's wrong?'

'They've put me with the men right in the front of this thing, look you, an' there's no air an' very little light down there. I've only been on a steamer once. That was round Colwyn Bay and then I was sick. I don't mind fightin' the savage Zulu, see, but this is different, isn't it?'

Simon sighed. 'Look. For most of the time, we're going to be steaming through tropical waters that are bound to be placid. It is not as though this is a paddle steamer. This vessel is fitted with propeller screws at the stern that make it go much more quickly and we should make good time. Your duties on board are bound to be light because I shall need very little. Treat it as a pleasure cruise.'

'Very good, sir. But it's so noisy, too. Look.' He rapped his knuckles on the bulkhead. 'This iron clangs all the time. An' it must be so heavy. Why don't it sink?'

'A good point. I have often wondered myself. Something to do with displacing water, I think. But you must ask one of the sailors. Don't worry. We're safe enough.'

Simon reported to the artillery major named Baxter who was the senior soldier on board, and learned that his duties during the voyage were to conduct daily arms drill for the motley collection of infantrymen sailing and also to be responsible for one of the emergency muster stations. What exactly he was supposed to do once the men were mustered seemed to be known only to the Horse Guards and the captain of the vessel.

The ship sailed on the evening tide, slipping away quietly from her berth with the minimum of fuss. Once clear of the Isle of Wight, she began butting into a channel westerly, confirming Jenkins's worst fears about seafaring and reducing the men's quarters for'ard and aft into dark holes, where low moans and the sound of retching emerged from the dim recesses of the closely positioned bunks. The *Devonia* put her head down and pushed into the foam-topped swell, sweeping spray as far aft as the bridge.

Simon's attempt at holding deck drill failed and the medical officer on board was of little use. He spent the first three days in his bunk, occasionally staggering on deck to empty his slops and then be sick again.

The weather worsened as the ship turned south into the Bay of Biscay. This time the swell took the steamer on the starboard beam and she rolled dismally, her sails reefed down and her funnel belching black smoke. Even Simon, who had enjoyed the first few days and had hungrily tackled his meals, now began to feel ill. His attempts to summon up visions of Alice, in her blue gown with her pearls matching her skin, failed to comfort him. Duties on board for the army contingent descended into unhappy anarchy, with few men able to stand on the deck, let alone carry out meaningless tasks for the sake of maintaining discipline. The artillery major had not left his bunk since the Isle of Wight had dropped astern. It was a bad introduction to the voyage south.

After the first day, Simon had seen nothing of Jenkins. The little man had disappeared completely into the black hold for'ard. It was not until the seventh day that he reappeared, just as a wan sun attempted to penetrate the clouds off the northern coast of Spain.

'Dereliction of duty, 352,' said Simon with relish as Jenkins put a woebegone face round the cabin door.

'Sorry, sir. I've been waitin' for this tropical stuff you told me about. There doesn't seem much of it about, does there? An' I 'aven't seen too much of this pleasure cruise business either, see. The Glasshouse at Aldershot was better'n this.' His haggard face looked up at Simon and was racked with another spasm. 'Ooh God. I gotta go again. Sorry, sir.' And he disappeared up the companionway as fast as his strong, short legs could take him.

The belated promise of fine weather was eventually redeemed on the eighth day, when the sky cleared, the swell subsided and the sun shone. Like moles surfacing, white-faced soldiers began to appear on deck, unsteady and uncommunicative, but alive again. Simon immediately called a parade of the infantrymen and some sort of discipline was re-established. Jenkins's tan also came back and he became oversolicitous of Simon's comfort, as though to compensate for the previous week's neglect.

The army officers messed separately from the ship's officers and there was no formal opportunity therefore for fraternisation, particularly as the sailors tended to keep to themselves – as though the soldiers were just another cargo of worthless emigrants. However, Simon was able to strike up an acquaintance with the Third Mate, a Scotsman roughly his own age. This gave him the chance of asking about mustering in an emergency. Once the men were gathered together, what happened then?

The Mate smiled. 'They should be kept at their mustering station until it becomes necessary to allocate them to a lifeboat,' he said.

'But shouldn't we be allocated to lifeboats now and even have some drill on how to launch them?'

'Mebbe. But it's no' as simple as that.'

'Why isn't it?'

The Third Mate looked forward and then aft, at the blue,

now friendly swell that rolled up behind the *Devonia* before slipping impassively down the length of the hull. 'Well,' he began evasively, 'I've not done the sums, but I should say that we don't have enough lifeboats to go round if we had to abandon the ship.'

Simon was horrified. 'Good lord. What a terrible state of affairs. Does the captain know?'

'I should think so. But och, this is no' unusual. In this sort of trade – and I'm talking about shipping emigrants, soldiers an' the like – there are never enough boats to carry everyone.' He wrinkled his eyes and looked up at the foretops'l, now drawing comfortably. 'An' it doesn't really matter. In storm conditions and wi' these sort of passengers, few small boats would stand any chance of surviving. The best hope is to trust to the ship. She's a good old tub and won't let us down.'

Simon frowned, not at all reassured. The *Devonia* was far from young, one didn't have to be a sailor to know that, and during the Biscay storm it had seemed to him that she had laboured disturbingly. 'But isn't it possible,' he asked, 'just to be told how the boats are launched?'

The Scotsman looked at him wearily. 'Yer a wee bit persistent, aren't you? All right. I'll show you. But don't go around upsetting the army, or we'll never get to the Cape.'

The two walked to where the white-painted boats hung from their davits and the Mate showed Simon how, by breaking out a handle from its lashing, it was possible to winch out a longboat and lower it into the sea and then uncouple the lowering cables. He pointed out the four pairs of oars lashed inboard and the casks of water stowed under the bow. 'But I shouldna attempt to drink the stuff unless you can lace it wi' a dram,' he confided. 'It's all o' two years old.'

The conversation disconcerted Simon, and despite the Mate's request, he felt bound to report it to the Major. Baxter was quite unmoved. 'I think we can trust the captain to know what he is doing,' he said. 'There will be enough boats to go around, I am certain of that. Anyway, I am sure that we are over the worst of the weather.'

But they were not. Another twelve days of clear blue skies and placid seas ushered them over the Equator and down the west coast of Africa, until, when they were a couple of days short of Cape Town and closing in on the coast, a cold wind sprang up from the south-west. It brought with it the icy malevolence of the Antarctic, causing spume-drifting crests to fly like tattered veils from the top of the waves.

The force of the wind increased and the vessel began to sustain a succession of keel-wrenching shocks from the seas breaking heavily on the starboard bow. The black hours of night brought no respite and there was no escaping the crashing noise as the seas pounded the iron plates. The ship pitched and rolled, creaking and sighing, her top spars swinging through an inconsistent arc as they seemed almost to kiss the white rollers. There was no sleep for anyone, and this time, sickness could not divert the soldiers from the fear they felt.

At about five a.m. a loud explosion came from within the ship, strong enough to boom above the howling of the wind and crashing of the sea. Unable to sleep, Simon was standing amidships, clinging to a stanchion by the main mast. He felt the vessel lose her momentum and swing around, presenting her starboard side to the sea.

'What's happened?' he demanded of a sailor rushing by. The man shouted unintelligibly and disappeared down a hatchway.

The ship was now rolling violently as the great broken-topped swells, surging unchecked across the South Atlantic Ocean, hit her hard a'starboard. The cross trees near the masthead were now swinging consistently in their obeisance to the waves. It seemed to Simon, clinging now to the main mast itself, that all way had been lost and that the ship was doomed to turn turtle. Then the *Devonia* began to tremble with engine life and slowly, very slowly, her head came round and she began to butt into the sea again, albeit with much less vigour, as though she was tired of the struggle.

The Major materialised out of the darkness. 'Get your men to their muster stations,' he half mouthed, half shouted above the roar of wind and sea.

'What's happened?'

'One of the boilers has blown. We are making way again but it is devilishly hard work. We must be ready for anything.'

Simon lurched his way across the corkscrewing deck and plunged below to the for'ard quarters. One lantern only swung from the deckhead, revealing a nightmarish scene of white faces and shrouded figures, some lying, some kneeling, a few standing and clinging to the bunk posts. The smell of vomit assaulted Simon's nostrils. He caught a glimpse of Jenkins, fully dressed and wearing his greatcoat. He nodded approvingly.

'Fall in at the muster station,' Simon shouted. 'Look lively. Break out your greatcoats and put them on. Leave everything else. Sergeant Laxer?' But the NCO in charge was lying uselessly on the deck. 'Jenkins.'

'Sir.'

'Make sure everyone is wearing his greatcoat before he climbs the ladder. It's freezing up there.'

'Where's yours, then?'

'Damn you, Jenkins. Do as you're told.'

Simon turned and climbed up the companionway. On deck he bumped into the Third Mate and caught his sleeve. 'What chance have we got?' he asked.

The young sailor put his mouth close to Simon's ear. 'We're running on only one boiler. The Chief is trying to repair the one that's blown.' He grinned. 'He's a Scotsman, so he'll do it. Trouble is that we're not really makin' enough headway to stop us from being blown towards the lee shore about ten miles away. So it's a bit of a race against time.'

'Can we help?'

'Nae, laddie.' He grinned again. 'This is man's work. It's no' for tin soldiers.' And he picked his way forward, oilskins glistening.

Simon made his way to the muster point where a wretched bunch of infantrymen were beginning to accumulate – all, he was glad to see, greatcoated against the biting south-west wind. Suddenly, something was thrown over his shoulders.

'Put that on, bach,' said Jenkins, 'and set a proper example.'

'To hell with you, Jenkins,' said Simon. But he buttoned up the coat. 'Pay attention now,' he shouted against the wind. 'There's a problem in the engine room but we are in no immediate danger. We have mustered you on deck now to save time in case we need to abandon ship. But this is most unlikely. Now line up in the lee of the deckhouse. No one is to move from here.'

He looked at Sergeant Laxer, who was leaning against the deckhouse, his eyes closed and head down, wretched from sea-sickness. There were no corporals in his batch. His gaze sought Jenkins. The little man, buoyed up by the danger and activity, had lost his own nausea and was now looking at Simon intently, water dripping from his black moustache. Catching Simon's eye, he nodded, almost imperceptibly.

'Private Jenkins 352 will be in charge until further notice,' yelled Simon.

'Is there pay, then?' enquired Jenkins, as conversationally as the storm would allow.

'Report to me any man who leaves this station.'

'Very good, sir.'

Simon staggered aft, looking for Major Baxter. He eventually found him on the bridge, talking to the ship's captain, who glared at Simon from under his soaking cap. 'Get off my bridge,' he shouted.

Ignoring him, Simon addressed the Major. 'I'd like a word, sir.'

Without argument, the Major followed him to the deck below. 'What is it, Fonthill?'

'I have no idea how bad things are, sir, but I think we should get the men dressed in greatcoats if they are to remain on deck in this wind. And sir . . .'

'Yes.' The Major had lost any air of superiority. He knew exactly how to withstand a concentrated barrage of shells but this chaos at sea presented problems that were beyond him. His nerve held – as, for the moment, did his stomach – for he was a brave man. But he felt powerless in these alien conditions. The skipper of the ship was taciturn, unhelpful and, of course, busy. Major Baxter did not know what to do for the best.

'It is possible, sir,' shouted Simon, 'that we may have to abandon the ship if we get caught on the lee shore. Do we have any instructions on how to launch the lifeboats?'

'No. I presume that the crew will do all that.'

Simon shook his head and saltwater sprayed from his nose and forehead. 'They may, but I know there are not enough boats to take all of our men. If the worst comes to the worst, we cannot afford to have a panic, and anyway, there may not be time for the crew to launch every boat or to show us how to do it.'

'So. What are you suggesting?'

'I know how to launch the boats. Let me show the other officers and let us muster by the boats to save time in case we have to use them quickly.' He looked anxiously into the doubting face of the older man. 'I do think it advisable, sir.'

'Oh, very well, Fonthill. Tell each muster station to detail two men to fetch greatcoats. Then we will re-muster. I will allocate the boats to each party.'

Dawn was now breaking weakly and the dim light, although only a slight shading of the sky to the east from black to grey, helped the soldiers to make their way to the boats. Deck hands were now attempting to set storm sails and bracing the yards round to harness some of the wind's force to claw a few points to windward. The attempt failed as the mainsail split with a crack like a whiplash.

Once the troops had huddled in detachments by the lifeboats, Simon visited each officer in charge and pointed out the handle lashed to the davits and passed on the instructions for swinging out and lowering. At each new muster point, his eye quickly estimated each group of soldiers and attempted to measure them against the size of the boat. He had no idea how exactly they matched but there were clearly too many men for the space available. He also realised that, if all the boats were to be used, then the ship would have to be either bow or stern on to the sea. A beam sea would tilt the vessel over and prevent at least half of the boats from being swung out. So perhaps the measurement of men to boat space was pointless anyway.

He hurried back to his own detachment. As he neared his men, he sensed a difference in deportment in them to the others. Jenkins was out in front, one hand swinging to and fro. The whole detachment was also swaying – but not in time to the ship's crazy convolutions. They were singing! 'Guide Me, Oh Thou Great Redeemer', reedy but unmistakable, could be detected above the roar of the storm. Even the Sergeant was attempting to mouth the words.

Jenkins looked up impassively as Simon approached. 'I thought we'd 'ave a bit of compulsory recreation while we was waitin' for our swim, like,' he shouted, half apologetically. 'It was better than doin' nothing, see.'

'Jenkins, you're a genius.'

'Oh, I know that. But is there money in it?'

The growing light seemed to bring a slight diminution in the storm. The wind had undoubtedly dropped a little, but the seas seemed as high. And it was clear that, try as she may, the *Devonia* was losing her battle to make significant headway to the south-west, away from the dreaded lee shore. Gamely she pushed her starboard shoulder into the serried waves, but the impression that she was being forced back was inescapable.

Simon climbed into the ratlines and, shielding his eyes against the spray, strained to look to the east. There was no horizon, only a few hundred yards of high, spume-tossed waves, marching and crashing towards the South African coast. Nothing more was to be seen, although . . . what was that? A new sound imposed itself above the roar of the storm. At first intermittent, it gradually became a dull, consistent booming. Breakers.

How near was the shore? He strained to see, but still could not penetrate that wall of sea and wind-driven rain. Obviously it was near, because he could hear the sound coming to him against the wind's direction. He leaped down and ran towards the bridge. The Major and the ship's captain were still together, the latter shouting something down the voicepipe, presumably to the engine room.

'Sir,' shouted Simon. 'Breakers on the eastern beam.'

'Damn,' cursed the skipper. 'What's the bloody look-out doing?' He rushed out on to the open eastern wing of the bridge and directed his binoculars, as though he had no faith in Simon's report.

'Breakers off the port beam, sir.' The call came dimly from the crosstrees above.

The captain swung round. 'I can see 'em now. Mr Blakeley,' he called to the First Mate. 'Get a sea anchor rigged directly and trail it from the stern to bring the bows into the sea. Major, muster your men and allocate them evenly to each boat.'

'I've already done that, Captain.'

The seaman gave Baxter a quick, appraising glance. 'Have you now. Good. We'll try and see if we can hold our own but we'll not be able to unless the storm abates. If we have to abandon ship, I'll allocate an officer to each boat. The lucky thing is that if we are where I believe we are, there's a gap in the reef ahead and the lifeboats will stand a fair chance of making the beach.'

He quickly looked about him, without expression. 'But this old tub is too big to get through without power in this storm. If she hits the rocks, we'll never be able to launch the boats. So it's a question of timing. Stand firm until I give the order.'

'Very good, Captain,' said the Major. He turned to Simon. 'You heard what the skipper said, Fonthill. Tell each muster party to stand by its boat but under no circumstances to try and board it or launch until we have the order. In any case, we should wait until a ship's officer arrives to direct us.'

Simon frowned. 'But . . .' he began, but thought better of it. 'Very good, sir.'

He half fell down the bridge companionway and relayed the order to each muster party, leaving his own until last. Jenkins was still in control and he looked keenly at Simon as he arrived.

'You all right, sir? No nerves or anything?'

Simon regarded him speechlessly. It had not occurred to him – so active had he been, so completely caught up in the dangers of the situation – that he had experienced no sinking sensation, no feelings of fear at all. His breathlessness came only from the hectic dash from the bridge. The only taste in his mouth was from the salt and the spray. He was elated, not collapsing. *He was not afraid!*

He laughed joyously at his staunch, bedraggled servant. 'Jenkins, look you, bach,' he cried. 'I am absolutely fine.'

Jenkins sucked in his moustache and raised his eyebrows in mock resignation. 'Oh, well then, everything's all right, isn't it? We're all goin' to drown, look you, but you feel fine. Things couldn't be better.'

The rigging of the sea anchor was completed and the contraption – an awkward triangle of heavy spars and tarpaulin – was paid out over the stern and had the immediate effect of turning the ship's head into the oncoming sea. There she stayed, stoically taking her punishment. But was she holding her own or was the sea still forcing her towards the rocks and the shore?

At this point, the cloud of spray and rain to the stern of the ship lifted for a moment and provided the answer. About two hundred yards away, the sea thundered in creaming white lines on to a row of rocks. They were partly submerged but revealed themselves threateningly as each breaker retreated. To the right, however, there was a break in the reef through which a beach could just be discerned in the distance.

Immediately, a steam whistle sounded from the bridge and seamen began running across the deck. From a companionway amidships grimy, blinking figures emerged and looked about them with white faces. If the engine room men were leaving their stations, reasoned Simon, then the whistle signalled Abandon Ship.

'Jenkins.'

'Sir.'

'Climb into the longboat. Look. See that winch? Be prepared to turn it to lower the boat once it has swung out. You,' he turned to the soldier standing next to Jenkins, 'do the same with the winch in the stern. Be sure to lower at the same rate or you will tip everyone out into the sea. But don't lower until the boat is full and until I give the order.'

Awkwardly, encumbered by their big coats, the two men climbed into the longboat and began inspecting the mechanism. Simon struggled with the lashing holding the winch handle that would swing the davits out. Eventually, it broke free. He looked about him.

'Fonthill.' The Major ran up. 'You must not launch until I give the order and until we have a ship's officer with us.'

'No, sir. But where is he?'

In truth, it was difficult to detect much on deck, so steeply was the *Devonia* pitching in the now shallower sea and so thickly was the spray being thrown aboard. Forward, however, a group of sailors could just be seen, swinging out a lifeboat while a bedraggled muster of soldiers watched them.

'See,' cried the Major. 'We must wait our turn.'

'No. No. Look!' They watched in horror as the seamen suddenly jumped into the boat and began lowering it. Belatedly, the soldiers moved forward and attempted to board the swinging boat. About ten of them succeeded. But another dozen or more tried to jump into the craft as it was being lowered some eight feet below the rail of the ship. Four of them fell into the white water below, their despairing cries hardly heard above the roar of the storm. The others crashed on to the sailors who were already overcrowding the lifeboat, tipping the boat fatally to starboard and precipitating all its occupants into the sea. The boat then hung there forlornly, crashing into the iron plates of the ship's side.

'Oh my God,' sighed the Major.

'Never mind them,' cried a strong Scottish voice clearly above the noise of the gale. 'They're the bluidy Laskars. Don't panic.' The Third Mate turned to Simon. 'Can yer remember what I told yer about swingin' out, launchin' an' all that?'

Simon nodded.

'Then get on wi' it. I'll help the others. Major, you'd better get in here. There's nae goin' to be too much room in the boats.' He gave a sad grin to Simon.

Baxter looked at Simon. 'You'd better carry on, son,' he shouted. 'You've got your first command now. Sorry it's at sea.'

'Very good, sir.' Simon called to Jenkins. 'Unlash the oars and distribute them to the men who man the middle thwarts, once they're on board. Oh, to hell, man. What's the matter now?'

71

'What's a thwart, then, when it's at 'ome?'

'The seats, dammit. The seats.'

'Oh, very goo— aye, aye, sir.'

Simon turned to his men. 'Climb on board in single file. Slowly, so you don't start the boat swinging. Fill up from the front. Go on. Move yourselves.'

He turned to the Major. 'Would you like to go amidships, sir?'

Baxter gripped his shoulder and smiled. 'No thanks, my boy. You'll do well enough without me. Did you instruct the others on how to handle the launching of these things?'

'As best I could, sir.'

The Major nodded. 'Good. Then I'll make sure everyone that can gets away. I will take the last boat. Off you go, Fonthill, and may God go with you. We will watch what you do.' He turned and lurched away up the pitching deck to the next boat.

Simon supervised the loading of the lifeboat and then came to the decision he had dreaded. Nine men, including himself, could find no room in the crowded hull. He turned to the little group left on deck. 'Any non-swimmers here?' Whether they had not heard the question or didn't comprehend it he would never know, but no hand was raised.

'Good. Now we will take off our greatcoats and boots and, once the boat is safely launched, we will jump into the sea.' He looked towards the shore. 'The beach is near enough to swim to, but I don't recommend it in these seas.' He tried to sound sanguine but his matter-of-fact manner was diluted by the need to shout. 'Each of you must strike out for the boat and seize those ropes hanging down.' He pointed to the tarred ropes that were looped along the side of the longboat. 'But don't just

72

hang there. Hold on and kick out. It will keep you warm and help to propel the boat.'

He inserted the handle into the winch and, with an effort, for the mechanism was rusty, wound the longboat out between its davits. 'Right, 352,' he shouted. 'Lower away carefully. Do it together to stop the boat tipping.'

Jenkins stood up, none too steadily. 'Come on board then, sir,' he called.

'No. You are full enough already. We shall jump into the water and swim to you and hold on to the loops. If any man in the water tries to climb on board, knock him back. You will swamp if you add to the people on board.'

Jenkins shook his head. 'Don't be stupid, bach,' he called. 'We must take you.'

'Don't be impertinent. Do as you are told. Once you are in the water, pull away to the right and back water with the oars – oh, for God's sake, that means rowing backwards to hold the boat steady – till we all swim to you and gain a handhold. Then keep the stern – the back – of the boat to the waves and pull as hard as you can. We can ride the waves on to the beach if we are lucky.'

He could not help but smile at the look of complete dejection on the face of Jenkins. 'Now, lower away steadily. Good luck. Think of Colour Sergeant Cole.'

The boat was bucking between its davits, matching the pitching of the ship, but by some miracle the lowering process went smoothly enough so that the keel kissed the water sweetly. As it did so, Jenkins and the other man at the hoists smartly disconnected the blocks and the boat was a free thing, pitching and rolling. Simon had a momentary impression of Jenkins, standing like some latter-day Bligh in the stern, urging on the rowers, and then the little vessel began to pull away from the *Devonia*.

'Now.' He turned to his soldiers, standing coatless and bootless on the wet deck, trying to keep their balance as the ship pitched ever more sickeningly in the shallow sea. 'Over with you. Strike out for the boat but don't try and board her. It'll be fifty lashes for anyone who does.'

One of the infantrymen demurred. 'But sir,' he cried, 'we shall freeze down there.'

'Not so,' Simon answered as he threw off his coat and unlaced his boots. 'We are cold now because of this south-west storm that comes from Antarctica. But it is only early autumn in these waters and the sea temperature has not had time to fall by more than a couple of degrees. We shall not freeze. Come on. Let's go.'

Not trusting himself to look down, Simon held his nose, climbed over the rail and leaped. The water was cold, green and shocking but not, as he had rationalised, freezing. Down, down, he went, pulled down as much by the weight of his clothing as by the force of his jump. Kicking frantically, he gained the surface, to be hit by the foot of one of the soldiers striking out for the boat. He looked around him. The side of the *Devonia* loomed above him and he kicked out away from it, filled by the danger of being caught by the big ship's propeller. In the trough of the giant waves he could see nothing and he had little idea of whether he was striking out for the lifeboat or towards the open sea. Then, as he was lifted by a roller, he caught a glimpse of the boat, desperately low in the water but still afloat, about a hundred yards away.

He swam as hard as he could, feeling impotent amidst the turmoil of the sea, until an oar materialised in front of his face. He grabbed it and then, realising that he might pull down the rower, released it. Somehow, above the storm, he heard the unmistakable bellow of Jenkins: 'No, no. Hang on to the bloody thing, man.' Gratefully he clung to it and was pulled to the side of the boat, close enough to grab a loop. He saw another man hanging in front of him and felt the presence of another, behind.

Jenkins was standing again in the stern. 'Now, boyos, pull, damn you all, pull. Pull like your lives depend on it, because, blast you, they do.'

Simon tried to shout to Jenkins to make sure that each of the swimmers had a handhold and that none were left behind, but he lacked the breath. He hung on to the rope and tried to kick. The boat yawed and pitched but Simon could tell that it was beginning to make progress. Then, as a wave caught it, it surged ahead, so that immense pressure was exerted on Simon's arm holding the rope and his feet were thrown up behind him, trailing in the wake. The soldier ahead of Simon suddenly lost his hold and disappeared and Simon realised that, unless someone was steering – and he had forgotten to give orders about this – the boat would be swept on to the rocks. He looked aft and saw the reassuring figure of Jenkins, his eyes bulging, water pouring over him, but standing erect, riding the roller-coaster and hanging on to the tiller for dear life.

He did not know how long the surging ride took but it seemed only seconds before the keel grounded on the shingle with a crash and he was thrown clear into the surf, to be tumbled over and over until, on hands and knees, he was able to crawl on to the beach. He turned his head to see the lifeboat now completely capsized, but with survivors lying about him. He tried to stand but sank back on to the sand.

The sky was lighter and the wind seemed to have abated a little, although the seas rushing on to the beach through the break in the reef still seemed to be mountainous. Far out, he could discern the black mass of the ship. She now seemed inanimate, no longer moving with the sea but firm and unyielding. He realised that she must have been thrown on to the reef. More importantly, however, the seas were dotted with lifeboats, sadly overloaded but surging towards the shore.

He looked about him. To his left but crawling towards him was Jenkins, greatcoat still buttoned to his neck, his hair plastered down and his moustache looking like some small black rodent he had caught with his nose. Simon felt a flood of warmth at seeing his servant.

'You all right, sir? Good.'

Simon held out his hand. 'Well done, Admiral. Welcome to South Africa.'

The little Welshman took the hand, shook it and then collapsed on to the sand. 'Thank you, sir. I enjoyed the pleasure cruise, indeed I did. Is this where the tropical bit starts?'

The two lay exhausted for a few minutes and then Simon rose to his feet and mustered the survivors to wade into the surf to catch the bows of the longboats that now began to approach the shore. Eight of them were brought in, some with soldiers still clinging to the lifesaving loops, but mostly unencumbered. In the last boat was Major Baxter, with the Third Mate. Of the captain of the SS *Devonia* there was no sign.

They had made their landfall only twenty-five miles north of Cape Town, agonisingly close to the harbour there. Of the 250 soldiers, sixty-three had perished, as had thirteen of the crew of twenty-five. The captain of the ship was among them. No one had seen him leave the bridge and it was presumed that he had gone down with his ship. For the *Devonia* had not lasted long on the reef. She had broken up quite quickly under the pounding of the waves, and once the storm had subsided, all that could be seen of her was the tip of her mainmast showing above the reef and a fragment of her stern.

Once the muster had been taken, the Major assumed command briskly. He was a different man on terra firma, back in his element and sure of himself. The dismal task of burying the bodies washed ashore was undertaken and wagons and oxen, with drivers, were commandeered from local farms to take the survivors to Cape Town. Two days after the shipwreck, Simon was accommodated in the officers' mess of the staff of the Commander of the Imperial Forces in South Africa, Sir Arthur Cunnyngham.

Shortly after his arrival, he was summoned to a small office that had been allocated to Major Baxter. The gunner shook his hand warmly.

'I want you to know, Fonthill,' he said, 'that I believe you behaved with gallantry and great presence of mind during this whole disaster. In fact, I would have recommended you for a decoration but, as you know, these can only be awarded for distinguished service in the face of the enemy.'

He smiled wryly. 'In fact, I never want to face an enemy which could put the fear of God into me as that sea did. But the fact remains that I cannot commend you in this way. However, I have mentioned you in my dispatches – and I have done so also for your servant, who steered that first boat so admirably and showed the rest of us how to do it.'

'That's very kind of you, Major,' said Simon.

'Oh – there's one other thing. I would like to write directly to your CO to tell him how well you behaved. Please give me a note of his name and where I might contact him.'

A slow smile spread across Simon's face. 'Thank you, sir, I will do that. He will be so gratified to hear from you.'

Chapter 4

Those first four days in Cape Town were happy ones for Simon. The Commander-in-Chief and the whole staff were up-country, so he was left to his own devices and was able to relax and begin to explore the strange and beautiful terrain surrounding the small town. Most of all, however, he warmed at the thought that Baxter would be mentioning him in his dispatches. 'Behaved with gallantry,' he had said. *Gallantry!* The word rolled off his tongue deliciously. What's more, it would stay on his record at Horse Guards and surely offset whatever calumny Covington would have entered. No cowardice. No more self-doubts. With a light heart, he requisitioned a horse and, with an eye to the future, set himself to regain some familiarity with the saddle. He intervened with the bored staff captain who was in charge of administration in Cape Town and secured the company of Jenkins for his rides of exploration.

His relationship with his servant had matured into one of easy familiarity – a relationship without embarrassment on either side but one that would have shocked any senior officer who witnessed it. For Simon, Jenkins had become an indispensable, warm part of his life, and although both would have died rather than openly acknowledge it, the association had deepened into one of mutual respect since the shipwreck. Drinking remained Jenkins's problem and, during the interminable months in the depot, only Simon's intervention with the Guard Commander had twice prevented the little Welshman from being put under arrest for drunk and disorderly behaviour. So far in Cape Town, however, Jenkins had remained surprisingly sober. A further surprise came when Simon realised that 352 was a more than competent horseman. The stocky infantryman mounted with the accomplished ease of a dragoon and sat erect, holding the reins with soft hands.

'Where did you learn to ride, Jenkins, for goodness' sake?' Simon asked as the two set out early for Table Mountain.

'It was the farm, see, when I was little. When he wasn't beatin' me, my da would let me sit on the horse when he was ploughin'. Then, later on, when I used to muck out the stables at the big farmhouse, they would let me ride the ponies sometimes.'

'Why didn't you join the cavalry, then?'

'I didn't fancy wearin' those tin shirts an' funny 'elmets. An' anyway,' he sucked his moustache reflectively, 'I didn't really 'ave much choice, see.'

'Why not?'

'I was bricklayin' in Birmingham, look you, and I'd 'ad a drink or two and got into a small discussion with the foreman. He 'it me with a shovel so I 'it him back with my hod. I didn't get paid off, see . . .'

Simon gingerly pressed his heels into his horse's flanks and nodded. 'That seems reasonable.'

'No. But I only 'ad threepence left.'

'So?'

'So I 'ad another drink to think about what to do next. The 24th was recruitin' outside the pub.' Jenkins grinned at the recollection. 'You'll never guess who was standin' there in 'is red tunic and polished buttons, shoutin' out the odds.'

'Oh, I think I can. Colour Sergeant Cole?'

'The very same. Except that 'e was only a sergeant then. Anyway, he says, "Come an' join the 24th Regiment of Foot and we'll make a man of you." So I says, "I'm a man already an' a better one than you." So 'e says, "I'm wearin' uniform, otherwise I'd knock the cockiness out of you, sonny." So I says, "All right then, I'll put the bleedin' uniform on an' then you can try." So that's 'ow I took the Queen's shillin'.'

'What happened then?'

Jenkins grinned. 'As soon as I'd signed, like, Cole put me on a charge straight away for impertinence. 'E always 'ad a sense of humour.'

The two picked their way through wild garlic and strange silver trees, the witboom, up the slopes of Table Mountain. At a little plateau below the summit they tethered the horses and scrambled up several hundred feet more to the flat top. Both men were struck silent by the view. To the south, the coastline meandered through wisps of low coastal cloud to the tip of the Cape itself. Seaward and to the north, the dark blue of the South Atlantic was studded with white sails and smoke trails as ships made their way to the haven of the artificial harbour. Coaling was taking place at one end of a quay and small black clouds half hid the vessels berthed there. The harbour bristled with masts and the water within the moles was criss-crossed with white wakes as the small crafts plied their trade. To the north and to the east, the mountain fell away in gullies of red sandstone, made more crimson by the patches of red disa orchids growing within. The air was clear and crisp and the coastal plain, dotted with farms and white-painted houses, seemed to march for hundreds of miles before it gradually gave way to smoky blue hills. Simon thought that, if he concentrated hard, he could see to India.

'Almost as good as Wales, bach sir,' said Jenkins.

Simon had hoped that his few days of leisure could be used to prepare for the task ahead. Apart from the horse riding, however, he found it depressingly difficult to discover anything about the Zulus and the threat they posed. Before sailing, he had ascertained that the 1st Battalion was not, in fact, in Cape Town, but had been posted some six hundred miles to the east to Kingwilliamstown, in British Kaffraria, at the very edge of the Cape Colony. There they were attempting to keep the peace in a border province that, although under direct British rule – as was the Cape Colony – was a polyglot pot of nationalities which now showed signs of boiling over. Natal, the British colony that bordered independent Zululand, seemed quiet. The glory, it seemed to Simon, lay with his old battalion in British Kaffraria and he had long since resolved to try and join them, if he could. There was a debt to be paid there.

Cape Town itself, in those first days after Simon's arrival, was not designed either to inform him or to advance his plans to join the 1st/24th. As the political, military and commercial hub of the Cape Colony – and virtually that of the rest of South Africa – it was temporarily leaderless and, it seemed to Simon, full of lassitude. The newly appointed Governor of the Colony, Sir Bartle Frere, had left for Kingwilliamstown and taken his staff with him, including the Army Commander, who, it was rumoured, was soon to be replaced anyway. However, the latter's chief of staff, Simon was informed, was on his way back to Cape Town and would give him his orders on his return.

On the fifth day after his arrival, Simon received a brief

note ordering him to report to the office of Colonel George Lamb CB, late Indian Army.

The office, for all its white-painted walls, was dark and sparsely furnished but it seemed to light up with the Colonel's smile as he stood and advanced to welcome Simon. A diminutive man, with colonial campaigning etched on his nut-brown face, he held himself as erect as a colour standard and exuded authority and bonhomie. Nevertheless, Simon regarded him with apprehension. How much did he know about the reason he was serving with the 2nd Battalion, and would his horsemanship be tested? He would never survive that. He need not have worried. This was no Covington.

'My dear Fonthill, a belated welcome to the Cape. I am sorry that you have had to kick your heels for a few days, but I had to travel with the C-in-C.'

'Of course, sir. Thank you.'

The Colonel pushed forward a chair. 'Do sit down. Cheroot? Sorry I can't offer you a decent cigar but we cleared out stocks to replenish the 1st/24th's mess at Kingbillystown.' His blue eyes sparkled. 'I'm sure you'd approve of that, though.'

'Very much so, sir.'

The little man bustled back to his desk, picked up matches and threw them to Simon.

'I've just been going through Baxter's report. Sad business. We shouldn't use these old emigrant tubs to transport our men. But you did jolly well. I congratulate you.'

Simon murmured his thanks.

'Right, now let's get down to business.' He pulled deeply on his cheroot and examined the papers on his desk. 'I see that you're a fine horseman and that, although you don't speak Zulu, you have one of the Bantu dialects?'

Simon swallowed hard and shifted from one buttock to the other on the edge of the chair. 'Er, not quite, sir.'

'Eh? What?'

'I can ride, of course, Colonel, but I've only got French and German and . . .' he tailed off, 'my German's not too good.'

'What the blazes!' The Colonel looked again at the document on his desk. 'It distinctly says here, "Has aptitude for languages and knows native dialect." '

Simon swallowed again. 'I think, sir, they might be referring to Welsh. I did learn it while I was at school in the country before going on to Sandhurst, although it is very rusty now. It must somehow have got on to my record.'

'To hell with the confounded Horse Guards! They get everything wrong.' Colonel Lamb frowned and looked hard at Simon. Then, gradually, his eyes softened and the brown face seamed into a half-smile. 'Welsh, eh?'

Simon nodded. 'Half Welsh, anyway. Borders.'

The smile broadened. 'Welsh meself, although I never did master the deuced lingo. Dammit all, Fonthill, if you can speak Welsh you can learn Zulu, can't you?'

'Well, yes. I suppose so, sir. But I was wondering if there was a chance that I could join my old battalion in Kingwilliamstown and serve as a line officer there?'

'Certainly not. The bloody place is full of Welshmen as it is. Now the Governor and the C-in-C are there, too. There's not room to breathe in the godforsaken hole. Best you stay out of it.' The Colonel tapped the ash from his cheroot and leaned forward. 'No. Kaffir wars are dirty businesses. Chasing bunches of natives through head-high thorn scrub; not seeing more than a foot or two in front of you and not knowing when a spear is going to be thrust into your privates from out of the bush . . .'

He winced and shook his head again. 'No. These are foot soldier policing actions. Not for a fine horseman like you.'

Simon groaned inwardly.

'Anyway, the damned war hasn't begun yet. And, of course, the Governor has gone down there to stop it starting.' The Colonel's teeth gleamed in the darkened room. 'No, my boy. We have something rather more interesting for you to do.'

He pushed back his chair and strode to a map that dominated one wall. 'Know much about South Africa?'

'Very little, I'm afraid, sir. There wasn't much time to do research before I left England.'

'Right. Perhaps best to start with a clean slate, anyway. You must first get the geography in your mind.' He picked up a pointer. 'Here we are.' He tapped the Cape Colony at the bottom of the map, the largest territory shown. Then his pointer moved upwards and eastwards. 'Here's British Kaffraria, where your Welsh boys are. You mustn't worry about Basutoland and Griqualand East and West, here. They're annexed and reasonably quiet. To the north of the Orange River here is a wilderness of desert, with a few bushmen and nothing else. No interest to anyone.'

He gripped his cheroot with his teeth so that it tipped up and the smoke curled clear of his eyes. The pointer swung in an arc from top right of the map to top centre. 'Here,' he said, wrinkling his eyes, 'here's where the trouble starts.'

The pointer jabbed at the middle of the map. 'Orange Free State, where the Boers trekked to fifty years ago to get away from us. See?' The pointer moved north-east. 'Here. The Transvaal. Huge territory. High plateau country. Both of 'em independent Boer republics. Got it?'

Simon nodded.

The pointer swung right and down. 'Natal. British but independent of the Cape Colony. Usual mixed bag of settlers but mainly British and natives. Lush, good country. And here . . .' The pointer moved up the coast to a rectangular strip of seaboard, fringed on the north by Portuguese territory, by Natal to the south-west and the Transvaal to the north-west. 'This,' said the Colonel, 'is Zululand. A completely independent nation, ruled by King Cetswayo.'

Lamb walked back to his desk and stubbed out his cheroot. 'The problems of this colony, Fonthill, are fundamentally those of every country in the world: people and land. We have European underpopulation and native overpopulation, of course, the same as throughout the Empire. But here the Europeans are an infernal mixture of anti-British, damned touchy Boers, British settlers and a poacher's bag of the sweepings of the rest of Europe.' He leaned forward. 'And the natives are another hell's brew: servile coastal Kaffirs, various tribes of Bantu inland, and up there,' he gestured over his left shoulder, 'the Zulu nation.'

Simon stood up and walked to the giant wall map. 'I can understand that, sir,' he said. 'But land? This is a huge country, and from the little I've seen of it, it is very fertile. Surely there is enough to go round?'

'Stuff!' The little man bounded to his feet. 'You know nothing of it yet. Yes, the territory is enormous.' He swept the map with his palm. 'Well-watered, grassy flatlands is what everybody – white and black man alike – wants. But there is not enough of *that* to go around. We've got steep mountain ranges and arid tracts eating up vast acreages, and great stretches of potentially fertile flatlands that are only usable when we get water trickling through the stony riverbeds for a couple of months a year. Winter pasturage is always a problem, and when we have a drought it can be as bad as India.'

The Colonel bristled with animation, his blue eyes shining from his seamed face as he jabbed the map in emphasis. Simon realised that this was a breed of soldier new to him. He had long been accustomed to the languid career officer typified by Covington: mannered, confident and arrogant from his breeding, able enough but with little interest beyond regimental matters, hunting and the social round. Lamb carried the missionary zeal of an empire-maker. He had, Simon remembered being told, served long years in India.

'As you would expect,' continued the Colonel, 'two hundred years of European settlement has meant that the white man has taken the best of the land and the water availability.' He gestured to the map again. 'Only here, in Natal, has any land been set aside for the natives, where we've pushed about three hundred thousand Kaffirs into reserves. But the Boers do nothing. They think that the Transvaal goes on for ever – and that it's all theirs.'

He sighed in exasperation. 'Here on the border of the Transvaal and Zululand, between the headwaters of the Buffalo River and the Pongola, there's been a land dispute between the Boers and the Zulus going on for years. God knows when it will be settled but there will probably be another Boer–Zulu war before it is.'

Simon peered pensively at the map. 'What's the answer to it all, then, sir?'

Lamb bounced on his heels. 'One word – confederation.'

'Confederation?'

'Confederation. Uniting all of the territories into one big

colony or dominion under the British flag, as we've just done in Canada. That way we can have central government and begin to impose some discipline and long-term planning. It will take time, but it's the only way to build this sprawling mess into a proper nation within the Empire.'

The Colonel took Simon by the arm and led him to his chair. 'In fact,' he said, 'the process has already begun. I am sure that the new Governor, Sir Bartle Frere, has come out with this intention.' He leaned forward confidentially. 'Can I rely completely on your discretion?'

'Of course, sir.'

'Shepstone is already in the Transvaal, preparing to annex it to the British Crown.'

'Shepstone?'

'Yes. Sir Theophilus Shepstone, formerly Secretary for Native Affairs in Natal – he knows Cetswayo well – has come out from the Colonial Office with a special mission.' Lamb smiled. 'As a matter of fact, Shepstone is a bit of a loose cannon crashing about the deck. He does tend to be a trifle unpredictable. But he knows the territory well and Sir Bartle should be able to handle him.'

'I see.' Simon nodded slowly. The history lesson and the tour d'horizon of South African politics was all very interesting, but what the hell had they to do with an infantry second lieutenant who spoke good French, some German and no Zulu? 'May I ask, sir, how I fit into all of this?'

'You may well. I spoke a second ago – perhaps a touch indiscreetly – about a loose cannon. Well, there is a whole battery of loose cannons also out there: Cetswayo and his Zulus. Know anything about them?'

'Very little, I have to confess, sir.'

'Well you should. Any soldier should. Damned fine people. Let me tell you about them.'

Colonel Lamb returned to his chair, threw a cheroot to Simon and settled back and lit another for himself. 'At the end of the last century, the Zulus weren't up to much. They were a small clan – only about fifteen hundred people – living a pastoral life in the Umfolozi Valley in an area of what we now call Zululand only some ten miles square. Then came Shaka. He was probably illegitimate and he had no privileges, although he was undoubtedly the son of a chief. He made his own way and became a fine warrior, allegedly killing a treed leopard when he was a young teenager.'

The Colonel sucked on his cheroot. He was enjoying the telling of a good story. 'He eventually became leader of his small clan and began building up the finest army that has ever been seen among the tribes of South Africa – perhaps the whole of Africa. He started with the weapons. He threw away the light throwing spears that he considered just toys and introduced the assegai, a short stabbing spear which became known as the iklwa. Know why?'

Simon shook his head.

'Because that's the noise it makes when the blade is twisted in the victim's body and drawn out. A sort of sucking sound . . . iklwa!' Lamb savoured the word and chuckled.

Simon swallowed and put a firm rein on his imagination. The story was too interesting to have it interrupted in any way. He leaned forward, fascinated.

'Anyway,' Lamb continued, 'he taught his troops how to hook the bottom of their shields around those of their enemy in personal combat and then, as the body is swung round and left unprotected, to sweep under with the iklwa so . . .' The little man danced to his feet and demonstrated the movement with his pointer.

'He introduced discipline and unquestioned obedience to orders: the fundamental of success in battle, as you know. He had to chop off a lot of heads along the way and he undoubtedly was a despot, but he knew what he was doing.' Lamb chortled again. 'Shaka felt that the leather sandals worn by his warriors impeded movement, so he had them all thrown away. When his men objected, he made 'em dance on thorns.

'He also introduced battle tactics which were revolutionary in their time and are still in use by the Zulus to this day. Look.' He took a piece of paper from his desk and gestured to Simon to look over his shoulder. He roughly pencilled two rectangular blocks opposing each other.

'Zulu warfare used to consist of two bodies of men facing each other and hurling insults and light throwing spears. Not many casualties. Shaka changed all that. He reasoned that warfare wasn't sport, it was a means of acquiring power. And to do that you had to kill.'

Lamb tapped the block on the right. 'Shaka's Zulus became a buffalo in battle. This was the chest of the beast, which faced the enemy in the traditional way. Suddenly, however, it developed horns.' He drew quickly. 'The top horns would break out of the main body from the rear, like this, and race quickly behind the enemy, while the bottom horn would do the same in the other direction, so that the enemy was suddenly surrounded and had to fight on all fronts. Sounds simple, doesn't it? But the skill lay in the timing of it and the speed with which it was done. They're still doing it and it's easy to be fooled.'

The Colonel wrinkled his brow in admiration. 'Shaka was a remarkable man. A complete innovator. He trained his impis –

they're Zulu divisions, or even corps – to move fast over rough country. They can trot for twenty or so miles and then fight a battle. But his most profound move was his complete reorganisation of the army.

'He structured his warriors into separate regiments, usually segregated by age and marital status. Each was separately trained, given names and shield insignia to distinguish them in battle. A remarkable esprit de corps and regimental loyalty was established, with great competition growing between the units.' The Colonel drew reflectively on his cheroot. 'Do you know, Fonthill, this savage intuitively established within four years the same regimental system which it had taken sophisticated European military theorists four hundred years to evolve.

'When he died, about fifty years ago – murdered, of course – the Zulus had established complete superiority over all clans within their reach. They had grown to be a nation of some quarter of a million and their territory had expanded from that original hundred square miles to a vast tract, stretching from the Swazi border on the Pongola River in the north to what is now called Central Natal in the south, and from the Drakensburg mountain range in the west to the India Ocean in the east.'

'And now, sir?'

'Now, Fonthill, Shaka's people have consolidated into a semi-pastoralist, semi-militarist nation, within their own borders. They've battled with the Boers over the years and, of course, with neighbouring tribes. But under Cetswayo they've been reasonably quiet. People here are a bit undecided about the Zulu king. Some call him a savage who poses a constant threat. Others suspect that he's a shrewd operator who has accepted the reality of the white man's presence and wants to find a way to live in peace and retain his independence.'

'So what's your view, sir?'

'I lean towards the latter persuasion, although I rather fear I am in the minority.' The Colonel rose to his feet, agitated once again.

'But that's not the point, dammit. It's not as simple as that. Firstly, Cetswayo maintains a standing army of about thirty thousand warriors, all disciplined, trained men, unlike most Bantu troops. They exist to fight – they call it "washing their spears" – and they get fretful when they don't. It's like keepin' a pack of hounds and not letting 'em hunt. They haven't had a run-out for some time now and the King must have a problem there.'

He approached the wall map again. 'Secondly, look at his frontiers. They stretch for miles with the Transvaal and Natal. We can't defend that sort of border. There's absolutely nothing to stop the Zulus pouring over into these settlements, marauding and killing, if they want to. It doesn't matter a damn that they may never do so. They can if they want to. That's the point.'

The Colonel slapped the map with his hand. 'Cetswayo remains a destabilising influence and a threat to confederation as long as he remains independent. If he will not accept annexation and control by us, then he will have to be put down.'

The two men regarded each other across the room in silence. Several questions crowded into Simon's mind – Why should the Zulu king accept annexation, and, if he didn't, what would world opinion think of him being 'put down'? – but he left them unsaid. Instead, he asked: 'And me, sir?'

The Colonel pulled up a chair and dragged it towards Simon,

sitting on it akimbo, the wrong way round, with his chin resting on the chair back.

'We know quite a lot about Cetswayo, but not enough. Shepstone was at his coronation and kept an eye on him for years but he's out of touch now. We think the Zulus have about thirty thousand men but we're not sure. We believe he is well intentioned towards the British – although not the Boers – but, again, we are uncertain how far this goes. Will he go to war if we put pressure on him to come under the flag? We don't know. You know what they're like, back home. We don't lightly want to start another native war, particularly one that would undoubtedly be a damn sight more serious than some Kaffir skirmish. No, these chaps would be a very different kettle of fish.'

'So you need information?'

'Precisely.'

'But surely you have informants, if not among the Zulus, at least across the border in Natal?'

'Well, we do and we don't.' Lamb shrugged his shoulders fatalistically. 'Everyone living anywhere near the Buffalo on the Natal side professes to be an expert on the Zulus. But they're mainly poseurs. Even Shepstone, who speaks Zulu well and has been close to them for twenty years or more, has lost touch with Cetswayo. And he's got his hands full in the Transvaal now, anyway.'

The Colonel edged his chair closer. 'But there is one man who knows as much as there is to know about the Zulu nation.'

'An Englishman?'

'Sort of – half Irish, actually. His name is John Dunn, or "Jantoni" as he's known to the Zulus. He is the son of a drunken Irish trader and while still a boy went off on his own to hunt and trade. He can read and write but he has little formal education, and although he's now in his fifties and is quite a rich man, he's never been accepted in Natal social circles.'

Lamb smiled. 'Mind you, it's no great accolade to be accepted in Natal social circles. However, Dunn has become Cetswayo's only European confidant. Years ago, he backed the wrong horse in the Zulu battle for succession and he even fought against Cetswayo. But somehow he made his peace. He now lives in some style in Zululand on a large tract of land north of the Tugela given him by the King. He has the full rights of a Zulu chieftain, and I am told that he rules over kraals with a population of about ten thousand Zulus. He has his original half-caste wife – at least, I think he married her – but also twenty or more Zulu wives and God knows how many children.'

Simon frowned. 'He sounds as though he has gone completely native. Whose side is he on?'

'That's just the point. We have to make sure it is ours, although this could be difficult, in that I understand he scorns what we might call the fat burghers of Natal. Nevertheless, he will know Cetswayo's thinking and also the state and location of his army. We must harness Dunn and gain information from him.'

'Why not just summon him to Durban and question him?'

'Can't do that. Firstly, he's not the sort of man one just orders about. Don't forget, formally he's a Zulu chieftain, and anyway, he has lived a life of great independence for years, having nothing to do with what you might call civilisation. Having said that, we are gambling that, if it comes to a fight, he will cast in his lot with the strongest side, which must be us. There is a second point, however. He has been deliberately evasive for some time. Shepstone, who knows him well, of course, has sent several couriers to him, who all returned saying that Jantoni was away hunting. The man ain't exactly being helpful to us, Fonthill.'

The little man smiled again, so infectiously that Simon was impelled to smile back, as though they were sharing some secret joke.

'And this,' said the Colonel, 'is where you really do come in, my boy.'

'You want me to go to him?'

'More than that. We don't want you treated as another messenger. No.' Lamb rose and strode back to the wall map. He indicated an area within Zululand, a few miles north of the Lower Drift of the Tugela, in the south of the country. 'This is where he has his kraal, although, of course, he could be anywhere in his territory. We want you to find him and live with him for a while – long enough, anyhow, for you to be able not only to win his confidence, but also to learn something of the Zulu tongue and see for yourself how things are there.'

'I am to be a sort of spy?'

'You will be a formally accredited agent of the British army. You will, of course, reveal your identity to Dunn. But if the Zulus discover who you are they could well kill you.' The Colonel regarded him keenly. 'That won't be a simple assegai thrust either. It's more likely to be impalement through the anus.'

Simon gulped. One half of his mind considered rationally what was being said, but the other noticed, with relief, that his reaction was not extreme: some dryness of the mouth, perhaps, but nothing more. He concentrated. 'Why should Dunn take me in, sir?' he asked. 'What's to stop him turning me over to the Zulus for, er, a spot of impaling?'

'Highly unlikely,' Lamb responded briskly. 'Firstly, he is, after all, British and there are those who say that he would never betray a fellow countryman. Personally, I think that's all stuff. Your main protection will be a letter that you will carry from the Governor, Sir Bartle Frere – I have it here – explaining your mission and asking Dunn to assist you in every way. It is tantamount to an order from Her Majesty's Government and if Dunn rejects it, then he knows that he has burned his boats and bridges behind him. He may or may not do that. We shall have to see.

'Of course,' Lamb went on, 'the letter itself poses a danger for you. If you are captured by Zulus before you get to Dunn's kraal and they find the letter, then you could be in deep trouble. They probably won't be able to read it, of course, but they will know it is some form of official – *and secret* – document. They will either kill you on the spot or take you to the King. Once there, you would have to talk your way out of it. Using your Welsh, of course.' The Colonel smiled wryly.

'So we must reduce the risk. The letter will be sewn into the lining of your jacket. It must not be found. Which reminds me. You will pose as a hunter and trader who is visiting Dunn to do business with him. That's why your horsemanship is important. Dunn is a fine shot and lives in the saddle. You must, too.'

Simon smiled weakly. 'Quite so, sir. With whom and how do I communicate?'

'With me and only me. Sir Bartle doesn't want Shepstone . . . at least, let's say that we want to avoid any danger of misunderstandings. Shame I can't read Welsh. We could have used it as a code. You'll just have to think of some way of getting messages out safely.'

Simon realised that he had been presented with a heaven-sent opportunity to make the case for Jenkins to accompany him. He did so carefully, against an obvious antipathy from Lamb, pointing out Jenkins's reliability and his conduct on the *Devonia* that had earned him a mention in dispatches. 'And, sir,' Simon concluded with heartfelt sincerity, 'he's a better horseman and shot than me.'

'Very well.' The Colonel scribbled on a slip of paper. 'Take this chit to the quartermaster and fit yourselves out with hunting clothes – they must be well worn, mind – and rifles, a pair of good horses and whatever else you need. The QM is experienced in bush conditions. There is a ship sailing for Durban tomorrow. From there, make for the Tugela at the Lower Drift and cross into Zululand there. Anyone should be able to tell you how to find Dunn's kraal. It lies about forty miles into the territory. Here is the Governor's letter. Get your man to sew it into the lining of your jacket.'

The Colonel stood up. 'To repeat: what we need is information about the size of Cetswayo's army; how it is broken down into impis; where they are stationed; and how quickly they might be able to react. Pick up all you can about the King's attitude towards us and whether he will fight if he has to, knowing the force of our weaponry. A lot depends upon you, Fonthill. You could save lives.'

'Of course, sir. I will do my best.'

The two men shook hands. 'Oh, by the way. It's a pity you leave tomorrow. The *Edinburgh Castle* has just set sail from England with Covington and the 2nd/24ths on board. He will be sorry to have missed you, no doubt.'

'No doubt, sir. Thank you and goodbye.'

Chapter 5

Alice Griffith pulled back the curtains of her bedroom and looked out at the grey cloud torn on the high tops of the pines of Brecon Beacons a mile away. The dismal scene – rain was obviously lurking within that dirty cotton wool, probing to get through – did not depress her because she did not register what she saw. Like most mornings, she was preoccupied with the great question of what to do with her life.

She slumped into the little brocaded chair before the dressing table and began to brush her hair with long, rhythmical strokes. The features reflected in the mirror had now acquired a certain beauty: long, clean lines from the high cheekbones to that firm and slightly overlarge jaw; lips perhaps a little too full but well coloured; the grey eyes set beneath perfectly arched brows. The overall effect was undoubtedly pleasing. Yet it was not a happy face. The period since her coming-out ball had not been fulfilling. She had been able to tolerate only a couple of weeks of the London season. The balls she found boring, her love of dancing far outweighed by the banality of the young men who partnered her. And she disliked even more the studied, artificial informality of the set-piece events, although she had only survived two – Ascot, and the Eton–Harrow match at Lord's.

She poured hot water from a jug into a bowl and then absent-mindedly rubbed her face, shoulders and neck with a square of soft flannel. Life in the country had its pleasures. She enjoyed riding and had joined the hunt, going out often with Charlotte Fonthill, whom she was now growing to respect. It was unusual to find a well-read, opinionated woman in the shires and particularly one who was not afraid to debate the issues of the day with men. For her part, Mrs Fonthill had gradually, if grudgingly, grown to accept the strength of Alice's mind and the lucidity of her expression. Their friendship had developed and had grown into an ill-formed, unspoken but real alliance against dominant males.

The hunt, of course, could not take all her time and there was only so much she could do in helping her mother on the estate, visiting sick tenants and packing baskets of groceries to take to the poor of the village. She would have liked to take an interest in the economics of farming but her father strongly discouraged this. What she wanted, she knew, was a career. But doing what? Universities were closed to women and she could see no way of acquiring formal training for any of the professions. Miss Nightingale offered some sort of career for young ladies in nursing but Alice disliked the thought of being a distaff attachment to the army. So demeaning!

She had taken to riding over to the Fonthills' about once a fortnight. Although, despite their new friendship, she still found Mrs Fonthill a little daunting, she was fond of the Major. His gentle uncertainty reminded her of Simon. Simon, ah yes! She smiled as she buttoned up her dress. Simon! She certainly did not love him, of that she was sure. And she had no intention of marrying him – or anyone else, for that matter. Nevertheless, she was aware of a certain ambivalence in her attitude to the

Fonthills' son. The wanton, wilful side of her smiled (smirked?) at the way he had been captured. Then this thought made her feel contemptuous, both of herself and of Simon. Deep in her heart perhaps she was no better than the pretty little things who set out their stall during the Season and had no other thought than that of snaring a man. Simon was no better for falling. She had hoped for more from him. Yet he was thoughtful, quiet and paid no superficial compliments. He was also vulnerable and needed help from a supportive friend – the sort of role she could play. And . . . she *had* enjoyed kissing him. The carnality of the thought intruded and she shook her head in self-reproach. Alice had not come to terms with the stirrings of sensuality that had been a disturbing part of her life for several years now. She loved their thrill but resented their random persistence. She liked her life to be controlled. She frowned.

Should she visit the Fonthills that day? They might have news of Simon to add to the dutiful, rather dull contents of the two letters she had received from him. More to the point, talking to the Fonthills would give her a chance of discussing the present situation in the Middle East.

The newspapers were full of talk of possible war again with Russia, with whom Turkey was now in conflict. It was rumoured that the Reserves would be called out and that the Fleet would be sent to the Dardenelles. What a pity if there should be opportunities for advancement there, while Simon kicked his heels in a colonial backwater in Africa! Yes, she would ride to the Fonthills' and debate the matter with them – if Mrs F would let her get a word in edgeways.

The rain held off, although the going was heavy and it took her almost an hour to reach the Fonthills' redbrick house. As always, the welcome was warm, although not effusive.

Charlotte was at home and the Major was expected back at any moment.

'Do sit down, Alice,' said Mrs Fonthill, ushering her into the drawing room. 'Have you heard from Simon, by any chance?'

'Not for about two months, Mrs Fonthill. You may remember that I received two letters, one from Cape Town and the other from Durban in Natal, but he was in a hurry on both occasions and hardly even filled one page.'

'Ah yes,' said the older woman. 'He was equally non-committal with us. It is a very strange business. Both battalions of the regiment are serving in the same overseas posting for the first time for many years and yet Simon is with neither. I do hope that that strange incident of his illness is not being held against him.'

'I am sure not. I have the feeling that he has been selected for some special duty that he forbears to write about.'

Mrs Fonthill smiled. 'If that is so, Alice my dear, then it would suit Simon perfectly. He has always been a romantic and rather a dreamer, you know. He imagines things, and when he was young, he always lived in his own world. Something to do with being an only child, I expect. We were a little surprised, although delighted, when he chose to go into the regiment. That is why . . .' She frowned. 'But no matter. My main concern now is that he is managing to keep his seat on his horse. He is a dreadful horseman.'

They were interrupted by the arrival of the Major, who strode into the room and bent to brush his lips against his wife's cheek. He extended his hand to Alice and gave her a wide, embracing smile.

'You will stay for luncheon, please?'

'Oh, I do not wish to impose.'

'Nonsense. There is no imposition. In any case, Charlotte and I want to hear your views on whether England should involve itself with the Turkish business.'

Alice was aware that her declared interest in foreign affairs was not always approved by older people and she looked at the Major sharply. But there was no sign of condescension in his kindly smile.

The luncheon was light: consommé and cold mutton. So too, at first, was the conversation. The Major confided that the gas lighting system that he had installed in the house only twelve years ago now seemed as though it would be out of date, since Mr Edison in America had now found a way of 'subdividing' electricity so that it could be harnessed to provide domestic lighting. They also marvelled at the fact that the Queen herself had recently had a practical demonstration of the magic of the new telephone, when Miss Kate Field had sung 'Kathleen Mavourneen' into an instrument in a cottage at Osborne while Her Majesty had listened through another in the main house. What times they lived in!

'In fact,' said the Major, 'as far as politics are concerned, anyway, there is now a word which, I understand, describes them.'

'Really, my dear, what is that?'

'Jingo, or to be more correct, I suppose, jingoistic.'

Mrs Fonthill frowned. 'And what does that mean, pray?'

'Well, as I say, it seems to be the latest term for describing the England of today – or, at least, what is supposed to be the popular mood of the times vis-à-vis our attitude towards Russia and whether or not we should intervene with their war with Turkey.' The Major looked a little sheepish and clearly wished that he had never embarked on this line of conversation. 'I understand that it comes from a music hall song which is current.'

'Oh really, Major?' said Alice mischievously. 'Do sing it.'

'I . . . ah . . . am not familiar with the tune but I believe that the words go something like this:

> 'We don't want to fight,
> But by jingo if we do,
> We've got the ships,
> We've got the men,
> We've got the money, too.'

'How vulgar!' said Mrs Fonthill.

'Yes,' agreed Alice. 'But it is rather a lovely word. Jingo. Jingo . . .' She repeated it ruminatively. 'It sums up beautifully the attitude of those thoughtless people of whatever class who believe that Britain should involve herself in any and every war. They want blood and glory and see opportunities in other people's conflict to add to the Empire. I am not sure that I would not even exclude Lord Beaconsfield, as we must now call him, from their ranks. The jingoes. Yes. It's perfect for them.'

Mrs Fonthill pursed her lips and ignored her husband's almost imperceptible shake of the head. 'My dear Alice,' she began, 'we must help the Turks. Russia is up to her old tricks again and only we have the strength to intervene and face her down. If she conquers Turkey then she has an additional route to the North West Frontier of India and Afghanistan. Now, these are commonly held and common-sensical views. Does this make me – what d'yer call it – a jim-jam?'

'Jingoist, dear,' corrected the Major diffidently.

Alice flushed. 'Oh, I had no wish to give offence, Mrs Fonthill. But I do believe that we tend to rush into conflicts too quickly. Really, you know, we cannot have defensible interests in every confrontation between countries and I do think it rather arrogant, if I may say so, to consider ourselves the peacekeepers of the world.'

'The Pax Britannia has served the world very well so far,' responded Mrs Fonthill, 'and I hate to think what state the benighted people of inferior countries abroad would be in if it were not for the British Fleet. Take slavery, for instance . . .'

The Major gently interrupted his wife's flow by asking for some more of her excellent onion sauce with his mutton. The intervention, however, failed to divert the conversation.

'Yes, take slavery,' said Mrs Fonthill. 'That abominable traffic has virtually ground to a halt because of our naval patrols off the coast of West Africa. We were the first nation in the world to ban slavery in our own country and our own empire. Goodness knows how big the loathsome trade would have grown if we had not made a stand. No other country would have done it.'

Alice nodded. 'I quite agree. But, if I may say so, it was only right and proper that on this issue we should take the lead. After all, it was the English who began the awful business in the first place. Bristol and Liverpool have grown fat on it over the years. And, while we may have reduced the international trade, the ex-slaves of the southern states of America are, I am told, still living in penury and, of course, are not recognised as citizens by their government. I presume that you would not wish to declare war upon the United States of America to remedy their lamentable position?'

'Tosh, Alice. That is quite a different matter, as you know

very well. Goodness, it would be intolerable if the vote was extended to *everyone*! Think of it – servants and manual workers who have had no education being allowed to decide the government of the country. Whatever next! No.' She shook her head. 'My point is that Great Britain has a moral right to intervene when wrong is being done in the world. And when it comes to wrongdoing, Russia is behind most of it. Everyone knows that.'

Both Alice and the Major drew in their breath to speak but Mrs Fonthill continued remorselessly. 'Well, I say everyone. But that's not true. The Liberals, of course, continue to seize every opportunity to undermine our position on foreign affairs, even though Gladstone, that awful old man, says he has retired to the back benches. I don't believe *that* for a moment, I can tell you.' She squared her shoulders and settled back in her chair. 'His influence persists. Why, only the other morning the *Morning Post*, which is usually so sound on these matters, carried an article that suggested that the Russians might have a point in their attitude to Turkey. Can you imagine—'

'Yes, I know,' interrupted Alice. 'I wrote it.'

A sudden silence descended on the room. 'What?' exclaimed Mrs Fonthill.

The Major beamed. 'I say. How very interesting, Alice. Congratulations.'

Alice felt herself colour. 'Yes, well, it was the first time that I have done this sort of thing, you know.' She looked at her lap and then smiled at them both. 'I received ten guineas for it, which I thought was rather splendid.'

Mrs Fonthill blew out her cheeks. 'I am surprised, Alice, that a well-founded institution such as the *Morning Post* takes offerings from, well, amateurs, on matters which are so, ah, complex.'

The Major frowned slightly. 'Oh come now, my dear. That is rather condescending. The *Morning Post* has very high standards and obviously Alice has met them, or her article would not have been carried. I read it myself, without,' he smiled, 'realising that its author was our neighbour. I thought it very well argued, although I did not quite agree with every point.'

Alice's pride was now retreating as she realised that her secret was out. 'Oh, Major, you are very kind. And Mrs Fonthill, I do understand your position. I had no intention of telling you about this and it rather, er, slipped out. I am not sure whether Mama and Papa would approve of my writing, although I intend to tell them very soon. For the moment, however, I would be most grateful if you would be so kind as not to mention it to them. I would like to do so soon, but in my own way.' She regarded them both anxiously.

Mrs Fonthill looked down her nose and flicked a crumb away from her lap. 'Well, I don't approve of children having secrets from their parents, Alice,' she said. 'But,' and she looked up and suddenly smiled, 'this one is safe with us.'

'Oh, thank you both. You are really very kind to me, you know, and I am most grateful.'

'We will say no more on the matter,' said Mrs Fonthill. 'However, it would be nice, you know, *if* you submit another article, perhaps to include one or two points of view from . . .' her smile became a little fixed as she sought the right words, 'the other side, so to speak.'

Alice exchanged a half-hidden smile with the Major. 'Of course, Mrs Fonthill, I do take the point.'

They took a cup of fine China tea in the conservatory, although it was really too cold to sit there, and then Alice made her excuses. 'I fear the weather may close in and Papa dislikes me riding when the light begins to fade.'

'I shall ride with you,' said the Major.

Alice resisted his offer. She felt embarrassed at having to beg the Fonthills' indulgence on the matter of her writing – something that she had resolved to keep to herself. To ride with him would leave the matter hanging between them awkwardly and she wanted now to get away from her faux pas as quickly as possible. A compromise was reached by summoning Owen to drive Alice home in the carriage, with her horse tethered at the rear. This was just as well, because the heavens opened shortly after she had left and the rain beat heavily on the roof of the coach. By the time the Manor was reached, Alice's mood was one of annoyance at her indiscretion and frustration as, once again, she considered her future.

She remained subdued through dinner with her parents in the panelled dining room.

'Have the Fonthills heard from Simon lately?' enquired Mrs Griffith brightly.

'No, Mama.'

'Strange,' said the Brigadier.

Alice frowned. 'Really, Father,' she snapped, 'it is not strange at all. He has only been in South Africa for three or four months. He is obviously very occupied, and anyway, the mail takes several weeks to travel the great distance involved.'

'Quite so, my dear,' said the Brigadier.

The meal continued in silence until Alice took a deep breath and addressed her father again. 'Papa, I really must have something to do.'

The Brigadier put down his knife and fork slowly. 'Do? Do? What do you mean, Alice?'

'I mean, Father, that I cannot remain here filling my days with trivialities. I cannot simply do good works. I must use my mind in *real* work – just as a man would.'

Mrs Griffith leaned forward comfortingly. 'My dear, you must be patient. The right man *will* come along. Simon—'

Alice exploded. 'Simon is *not* the right man. Nor is any man. I am not going to sit at home waiting for some young barbarian to propose to me. Papa,' she turned back to her father, 'you know what I mean.'

Brigadier Griffith had the reputation among his neighbours of not being able to refuse his wilful daughter anything. Nevertheless, the officer had been renowned throughout his career for being a strict disciplinarian. His attitudes were those of his station and his time: he was illiberal and High Tory. His eyes narrowed now as he addressed his daughter.

'How dare you speak to your mother in that intemperate manner. You will go to your room immediately. I shall think of something for you to *do*, in due course.'

Alice recognised the storm signals. 'Very well, Papa. I am sorry, Mama.' She rose and left the room.

In her bedroom she walked to the window and looked out at the rain. She pursed her lips and reviewed her situation yet again. Her parents could say and do what they liked but they would *not* imprison her or present her as a slave on the country marriage market. To hell with that! If her determination to employ her brain in more demanding tasks than planning dinner menus led to conflict, then so be it. It was a confrontation she would win!

Slowly, Alice turned to her writing desk. She picked up a copy of that day's *Morning Post* and read once again the leader on the Russian–Turkish crisis. Rubbish of course. Impulsively, she reached for her pen, dipped it in the ink and began writing.

> To the Editor of the *Morning Post*.
> Dear Sir,
>   I read your leading article of today's date with growing disquiet . . .

Chapter 6

The two horsemen crested the hill with care, keeping a patch of high scrub behind them so that their silhouettes would not be exposed on the skyline.

'Sorry, sir, but you're still not relaxin',' said Jenkins with exasperation. 'You're grippin' too tightly with your calves an' ankles instead of your knees an' the poor beast doesn't know whether to walk or trot. If you go on like that, you'll ache like you've bin on a twenty-mile march, see, an' we'll never get to this kraal place.'

'To hell with it, man,' snarled Simon. 'Leave me to sit on the damned animal as I like. And don't call me sir. We're supposed to be traders.'

'What am I supposed to call you then, sir?'

'Call me bach. Or Fonthill.'

'Very good, sir.'

'Are you deliberately trying to annoy me, 352?'

'No, sir. But you shouldn't call me 352, then, should you?'

'Damn you, Jenkins.' Simon dug his heels into the flanks of his horse and cantered on, raising a small cloud of red dust. The Welshman urged his mount on and overtook Simon.

'Seriously, though, sir. I don't think we should raise dust. It can be seen for miles on this plain.'

Simon sighed. 'You're quite right,' he said, and the two riders slowed to a walk. Little remained to show that they were soldiers. They wore Afrikaan-type slouch hats and leather jackets worn smooth, particularly where their bandoliers of ammunition crossed their shoulders. The only hint of their military roles was their .44 calibre Martini-Henry rifles, which, after careful thought, Simon felt they should keep. These had been issued to the British army only four years before and, at eight pounds ten ounces, they were the lightest rifles ever produced for the military. More importantly, however, they were accurate up to 700 yards and deadly at 250 or less. Only one bullet at a time could be inserted into the breech but they were potent weapons and too good to leave behind, even if they were unlikely rifles for traders to carry.

The terrain through which they rode now was very different from that which they had left behind at the Lower Drift of the Tugela. Instead of sugar cane plantations and moist, wooded valleys, here the red-earthed plain was broken by jagged escarpments and conical, brown-grassed hills that rose haphazardly as though a giant had plucked them up at random, as a child pulls at a tablecloth. The track that they had followed from the river crossing had long since disappeared and they made their way now by compass, on a NNE bearing that they had been assured would eventually bring them to Dunn's kraal. It was not easy riding, for the plain was studded with thorn scrub and ant-bear heaps and crossed by dried riverbeds, or dongas, often forcing them to dismount and lead their horses. It also provided easy cover for a possible ambush.

They had been riding most of the day after crossing the river. At first they had met scattered groups of Zulus, some herding cattle, others regarding them stoically from their beehive-shaped huts. Simon was relieved to find that they seemed to take no interest in the two horsemen. As they penetrated further into Zululand, however, all signs of habitation disappeared. Occasionally they disturbed a small antelope but otherwise they seemed to be the only living things on the plain. Only the cries of raven-type birds wheeling high overhead disturbed the silence. The very quietness was discomforting.

The shock when they met the warriors, then, was all the greater.

Jenkins was leading and had wearily dismounted to lead his horse down the bank of yet another dried-up donga when, suddenly, they were no longer alone. From the riverbed appeared some thirty Zulus, who deployed to surround them with a speed that exuded military discipline. Simon observed them closely, for they were the first warriors he had seen. He had expected extravagant feathered headdresses and brightly coloured beads, but these men were unadorned, naked except for thongs around their waists from which hung flaps of animal skin front and back and tufts of what appeared to be grass tied above their calf muscles. Their black skins glistened in the evening sunlight. Most of them carried short stabbing spears – the famous assegai. These weapons looked quite as fearsome as their reputation. The blade was about ten inches from tip to shoulder and about three thick fingers wide at the broadest part, near where the tang, the slender point at its base, had been rammed into the hollowed haft and bound with what looked like resin over a tube of hide. The haft was some three feet long, broadened into a slight bulb at the bottom. The warriors carried long, dappled shields, probably made of cowhide, behind which Simon glimpsed other spears and clubs clutched in their left hands. Looking at them, he received an impression of great individual strength. Although the warriors were only of medium height, they all had thighs like young oaks and chests that were wide and deep. The Zulus he had met in Natal were nothing like this.

No Zulu spoke but their assegais, all held underhand, were pointed at Simon and Jenkins. 'Don't touch your rifle, 352,' said Simon, quietly.

'I thought you weren't goin' to call me 352,' murmured Jenkins.

The tallest of the Zulus, who wore a headring waxed into his short, tightly curled hair, raised his spear to Simon and spoke several words in Zulu. There was no reaction from the other natives, so Simon presumed it was a question.

He rose in his stirrups and pointed ahead. 'We go to Jantoni,' he said. 'We are English, not Afrikaaners. Not Boers. English.'

Slowly, the Zulu repeated the name. 'Jantoni.'

'Yes. We go to Jantoni. To trade.'

The leader gestured to Simon with his assegai in a motion that clearly ordered him to dismount. He did so and the Zulus immediately closed in on the two men. 'Don't let go of the reins,' said Simon. 'We may have to leave quickly.'

'If we have to leave quickly, you'll fall off,' replied Jenkins, keeping his eyes on the tall Zulu.

The leader now approached them and slowly, with the end of his assegai, thrust open the leather coats of first Simon and then Jenkins. He gestured to another Zulu and gave a low order. Immediately, their saddlebags were opened and the contents scattered on the ground. They were briefly examined by the chief, who uttered another command, and to Simon's surprise, the contents were then carefully replaced in the bags, which were then buckled up again.

Out of the corner of his eye, Simon noticed a Zulu lay a hand on one of the rifles and begin to withdraw it from its saddle holster. Unhurriedly, Simon raised his hand and touched the Zulu's shoulder. 'No,' he said and shook his head.

The man jumped back and raised his assegai. With startling speed the leader leaped forward and plunged his own assegai into the man's stomach, twisting the blade and withdrawing it in one smooth movement, so that it was free long before the warrior doubled up in agony and sank to the ground. For the first time, Simon heard the iklwa. Everyone stood motionless and watched as the Zulu, in grotesque silence, writhed at their feet, his hands vainly attempting to stem the blood which pumped from his terrible wound. Without a word, he curled into the foetal position and died in the dust before them. The incident had lasted perhaps only forty-five seconds.

The silence was eventually interrupted by Jenkins. 'Fancy that,' he murmured.

The speed and gratuitous barbarity of the act had transfixed Simon. He had never before witnessed violence so brutal and final. It had happened at such speed that there had been no time to feel afraid or even threatened. Nor did he feel fear now, only curiosity at what would happen next. He looked at the Zulu chief, who returned his gaze imperturbably, with eyes black and quite expressionless.

Then the leader uttered another command and gestured and the body was dragged into a patch of scrub. He turned to Simon and spoke quickly in Zulu. Simon thought he heard the name Jantoni as the chief pointed with his red-bladed assegai in a more northerly direction than that which they had been following. It was a clear command and the party set off, Simon and Jenkins leading their horses and the Zulus, still surrounding them, setting a brisk pace, half walk, half trot.

'I don't think I'm goin' to like this,' said Jenkins. 'I was told we'd be cruisin', not marchin'.'

'It will teach you to criticise my horsemanship,' replied Simon. 'Come on. We'd better keep up if we don't want an assegai in our bellies.'

They marched for about another two hours, until the sun was brushing the low hills to the west. Then a halt was made in the trench of a donga that still contained a trickle of water. Without paying any attention to the two white men, the majority of the Zulus squatted on their haunches while three noticeably younger men, who, Simon noticed, carried no weapons, shook out a bundle and began distributing cloaks and straw sleeping mats. As the elders took snuff, the young men set about collecting dried dung and what little thorn bush kindling they could find and began making a fire, upon which they stood a blackened cooking pot containing what appeared to be mealies.

Simon and Jenkins slowly unsaddled their horses and hobbled them, making sure that their movements were un-hurried and deliberate. The Zulus made no attempt to restrain or direct them, but Simon noticed that the chief rarely took his eyes off them. When wooden bowls full of mealies were handed to the warriors, the leader gestured to them and, hungry as they were, they squatted and dipped their fingers into the mess.

'That's sociable, like, then, isn't it?' said Jenkins, settling himself against the side of the riverbed. 'It looks as though they're not goin' to open up our tummies just yet. They wouldn't be wantin' to waste good food now, would they?'

'No. But I can't see why they should want to kill us anyway.

116

We're not at war with them and killing white men is not Cetswayo's style, from what I've heard.'

Simon mused for a moment. He nodded to the leader. 'I think he's taking us to Dunn,' he said. 'But the way he was pointing was not the direction we were given for Dunn's kraal. It was too far north.' He pondered. 'I wonder if Dunn is with the King and we are being taken there. Now that would be a stroke of luck.'

Jenkins raised his eyes to the heavens. 'Oh yes. Oh yes indeed. What a great stroke of luck. I can hardly wait. We'll probably be served for the royal breakfast.'

'Rubbish. Zulus aren't cannibals. In their own way, they are very civilised people, although I must confess – I don't much like the chief's way of restoring discipline.'

The two men had been sitting half in, half outside the circle of Zulus, and speaking quietly, although the warriors paid no attention to them. Simon regarded the chief covertly in the gathering dusk. Apart from his headband – no one else wore one – there was no obvious sign of rank, although a few flecks of grey could be seen above his ears. He was about forty-five years old, the oldest of the group by far, and his comparative age had not seemed to impair his easy, loping stride. He sprawled now, not ungracefully, the firelight flickering along his blue-black skin and illuminating his round face. Simon noticed that, although the nose was flattened and negroid, the jaw was firm and the eyes were well set apart. Even in repose, his manner exuded dignity and authority.

Simon climbed to his feet slowly and unhurriedly walked to where the saddlebags lay, near the horses. A guard had been posted at this point, and as he approached, Simon saw the young warrior look quickly at his chief. However, no instructions seemed to be conveyed and the Zulu stepped back to allow Simon to rummage in his pack. He found what he was looking for and sauntered back to the circle, squatting near the chief. He produced a silver flask and, looking expressionlessly at the chief, took a draught of the whisky inside. Wiping the neck of the flask, he reached out and offered it to the chief. The Zulu sat upright and gingerly took the flask and smelled the contents. He looked at Simon and the big round face slowly broke into a smile, revealing two rows of even white teeth as big as tombstones. He tossed his head back and drank deeply from the flask.

Simon smiled and gestured to the north-east. 'Jantoni?' he asked.

The chief nodded. 'Jantoni,' he affirmed. He reached for a stick and began speaking slowly and distinctly as he drew in the dust. The language was meaningless to Simon but he thought he detected the word 'Ulundi'. The chief drew a large circle with many tiny beehive-shaped symbols within it. Outside the circle he scratched numerous crosses, tailing them impatiently as though extending them into infinity. Then, with practised strokes of the stick, he outlined the shape of a bullock or buffalo's head, complete with horns. Turning to Simon, he gestured with his hand to the ground on which he was sitting, then to the circle in the dust, and held up two fingers.

Simon frowned for a moment and then understanding came flooding in. He pointed to the circle and asked, 'Ulundi?'

The chief nodded and held up his fingers again.

'Two days' march,' said Simon and nodded. He turned to Jenkins. 'Dunn is with the King at the royal kraal at Ulundi and he's taking us there. It's two days' march from here.'

Gravely, the chief wiped the top of the flask and handed it back to Simon. The Englishman nodded and solemnly took another draught, wiped the neck and once more handed it back. The ritual continued with great formality until Jenkins could stand it no longer.

'If what's in that flask is what I think is in that flask, bach sir, I could do with just a wetting of it myself, if you think that's in order.'

'Certainly, Jenkins.' Simon ceremoniously handed the flask to the Welshman, who raised it, nodded to the chief and Simon and drank. Grimacing in appreciation, he wiped his mouth with the back of his hand and returned the flask to Simon, who, in turn, wiped the top again and handed it to the Zulu.

'Bloody 'ell,' exploded Jenkins. 'Don't be wastin' good liquor like that on an 'eathen. We shall need every drop of that before we've finished this trip.'

'Don't talk like that,' said Simon evenly, smiling at the chief. 'He may not speak English but he can understand your tone. So smile, damn you. This is a good investment, Jenkins, and anyway, I've got two more flasks full.'

So the drinking continued until, to show good faith, Simon upended the flask to allow the last drop of liquor to disappear into the dust at their feet. Without a word, the chief rolled over, pulled his cloak over his head and fell asleep instantly.

Simon rose to his feet rather unsteadily. 'I think that the bar is now closed, 352,' he said, conscious that the rest of the Zulus were watching him with a new interest. He walked to the saddlebags, replaced the flask and pulled out two blankets. 'I shall have a thick head in the morning but I think that, on the whole, it has been worth it.'

The two men slept soundly and the party was on the march well before dawn. As the day wore on, there was even less attention paid to the two white men, the Zulus' mile-consuming gait setting a pace that soon had Simon and Jenkins lagging well behind. It was punishing for them, for they had to lead their horses down each donga, picking their way through stones over which the Zulus hopped quite unconcernedly. The sun was hot but it was the humidity that caused the most discomfort, rendering their shirts rags of wet cotton as the day progressed. Simon felt that he dared not remove his leather jacket and be parted from the important letter sewn into the lining. At one point, he and Jenkins mounted their horses to catch up with the main party, but seemingly within seconds, they were surrounded again and gestured to dismount.

They camped once more that night and were up again at sun-up. Now the country they traversed was easier. They moved across vast paddocks of grassland where herds of big horned cattle, tended by lithe adolescents, munched disinterestedly as they passed. The hills that broke up the horizon were lower, although still rocky and stark. Great clouds of pure white cumulus bunched together against the blue, reminding Simon of languorous August school holidays back home at Brecon. The humidity was easier now that they were further away from the coast, but the pace was unrelenting.

The longed-for midday snuff break had just ended when the warrior at the head of the party raised his assegai and gestured ahead, calling to his chief. Simon lifted his head and saw the tiny figures of three horsemen descending a mound about a mile away, raising dust as they rode towards them. The chief grunted and increased the pace to a jog to meet the riders.

'It must be Dunn,' said Simon, the perspiration running down his chest and darkening his shirt at the waist belt. 'Few Zulus have horses. He's come to meet us.'

'Very kind of 'im, I'm sure,' panted Jenkins. 'Now perhaps we can ride these blasted 'orses instead of pullin' 'em along.'

Very soon the dots took shape into the figures of two black riders, looking like Zulus but carrying distinctive red and black shields, flanking a tall European. The horsemen reined up in a flurry of dust and the European dismounted and addressed the chief in fluent Zulu. He was a big man in his late forties, deeply tanned and with a full beard covering the front of his hunting shirt. Old cotton trousers were tucked into fine leather boots and a Boer-type slouch hat hung between his shoulder blades from a thong around his throat. Simon noted with interest that a modern army Martini-Henry rifle was slung behind his saddle. If the newcomer's appearance was raffish, his manner exuded confident authority and it was clear that the chief was treating him with respect. Simon and Jenkins waited diffidently as the two men talked. Then the big man turned and strode towards them.

He held out his hand. 'G'day, gentlemen,' he said in a voice that carried the nasal twang of a native Natalian. 'Dunn. John Robert Dunn.'

'How do you do,' responded Simon awkwardly. 'Simon Fonthill. This is my, er, associate . . .' With a surge of embarrassment, he realised that he did not know Jenkins's Christian name. 'My associate, ah, Mr Jenkins.'

The brown eyes of Dunn betrayed no sign of surprise. 'G'day, Mr Jenkins.'

'Glad to meet you, Mr Dunn.'

The tall man's gaze travelled quickly over their horses and

packs and took in their dishevelled appearance. 'Rough journey, then, eh?'

'The Zulus prevented us from riding,' said Simon. 'And it's been rather warm.'

Dunn smiled in a not unfriendly way. 'So it has.' He gestured to them to sit down and lowered himself easily on to the coarse grass. 'You seemed to be wandering a bit, so the King sent this inDuna . . .'

'InDuna?'

Dunn looked at him sharply. 'Yes, inDuna. It means chief or commander in Zulu.' He smiled again. 'I guess you could call me one. Anyway, the King sent this party to get you, since you didn't seem to know exactly where you were going. You might have got into a bit of trouble. Some of the kraals are a bit touchy just now.'

Simon looked at Dunn in disbelief. 'You mean the King knew we were here?'

Dunn nodded, the tolerant half-smile still on his face. 'Oh yes. I guess he must have known as soon as you crossed the Tugela. Not much goes on here without him knowing about it. What are you doing here, anyway?'

'Well, as a matter of fact, we were looking for you.'

'Looking for me?' The smile dropped from Dunn's face and his eyes narrowed. 'You were way off track. What do you want with me, then?'

Simon looked at the Zulus. The whole party, including the warriors who had arrived on horseback with Dunn, were squatting on the ground, all regarding the white men with interest. There was no way of knowing whether or not they understood the conversation. Certainly they were within earshot.

'We have, ah, come to trade.'

'Trade!' Dunn threw back his head and roared with laughter. 'You are . . . traders?'

'Certainly,' said Simon with desperate dignity. 'We wish to trade with you.'

Dunn looked at each of them in turn for some seconds, the half-smile back on his lips. He took a breath to speak and clearly changed his mind. He shrugged. 'Ah well. That will disappoint the King, anyway.'

'Why?'

'He thought you were emissaries.'

'No, no,' Jenkins intervened helpfully. 'We're English – well, at least he is. I'm from Wales, see.'

Dunn looked blankly at Jenkins and Simon hurriedly continued. 'Why on earth should the King think we were emissaries?'

Dunn languidly stretched a long leg along the grass and rested his elbow on a rock. 'Because the word came from the border kraals that two soldiers in – what d'yer call it? – mufti, that's it, had crossed the Tugela and were heading in the general direction of Ulundi, although off the right route.' He looked at Simon and smiled again. 'He thought that one of you, at least, was quite an important inDuna because he couldn't sit his saddle like the horse soldiers do. No offence, mind.'

'None taken,' said Simon stiffly. He lowered his voice so that the watching natives could not hear. 'Do these Zulus understand English?'

'Not a word. Why?'

'We *have* come to see you and I would welcome a chance of speaking to you in private.'

Dunn slowly got to his feet. The effect was that of a bear stretching. 'Well, all right. But King Cetswayo wants to see you so you had better think of something to tell him that doesn't arouse his suspicions. You don't look like traders to me and you won't look like traders to him.' His voice took on a sharp edge. 'He's no fool, you know. You redcoats seem to think that just because he's a black heathen he can be fed any old line. That's just not so. He's a shrewd, intelligent man. I think he's a good man, too. So you'd better put your thinking caps on. Let's mount up. The King's waiting.'

Dunn took the lead on his large bay and as Simon and Jenkins fell in behind, so the two Zulu horsemen, riding effortlessly with bare feet in the stirrups and with shields slung over their left shoulders, completed the party in the rear. The big man set a fast pace and pulled away a little.

'What are we going to tell the King, then?' asked Jenkins from the corner of his mouth.

'We must stick to our story that we are traders. It's too late to think of anything else credible. Above all, we must not admit that we are soldiers.'

Jenkins smiled. 'Well, bach sir, they're not goin' to think that you are cavalry, that's for sure.'

'Be quiet. People from the Glasshouse shouldn't throw stones.'

The party rode for half an hour, picking their way through herds of the most indolent, well-fed cattle, which Simon presumed must belong to the King, until they topped a gentle rise and looked down on the King's kraal at Ulundi.

To Simon and Jenkins, used to the small groupings of beehive huts that constituted the few Zulu villages they had seen so far, the capital presented an amazing sight. It stood on a gentle slope that rose from the banks of the White Umfolozi River and, observed from a distance of just under a mile, resembled a giant anthill. The kraal was defined by a thorn fence that must have enclosed at least ninety acres of land, corralling hundreds of hive-shaped structures, grouped, in turn, around a central cattle pen. Tiny black figures could be seen between the huts and spilling out beyond the thorn barrier on to the surrounding plain, where more cattle grazed. Scores of smoke spirals curled into the sky and merged with the dark blue hills in the background. Ulundi was vibrant and as alive as a termites' nest. It was an aboriginal metropolis.

Dunn turned around in his saddle and waited for the others to draw alongside. He nodded ahead. 'This is the royal kraal.' He spoke with what could be construed as pride in his voice. 'About one third of a million people live here, and King Cetswayo has absolute authority over them.' His mocking smile returned. 'That means that quite a few people die here, too. So if I were you, I wouldn't let on that I was in the British Army – if you are, that is.'

He looked quizzically at Simon. 'But I don't want to give the wrong impression. The days when people were put to death on a whim have long since gone. Shaka and Dingane did that but Cetswayo does not. He's a fair man and the ways of the Zulu can teach the people of Durban a thing or two.' Dunn spat in emphasis. 'The King doesn't want trouble with the British and it's part of my job here to keep him out of it.'

Simon gestured ahead. 'Do you live here, then?'

'Good God, no. I am visiting at the moment. I've got a few acres of my own near the coast. I'm my own man and the King knows it. But I can be useful to him and he knows that, too.'

The party began to trot towards a drift in the river and the city fell away from view.

'Are we seeing the King now, then?' enquired Jenkins, a trifle anxiously.

'You are. I was sent to get you.'

Jenkins pulled on his moustache. 'I don't fancy crawlin' on me belly or any of that stuff,' he said. 'We don't 'ave to do any of that when we meet the King, do we?'

'No. Just bow your head.' Dunn's teeth flashed through his whiskers. 'Just like when you say hello to Queen Victoria.'

'Ah, righteo, then,' said Jenkins, now riding straight, like a Guardsman. 'I'll throw in a curtsey too, if you like.'

The horsemen cantered through thicker herds of cattle, tended by slim young boys who now watched them with undisguised interest. Simon had the impression that not many white men visited Ulundi. The kraal reappeared as they rounded a low spur and immediately they were surrounded by Zulus, who raised their spears and sticks in salute to Dunn and fell into step with the horses, forming a trotting mass several hundred strong, to usher them towards a wide gap in the stockade. Dunn rode to the central cattle pen and dismounted, gesturing to them to tether their horses to a low rail.

'What about our packs and guns?' asked Simon.

Dunn gave him a keen look. 'They're safer here than in Piccadilly Circus. I've heard what happened to the young buck who fancied your rifle back there. You're the King's guests here, so no one will touch your possessions. Come.' He gestured towards a large, low mud hut, built in rectangular European style and by far the largest dwelling to be seen.

The big man led the way and pushed open the unpainted door. The others followed and immediately began coughing as the smoke of the interior engulfed them. Dimly, they perceived a beaten earth floor, leading to simple wooden furniture grouped on woven matting at the far end of the room. The light was poor, for there were no windows, but the glow from the fire, burning despite the heat outside, picked out a number of women of uncertain age grouped around a large Zulu who reposed on a roll of matting.

He rose as they entered and Simon regarded him closely. He was as tall as Dunn – about six feet two inches – broadly built and clearly had possessed a fine athletic stature in his youth. Now, in early middle age, he had developed a large stomach, and rolls of fat followed the contours of what had once been sharply defined pectoral muscles in his chest. His legs were finely proportioned and he stood with an air of erect nonchalance, a handsome shawl thrown over one shoulder and a brightly coloured cotton cloth wound round his waist. His feet were enormous, with widely splayed toes and the gaps between almost white. The King's face was round, with wide-set eyes and a snub nose under a broad forehead, which was topped by a ring waxed firmly into his short black hair. His beard and moustache were neatly clipped short and bore no hint of grey. His expression was serene as he observed the newcomers.

Cetswayo made no movement as Dunn approached. The Natalian bowed his head and spoke quickly in low, guttural Zulu. The King raised his hand languidly and Dunn turned to Simon and Jenkins. The two intuitively took two paces forward and bowed their heads in unison. 'Your Majesty,' said Simon.

The King regarded them with obvious interest and spoke slowly and quietly. 'The King says that you are welcome to Ulundi,' Dunn translated, 'as are all men who come in peace.'

'Please thank His Majesty and tell him that we certainly come in peace,' responded Simon. 'We have nothing but respect for him and his people. We did not expect to meet him so have no gifts worthy of his status. But . . .' Simon fumbled in the small haversack at his hip, 'if he will accept this small and inadequate token of our respect we will be highly honoured.' And he handed Dunn his small silver hip flask.

Dunn bowed, translated and handed the flask to the King, who slowly unscrewed the cap, smelled the contents, replaced the cap and expressionlessly handed the flask to one of his women attendants.

'You should have consulted me about that,' said Dunn evenly without taking his eyes off the King. 'He doesn't drink much alcohol but silver is a good idea. You could have insulted him, but as it is, I think you have got away with it.'

The King spoke again and, with a small movement of hand and head, gestured for them to sit on a mat that was unrolled at their feet. A chair was brought for the King, who lowered himself into it, picked up an assegai and toyed with it as he addressed them.

'The King would like to know,' said Dunn, 'what you are doing in his country. As a matter of fact,' he added, his eyes twinkling, 'so would I.'

'Good luck, bach,' murmured Jenkins softly without moving his lips.

Simon looked the King firmly in the eye and spoke slowly and clearly. 'We are traders,' he said. 'We have come to your country to trade.'

Dunn's face was expressionless as he translated. Not so the King's. Immediately he frowned and spoke with animation, jabbing the assegai towards the two men in emphasis.

'The King says,' Dunn relayed, 'that he cannot understand how you can be traders when you come to his country without knowing it – that was clear because you seemed to be avoiding kraals but were going in no clear direction – and without knowing the language of his country. He also says that you do not look like any traders he has met before.'

Simon had not relaxed his eye contact with the King. 'We are new to the ways of this country because we came to South Africa only two months ago,' he said. 'We wish to set up a business trading cattle in Natal but we need stock. We heard in Cape Colony that Jantoni in Zululand had good cattle and we came to find him and buy cattle from him.'

The King considered this for a moment and then his eyes narrowed as he addressed Dunn. 'The King wants to know why you don't want to buy cattle from the Zulu people. The King himself has the best herds in the whole of Africa.'

Simon swallowed but maintained his gaze. 'We do not have the Zulu tongue, so we could not talk to Zulu people in their kraals. And we did not presume to think that we could buy from the King. We know he is not a trader.'

Dunn allowed one eyelid to drop. 'Smart answer, sonny,' he said before turning back to the King.

King Cetswayo nodded at the reply but his bearing remained stiff as he sat in his wooden chair. His movements were no longer languid and he fidgeted with the assegai, one thumb constantly rubbing the edge of the blade. He was clearly disappointed in his visitors. He began speaking again.

'If you are traders,' translated Dunn, 'how is it that you have the very latest army rifles, the Martini-Henry. He knows that the army does not sell them.'

Simon did not hesitate. 'We bought them in England before we set sail – directly from the manufacturer. Anybody can do that if they have the money. Please point out to the King that not everyone who has a Martini-Henry is a soldier. Jantoni has one and he is not a soldier.'

Dunn shot him a quick glance. 'You've got nerve, I'll give you that,' he said, before relaying the answer.

Immediately, the King's expression of annoyance changed and he spoke quickly.

'Very well,' said Dunn. 'If you can get rifles that easily, the King is happy to trade with you. He will sell you as many cattle as you want in return for rifles. But he is anxious to tell you that these will not be used for aggressive purposes, particularly against the British, whom he regards as his brothers. He wants them to defend his people against the Boers, who are trying to take his land in the north-west.'

Simon took a deep breath and this time addressed the white man directly. 'Mr Dunn, you know that the authorities in the Cape will not allow the trading of guns with the Zulu.' He took a calculated risk. 'Although I believe that there have been exceptions in the past and you have been involved in them.' He saw Dunn's eyes flicker and presumed that his guess had been correct. 'But it is something with which we could not be involved. We trade in cattle. We do not sell guns.'

As Simon's words were relayed, Cetswayo's expression hardened and he fell silent. Only the sound of the flies buzzing in the smoke disturbed the quiet. Eventually, the King spoke.

'The King wishes to know if you have seen Somtseu and if you bring any message from him.'

For the first time, Simon was wrong-footed. 'Somtseu?' he repeated.

Dunn became impatient. 'You really don't know much about this country, do you? Somtseu is the Zulu name for that pompous old bastard Shepstone. He used to be Secretary for

Native Affairs in Natal. He knows the King well – as a matter of fact, he crowned him.' Dunn snorted. 'Although he'd got no right to. Now he's in the Transvaal, stirring up more trouble. But the King knows he is important and I suppose he is.'

'No. Please tell the King that I have never met Shepstone. We are just traders.'

The King had been growing impatient at the exchange between the two white men, and when the translation was made, he got to his feet and, with an irritable gesture of his assegai, indicated that the audience was over. The trio bowed and made for the door but Cetswayo called Dunn back and spoke to him quietly for a moment as the others thankfully stepped into the clean air outside the building.

'You did well, bach sir,' exploded Jenkins. 'I didn't think that you could be such a good liar.'

'Thanks, but I am not sure that the King believed me. We've just got to rely on Dunn to keep us out of trouble. If he is on our side then I think we will stay alive. But I must talk to him – I can't fathom him out yet.'

Within a minute Dunn joined them. 'Can we talk?' asked Simon anxiously.

'I think we'd better,' said Dunn, striding on. 'But not here. Follow me.'

The big man led them through a rabbit warren of lanes between the conically shaped huts. The kraal teemed with Zulus: men, obviously of various warrior castes, judging by their ages, lying in the shade, smoking or taking snuff; while the women ground grain or bustled by carrying loads, always busy. Children were everywhere, playing in the dust, fighting with sticks or – the smaller ones – crawling over patient male adults. Simon noticed that the children always seemed to be indulged, and found, in the four-minute walk to Dunn's hut, not one man who seemed to be employed. Everywhere the women seemed to be toiling while the men lay resting. Dunn was clearly known and drew respectful nods as he strode by. Jenkins and Simon, on the other hand, were objects of great interest. The Zulus made no effort to conceal their curiosity and the children gaped in wonder as the strange trio, in their layered clothing and heavy boots, walked by.

They came to a beehive that was a little larger than the others and set slightly apart. Here Dunn gestured and dropped to his knees so that he could crawl through the low opening. The others followed and found that they were in a cool dwelling made of a light framework of woven saplings and grass thatching. It was supported by a central pole, but to Simon's relief, there was no fire. The floor had been beaten to a polished surface of clay and cow dung and mats hung from pegs in the walls. There was no sign of formal furniture.

A young girl stood as they entered. She approached Dunn and they exchanged a few words in Zulu before she kissed him lightly on the cheek, European style. As Simon's eyes became accustomed to the gloom he saw that she was taller than most Zulu girls and considerably lighter in colour. As they had scrambled through the entrance, he had caught a glimpse of naked breasts, but she had covered herself with a simple cotton garment, although her legs and feet were bare, apart from tufts of grass worn, Zulu-style, above her calves. Her hair was Zulu black but long and straight and not crinkled close to the scalp. Her features were open and un-negroid. Only her style of dress, her coffee-coloured skin and a fullness of her lips betrayed her half-caste origin. She smiled at the visitors without shyness.

'This is my daughter, Nandi,' said Dunn.

'How do you do,' said Simon, taking the hand that was thrust confidently towards him.

'Very pleased to meet you, miss,' echoed Jenkins, sounding very much as though he meant it.

The girl gave no word of greeting but smiled at them warmly, revealing rows of strangely small, white teeth behind the full lips. Dunn spoke to her in Zulu and she immediately left the hut. Simon could not help noticing how tight were her buttocks under the shift as she crawled through the entrance.

'Nandi,' repeated Simon. 'Is that a Zulu name?'

'Very much so,' said Dunn. 'I named her after Shaka's mother in tribute to the Zulus. The King was pleased. He took it as the compliment it was meant to be.' He unhooked a mat and threw them mats of their own. 'You might as well know. I've got twenty-four children, so far, and she's the brightest of them. I've also got ten wives – also so far – and all of them are Zulu, except one, the first.'

He began to fill a pipe and looked across at them. 'You shocked?'

'Er . . . no,' said Simon. 'Not at all.'

'No, bach,' said Jenkins readily. 'My da had four wives. Mind you, he had them one at a time, like . . .' He tailed off. 'That was in Wales, see, and I suppose things are different 'ere.'

Dunn smiled easily. 'I suppose they are. They say in Durban that I've gone native. So I have and I don't care a pot of buffalo dung what they think of me there. I left what I suppose you would call civilisation about twenty-five years ago, crossing the Tugela with Catherine. She was fifteen and I wasn't much older. She was the half-caste daughter of my father's old associate. Both of our parents were dead and I'd been cheated out of wages by a Dutchman. So I took off to live with the Zulus.'

Dunn put a match to the tobacco and drew on the pipe. 'It wasn't easy at first but I built us a kraal and broke in oxen for a living. Later I traded cattle and gradually built a herd. I kept myself to myself under the reign of old Mpande, Cetswayo's father, but I backed the wrong horse for a time when the family was brawling for the succession.

'I just about escaped with my skin when Cetswayo crushed the iziGqoza at Ndondakusuka in '56.' He smiled at the memory. 'In fact, I only got across the river by holding on to the tail of my horse.' His face hardened. 'Jehovah! There was killing that day. The skeletons are still there. They call it the Mathambo, the Place of Bones.'

He sat up. 'But enough of this. What do you want of me?'

Simon leaned forward. 'Is it safe to speak here?'

'As long as you're not going to break into fluent Zulu at the top of your voice, it is.'

'Very well.' Simon took off his jacket and slipped the tip of his knife into the lining and withdrew the letter. He handed it to Dunn – and then paused in embarrassment. 'Forgive me,' he said, 'but you do . . .?'

'Yes, I do,' said Dunn, taking the letter. 'I haven't gone *that* native.' With broad fingers he tore it open and his eyes went immediately to the signature at the bottom. His lips pursed and he whistled noiselessly. 'From the Governor himself, eh? I must be becoming important. I half feared that it was another note from old Somtseu – and *that* would have gone the way of all the others.'

Dunn read the letter silently. Eventually he looked up and

frowned. 'I don't like this. I don't like this at all. You know what this says?'

Simon nodded.

'Well, it's nonsense. I am supposed to harbour you both while you gather information about the King, his army and his intentions. There are several things wrong with that.' Dunn slapped a broad forefinger into the palm of his left hand. 'First, you can't speak the language, you don't know the country and you can't just go blundering around Zululand.' He scowled. 'Second, the King needs persuading that you are traders and not spies, so he will be watching you – and, dammit, I shall have to sell you some cattle to make you look genuine.'

This clearly pained Dunn as much as, if not more than the other factors and he sat silently for a moment in glum contemplation. Simon opened his mouth to speak but Dunn silenced him with a gesture.

'Third, all of this sounds as though the authorities are preparing for war, and that's the bit I like least of all.'

'No,' said Simon eagerly. 'I believe that you are wrong about that.' He checked himself. 'At least, I am not privy to policy, of course, but it could well be that the information we supply will lead to a peaceful solution to all this.'

Dunn continued as though he had not heard a word. 'And why do I like it least of all? I'll tell you.' He leaned forward on his crossed legs and his brown eyes burned into each of them. 'There are two reasons.

'The first is that the redcoats in Durban and the Cape have no idea what they will be taking on if they clash with the Zulus. This is not just a bunch of Cape Kaffirs, you know. This is a highly disciplined, well-trained military nation.' Dunn rocked back. 'The Zulus have the biggest and best standing army this side of the Equator – perhaps in the whole of Africa . . .'

'How many men?' Simon enquired quickly.

'Never you mind that for the moment. Take my word for it, the Zulu army is huge and it hasn't washed its spears for some years now. There are hotheads who would just love the chance. And they would be formidable. Ask the Boers about that.'

'And the second reason?' asked Simon quietly.

Dunn reflected silently for a moment. 'The second reason is the most difficult part for me. You see, these are my people now. Even though I backed his brother against him twenty-two years ago, Cetswayo never held it against me. He gave me land, he allowed me to have my own men – the red and black shields you saw this morning – and he let me live my own life in his country.' He gestured with his pipe. 'Of course he used me. I've been a kind of link with the Europeans, and once – you were right – I was able to get him rifles. But it was only a hundred and sixty and Shepstone knew all about it. The fat farmers of Durban think I smuggle guns all the time into Zululand. But that's not true.

'No. The King has been good to me and I don't want to betray him. Anyway,' he looked up defiantly, 'if there is a war and the British win it – which is by no means certain – then I lose all I have built up here.'

A silence hung for a moment and was broken as Nandi crawled through the entrance, this time awkwardly because she was pushing before her a tray holding three gourds and a large bowl of liquid. Dunn's face brightened.

'Let's have a drink,' he said. 'My mouth's dry after the ride and you must be thirsty too.'

'That is very, very true, sir,' said Jenkins, scrambling to his feet, taking the bowl from the girl and giving her one of his huge, face-breaking smiles. Simon noticed the 'sir' and reflected that Dunn had won Jenkins's respect, anyway. He accepted a gourd and, following Dunn's example, dipped it into the bowl.

'What is it?' he enquired.

To his surprise, the girl answered, in perfect and accent-free English. 'Zulu beer,' she said, smiling politely and offering the bowl to Jenkins.

'Nandi made it herself,' said Dunn with obvious pride. 'She's a good beer-maker. All Zulu women have to make beer; it's absolutely essential. But some of them do it less well than Nandi. Try it.'

Simon sipped obediently. It tasted blessedly cold, slightly sour, but not unpleasant. Jenkins sucked his moustache and nodded his approval. 'Jenkins here is an expert on beer,' Simon said with a smile. 'If he likes it, it must be good.'

Dunn turned to the Welshman. 'What exactly do you do in this outfit, then, Jenkins?' There was a touch of condescension in his voice.

'With respect, Mr Dunn sir, I'm Jenkins to Mr Fonthill but *Mister* Jenkins to anyone else. What do I do? I look after the Lieutenant, here.' Jenkins's eyes narrowed. 'But I also kill people for a living. I'm a soldier, see.'

The two men regarded each other silently for a brief moment, then a slow smile crept over Dunn's face. 'Very well, Mr Jenkins,' he said. 'I think we understand each other.'

Simon took a deep breath and leaned towards the South African. 'Mr Dunn, as I have said, I have no inside knowledge of the British Government's attitude towards the Zulus. I do know that their militant state causes concern to the Governor and his staff in the Cape, but, as I expect you are aware, the Foreign Office and the Horse Guards back home have their hands full at the moment with the Afghans to the north-west of India and I cannot conceive that they are planning a full-scale war with the Zulus.'

Dunn listened impassively and took a deep draught of beer, so, with a little more confidence, Simon continued. 'You are wrong, by the way, if you believe that the army underestimates the Zulus. The same views you have just expounded about their strength were expressed to me by the Chief of Staff in Cape Town. In fact, it is the very respect in which they are held that has prompted my mission here. You see, not enough is known about them, their military capacity and their intentions. And every command must have this sort of information at its fingertips. It does not necessarily mean war. In fact, it can mean the opposite. The very efficiency of the Zulu military structure, when it is known and digested, can be a safeguard against border blunders, for instance, leading us unintentionally into war.'

Simon suddenly became aware that his audience was more than Dunn and Jenkins. Unnoticed, the girl had sat quietly against the wall of the hut and was watching him now intently, black eyes unblinking. Presumably she could understand every word. Simon inwardly cursed himself for speaking so freely – here, in Cetswayo's kraal, of all places! One cry could summon enough warriors to drag them away to the stake. He gulped – but he couldn't stop now. He looked closely at Dunn. The man's face was quite expressionless. Simon decided he had to play his main card.

He leaned forward and sensed Jenkins's tenseness by his side. 'I understand what you say about your loyalty to the

Zulus and their king. If I may say so, it does you credit. But . . .' He let his voice fall away. 'There may well come a time, Mr Dunn, when you have to decide what nationality you are.' Simon let the point sink in, but there was no reaction from Dunn. 'Heaven forbid that there will be hostilities. But if they do break out, I do not see how you can remain neutral. You will have to make a choice.' He paused for a moment. 'I suppose, in a way, we are forcing you to make that choice now. Are you British or Zulu?'

Dunn made no reply but sat puffing his pipe, looking unblinkingly at Simon. Eventually he spoke. 'Do you know what the King said when he called me back, just there?'

'No.'

'He said that he didn't know what to make of you – whether you were a new kind of trader or army spies. He asked me to find out.' Dunn threw back his head and laughed, although the tension within the hut remained unbroken. 'So he's forcing me to make the same decision. I'm being pressurised from both sides, dammit.'

Suddenly the big man rose to his feet. He seemed twice as tall in the dark hut. 'Well,' he said. 'I'll tell you one thing. I have absolutely no intention of making that decision until I have to.'

'But what are you going to tell the King?' asked Simon.

'Nothing yet. In any case, he has told me to take you to my kraal because he doesn't want you hanging about Ulundi. So we will start at sun-up tomorrow. It's a good day's ride. You can stay at my place as long as you like but, at least at this stage, I don't feel inclined to feed you information. But we can talk about that later. I've a lot to think about.'

Dunn moved to the door, where he paused. 'The Governor

wants me to teach you Zulu and says you have an aptitude for languages. Well, you're going to need it, because I won't have the time to nursemaid you with that. You'll just have to pick it up, like I did.'

'I can teach him, Father.' The quiet tones came from the wall, where Nandi still sat, cross-legged.

'We'll see about that, too,' said Dunn. 'You can't neglect your work any more than I can.'

Simon stood and smiled at the girl. 'Thank you. I don't wish to be any trouble.'

'We could teach you Welsh, in return,' said Jenkins. 'Well, at least, Mr Fonthill could.'

Dunn led them to a vacant hut nearby and threw them two sleeping mats. 'There's a well just here for washing and drinking. It's a bit brackish but you'll soon get used to that. Don't get talking to any of the Zulus. You've dressed yourselves as Afrikaaners. *I* don't think you look like Afrikaaners but *they* might – and they don't like Boers. While you are here you are living on a bit of a knife edge. So: take no risks.'

With a nod he was gone. The two soldiers crawled into their hut and found, to their surprise, that their packs and rifles had been placed inside. Nothing seemed to have been taken. While Jenkins fetched water, Simon prepared a little biltoeng for them to eat, and as darkness descended, they settled to sleep.

'Well, bach sir,' said Jenkins, from beneath his blanket. 'I have to tell you that I like what you said back there and the way you said it. It doesn't matter about ridin' a horse well, if you can talk like that. Any fool can ride a horse – though it would be nice if you could stay on if we have to gallop, look you.'

'I'll try and remember that, 352. Now shut up.'

Chapter 7

They rose before the sun but Dunn was saddled, loaded and waiting for them as they collected their horses. Nandi was also on horseback, as were the two Zulus, who were clearly part of Dunn's personal bodyguard. They set off to the south-east at a pace that made Simon anxious. This time, however, the going was easier because Dunn seemed to have the knack of picking out trails that were invisible to the others. Not once did he consult a compass. Now they skirted dongas instead of crossing them and Dunn avoided rutted, well-used tracks and the dust clouds their use would have caused. Instead, he picked his way through tussocks of grass at a pace twice as fast as that managed by Simon and Jenkins on their first day in Zululand. The sun was touching the black serrations of the mountains to their right when Dunn stood in his stirrups and gestured ahead.

'There's home,' he cried.

They cantered through the familiar herds of cattle, taking waved greetings from the black boy tending them, and approached a long, single-storeyed thatched dwelling, looking inviting behind its veranda or stoep, fringed with bougainvillea and clematis. It could have been Kent or Sussex, except for the clusters of typically African round mud huts, also thatched, that meandered in scores behind the main building. They stretched away to a distant cattle pen, and in the other direction, what looked like sugar cane plantations marched away to the blue hills.

As the horses reined in, a platoon of small brown children rushed from the nearby huts crying out greetings and dancing in excitement. Dunn picked up a couple and deposited great kisses on their dusty faces and ran his hands over as many of the other curly heads as he could reach. Nandi did the same. Dunn looked back at Simon with an expression of some embarrassment.

'Hell, man,' he said. 'They always make a fuss when I get back.'

'You're a lucky man, Mr Dunn,' replied Simon. And he meant it.

Zulus took the horses and led them away and Nandi quietly disappeared. Dunn led the two visitors across the stoep into a large room with a polished wood floor, strewn with native mats, and walls covered with trophies: heads of antlered deer, impala, a lion and three huge buffaloes, the horns of the largest of which curled above a long, low stone fireplace. It was a lived-in, welcoming room; that of a countryman of affluence.

'Catherine,' cried Dunn loudly. 'We have guests.'

After a pause, Catherine Dunn came into the room. She was about a foot shorter than Dunn and so thin that he could, it seemed, have picked her up with one hand. The climate and toil of life in Zululand had treated her less well than it had her husband. Her thin hair had turned grey and was pulled back into a bun, and whatever the original colour of her skin, it now looked a sallow yellow, with brown age spots marking her hands and forearms. She was wearing a simple cotton shift and was barefoot. But her eyes were bright blue and shone with interest as she greeted her visitors.

'You are welcome, gentlemen,' she said, echoing the nasal, clipped speech of her husband. 'Forgive me for not wearing shoes but I was not expecting John back today. Will you take some beer?'

'I don't think so, my dear,' said Dunn. 'We would all like to eat and, I expect, take a bath first. So would you please see that the boilers are lit straight away.'

He turned with a proprietorial air. 'We have three bathrooms here,' he said, 'and they are all piped to individual boilers but they take a little time to heat up and for the boys to pump the water through.'

'Three bathrooms!' exclaimed Simon. 'Now that really is luxury. I never expected to find that in Zululand.'

Catherine Dunn looked pleased. 'It's not always been like this,' she smiled. 'But I think we can say now that we are as comfortable as anyone living in Durban.'

'Ach, no,' growled Dunn. 'Better.' He shouted commands in Zulu and a native, clad incongruously in what seemed like nothing but an apron, came running. 'Benjamin here will show you to your rooms. We will serve dinner in an hour.'

The boy led them along a corridor and gestured to adjoining rooms. Simon's was spartan but made more than adequate by the tin bath set in a little annexe. Two crude clay pipes ran from it through holes punched in the mud wall, and after a few minutes, hissing hot water began to emerge from the first, filling the bath with a brownish liquid. Then clearer cold water poured from the second. In a moment, Benjamin reappeared.

He dipped his finger into the water and looked up. 'Is good?' he enquired. Simon tested it. 'Very good,' he smiled. Benjamin's face lit up and he was gone, presumably to perform the same service for Jenkins. Simon smiled again as he reflected that this was probably the first time that anyone had ever run a bath for the little Welshman.

Brown or not, the water was magnificently relaxing. He stirred the surface with his toe and his thoughts dwelt on Dunn. He seemed friendly enough – and, more to the point, European enough. But was he playing a double game? How could a man as close to Cetswayo betray the King? – because that was what they were asking him to do. Simon stirred uneasily in the relaxing water. He disliked the fact that the action now lay with Dunn and that all he could do was wait. But what to do? Learn Zulu? The thought of tackling that guttural tongue, with its back-of-the-throat clicks and grunts and impenetrable vocabulary, was daunting, to say the least. Perhaps Nandi really could teach him. Luxuriantly, he let his thoughts dwell upon her. She was pretty, there was no doubt about that, and he mused about her lineage. Was she Catherine's daughter? No, her skin was too dark for that. Her skin ... He remembered the flash of breast in the darkness of the hut in Ulundi and the firm buttocks undulating through the low entrance. Simon felt arousal in his loins and a rude desire that he had not experienced since he had bought a weird concoction of lemonade and sherry for a tart in a pub near Sandhurst. Almost immediately, he experienced a sense of shame. He had never felt quite that way about Alice. Alice ... He had not thought about her for weeks! He tried to conjure up her face but it refused to appear; all that he could recall was a montage of white skin and coiled fair hair. Did he love her? He sighed. How could you love someone whom you couldn't recall? He rubbed his body savagely with a coarse sponge in admonishment.

If the bathroom was a surprise, the dinner was a revelation. Simon had put on his best, unworn shirt and he was pleased that Jenkins had similarly changed. In fact, despite his lugubrious moustache, Jenkins looked like a cherubic, well-scrubbed schoolboy. His black hair was plastered down, he had somehow polished his riding boots and his brown face exuded bonhomie and pleasurable anticipation.

'Let's have a drink before we eat,' said Dunn, clapping his hands.

Catherine, now wearing a well-cut gingham dress and laced shoes, joined them around the long fireplace, as, too, did Nandi, looking quite European in a simple white dress which showed off her skin to perfection. She had tucked a white orchid into her hair and was wearing leather sandals. The party was completed by James, a tall, well-built half-caste whom Dunn introduced as his eldest son. Simon looked closely at the boy, who must have been only a year or two younger than himself. There was more of the Zulu in him than was evident in Nandi. They shared the snub nose and the dark eyes, but his skin was darker than his sister's and his limbs had the massiveness of the native. Yet, from the affection with which he was treated by Catherine, he might have been her son.

The ubiquitous Benjamin – this time wearing a loose-fitting white jacket and trousers, with a red sash around his midriff, and looking like a waiter at any of the white man's clubs to be found from Cairo to Singapore – appeared carrying a tray, two bottles and six glasses.

'Have some champagne,' said Dunn gruffly and gestured to Benjamin to open and pour.

Simon stole a glance at the bottle. 'Good lord!' he cried involuntarily and lapsed into an embarrassed silence.

'Oh, don't worry,' said Dunn with a grin. 'All new visitors are surprised that I serve good champagne. This is Bollinger '65. I get it through a merchant in the Cape. Now, Mr Jenkins, I am told you're an expert on beer. What d'yer think of this stuff, eh?'

Jenkins studiously sniffed the bouquet (Simon could smell nothing), took a sip, rolled it around his tongue and nodded appreciatively. 'It's travelled very well, Mr Dunn,' he said. 'There are them that say that good bottles can't cross the Equator. But it all depends upon how they're packed into the 'old of the ship, look you. If they're right at the bottom, see, right near the keel, so as they don't swing and sway so much, and lain horizontally so that the champagne don't move in the bottle with the pitch of the ship,' he sniffed, 'then they don't get agitated much and they're far enough down to get away from the 'eat and be cooled by the ocean itself, see.' He looked round and, seeing that he had everyone's attention, went on with confidence. 'That means that they 'ave the minimum of disturbance on the journey and, again, if they're laid down properly in a cellar or somewhere when they arrive, they can recover their equil . . . equilaborom, so to speak, before bein' served.'

He held up his flute glass. 'An' another thing. It's good to drink from a proper glass, which keeps the bubbles in – not one of these wide-open things that lets all the fizz out, so to speak.' He took another appreciative sip. 'There's people who think that keepin' good wine is about 'avin' it cool all the time. Now it's true that 'eat doesn't do a bottle any good at all, but it's more important to keep the temperature as even an' unchangin' as possible.' He held up the glass. 'I can see that you keep your bottles laid on their sides, like, undisturbed an' probably in a cellar.'

'I do indeed, Mr Jenkins,' said Dunn warmly. 'And it's rewarding to have good wine properly appreciated. Here, have some more.' And he took the bottle from the tray and filled Jenkins's glass to the brim.

Simon looked on incredulously as Jenkins carefully wiped his moustache and half drained the glass. What sort of man was this who could hardly read but could survive the Glasshouse of Aldershot, ride like a Hussar and discourse knowledgeably on the problems of shipping and laying down champagne? He smiled and nodded courteously as Jenkins raised his glass in approval.

The large dining room had more pretension than the drawing room. Candles set in silver candelabra reflected in the dark red mahogany of the table, which had been elaborately laid. A cream Sèvres dinner service was set inch-perfectly at each place and two wine glasses and a brandy goblet stood as sentinels by each soup spoon. The chair backs were elegantly shaped and cut as fine as filigree and the seats were of crimson velvet. Dark paintings, mainly of animals and still life, hung on the walls, and a huge, seemingly French gold-framed mirror dominated the fireplace. Simon felt that they could have been dining at the Queen's new castle at Balmoral.

General conversation at the table was perfunctory, not least because the food was so good: a fish from the coast that tasted like sole, followed by roast pig cased in golden crackling. The wine, of course, was superb – an 1865 claret had been carefully decanted. Simon noticed with a twinge of annoyance that Jenkins was spending most of his time talking quietly to Nandi, who was seated at his side. He turned to Dunn.

'You told me earlier, Mr Dunn, that the Zulus hated the Boers. Why is that?'

Dunn put down his knife. 'It would take too long to go into all the details from the past. But when the Dutchmen left the Cape and went on their Great Trek to get away from the British, they set off northwards and easily put down the Basuto and Matabele they met on the way. Most of them settled in what is now called the Orange Free State and then the Transvaal. But some of them peeled off to the south-east and took their wagons through the Drakensbergs – know where they are?' Simon nodded. 'They came up against the Zulus for the first time. Old Dingane, the King at the time, tricked the leader of the Boers and sixty of his followers and impaled the lot. Then he wiped out the women and children waiting in the wagons and, because the British in the south had somehow got involved, turned on the little settlement of Durban – it was called Port Natal then – and burned that.'

Other pockets of conversation around the table had died away and everyone now listened to the big bearded man.

'I remember that well, although I was only five. For a week Dingane's impis torched the town. They killed my grandfather on the beach but my father was somehow able to get my mother, my three younger sisters and me on to a little schooner in the harbour and we got away. We had come to settle there, you see, so it wasn't a very good welcome. But we all came back.'

He smiled and mopped up gravy with a crust of bread. 'The Boers came back as well and they defeated Dingane at Blood River, where they laagered their wagons and held off twelve thousand Zulus, killing three thousand of them. Then the territory sort of swayed back and forth between the Boers and the Brits over the years – not least because the Afrikaaners may be damned good fighters but they can't organise brooms in a broom cupboard. It has, of course, ended up with your lot.' He looked up. 'Am I boring everyone?'

'Not at all,' said Simon.

'Fascinatin',' said Jenkins. They both meant it.

Gratified, Dunn continued. 'Well, the old enmity between the Zulus and Boers goes back, of course, to Dingane, Blood River and all that. But it's been revived over the last few years. There's a dispute which has been rumbling for ages over a large tract of land east of the Blood River to the north of here.' He gestured over his shoulder.

'The Transvaal Boers claim that it was ceded to them by Mpande, Cetswayo's father. The King denies this and is looking to the British and his old friend, Somtseu, to back him up. So far, they have, but . . .' Dunn let a pause hang in the air for a moment. 'If Shepstone wants to buy the Boers' friendship for annexation of Transvaal, then he could switch sides.'

He looked at Simon. 'That's why the King was so tetchy when he met you. He thought that maybe Shepstone had sent you to reassure him. There is a rumour that some sort of commission is going to sit in London to sort out this land business. But I'm worried about it all. As I've said, there are many of Cetswayo's warriors who have never washed their spears. If this tribunal thing goes the wrong way, that could give them the excuse. And then we could all be involved.'

Simon nodded silently. Listening to the big man's fears, his thoughts had fled back to that darkened room in Cape Town and Colonel Lamb's talk of confederation and conquest. Either way, it was difficult to see how the future could deny the King's impis the chance to earn their manhood. He needed to think.

The pessimism in Dunn's voice had settled like a pall over the table and even Jenkins could think of nothing to say. Simon pushed back his chair. 'I am most grateful to you, Mr Dunn, for your clear account of events.' He turned and bowed to Catherine. 'And to you, ma'am, for a most delightful dinner.'

'Hear, hear,' growled Jenkins.

'Oh, don't go yet,' said Dunn. 'Mr Jenkins, you must have another brandy.'

Jenkins beamed. 'Well, I don't mind if—' he began. But Simon cut in quickly.

'That's very kind of you, but I think we should retire. It's been a long day.' Bowing again to Mrs Dunn and to Nandi, Simon led the way to the door.

As they parted at their bedroom doors, Jenkins beamed at Simon. 'I'm not sure what exactly is goin' on 'ere, bach sir,' he said, swaying slightly on his feet, 'but for the moment, I rather like this postin'.'

'Well, don't get to like it too much,' hissed Simon, 'because I don't know what's happening either. But I don't like the sound of any of it. We could still be dropped like a hot potato by Dunn – and straight into Cetswayo's lap. And here.' He grabbed Jenkins's arm and pulled him close. 'Where on earth did you learn all that stuff about champagne? Were you making it up?'

Jenkins withdrew his arm with unsteady dignity. 'Cerdenly not,' he said. 'As smadder of fact, I was officers' mess corporal in the 1st Battalion and me an' old Captain Talbot used to do all the buyin', see. I got to know the merchant very well.' He smiled reminiscently. 'As smadder of fact, I got to know some of the wines as well.' He leaned forward confidentially. 'To be honest, bach sir, that Bollinger '65 wasn't as good as I made out, see. He's bought the wrong year. Now the '67 . . .'

'Oh, do shut up, 352, and go to bed.'

'Very good, sir. As you say, sir.' Jenkins executed an immaculate about-turn, crashed into the doorpost and fumbled his way into his room.

Simon was in a deep sleep when a steady, insistent shaking dragged him back into consciousness. A fresh-faced Jenkins, his black hair slicked down and his eyes bright over the bristling moustache, was beaming down at him. 'Better get up, sir. The sun's been up for nearly an hour and Mr Dunn's ridden off somewhere. Everyone's up an' about. I've done my best with your boots but I can't get 'em to shine 'ere for some reason.'

'To hell with the boots. I don't want to look like a guardsman here. Why on earth didn't you wake me?'

'As a matter of fact, sir, as you probably just noticed, like, I 'ave woken you.'

'No, you fool. I meant earlier.'

'Ah well. I felt that we both deserved a bit of a lie-in, after all that ridin' an' all.'

Scowling, Simon pulled on his clothes, washed his hands and face in the china bowl on the washstand and hurried into the kitchen, with Jenkins scurrying behind. There, they were given eggs, bread and bowls of coffee by a huge Zulu woman who was obviously mistress of the kitchen. As they finished their coffee, a smiling Nandi appeared, her hair tied back, looking as fresh as the morning.

'Father has had to leave,' she said, 'but he has asked me to say that you are free to do as you please. Except that he does not think it wise for you to ride further than, say, ten miles from the house.' Her smile grew wider. 'But I thought, Mr Fonthill, that it would be a good idea if we begin the Zulu lessons right away.' She turned to Jenkins. 'And my brother

James is happy to take you, Mr Jenkins, with him to herd some cattle, if you would like that. It would give you a chance to see more of the country.'

'Good idea, Jenkins,' said Simon, as the Welshman opened his mouth to protest. 'Get to know the country and all that.'

'Oh, if you say so.' He turned sullenly to Nandi. 'I rather thought that I would like to learn Zulu too, look you.'

'Some other time, Jenkins,' said Simon. 'Now just go and get to know the country like a good chap.'

After Jenkins and James had ridden off, Simon was surprised to find that Nandi had provided two saddled horses for them, too. 'Don't we go to the schoolroom?' he asked.

Nandi shook her head gravely. 'Oh no. I know a nice place away from the house where we will not be troubled. It is not far and we can concentrate there.'

They rode through pleasant, undulating countryside, well watered and grassed. Simon reflected that Dunn had carved out for himself what surely must be some of the best grazing and sugar-growing territory in Zululand. He speculated that they were not far from the coast, and although the humidity was higher than at Ulundi the sun was not too hot. For once, Simon thoroughly enjoyed being on horseback. He followed Nandi, who sat in the saddle with supreme confidence, riding with her bare feet thrust forward in the stirrups. They spoke little.

They followed a small stream until it widened out into a dark green pool beside a hollow that was covered with moss and coarse, springy grass. 'This is my favourite place,' said Nandi as she dismounted. 'Come and sit under this tree.'

They tethered their horses to a low branch and then sat under the tree's cool shade, Simon beginning to feel slightly disconcerted by the intimacy of the surroundings, but intrigued by the matter-of-fact assurance of the young girl.

'Now, Mr Fonthill,' said Nandi, once they were sitting together.

'I think you should call me Simon, if you would like to.'

She clapped her hands girlishly. 'Oh, Simon! Simon. It's such a lovely name. So . . . English.'

'Is it? I've never really thought about it.'

'Yes, it sounds very . . . what is the phrase? Anglo-Saxon. Yes, that's it.'

'Anglo-Saxon! Nandi, where did you learn your excellent English? Surely not here, in Zululand?'

'Oh no. Papa sent me to boarding school in the Cape when I was very little. I was taught in a convent.' Her face clouded over for a moment. 'I hated that and I was glad to come home when I was sixteen. Father sent James away too – we are the two oldest, you know – but he disliked it as well, so now, although he has a lot of money, Papa doesn't bother to send any of the other children away. I try and teach them here.' She chuckled ingenuously.

'May I ask . . .' began Simon nervously. 'You are not, I think, Catherine's child?'

Nandi shook her head. 'We are all Catherine's children in that she is the head wife – and she is good to us all. But she and Papa never had children. My mother was the second wife and I think Father loved her very much. She was of very fine and pure blood and was the daughter of an inDuna.' She dropped her head. 'But she is dead now.'

'Oh, I am sorry.'

Simon looked at the face before him, now dappled by the shade. Nandi's skin was the colour of coffee after a dash of cream has been added to it and there wasn't a wrinkle or a line to be seen. Her hands were cupping her cheeks now, and the fingers were slender, not splayed at the tips as with many Zulu women, and he noted that she had polished her nails. Simon could clearly see the hard protuberance of her nipples as they pushed against the shift she was wearing. He wondered if she went bare-breasted when there were no visitors at the house.

To his amazement, he heard himself asking the question.

'Oh yes,' said Nandi, quite unfazed. 'It is much easier when working. Most Zulu women do. And I have good breasts. Look.' In a smooth, fluid movement she pulled her shift over her head and proffered her breasts. 'They are quite firm,' she said. 'Men like to touch them, though Papa doesn't like it and has told me that I should wear a dress when men are present, like white women do. But I don't mind you touching them, if you would like to.'

The invitation hung limpidly in the air as Nandi sat perfectly still facing Simon, a smile playing on her lips. A cavalcade of emotions flashed across Simon's brain: surprise, embarrassment, lust and then a dull warning of danger.

He licked his lips. 'As a matter of fact, I think it's French,' he said weakly.

She frowned. 'What is?'

'The origin of Simon.'

'Oh, really. How interesting! Are you part French, then, as I am part Zulu?' The breasts stayed tantalisingly close, beautifully formed, tip-tilted to the nipples and still, so to speak, on offer. He wondered if she was teasing him. The little smile was still there, now more in the eyes than on the lips. If she was quite innocent, some sort of noble savage, then those black eyes would surely not twinkle so. She had moved almost imperceptibly closer.

Slowly, Simon leaned forward, his mouth slightly open. Then he stopped. With a sharp inward breath he sat bolt upright and turned his face upwards and stared desperately at the blue sky framing the tracery of leaves.

'I think you had better put your dress on again, Nandi,' he croaked.

'All right,' she responded cheerfully. 'You are quite right. I did not bring you here for ukuHlongonga – although, Simon, that would be very, very nice, you know.'

'Uku . . . what? I don't understand.'

'I will tell you another day. Now.' She had been kneeling but now she crossed her legs underneath her and sat upright in a businesslike kind of way. 'I have something important to say to you, Simon.'

'Ah, yes. The Zulu lesson.'

'No – although you must begin to learn and I *will* teach you, because you cannot do your work here properly unless you know the language. But first there is something more important.'

Simon made an effort and tried to look at her dispassionately. He did not know how old she was – perhaps seventeen, eighteen? – but the serious expression she had now adopted made her look even younger. She was, he realised forlornly, quite remarkably beautiful. She was also probably quite primitively amoral. And, most importantly, she could ensure quicker than any other factor in this complicated equation that Jenkins and he would end up with assegais in their stomachs. But now Nandi was talking and he composed himself to listen.

'When you spoke to my father in Ulundi about information that you needed, were you serious about it not being used for war but, in fact, to stop any fighting?'

'Of course. But why do you ask?'

'Well, I think that I have most of the information that you need.' She frowned earnestly. 'Not about the King's intentions. I don't know about that. But I do know roughly how big the army is and where the impis are.'

'Good lord, Nandi. How do you know all this?'

Her smile was back now and she was very aware that she had Simon's full attention. 'Well, you see, my father sells cattle to the King. Papa has some of the finest beef in the country and the King buys from him regularly to feed his army. The King cannot supply the impis properly from his own herds because many of them are made up of ceremonial cattle that he cannot kill. So he buys from Papa.'

Nandi began rocking to and fro as she spoke, so that the dappled sunlight moved across her face and gave a magic lantern effect. 'As well as teaching the children,' she threw back her head and laughed loudly, 'at least, some of the time, I help Papa with this business. This means that I have to keep records for him because he does not like that side of it at all. He does not have to pay – what do you call them – taxes, yes, but he must be careful when he trades with the King. I write down which cattle go to which regiment and where they are living in our country. Soooo . . .' she drew the word out teasingly and gazed upwards at Simon through her lashes, 'I know very well how the army is made up and where it is.'

Simon blew out his cheeks in astonishment. 'Nandi, you continue to amaze me. But why should you want to give me this information and why cannot your father supply it?'

Nandi frowned. 'I know Papa very well and he is not very – how shall I say it? – decisive. He will not want to get involved with you in this way. He may give you little bits of information to be polite and keep in with the British but he will want to stay on the fence, as the English say. I heard what you said about knowledge preventing a war and I would like to give you that knowledge, if it will stop the war. Will you promise me that, Simon, if I give it to you?' There was no coquettishness in her eyes now as they looked into Simon's. Simon realised that she was completely in earnest.

He took a deep breath. 'Nandi, I am not in a position to give you guarantees or even assurances. I am not a general, only a very humble lieutenant. It is the generals who take the decisions. I only carry them out. But I can promise you one thing. If you can help me, I do believe it will reduce the risk of war and I will do everything in my power to make sure that the information is used for peace.'

The girl stared at him silently for a moment. 'But do you *yourself* really believe that information about the Zulu army would, as you said, reduce the risk of some silly accident – at the border, say – setting off a war? I ask this because I know these people and that is just what might happen.'

Simon became aware that he was on the edge of a moral maze and disliked the feeling. Yet he was committed. He had to go on.

'Yes, I do. If the size and preparedness for war of the Zulu army is known and if, as I suspect, those facts are impressive, then I do believe that it could make hot-heads on our side, at least, think twice and three times before they commit the army. You see,' and now he felt on surer ground, 'our government in London is far more concerned about the threat to India from the Russians who are stirring up trouble in Afghanistan. I cannot see them starting a war in South Africa against a nation they know to be well prepared militarily.'

Nandi looked relieved. 'Very well, Simon. Then I shall tell you all I know. But you must not make notes. That would be very dangerous. You must remember everything I tell you.'

'Oh dear, Nandi. That will be difficult. But I take your point. No notes. Right. First of all, how many men are in the army – in a state of readiness, that is?'

The girl frowned. 'Well, as you probably know, the Zulus have the same basic structure as the British Army – divided into regiments, and that sort of thing. So there are thirty-three regiments serving the King now. That is just under fifty thousand men.'

Simon whistled. 'As many as that?'

'Yes. I do not know about readiness but not all of them would be very good in a battle, I think. About seven of the regiments date from the days of Shaka and Dingane and the men in them are too old to frighten anyone. But,' she looked at Simon with wide eyes, 'they *would* fight. Every man is trained to fight, from the time they join their iNtanga groups as boys. When the boys of various iNtanga reach military age, they are formed into regiments from the same age-group and district. The number of warriors in a regiment might vary from, say, five hundred to six thousand, but I suppose the average is about fifteen hundred.' Nandi leaned forward. 'Do you know about celibacy?'

'A little, but tell me.'

'Well, Shaka said years ago that the first duty of young warriors is to protect the nation, not to marry and grow fat. They could do that later. So that has been the practice ever since: warriors must stay celibate either until they are about forty or until they have proved themselves in battle. Of course . . .' and here Simon could have sworn that Nandi blushed, 'there is ukuHlongonga. But that doesn't matter for now. The point is,' and she regarded him again with that frown which made her look like a schoolgirl relating a lesson, 'all the young men who do not wear the isiCoco – that is the circlet of fibre woven into the hair which a man is allowed to wear when he takes a wife – all of them are anxious to wash their spears to gain it. And, Simon, there has been little chance of washing spears in recent years, so there are many men anxious to go to war.'

Her eyes were wide in their anxiety to impress. Simon wanted to kiss them.

'Er . . . how many celibate warriors would there be, then?' he asked instead.

Nandi frowned in concentration. 'About eighteen of the thirty-three regiments consist of married men, but these include the seven made up of the old men I told you about. But the King mixes these regiments up to give the young men the support of the experienced ones. For instance, the Undi corps consists of five regiments, three of which – the uThulwane, the Mkonkone and the Ndhlondhlo—'

'I shall never remember these names,' said Simon despairingly.

'It doesn't matter about the names. These three range in age from about forty-three to forty-five; one, the inDluyenge, has men of about twenty-eight; another, the inGobamakhosi, has younger men, aged twenty-four. There are about ten thousand men in this corps.'

'Where is this corps?'

'It is kept in a special military kraal, near Ulundi. But many of the older men are allowed to live in their home kraals with their wives.'

'And where are the older regiments – those that are in military kraals, that is?'

'They are scattered about the country. Some are in the north, facing the Boers across in the Transvaal and the Orange country; some are in the south, guarding the Tugela.'

'Are they armed? I mean, do they have firearms?'

Nandi laughed. 'Oh, yes, some of them. The Zulus are very proud of their guns, those that have them. But Papa says that they could not hit an elephant in a hut. The guns are very old and have to be loaded at the end, what do you call them . . .?'

'Muzzle loaders.'

'Yes. They are very inaccurate and there is not much ammunition for them. The warriors know this really and prefer to fight with their spears and their knobkerries. But they are still very proud of their guns.'

Simon picked up a pebble and threw it into the stream. They watched as it sank out of sight in the green water. Somewhere on the other bank the ha-de-ha bird gave its eponymous cry. It was incongruous – no, it was downright ludicrous – to be sitting in this idyllic place talking of war with a young woman who had skin the colour of drinking chocolate and breasts like . . . Simon frowned and tried to concentrate.

'How quickly can they be deployed?' he asked.

'What does that mean?'

'Sorry. How quickly could each of these regiments go into battle?'

'Ah. Before going to war, they would all go to the King's kraal to be treated by the witch doctors to give them strength and protection in battle. It would take perhaps a day for the ceremony, then they would be ready to go wherever they were wanted. But, oh, Simon,' her eyes were big in emphasis again, 'how they can move! An impi can cover thirty to forty miles in a day and then fight a battle.'

Simon smiled ruefully. 'Yes. I can well imagine that.'

'So you see,' continued Nandi, 'it does not matter very much where they are in Zululand because they can move very quickly to launch an attack or make a defence.'

'Nandi,' said Simon, 'you have a remarkable grasp of strategic necessities. Are you sure that you are not a Zulu inDuna in disguise?'

'Oh no.' And then she smiled, seeing the joke, although clearly a little embarrassed, both by being teased and by the unwomanly nature of her accomplishment. 'It is just that,' she shrugged, 'I have to know the size of the regiments and where they are so that we can send the cattle there.'

'Last question,' said Simon, 'because I don't think my brain can take in any more. Once the warriors are committed to battle, is there any way of knowing which regiment is which – or, at least, which are the experienced men and which the young ones?'

'Yes, there is. This is shown by the shield colours. The very youngest warriors have all-black shields and white is added as the men gain experience. Red shields show married or mixed regiments, but the whiter the shield, the more senior and more experienced the soldier.'

Simon nodded slowly. 'Thank you very much, Nandi.' He leaned forward quickly and kissed her, in brotherly fashion, on both cheeks. Immediately, Nandi snaked her arms around his neck and pulled him close, but he firmly disentangled himself.

'Nandi,' he said, looking closely into her eyes, 'I have a lot to think about and I think we should get back. And, much as I like you, I think it would be unfair to your father if I were to . . .' He tailed away awkwardly. 'I am his guest here and there are rules about this sort of thing. At least there are back in England.'

The girl pouted petulantly for a moment and then gave her wide, forgiving smile. 'Of course, Simon. We should go now.' Then the archness came back. 'But you must learn Zulu. You told my father that it was necessary. And I said that I would teach you, so I am your schoolmistress.' She threw her head back and laughed, much more melodiously than the ha-de-ha bird and so infectiously that Simon joined in, so that they sat for a moment by that green pool, hand in hand, and laughing at the blue sky together.

On their return, Simon excused himself and went to his room. Neither Jenkins and James or Dunn were back, and he was glad of that because he wanted to think.

He had to take the risk of committing Nandi's information to paper. An oral message could so easily be distorted by the time it reached Colonel Lamb. Somehow he would have to smuggle a written report back to Durban, for onward transmission to the Cape. But how? And could he remember all Nandi had told him? The names of the regiments were impossible but the overall content of the message was clear. The Zulus had around 50,000 men available, nearly twice as many as suspected by the British; their army was structured on a basis similar to that of European forces, with regiments and corps; it was stationed to cover the invasion routes into the country, with strong support which could be deployed quickly; and the shield marking system would show in battle where the main points of inexperience – and therefore weakness – lay. He could not return with this information himself, because he still lacked the main nugget he needed: how likely Cetswayo was to resist the British demand for annexation.

Nandi could not help here. And goodness knows, she had been helpful enough already! The sequence of his thoughts brought him to his own role. He put his head in his hands and stared hard at the floor. He had misled the girl, there was no doubt about that. Did he really believe that giving information to the army about the enemy's size and deployment would reduce the chance of invasion by the British? Well, perhaps up to a point, but no further. After all, the main reason for his presence in Zululand was to prepare the British so that they could more easily destroy the Zulu army. Simon mused on this for a while then sat up and squared his shoulders. It couldn't be helped. He was a soldier and he had taken a vow to serve the Queen. The kind of detail that he must now smuggle back to Lamb could save British lives. The feelings of an eighteen-year-old girl could not be taken into account. With a sigh, he threw himself on to the bed and dozed fitfully.

Dunn returned in the middle of the next morning. He rode in at some speed and sent Benjamin to find Simon and Jenkins. They found him sitting on the edge of a cane chair in the large drawing room, sipping from a native-style gourd.

'Beer?' he offered as they came in.

As they sipped, he began to speak. 'I have returned earlier than I expected,' he said, 'because I have heard that an inDuna from the King, with a number of warriors, is on his way to see me. They should be here in the late afternoon.'

'What do they want?' asked Simon, unable to keep a note of anxiety from his voice.

'Could be you.' The bearded face was expressionless. 'The warriors would be needed as an escort to take you back. But I doubt it. More likely the King wants to know whether I have made up my mind about you yet – whether you are traders or British Army spies.'

'So you are being forced to make up your mind, then?' enquired Simon softly.

'I am and I have.' Dunn stood up and leaned with one hand on the low mantelshelf. 'I had hoped to have a few more days to think it all through.' He smiled. 'I hate to be rushed on important decisions, but there's no choice now.'

He seemed bigger than ever as he looked down on them. 'I am sure that you realise just how compromising your arrival is to me?' They both nodded. 'The obvious thing is for me to hand you over to the King and simply tell him that I'm not sure about you. I doubt very much that you would end on the impalement stake. He wouldn't want to upset the British. No, more likely he'd take you to the Buffalo or Tugela, push you over and tell you never to darken his doorstep again. But, anyway, I am not going to do that.'

'Thank you, Mr Dunn,' said Simon.

'Much obliged, I'm sure,' nodded Jenkins.

'I am not going to do that for two reasons,' continued Dunn, as though they had not spoken. 'Firstly because I can't afford to upset the Governor, who, after all, has made a direct appeal to me. Secondly, because I am British – although nearer Irish than English, I suppose – and I certainly won't put people of my own kind into danger. So I shall lie to the King and say that you *are* traders.' He sucked on his pipe. 'Now, this gives me certain problems. The obvious one is that if the King discovers I have been lying to him, I will lose all influence here and probably my land and possessions too. The second is: what do I do about you two?'

The question hung on the air. Simon felt that it would not be opportune to intervene. Dunn had made up his mind on a course of action. Best to hear him out.

Dunn hitched up his trousers, as though he was gathering all his resources to answer the question. 'If I say you are traders, you have to be seen to trade. So that means you will have to buy some of my stock – at my price, mind you, because I didn't seek to trade – and drive the cattle back to Natal. But, of course, you are soldiers and have your duty to do, so you will try and gather the information that you were sent here to obtain. Right?'

Simon nodded, thinking guiltily of Nandi.

'Right. I cannot throw you out to let you roam around the Zulu kraals, camping out, trying to gather that information. You will be picked up in no time and find yourself back in Ulundi, and that will reflect on me. So, you must stay here. But there has to be a time limit – let us say three months. There is one more thing.' The long, bearded face looked pained. 'I will lie to the King to protect you, but I will not help you to gather information that could bring about his downfall. I cannot do that to a man who has been so good to me. The Governor must understand that. So you must do your dirty work without my help, although I will provide shelter and food for you. I do not wish to know what you do.'

The concentration demanded by his unaccustomed eloquence had led Dunn to neglect his pipe and he now made a great fuss of relighting it. Simon was not sure that this was the time to intervene, and he laid a warning hand on Jenkins's knee as the Welshman stirred to speak.

The pipe alight again, Dunn looked over the glowing embers and, for the first time, spoke in a lighter tone. 'All I can say to you is this: for God's sake, don't get caught! Now, do you accept, for if you don't you had better clear off now before the inDuna from Ulundi arrives.'

'There is no question of that, Mr Dunn,' said Simon, getting to his feet. 'I understand well your position and we accept your terms.'

Dunn put out his hand and both men shook it in turn.

'There is one last, small point,' said Simon, hoping that he was not blushing. 'We would have less chance of getting into trouble if I had at least a rudimentary knowledge of Zulu. Nandi did offer to teach me. Would this, er, be acceptable to you?'

Dunn showed his teeth gripping the stem of his pipe. 'I have no problem with that,' he said. 'I doubt if you taking lessons in Zulu from my daughter will bring this great nation crashing down. Anyway' – was there a glint in his eye at this point? – 'I think that Nandi might find it amusing.'

Chapter 8

The Zulu party trotted in about an hour before they were expected and Simon watched them from the window of his room. There were about twenty of them, all carrying assegais and shields, and all – Simon noted with care – with black and white hides, except the inDuna, who wore the isiCoco in his hair and carried an all-white shield. They all looked as though they had been out for a Sunday afternoon stroll.

'Is it a hanging party, do you think?' Jenkins had entered silently and observed the Zulus from over Simon's shoulder, his chin almost resting on it. His breath lay heavily on Simon's cheek.

'What the hell have you been drinking, 352?'

'Only keepin' young James company in a bowl or two of beer, sir. He's a nice enough boyo, though he doesn't say much. I thought I might get him to talk a bit, see, an' learn somethin'.'

Jenkins had the grace to look uncomfortable at the obvious lie. His eyes were bright – brighter than Simon had seen them before. They glistened like black coals in the gloom of the room. But he held Simon's gaze steadily enough, even, perhaps, with a touch of truculence.

Simon pulled back from the window. 'Look,' he said, taking Jenkins's arm and turning him around. 'We're living on a knife edge here. We are very much on active service even though we are not wearing uniform. There's to be no drinking beyond the dinner table.' His grip tightened on the Welshman's arm. 'Is that clear?'

A half-smile played around Jenkins's mouth but it did not reach his eyes. 'Don't worry, bach sir. I can hold it, you know. You'll see.'

The two men stood for a second or two longer, each holding the other's gaze. Simon noticed for the first time an absence of the friendly jocularity that was never far from the surface in his relationship with his comrade. He remembered Jenkins's reputation for drinking and then getting into trouble. The sour odour of the Zulu beer hung like a cloud between them.

Simon spoke quietly. 'It's not a question of holding it. It's a question of not taking it at all when we are on duty. Is that understood?'

Slowly, unsmilingly, Jenkins nodded. Then he turned on his heel and left the room. Perturbed, Simon returned to the window and saw John Dunn talking quietly with the inDuna, while the remainder of the Zulu party squatted on their heels. As he watched, Nandi and two other Zulu girls – if they were half-sisters, they lacked her distinctive colour – approached carrying empty gourds and three large pitchers. Smiling and chatting to the warriors, as if with old friends, they dispensed the beer to them.

Later, Dunn came to Simon's room. He sat on the edge of the bed and smiled reflectively.

'Well,' he said, 'I've done the dirty deed. I've told the inDuna that I am satisfied that you are who you say you are and that I'm prepared to trade with you.' He pulled out his empty pipe and sucked it. 'That means we'd better round up some cattle for you to show that this is serious and you had better make some arrangements to get them back to Natal before the King smells a rat. The inDuna will take my message back to Ulundi, but make no mistake about it, the King will be keeping an eye on you.'

'Thank you, Mr Dunn,' said Simon. 'I appreciate very much what you have done.' He thought for a moment. 'If you will draw up a proper document of transaction for the sale of the cattle, Jenkins can take them back to Natal, if you will be kind enough to lend us some of your youngsters to act as herdsmen.' He smiled. 'Jenkins was brought up on a farm, so he should be able to handle cattle.'

Dunn rose to his feet. 'Very well. I will break out two hundred head for you. They are going to cost the Government five sovereigns each, my boy. There'll be no haggling. I don't want to sell, so it has to be my price. Understood?'

Simon shrugged. 'We are in your hands, Mr Dunn.'

'Good. Now, we are giving a bit of a feast for our visitors and of course you must join us.' He gave his resigned half-smile, as though in apology. 'No champagne tonight, though. We'll be squatting round the fire and drinking beer. In about half an hour. Right?'

'Right.'

As Dunn left the room, Simon raised his eyebrows fatal-istically and sighed. So now he was in the cattle business! How would Colonel Lamb react to having to pay one thousand of the Queen's sovereigns for cattle that, no doubt, he did not want? Simon had been in the army long enough to be under no illusion about the fuss this would cause. Better to shoot two hundred Zulus out of hand than to buy two hundred cattle without authority! Oh lord! He put his hand to his head. But there was no way out – and the cattle did provide a genuine excuse for dispatching Jenkins back to Colonel Lamb with the information he had been able to gather so far. He reached for his saddlebag and withdrew paper, pen and – carefully wrapped and plugged – a horn of ink.

Wrinkling his brow in concentration, he began to write. He decided that, as a last defence in case Jenkins was accosted, he should disguise his message somehow. After explaining the purchase of the cattle and – here he winced as he wrote – the price that had to be paid, he devised a crude method of referring to the size of the Zulu army in terms of cattle numbers and its disposition within Zululand by equating the regiments to cattle herds. The ages of the various army units, and therefore their potency in battle, he linked to the colour of the beasts' hides, and he explained that these herds could be moved very quickly around the country. He closed by saying that he was still attempting to determine the King's propensity to sell further cattle – in other words, fight invaders.

He read it through with dissatisfaction. He was sure that Lamb would understand the references – in fact they were probably not obtuse enough to save Jenkins if he was captured and the message read. But the risk had to be taken. He licked the envelope and sealed it down firmly.

The feast for the visiting inDuna and his escort was certainly that. It was clear that Dunn kept a good table whoever the guests were. Two cows had been specially slaughtered and the visiting Zulus sat around in a circle, mingling with Zulus from Dunn's own kraal, as the meat was roasted on spits. Simon was put on Dunn's left, while the inDuna sat on the big man's right. Catherine Dunn sat on Simon's other side and Jenkins had been placed, Simon noticed with annoyance, next to Nandi across the other side of the gathering. In all, about forty people sat out of doors, talking and drinking beer as the fat fell sizzling and steaming from the meat carcasses on to the flames. The smell was delicious, and although he tried not to drink too much from his beer bowl, Simon felt a warming sense of well-being creep over him. The inDuna displayed no interest in him and mostly exchanged monosyllabic grunts with Dunn, while Catherine, after a few desultory words about sugar growing, was now talking on her left to a middle-aged Zulu from the visiting delegation, who seemed to have some rank. Simon smiled at the incongruity of it all: it was just like a dinner party at home. The pecking order of seniority had been strictly observed, and here he was once again, looking around with affected ease but feeling awkward in reality, because neither of his partners was free at that moment to converse with him. He could have been in Brecon or London.

Then he stiffened. Across the flickering firelight he observed Jenkins, almost directly opposite him. At least, it was Nandi who caught his attention first. She had taken Jenkins's right arm in her left hand and the wrist of the young Zulu on her right in her other. Her face was animated and she was talking quickly to Jenkins while seemingly straining to keep her companions' hands from reaching across her. But neither Jenkins nor the Zulu was looking at Nandi. They glared across her, in confrontation, their faces contorted with expressions of mutual antagonism. As he watched, Simon saw Jenkins snatch his hand free and grab the necklace of wooden beads around the Zulu's throat. It snapped, and with a roar that caught everyone's attention, the Zulu sprang to his feet and smashed his beer gourd on to the glistening black head of Jenkins.

Simon scrambled upright, but not before Dunn had rushed across the circle and pulled the Zulu back from the Welshman, who, on hands and knees, was desperately trying to stand. As Dunn stood before the young warrior, addressing him sternly, Simon hauled Jenkins to his feet. 'What the hell is going on?' he hissed. The beer on the Welshman's breath hit him like an odorous wall.

'Look you, bach' – Jenkins's Welshness had, it seemed, increased in proportion to the beer he had drunk – 'this black bastard has been layin' hands on Nandi, see. She didn't like it and neither did I. An' I'm not 'avin' it.'

'Please, Simon,' Nandi looked at him imploringly, 'it was nothing. Nkumo here,' she nodded at the Zulu, who was speaking fast and low to Dunn, 'is a friend of my brother, James. It was nothing. He has had a little too much beer, that's all.' She glanced across at Jenkins. 'I think they both have.'

Simon was aware that the entire gathering had now fallen silent and was watching events with mute interest. He sensed, however, an antagonism towards Jenkins, the white foreigner. Most eyes were on the Welshman and there were more scowls than smiles.

Dunn left the Zulu and turned to Simon. 'Look,' he said, with anger in his voice, 'this is serious. This man says that Jenkins was pawing my daughter and that he tried to stop him. He says that he has been insulted by the white man.'

'Rubbish, Mr Dunn, sir.' The slight slur had now left Jenkins's speech, and the glazed look had gone from his eyes. His head was now thrust forward, and although he spoke to Dunn, his eyes never left the Zulu's face. 'This boyo did the pawin' and now 'e's doin' the lyin', like. 'E 'ad 'is 'and on your daughter's knee, see – an' not on the outside but on the inside.

Now that wasn't bein' respectful, so I told 'im to lay off. He didn't, look you, so I gave 'im a slap across the wrist.' Jenkins narrowed his eyes. 'It was only gentle, like, but 'e seemed to get a bit upset and 'it me with that bowl thing. Now, sir, that 'urt a bit and I don't take kindly to it – nor 'im tellin' lies about me, see.'

Before anyone could move, Jenkins took two seemingly unaggressive steps forward and then, coolly and with accuracy, spat into the Zulu's face. Immediately a growl went up from the Zulus watching. Beginning as an involuntary grunt, it swelled up the register until it ululated like a war cry.

The warrior slowly wiped the saliva from his face, his eyes on Jenkins. Then he spoke quickly to Dunn, turned and left the circle.

Jenkins's smile lit his face and he turned to Simon and Dunn. 'There you are, then, gentlemen. That chap 'as no guts. Men who are in the wrong never 'ave no guts, do they?'

John Dunn sighed. 'I am very much afraid, Mr Jenkins,' he said, 'that it will be you who won't have any guts in a minute.' He went on as Jenkins tried to interrupt. 'I mean that literally. He has gone to get his assegai. He won't get one for you because he will presume that you have one already. By spitting in his face, you've just invited him to fight you to the death.'

Jenkins regained his smile. 'Well, there's friendly for you, isn't it? Ah well, I'll just 'ave to teach the young feller a lesson.'

Simon grabbed Jenkins's shoulder and swung him round. 'You'll do no such thing, Jenkins. I'll have no fighting here. It could upset everything. You will apologise to that man when he returns. And that's an order.'

'For God's sake, man.' It was Dunn's turn to get angry and he thrust his head a few inches from Simon's face. 'Don't you realise that you are not on the parade ground now? You don't have any soldier boys over the hill waiting to ride to the rescue. You're in Zululand.' He gestured to the warriors, who had now approached, forming a loose circle around the three white men. 'This is their country and their customs. This bloody fool has caused offence and there's no way an "I-am-very-sorry-I'm-sure" is going to get him out of it. He'll have to fight or just be speared on the spot as a coward.'

Simon swallowed hard. The thought of losing Jenkins was frightening. Drunkard or not, he was his friend, mentor and vital companion on this mission. He took Dunn's arm in appeal. 'Look. I can't risk losing Jenkins. He is important to my work. Besides which, he is a good man really and he thought he was protecting Nandi. Can't you do something?'

Dunn shook his head. 'Sorry, Fonthill. The fool will have to fight or be killed – probably the same thing in the end, I fear.' He turned to Jenkins. 'I'm sorry about this, man, but you'll have to fight. I'll get you an assegai.'

'No thank you.'

'Don't be a fool. You'll not be allowed a rifle and bayonet, even if you have one.'

Jenkins spoke evenly, all trace of drunkenness now gone. 'I've got no bayonet, Mr Dunn sir, which is a pity, because I could have handled this boyo better with one. But I want no 'eathen spear – beggin' your pardon, sir, that is. No, I'll just 'ave to use me 'ands, see.'

'For God's sake, 352,' Simon implored. 'You can't fight a spearman with your bare hands. And you can't fight anyway, dammit. You're drunk.'

For the first time, Jenkins showed real mirth. 'Ah, bach sir,' he said. 'You don't really know me, do you?' He spoke now slowly and with emphasis, as though explaining something complicated to a child. 'It's the way for me *to* fight, see. The drink gets me dander up. Now don't worry about this black lad. I've bin fightin' since I was three an' nearly always with me bare 'ands, look you. Lads with bayonets, knives, pickaxes, shovels, hay forks: I've fought 'em all. And, see, I'm still 'ere. So don't you worry. I'll try not to 'urt this feller too much.'

In despair, Simon turned again to Dunn, but the big man shook his head silently and walked away, his arms held wide, talking in low, urgent tones to the onlookers and making them form a wide circle away from the fire. As they did so, Nkumo entered the ring. He had stripped away the body decorations that he had put on for the feast and wore now only a loincloth, and cow tails hanging from his biceps and calves. He carried his war shield and a short stabbing assegai. He looked in puzzlement at the unarmed figure of Jenkins, who walked over to join him in the ring.

The combatants looked an incongruous mismatch. The Zulu stood about six feet tall and was muscular across the shoulders and in his thighs. He was young – about twenty-one years old – and he wore no isiCoco, of course. But his posture was one of quiet fury and he faced Jenkins with a confidence only slightly confounded by the unusual appearance of his opponent. Jenkins looked somehow shorter in the firelight than his five feet four inches and proportionally squatter and broader. He was wearing his old corduroy breeches tucked into his riding boots, but he had put on, Simon noted sadly, his best cotton shirt for the feast. He stood now facing Nkumo, his body well balanced on legs slightly apart, his weight thrown forward on to the balls of his feet and his arms hanging quite motionless by his sides.

Simon caught a glimpse of Nandi on the edge of the crowd, her eyes wide in apprehension. Next to her was Catherine Dunn, her face quite expressionless. How many times, he wondered, had she seen scenes of this kind of brutality since she had first crossed the Tugela with John Dunn? His reverie was broken by Nkumo speaking to Dunn.

Dunn turned to Jenkins. 'He says he can't fight you unless you have an assegai.'

'I could fight 'im with a straw,' replied Jenkins, keeping his eyes fixed on the Zulu. 'But I'll tell you what, Mr Dunn sir. As I 'aven't got a spear an' 'e 'as, like, it might make it a bit more fair if he does without that shield thing. But he can keep his spear.'

Dunn translated and Nkumo frowned for a moment and then threw his shield to one side. He stepped a little closer to Jenkins, who moved not a muscle.

It was clearly disconcerting for the Zulu. From childhood he had been taught to fight, first with sticks and then with assegai, but always against an opponent who was similarly armed. To face a man who had no weapon was unbalancing, somehow, and it was clear that he did not know how to begin the combat. Eventually he held the assegai over his shoulder with a downward, stabbing grasp and made a few passes across and down Jenkins's face, but narrowly out of range.

The Welshman did not flinch and made no obvious movement to defend himself. Keeping his eyes fixed on those of Nkumo, he almost imperceptibly swayed backwards, making the Zulu's movements seem perfunctory opening gambits – which, of course, was what they were. The crowd made a low hissing noise and Simon had no idea if they were applauding or showing disapproval. Whatever the motive, it seemed to stimulate the Zulu, who suddenly changed to an underhand grip on the assegai and lunged towards Jenkins, thrusting towards the chest in two lightning feints and then, for real, to the stomach.

With remarkable grace, Jenkins pirouetted on his toes like a matador, moving his arms across his body stiffly, as though holding a cape, but not moving them up in defence. The last, meaningful stab passed his arms by some six inches and Jenkins, as light on his feet as a cat, slipped away out of reach and stood waiting, as before.

A communal gasp rose from the crowd, followed by, this time, an undoubted murmur of approval. Dunn looked across at Simon and drew his eyebrows up in surprised admiration.

Provoked, Nkumo whirled to the attack again in a flurry of stabbing motions. This time the Welshman extended his left hand towards his attacker's spear, as though to judge its distance, and danced away from the thrusts again, his feet a twinkle of movement in the light from the flames.

'Well done, 352,' cried Simon involuntarily and then fell silent, realising that he sounded like a prep-school spectator on the touchline. This was no game. Jenkins was concentrating like fury to stay alive.

The combat had only lasted for a couple of minutes yet both gladiators were perspiring. The young Zulu, his wide eyes showing yellow in the half-light, was glistening all over. Jenkins's hair, already drenched in beer from the gourd, was plastered to his forehead and the big black moustache had half disappeared as the Welshman sucked it below his lower lip in deep application.

The problem for the Zulu was how to circumvent his opponent's probing left hand, thrust forward almost like a bargaining counter, to get close enough to stab before the little man danced away. Even so, it was a one-sided contest, for Jenkins could make no aggressive move and it could only be a matter of time before the assegai found flesh.

It did so as Nkumo attacked again, this time feinting towards the body and then deliberately aiming the sharp point towards the extended left arm. Even then, Jenkins's reactions were almost a match for the thrust. As the spear tip sought his forearm, the back of his fingers deflected it so that it tore along his biceps, sending a spurt of blood along the ground. Jenkins stumbled on to one knee with the force of the thrust, his right hand touching the ground and his bleeding left arm held up, as though in surrender. Quickly Nkumo swung his spear arm back for the fatal jab. As he did so, Jenkins suddenly transformed into the aggressor. Rising from the crouch, he flung a handful of dust into the Zulu's eyes, momentarily distracting him, and then, ducking inside, delivered a short punch with his good hand into the black man's stomach. With frightening speed, he head-butted his opponent just below the ribcage and swung a sideways back-handed chop into the Zulu's throat as his head went back.

With a sigh, Nkumo collapsed completely, thumping on to the sandy ground with a force which left him prostrate and, it seemed, completely unconscious.

Immediately, Jenkins leaped astride the fallen figure and, with his left arm streaming blood, attempted to lift the head as though to deliver one more, mortal blow.

'No,' cried Simon, rushing forward. 'Don't, Jenkins. Don't kill him.'

'Kill 'im be buggered,' gasped Jenkins, trying to work his injured hand underneath the black head. 'Quick, help me. Get his head forward and his tongue out. I think he's swallowed it and he can't breathe.' He looked up at Simon and went on, conversationally: 'They tend to, y'know, when you 'it 'em in the throat. It can kill a chap. That's it. Get 'old of the tongue and pull it out.'

The little Welshman, kneeling across his victim with sweat pouring down his face, looked across at the crowd. 'Hey, you silly buggers, can someone bring some water? Or better still, beer. We've got to get 'im swallowin' again. Nandi . . .'

Dunn quickly gave orders and a gourd of beer was brought. Gently, Jenkins lifted Nkumo's head and began to pour a little of the liquid into the unconscious man's mouth. The beer spilled down the Zulu's chin but, almost immediately, he began to gulp and splutter and then opened his eyes. The two erstwhile opponents stared at each other across a distance of about seven inches.

'There, that's better, boyo,' said Jenkins soothingly. 'Nice old fight, wasn't it, then? You did very well for a beginner, like. Sorry if I 'ad to 'it you a bit 'ard but I 'ad to end the entertainment because you was gettin' a bit good at it, see.' He looked up at Dunn. 'Is there a drop more of that beer left, then, d'you think? I'm a bit dry.'

Wordlessly, Dunn handed Jenkins another gourd. The Welshman was about to drain it, but he paused, looked up at Simon and then took a couple of gulps before passing the rest to the Zulu, whose head he was still cradling. Nkumo drank quietly, his wide eyes never leaving Jenkins's face. The Welshman then put his other, good hand around the black man's shoulders and, with Simon's help, raised him to his feet. The big Zulu stood for a moment, gulping and swaying and looking around him with a puzzled expression. He spoke a few words to Dunn, who smiled and replied equally tersely.

'Is he all right?' asked Simon. 'What did he say?'

The Natalian nodded. 'He's going to live all right,' he said dryly. 'He wanted to know where the white man kept his knobkerrie. I told him he had no club. He just used his hands. Nkumo can't quite work it out, I think . . .'

'This lad's trouble,' interjected Jenkins, anxious to be helpful, 'was that he didn't watch me eyes, see. You 'ave to watch the eyes. It gives an idea of what's goin' to 'appen next – what a feller's goin' to do, like.'

Simon shook his head in resignation. 'Jenkins, do shut up. I don't know whether to put you forward for a court martial or for a medal. No. I do know. It has to be a court martial. You were drunk.' He turned to Dunn. 'Has any lasting harm been done, do you think?'

Dunn looked around him. The ring of onlookers was breaking up into animated, gossiping groups. No one paid the slightest attention to Nkumo, who stood where he had been raised, feeling his throat and still swaying slightly. 'No, I don't think so,' said the big man, pulling his beard. 'To be honest, I think that that was the best show these fellers have seen for years.' He turned to the Welshman. 'So, Mr Jenkins, I reckon that you've got away with it this time. But I do recommend that you go easy with our beer and keep your temper under control. You're quite a battler. But an even-tempered fighter is always better than one who loses his rag. And a sober one is best of all.'

Jenkins opened his mouth to remonstrate but Simon cut in quickly. 'You are absolutely right, sir.' He turned to Jenkins. 'We'd better see to that arm. You've got a big job to do in the next few days, although, after what I've seen tonight, I'm damned if I know if you're up to it.'

For the first time Jenkins looked concerned. 'Well, I'm sorry, bach sir, if I stepped out of line for a minute there. I 'ad to defend myself, look you, though perhaps I did 'ave a tiddle too much liquor. I'll make sure it doesn't 'appen again on this postin', though. With great respect, though, sir, I don't think you would 'ave much of a chance with a court-martial charge. See, we *was* on active service and this black chap *was* the enemy, wasn't 'e? Queen's Regulations say—'

'To hell with Queen's Regulations. We've got more to think about than that. Come on.'

But Catherine had now materialised with a bowl of water and a cloth, and with a crestfallen and ruefully silent Nandi in attendance. As Nandi held the bowl, her eyes downcast, Mrs Dunn began wiping the blood away from Jenkins's arm.

'Very kind, I'm sure, ma'am,' said Jenkins. 'It's only a scratch – but 'old on a minute, if you don't mind.'

He stepped to where a still shaky Nkumo was stooping to retrieve his assegai. 'Hey, Oomkoomi, feelin' better then?' The Zulu half flinched as the Welshman extended his hand. 'Come on. Let's shake on it. Like Englishmen do.' The little man's teeth flashed from beneath his moustache. 'Though you're a Zulu and I'm Welsh.'

The Zulu stood puzzled and motionless, so Jenkins took his hand and shook it vigorously. Then he turned to stand side by side with Nkumo and raised their clasped hands high above his head. Facing the Zulus, who were now drifting back to the fire, he shouted: 'Hey, fellers. Give a hand to the champion and the gallant loser then, hey?'

The crowd paused in surprise for a moment, then black faces began to crease into smiles at the sight of a bedraggled Jenkins, his face beaming, waving aloft the hand of a sheepishly grinning Nkumo. At the back of the dispersing ring, someone began to stamp his foot. The action spread and soon, it seemed, the whole camp was stamping their feet and crying, 'Usuthu! Usuthu!'

Dunn shook his head in mock despair. 'He's some man, your . . . associate, Mr Fonthill.'

'I'm afraid so, sir. I'm sorry about all this. I just don't know what to think.' Simon called to Jenkins. 'For God's sake man, come here. Who do you think you are, Tom Sayers?'

Jenkins hurried over. 'Funny you should say that, bach sir, 'cos I did see 'im fight once, in Hereford. O' course, 'e wasn't champion then, but, goodness, 'e was a rare fighter. Only ten stone nothin' he was, see, but 'e 'ad a left 'and like nothin' you've ever—'

Simon pushed the Welshman towards the women. 'Get on with you and stop talking. Get the arm bandaged and get to bed straight away. And no more beer. We must talk tomorrow. I have to tell you about a most important journey you're about to start. Perhaps the most important of your life.'

Jenkins looked up with interest. 'Oh yes, sir. What would that be, then?'

But Simon just shook his head and led the little champion towards the women.

Chapter 9

Alice Griffith tapped her foot with impatience on the wet cobblestones outside Paddington station. It was always the same. When it rained, one could never get a hansom cab in London. Mind, she reflected, it was never easy for a woman alone to stop a cab at the best of times. Perhaps women didn't tip as well as men. Ah, well . . . 'Cabby!'

The horse clattered to a standstill opposite her and the driver, perched high at the rear, the rim of his bowler hat just peeping out from under the glistening black cape that covered him, raised a mittened finger to his moustache in acknowledgement.

Alice paused, her umbrella aloft, one foot on the step of the cab. 'Do you know the offices of the *Morning Post* newspaper in Fleet Street?' she enquired.

The cabby nodded glumly.

'Then please take me there. I am a little late and would be greatly obliged if you could make whatever haste you can in this dreadful weather.'

Alice stepped up and the cab sashayed backwards on its high springs as she settled into her seat. Then it was off. The young woman adjusted the hat pinned on to her piled hair and wiped the condensation from the little window so that she could see the crowded pavements. How she loved London, even in the rain! The city was always so alive. Everyone seemed to have a purpose, unlike the country, where the set rhythm of the seasons gave a sleepy certainty to everyone's movements so that there was never any need to bustle. The crops would still be there to cut down and take in, even if the harvest was poor and late. Her eyes sparkled as she observed a middle-aged man, elegantly spatted and top-hatted, running – yes running! – down Park Lane as if his life depended upon it. Perhaps it did. Perhaps he had news of some vital development in the Empire that had to reach the City before the markets closed. Alice looked at the watch on her fob. Fifteen minutes to three. He did right to hurry. She sat back and then remembered to be nervous again. She must try and look older, and she settled her hat at a slightly less rakish angle. The appointment that faced her was quite as important as any which impelled that gentleman.

The cab reached the *Morning Post* with just three minutes to spare and she composed herself before stepping down and paying her fare, making sure that she tipped adequately. The tall commissionaire, looking like a major general, saluted her, opened the door and ushered her to the reception desk. The clerk behind it, with his high collar and loosely knotted black tie, might have stepped from one of Mr Dickens's novels.

'I have an appointment with the editor,' Alice said firmly.

'Yes, madam. Which editor?'

'What do you mean, *which* editor?'

The clerk sighed. 'Well, we have an editor for the news, one for the letters page, one for what we call features, and indeed, madam, we even have an editor for ladies' affairs. No doubt it is he you would wish to see?'

Alice flushed. 'My appointment is with *the* editor, the editor of the *Morning Post*. And if we are not careful, I shall be late for it.'

The clerk looked at her sharply, gave a half-bow, half-nod, and summoned a diminutive pageboy, whose brightly polished buttons ran from throat to midriff like illuminated vertebrae. Within a minute, Alice was sitting in the editor's anteroom. The door opened and a middle-aged man with cigarette ash down a badly buttoned waistcoat enquired politely, 'Forgive me, madam, but you did say *Miss* Griffith?'

'Yes.'

'Miss A.C. Griffith?'

'That is my name, yes, and I have a letter from Mr Cornford, the editor, agreeing to see me at three p.m. today.'

The man bowed and retreated. It was five minutes before he reappeared. 'The editor will see you now, mad— miss.'

Alice was ushered through the door and announced: 'Miss . . . ah . . . Griffith, sir.'

The room was large and wood-panelled. A table piled high with that morning's newspapers stood against one wall and a cheery coal fire burned from a grate in another. Opposite the door a large desk dominated, from behind which a portly man rose to greet her. She observed a well-cut morning coat, carrying a yellow carnation in the lapel, and two blue eyes smiling at her above a full beard and moustache. He looked, she thought, like an older version of the Prince of Wales.

'Charles Cornford,' he introduced himself as he held out his hand. 'Please do sit down, Miss, or is it Mrs Griffith?'

'Miss,' said Alice firmly, arranging her dress and sitting.

'You must forgive the slight delay in receiving you, Miss

Griffith,' said Cornford, a faint smile playing behind his whiskers, 'but, you see . . .' His voice trailed away.

'You were expecting a man.'

Cornford bowed his head. 'I fear that there has been some mistake, my dear young lady.'

'No, sir, not at all.' She had rehearsed this confrontation so many times that it was almost a relief that it was going exactly as expected. 'You see, I always sign my writings with my initials.' She smiled at him in turn. 'As do most men, I believe – when they are fortunate enough to write above a by-line, that is. There has never been any attempt to deceive – as, one must admit, there has been with Miss George Eliot, for example.'

Cornford bowed his head courteously again. 'Quite so. But my letters, I seem to recall, were addressed to A.C. Griffith *Esquire*. Our meeting was delayed a moment or two because I took the trouble to check.'

Alice felt her cheeks colouring annoyingly. 'Really? I fear I did not notice.' She leaned forward and spoke quickly. 'Mr Cornford, you have been good enough to print four of my articles on the Afghanistan situation and one on South Africa, and kind enough to write and congratulate me on their tone and accuracy. Surely the fact that the author of those articles is a woman makes not the slightest difference to their validity?'

Cornford rocked his chair back and nodded in affable agreement. 'Quite so. Quite so. However,' his blue eyes sparkled as though he was enjoying the debate, 'it does make every difference to your request that we should send you to north-west India as our correspondent there.'

'But why should it?'

The editor shrugged his shoulders and spread his hands. 'Because, my dear young lady, the frontier is no place for a woman.' He leaned forward. 'I know of no newspaper in the world which employs a woman on its staff to report from a war – no, I am wrong. *The Times* did it once, but that was most unusual. In the first place, you would cause embarrassment to the general staff there and they would never give you accreditation. In the second, during the course of your duties, you would have to live like a trooper and endure virtually the same privations on campaign as he does – rough living, rough riding and great danger. No,' he shook his head sorrowfully, 'a war is no place for a woman, however well she can write and comprehend military strategy.'

Alice gripped her hands in her lap tightly. 'Mr Cornford, I ride to hounds regularly over some of the roughest terrain in the Welsh Borders. I am told by the Master that I ride better than most men. When I was in Switzerland, I climbed six Alpine peaks over ten thousand feet in four months. I was accompanied only by a guide in each case and, because I rather anticipated your reservations, I have in my handbag a letter from him confirming this. Although this may not help me in Afghanistan, I speak fluent French and German, and, I can assure you, I am as fit as any man. I have not only lived rough in the mountains of Switzerland and Wales but I have positively enjoyed doing so.' Alice sat back, flushing a little. She disliked having to make claims for herself.

Mr Cornford sat forward and selected a cigar from a box on his desk and struck a match. 'Ah,' he said, in some confusion. He offered the box. 'Do you . . .? Would you care to . . .?'

Alice shook her head. 'Not a cigar, thank you. But perhaps if you have a cigarette . . .?'

'Of course.' The editor fumbled in a drawer and produced a silver box that he took to his guest, carefully lighting her cigarette for her. Alice puffed blue smoke towards the ceiling.

Cornford returned to his chair and to the attack. 'I fear that I haven't made myself quite clear,' he said. 'The rigours of campaigning are only part of the problem.' He sighed. 'Our world is changing so much that I do not doubt that there are women who can compete with men in handling the more, what shall I say, physical side of reporting. Your achievements seem remarkable and do you credit. But there are other considerations I must take into account.'

He leaned back in his chair and pulled on his cigar. 'You write very well on the issues. Why,' he waved his cigar in emphasis, 'only the other day Hicks-Beach, the Colonial Secretary, stopped me in the House and complimented me on your piece on the dangers of moving too quickly towards confederation in South Africa. But – there is a great deal of difference between contemplatively penning an article on policy in the comfort of an office or living room and in reporting hard facts from a battlefield, usually in competition with other reporters on the spot. Eh? What? Do you take my point?'

Alice nodded. 'Yes, I do, Mr Cornford.'

'And there are other factors. Our man in the field must be accepted by the army. D'you know, the Horse Guards and our generals are the most conservative – some would say reactionary – bunch of people in the whole of the Empire. I have to acknowledge that Russell of *The Times* pioneered the way for us to report directly, and sometimes critically, when he was in the Crimea and in America for the Civil War. But the idea of the press being on the spot to report mistakes as they are being made, so to speak, is still not completely accepted. Our people in the field need to tread warily and they need contacts in the army to do their job. I fear a feminine presence in this hard male world would complicate things frightfully.

'One last point.' Cornford spoke now with the air of a man who had made his case convincingly. 'We already have a man out with General Browne in Afghanistan. We could certainly not afford two.' He settled back in his chair.

'Why then, pray, did you agree to see me?' asked Alice.

'Ah yes, well, I have to confess that I wished to meet this Mr Griffith who had been writing for us so perceptively from the far-flung borders of England.' He smiled, half apologetically. 'It might have been possible to have offered him something abroad, as it happened, if he proved to be suitable. But, for the reasons I have already explained, I am afraid that it is out of the question, Miss Griffith.' He put a very faint emphasis on the word *Miss*.

Alice breathed deeply and stubbed out her cigarette. 'I quite understand all that you have said, Mr Cornford, and I am grateful to you for seeing me and for explaining the situation so frankly. But I must be frank with you, in turn.' She smoothed her dress and sat bolt upright. 'I am determined to become a professional journalist on one of the great newspapers of this country – even, perhaps, one day becoming as great and powerful an editor as you.'

Cornford inclined his head and smiled, more with amuse-ment than appreciation of the flattery, but he listened attentively as Alice continued.

'I have fixed my mind on reporting on great matters from abroad. If you will not have me, then I shall try *The Times* and the other newspapers in London until I find one that will allow me to exercise my talents. However, the *Morning Post* suits me well. Perhaps I am not fully supportive of its political stance but I do feel that I have a small, shall we say, investment in it as a result of my articles. Indeed,' Alice's eyes held those of Cornford, 'I believe that I may claim even to have built up a modest following among your readers.'

Cornford gave a gentle acquiescence with his head. 'That may well be so, my dear.'

'And so, Mr Cornford, I have a proposition to put to you. The North West Frontier may perhaps not be for me at this stage. But why can I not go to a less active theatre, which has news potential but where you are not already strongly represented and where, so to speak, I might win my spurs before going on to greater things?'

Cornford raised his eyebrows. 'Such as?'

'From my readings of the *Post* you do not have a strong representation in Cape Town. You only have there a stringer, if I have the terminology correct?'

'Both your terminology and your presumption are correct.'

'Good. Then I propose, sir, that I become your accredited correspondent in South Africa, with the task of reporting upon all of the developments there, from the Cape to the Transvaal to Zululand, and covering matters political, economic and military.'

Cornford made to speak but Alice went on quickly. 'Of course, I would prefer to be in Afghanistan, and South African affairs are undoubtedly of less importance to your readers. There is no Russian threat there, for instance. But I sense that this land dispute between the Boers and the Zulus could be the catalyst that could make the Cape of greater interest to us back home. And I have studied the matter, as you may know from my last piece.

'You mentioned that your representative in the field must have contacts. Well, I am a brigadier's daughter and he served in the 24th Foot, both regiments of which are out in South Africa at this very moment. If war did break out there – and even if it didn't – I would have the most splendid contacts among them which I would have no hesitation in exploiting in reporting on events.'

A smile had now spread completely across Cornford's face, lifting his whiskers and bringing a mischievous twinkle to his blue eyes. Alice, however, failed to notice. Engrossed in the urgency of her argument, her eyes fixed on his waistcoat buttons as she concentrated, she ploughed on.

'Now. I accept your point about my inexperience and I appreciate that you would be taking a risk with me. I do not think, therefore, that it would be fair for you to shoulder the not inconsiderable expense of my steamer fare to the Cape and back. I have modest means of my own and such a cost is well within them. So I am prepared to meet it. But that is the only indulgence I am prepared to allow. I must be paid whatever is the fair rate for a junior correspondent, together with the necessary allowances for living expenses, travel within the country and so on.'

Alice finished with a rush and the room fell silent, except for the crackle of the coal in the fireplace. Cornford stroked his beard reflectively, the smile still in his eyes.

'I confess, Miss Griffith,' he said, 'that I don't quite know what to say to you. I have never met so, ah, determined a young woman before. You make a good case. But what of your parents? Forgive me, I do not wish to pry, but you cannot be very old. I presume you live at home. Would your parents give their consent?'

Alice's heart leapt slightly. Was he relenting? Then she frowned at the condescension. 'My age, Mr Cornford, has nothing to do with it, except that I assure you that I am over the age of consent. I do not need my parents' permission to work for you, but if I did, I am sure that it would not be withheld. I am an only child and I am determined to make my own way in the world.'

Cornford coughed. 'I can quite see that, madam.' He rose to his feet. 'Do you know, I am rather taken by the idea of being the first editor formally to employ a woman as an overseas and, possibly, a war correspondent.' He chuckled. 'Perhaps it is the *only* thing for which I shall be remembered.' He held out his hand. 'Very well, young lady. I accept your terms. If you prove a success – and I must be the judge of that – then the *Post* will reimburse the cost of your fare to and from Cape Town. If you fail, then it shall remain your cost.'

Alice rose to her feet. She felt that her cheeks were burning bright red. 'Oh Mr Cornford,' she said, 'I am so very grateful to you for giving me this chance. You will not regret it, I promise.'

'I do hope not, my dear. Certainly my colleagues, when I tell them, will feel that my judgement is failing in my old age.' He smiled genially. 'But somehow I think I shall prove to be right. Now, I shall write you a formal letter of appointment and you must respond agreeing to my terms – we won't discuss them now but I think you will find them satisfactory. Please consult the steamer schedules and let me know the earliest time you can leave for the Cape. Bear in mind, however, that we shall need you in the office here for a few days before you embark, working with the foreign editor and so on to learn some fundamental ropes. He will advise you on the sort of kit to take, though . . .' his eyebrows rose in further merriment, 'I don't suppose for a moment that he will have much idea of what advice to give to *you*, my dear.'

He ushered her to the door. 'Can you be back here in, say, a week's time?'

'I certainly can, sir.'

'Then best of luck to you, Miss Griffith. Please don't make a fool of me, there's a good young lady.'

The journey back home on the Great Western Railway, changing trains at Cardiff on to the branch line to Brecon, was one of the happiest of Alice's young life. Her heart sang at her success. She had embarked on the interview quite convinced that she would fail. There was no precedent for her appointment and she had only her previous articles and the force of her personality to support her. She had had no real faith in either. But she had won!

Of course, she mused, South Africa was a backwater compared with Afghanistan and she had exaggerated to Cornford the importance of the border dispute. It would probably fizzle out and become just another footnote to the story of South Africa's growth. But the posting would enable her to gain experience: of recording events as they happened, rather than interpreting them from afar. It was much more exciting – and she might even see Simon!

She stared unseeingly out of the rain-streaked window. Not once in the talk of South Africa had she thought of him. Not even when she was boasting so grandiloquently (and rather falsely) about her contacts within the army at the Cape. Well, it would be good to see him again, if that was possible – why, he might even be useful to her in her work! Alice smiled at the thought. She had no idea of where Simon would be. There had been no further news since a rather boring and short letter had arrived from Durban. She gave a shrug. It was of no real import.

She had far more important things to think about now – not least the difficult task of explaining to her parents that she had suddenly become a foreign correspondent for a newspaper. She smiled again. She could do that. It might take all her skills but, after convincing Cornford, the task of winning over her mother and father would be comparatively easy. She pressed her nose against the cold window pane and began to hum to herself.

Chapter 10

At roughly the time that an apprehensive but excited Alice was boarding the vessel in London Docks that would take her to Cape Town, Simon was lying disconsolately on his bed in John Dunn's kraal. Late winter in Zululand had brought some relief from the humidity but it was boredom and a feeling of frustrated inadequacy that accounted for his discomfort now. It was four weeks since Jenkins, his arm bandaged, his hair freshly slicked back and Simon's letter stitched into the lining of his coat, had set off with the cattle to the border. There had been no news of him since, except that the boys who had accompanied him had returned and reported that the cattle had been safely delivered to the army pens in Durban. Jenkins had disappeared without trace.

More to the point, Simon realised sadly, he also missed Nandi. She had disappeared too, on the morning of Jenkins's departure. After two days, Simon had casually enquired about her and Dunn had told him gruffly that she had gone up-country for a few days to stay with her mother's relatives. It was clearly a banishment for her part in the Jenkins fracas. Dunn, too, was rarely at home and Simon's frustration stemmed from lack of meaningful activity as much as loneliness. His horsemanship improved considerably as a result of daily rides near the farm, but they brought him no information about the King's intentions towards the British or his possible preparations for war. All he saw were cattle, herdsmen, dongas and scrub. No warriors. No drilling impis. As a spy he was worthless! Yet he dared not ride towards the Zulu heartland, for he was useless without an interpreter. If only Nandi . . .

As if on cue, there was a gentle knock on the door of his room. 'Simon,' called a soft voice.

He sprang from his bed and opened the door. There she was, dressed in that familiar white shift, small white teeth gleaming, a wild orchid tucked into her hair, her whole manner radiating youthful happiness. 'Nandi,' he cried. 'Where have you been?'

She pulled a face of lugubrious misery. 'I have been in disgrace because Papa said that I had caused the fight between Mr Jenkins and Nkumo. So he sent me to stay in Mama's village in the north.' Her eyes widened in youthful innocence. 'But Simon. It was not my fault. I was not encouraging them, you know.'

Simon frowned momentarily. He was quite sure that she had played the coquette on that evening. She was a flirt, there was no doubt about it – but he needed her. 'Of course,' he said. 'Sit down.'

Nandi shook her head. 'No thank you. Papa says I must not go into your room. I called because I thought you might like to ride and . . .' she grinned, 'start your lessons in the Zulu language.'

'What a good idea, but what about your father? He has said precious little to me over the past few weeks and I fear that I am becoming an embarrassment to him.'

Nandi shook her head. 'No, I don't think so. He left early this morning for Durban; something to do with this Boundary

Commission which has been meeting at Rorke's Drift for a long time now. I asked him last night and he said that if you really wanted to learn, then I could begin teaching you.' The smile came back, seeming to tilt her nose and illuminating her brown face. 'So, you see, it's all right. I have the horses saddled.'

They rode, as before, along the track that led to the shaded pool, and sat together on the mossy bank. Nandi stretched out luxuriously and put her hands behind her head. 'Isn't this a wonderful place?' she said. Then she stretched out a languid hand. 'Simon . . .'

'What about my lesson, then?'

Nandi sighed and sat upright, resting her chin on her knees and looking at Simon through her lashes mischievously. Simon thought that he had never seen anything so lovely. She had tucked a cotton scarf around her neck and its bright orange seemed to make her skin more lustrous, her teeth whiter. 'All right, then. You are my pupil. You must listen carefully.'

'No textbooks, ma'am?'

'No. We don't have a written language, Simon. Although we do in a way.'

'What do you mean?'

'Well, we can communicate by colour. By sending you certain beads on a string, I can say things to you. Basic things, but you would understand – just like a letter, really. For instance, if I sent you a string of beads painted white, I would be speaking of love.' Unusually, she betrayed just a touch of embarrassment. 'If they were black I would be yearning and thinking of the night. Yellow means a house and a family, green is domestic bliss . . . and so on,' she finished rather lamely.

'How fascinating,' said Simon. His eyes drifted to her cleavage, where the ends of the scarf were tucked into her shift.

She was wearing nothing underneath again. Oh God! 'What, er, what about the language, then?' he enquired weakly.

'Yes, Simon. It will not be easy for you.' She curled her legs underneath her like a schoolgirl and her face wore that air of innocent concentration that reminded Simon of the Sunday school teachers of his youth. 'We have no books so I will have to teach you by mouth, so to speak.'

'How charming,' murmured Simon.

'What? Oh yes.' She grinned. 'But not by kissing, Simon. You said that there were rules about that. No, be serious and listen. The first thing is for you to learn how to make the sounds that are very different from English. For instance, we have three sorts of clicks. Look.' She threw back her head and opened her mouth wide.

'One is made like this, so.' She made a sound like the English tut-tut, by pressing her tongue to the back of her front teeth and pulling it away sharply. Simon came closer, moved his head down and looked into the roof of her mouth.

'How very fascinating,' he breathed.

She did it again. 'Now try for yourself. Look, see. Now you do it.' He tried and did quite well.

'Good. Now I suppose you could call that our letter "c". The second one is . . . let me think how I do it first.' She frowned and clicked for a while, looking quite adorable to Simon in the soft dappled light. 'Yes, I have it. You put your tongue to the back of the roof of the mouth and move it so that you make the sort of noise that I've heard Afrikaaners do to make their horses go faster. It's another kind of click really. Listen.' She clicked away while Simon solemnly rested his head on her lap, looking up between her breasts into her mouth. 'Now that's our sort of "x". Can you do it?'

Simon closed his eyes, pressed his nose into her stomach and clicked.

'That was quite good. Now – please move your head and look. This next one is how English people spell names or words beginning with their "q". It's the easiest, really. Come closer and watch my mouth. You put your tongue further back on the roof of your mouth and flip it down to the bottom. It's a deeper sort of cluck. Look.'

She lowered her head so that Simon could see. Before she could cluck, however, Simon's lips were upon hers, his tongue thrusting deep into her mouth, his arms around her. For a startled split second she sat inert. Then she coiled her arms around his neck and responded ardently. This time there was no pulling back by the young Englishman: his loneliness, his boredom, his sense of frustration were all sublimated by the desire he felt. Coquette or not, he wanted her. He kissed her mouth, her eyes, her cheeks, her ears, soundlessly but with a passion he had never evinced before. He rolled on top of her and began working himself against her slim body. Gently, she pushed him away.

'Simon,' she whispered into his ear, 'we must not make a baby. But – do you want ukuHlongonga?'

'What? God knows. But yes. I'm sure I do – whatever it is.'

'Oh yes. Let us do it, then. Here, give me your hand. Put it here.' She pulled up her shift and led Simon's hand between her thighs. 'Now . . .' She fumbled with the buttons on his breeches. 'There. There. That's it. How lovely. Yes.'

For minutes, the two lay in the glade, making gentle love under Nandi's tuition until they both climaxed, he with a gasp and a groan, she quietly, with a sigh and then a smile. She licked her fingers sensuously and then rolled on top of him and kissed him deeply on the mouth. 'Oh Simon,' she murmured, and began to whisper to him in Zulu as she snuggled her cheek beneath his chin.

Simon lay back, his hand gently running along the vertebrae he could feel through the thin cotton of her shift, his eyes staring into the tracery of leaves above him. A feeling of depression came over him. Had he seduced his host's daughter? He was not sure whether what they had done amounted to seduction, but whatever it was, he had compromised his position. He groaned aloud and Nandi pressed closer to him, murmuring soft, guttural endearments. And what about Alice? For the first time for days he thought of her but once again could not recall the details of her face, only the whiteness of her skin – so very different from . . . He groaned again.

Nandi sat up. 'Simon,' she smiled, gently patting his loins, 'don't worry. We have not made a baby so you will not have to marry me. I know that you would not like that.' She looked across at him with eyes that were now sorrowful. 'That is why I thought we should make ukuHlongonga. It is better that way, although, not, I should think, as much fun as making a baby.'

'So you have never . . .?'

'No. Have you?'

Simon shook his head. 'No. There has never been anyone.' He frowned. No. Surely he could not count his ineffective fumblings with that whore in Sandhurst? Of course not.

Nandi clapped her hands joyously. 'Oh good. I am so glad, Simon. Perhaps we can make a baby together then . . .' she tailed off and paused for a sad moment, 'some day.'

Simon kissed her hair. 'Perhaps we can. Some day.'

They rode back together in silence. Nandi, in a fit of responsibility – either feigned or real, Simon could not be sure

– had wished to continue with the language lesson but he had demurred. His mind was too disturbed, and anyway, he doubted whether he could ever make headway in a language that progressed in clicks, however sweet the teacher. And she *was* sweet. Simon studied her as she rode a length ahead of him along a donga. She sat perfectly erect, her big toes hooked into rawhide stirrups in what he had heard was the Basutho style, her slim body rising easily with the movement of the pony. She was beautiful and desirable – but he cursed himself silently. Now, in addition to spending his time indolently when he should have been gathering information, he had compromised himself with a Zulu half-caste. What would Covington make of that? He must, he *must* get out of here. He *must* get on with his job.

That evening, Catherine, James, Nandi and he sat down at dinner, in Dunn's absence. There seemed to be a tension in the air and Simon wondered guiltily if Catherine and James somehow suspected what had happened that afternoon. But how could they, unless Nandi had let something slip, perhaps in a moment of gleeful pride of conquest? No, she was unlikely to do that. They munched on in silence, until Catherine turned to him.

'You must forgive us, Mr Fonthill, if we seem a little gloomy tonight,' she said. 'But we are unhappy about what has happened at the frontier at Rorke's Drift, to the north of here. My husband has gone to Durban, on behalf of King Cetswayo, to see if he can intercede with the British about it.' She paused, looking for words. 'Nandi, you explain. My English is getting worse and worse.'

Nandi put down her knife and fork. 'It happened a few weeks ago now. A chieftain named Sihayo, who lives on the Buffalo River near Rorke's Drift, is a favourite of the King and visited him at his kraal. While he was there, his son discovered that Sihayo's Great Wife, Kaqwelebana, and another wife had taken lovers. Now, Simon,' Nandi's eyes widened again, in that familiar earnest look, 'adultery is a terrible crime in the Zulu nation, so Sihayo's relatives decided that, of course, Kaqwelebana had to be killed.'

Simon found himself nodding gravely and saying, 'Of course.'

'They went to look for her but found that she, the other wife and their lovers had escaped across the river into Natal. Now, once a Zulu crosses the river he can become a Natal Kaffir, if he wants to, and he is not therefore under the King's justice. It is different for wives, who, of course, belong to their husbands, but they all thought they were safe. But they were not.' Nandi shook her head gravely. 'Oh, no. Sihayo's son led a party of Zulus and they crossed into Natal and found the women and their lovers. They obeyed the British law, as they understood it, and let the two men go, because they had become Natal Kaffirs. Then they took the two women back and killed them – but not before they were on Zulu soil.'

Simon nodded. 'I see.'

Nandi shook her head. 'No. There is more. A few days later two white men were seen carrying out some sort of survey on the banks of the Tugela. They crossed the river to a rock very near the Zulu bank and refused to answer the questions of some warriors who were on the Zulu shore and who wanted to know what they were doing. So the warriors surrounded the men and made them turn out their pockets. They were not harmed and they were released in under an hour.'

Clenching her fists, Nandi now beat them gently on the table to emphasise her points. 'Now, the British Great Governor in Cape Town, Sir Something Frere, is saying that both these happenings are aggressive acts by the King and he is claiming large compensation and even hinting that the British will go to war over this.' She turned big eyes on Simon and he saw that they were blinking back tears. 'Simon, these are little things – the sort of things that have happened many times in the past without anyone worrying. Now your people are turning ... what do you say, an ant hill into a mountain?'

Simon stifled a smile and nodded.

'Yes, and they are using it as an excuse to attack our people, because they are obviously trying to push the King into war. It seems that you British want war after all, Simon.'

She was now looking at him half accusingly, and he realised that this news must have reached her after their afternoon tryst. He also noted Nandi's reference to 'our people' when talking about the Zulus. For the first time it occurred to him that she regarded herself as Zulu, not English, or even half-caste. Simon felt uneasily guilty and thought again of Lamb's question: 'Will he go to war if we put pressure on him to come under the flag?' Was this the pressure, the beginning of a cat-and-mouse game with the Zulu king? Or had the decision already been made to go to war as soon as an excuse could be contrived? Either way, he felt ashamed of the politicians and generals in Cape Town, playing their imperial games.

He coughed and asked, 'What is Mr Dunn hoping to do in Natal?'

Catherine answered. 'The Governor of Natal, Sir Henry Bulwer, is a reasonable man who knows my husband. John is hoping to see him to find out what is at the bottom of all this. You see, the King cannot understand why the British seem to want war.'

Again, Simon's thoughts flashed back to Cape Town, to the big map on the wall and the talk of confederation. 'Will the King go to war against the British?' he asked.

Catherine Dunn looked at her stepchildren. 'None of us know,' she said, replacing an errant wisp of grey hair. 'He has always been a wise ruler and not a bloodthirsty man. But it is a long time since his warriors washed their spears in a big, proper battle and probably there are many in his council who would wish him to teach the British a lesson.'

'It would be difficult for you if that did happen,' Simon murmured. In silence, the three of them nodded.

There was little further conversation and Simon retired to his room as soon as the meal was ended. Once again he needed time to think. The moral dilemma of his dalliance with Nandi was relegated to the back of his mind as he considered what he could do to stop the impending invasion of Zululand. It was no longer a question of discovering the King's intentions if a challenge was to be made. It sounded as though the provocation had been delivered now just as surely as if Sir Bartle Frere had slapped Cetswayo across the cheek with a glove. The time for speculation had long since passed. Now, somehow, the King had to be persuaded not to retaliate. How? Simon sat on his bed, his chin in his hand. He could think of no alternative. He must go to Ulundi and talk to the King.

Simon rose early but found Nandi already working in an outhouse, churning milk in a large pot to make butter. She gave him a sad, sweet half-smile. Immediately, his heart went out to her. She looked so poignantly unhappy and vulnerable, her bare feet on the beaten earth, her slight body beneath the simple shift working hard at the churn. He swallowed hard. He had to concentrate on his mission.

'Nandi, I have been thinking about what you said at the dinner table last night and I have been wondering how I might help.'

Her hand went to her mouth. 'Oh Simon. If only you could. But how? What can you do?'

He turned his back in thought and walked away for a moment, and then returned. 'Look, I know it sounds stupid, but I think that if I could get to Ulundi and see the King, I might be able to persuade him that fighting would be the wrong thing to do, whatever the provocation. If he knows exactly how strong the British are, then he might not accept the advice of those inDunas who want him to wash the spears.'

Nandi's eyes widened. 'No, Simon. No. You would be killed. No white man, except Father, has ever gone to the King's kraal without an invitation. It would be seen as an insult, a . . . what do you call it? Yes, intrusion, that's it. You could not go alone, and anyway, who could interpret for you?'

Simon shrugged. 'When will your father be back?'

'We don't know – but it is likely to be weeks.'

'What about James?'

'He rode out earlier for the south, where we have a herd with a diseased bull. He will be away three days or more.' Nandi's face was now completely crestfallen. 'Simon, you cannot go, for neither Catherine nor I could come with you. A woman cannot ride in to see the King, whatever the excuse.'

Simon thought for a moment, put his hands on her shoulders and looked into her eyes. 'Nandi, you would have told me if there was any news of Jenkins, wouldn't you? He has not been killed trying to make his way back here, has he?'

Nandi shook her head. 'Oh no, Simon. We would have heard if something terrible like that had happened. Papa knows everything that happens in Zululand, I promise you.'

He smiled. 'Yes, I can imagine that. One more question. Is there anyone in the King's kraal who speaks English? One of the inDunas, perhaps?'

She frowned for a moment. 'Yes, there is one man. He lived as a Natal Kaffir for some years before returning to Ulundi. He is much respected and he is on the King's council now. His name is Mapitha.'

Simon repeated the name. 'Right, that settles it. I will ride to Ulundi and ask him to translate what I have to say to the King.' He smiled wryly. 'It's a gamble but I have to take it. I cannot stay here and do nothing. Now, if Jenkins returns before I get back, tell him to stay here. Perhaps, Nandi, you would be good enough to let me have something to eat on the journey and some water to take.'

Tears were now coursing down the girl's face, and he drew her to him and kissed her, gently and chastely. 'Don't worry,' he said. 'I will be all right. I think I can find my way to Ulundi without starting the war on my own. But fetch my horse quietly for me, because I want to leave without fuss – just as though I was going on one of my rides.'

She sniffed, her eyes bloodshot, and nodded.

'Thank you, Nandi,' he said. 'For everything you have done for me – but most of all for wanting to help your country.' He smiled, kissed her quickly again, turned and strode away to his room for his compass and rifle.

Once out of sight of the Dunn kraal, Simon set a course to the north-north-east and put his horse into a canter. The journey would take him a full day and he was anxious to make as good time as he could over the easy riding terrain of Dunn's land, before he met the broken ground of the north. As he rode, he looked about him keenly. He was unsure what to do if challenged by Zulus. He disliked the idea of being taken in by a patrol as a prisoner. That way there would be no guarantee that he could get to see the King or even call for Mapitha. Indeed, he might get an assegai in his stomach on sight, for nerves must be stretched to twanging point in Zululand at the moment, and if he was taken, he would have no means of explaining his mission. In any case, he wanted to arrive at Ulundi with dignity, as his own man, riding in with an important message for the King. He decided that if he met a hostile party, he would attempt to outride it – and then smiled at what Jenkins would have thought of that.

The morning was uneventful and he stopped at noon in a shallow donga to eat the cold chicken that Nandi had provided. He ate standing, with one hand on the saddle, constantly turning his head. Even so, the flash of steel that he saw out of the corner of his eye was too close for comfort. It came as sunlight reflected from an assegai blade, and the Zulus, at a distance of about 150 yards, seeing that they had been detected, rose quickly and ran towards him, fanning out to surround him.

Simon hurled away his chicken, inserted his foot into the stirrup and put one hand on the pommel of his saddle and the other on the rifle butt protruding from its holster. As he did so, the first of the throwing spears bounced off the rock at his side. The noise startled his horse and she shied, twisting his foot out of the stirrup and throwing him down. The horse whinnied and trotted away up the donga, reins trailing, and Simon found himself flat on his back but, miraculously, with his rifle in his hand. Another spear quivered in the face of the donga and Simon scrambled to his feet and turned to face the nearest Zulus, now about a hundred yards away. His brain now raced. Should he run, stand and fire, or raise his hand and attempt to parley? The decision was taken for him as a shower of spears – flung on the run and therefore erratically – clattered about him. These Zulus were out to kill.

Carefully, he took aim at the nearest man and pressed the trigger. The native sprawled forward, scattering shield and spears and tripping one of his companions. With nervous speed, Simon fumbled open a cartridge pouch on his bandolier, pulled down the ejector handle behind the trigger of his rifle and inserted another bullet. The second shot was as lethal as the first and it acted as a deterrent, for the band – perhaps eight or nine men – halted uncertainly and then scrambled up the donga and took cover. But where were the others, the horns of the buffalo?

He reloaded and cautiously poked his head above the edge of the donga. To his left, five men were trotting in a wide arc to get behind him. To his right, a similar number were doing the same. The horns were closing in. Carefully he took aim and brought down the leading Zulu of the right horn, and then his second bullet kicked up dust in front of the leader of the left. Both groups immediately dropped to the ground and took whatever cover they could find. Good. The surrounding tactic had been halted for the moment – but where now was the main group, the chest of the buffalo?

Ramming another cartridge into the rifle, he slid down the wall of the donga to the bottom and nervously approached a blind bend ten yards to his left, the direction in which the main party were heading when he last saw them. He stood for a moment and found he was trembling. He ran a dry tongue over his lips. Would they be running along the streambed, and if so, how many? He swallowed. No point in waiting. He put the rifle butt to his shoulder and sprang round the bend. The nearest Zulu was only ten yards away and running towards him, spear upraised. He caught a glimpse of a yellow eyeball and a surprised face before he fired and brought the man down. The others were trotting along the donga in a bunch some twenty yards back. He pushed another cartridge into the breech and fired into their midst but turned and ran before he could see the effect. He had no time to reload, and as he ran, he realised that this was a game with only one ending. Shrewdly, the Zulus were attacking on three fronts and, on his own and with only a single-shot rifle – however accurate – he could not hold them off for ever. Would one of the horns have doubled back and slipped into the other end of the donga? If so, he would be running full tilt into them with an unloaded rifle. There was little choice, so, sick with apprehension, he rounded a bend in the streambed – and there stood his horse, reins dangling and her eyes wide with fright at the noise of the rifle shots.

Breathless, but his heart singing with relief, Simon approached her with care. He took a precious moment to pat her flank to reassure her, then he was in the saddle. Which way? He could not put the horse to the steep side of the donga – better to turn and gallop the way he had come, and with the element of surprise, perhaps he stood a chance of riding down the smaller of the three parties. He hauled on the left rein and dug in his heels. The mare took off in a flurry of stones and rounded the bend at a gallop to meet some six Zulus running towards her only a few yards away. The sight of the big horse thundering towards them in the confined space of the donga was too much for the Zulus and the party split, three flattening themselves to one wall and three to the other. Simon was through them in a flash, his head down, his heels beating a tattoo on the horse's flanks. He zigzagged at perilously high speed along the bed of the donga until he found a drift where he could pull out and up on to the plain.

There he reined in, his heart pounding and perspiration running down his cheeks, and stood in the stirrups to look around. The plain was deserted. There was no sign of the Zulus. It was as though they had never existed and the whole frightening clash with them – which had only lasted about four minutes – had been a figment of his imagination; some hangover from the lonely games he had played as a boy, back in Brecon. Simon swallowed hard and dug his heels in again. He lost no precious time in consulting his compass; he just wanted to put as much distance as he could between himself and that war party.

He rode as fast as the terrain allowed, heading towards the sun and to the right. After a while, he pulled out the compass and adjusted his direction somewhat, so that he returned to his north-north-east course and trotted through broken ground, every fold of which he knew could conceal scores of Zulus. But he met no one until, as the sun was sinking, he began riding across billows of well-grassed country, containing herds of cattle under the care of the inevitable Zulu boys. They watched him with curious eyes and he realised that he must be nearing Cetswayo's capital.

Simon fumbled for his watch. If his encounter with the Zulus had taken place at noon, that was about six hours ago now, and fast as they moved, they could not possibly have beaten him to Ulundi. Good. He must have time to reach the

King before the news got to him that some of his subjects had been shot by this 'trader'. How many had he killed? Three . . . four? *Killed!* The thought made Simon sit up suddenly in the saddle. Although he had served the Queen now for more than three years, this was the first time he had killed a fellow human being. He let the mare find her own pace as his mind pondered the enormity of it. As a soldier, he had always known the time would come when he would have to take life, and in the recesses of his being, he had always wondered whether he would have the guts to do so. Well, it had happened and he had shot instinctively and with effect. It wasn't a question of guts, he reflected wryly; it was more a matter of kill or be killed. There had been no time for moral debate – or for fear, for that matter. Yes, he had trembled. But he had not been afraid.

The thought gave him satisfaction, but as the growing number of cattle showed that he was nearing Ulundi, his mind now turned to how Cetswayo would treat him when he heard – as he was bound to, sooner or later – that Simon had fought like a soldier. Simon shrugged. Better, perhaps, to tell him exactly what had happened and trust to what Catherine had said about the King. What was it? 'A wise ruler and not a bloodthirsty man.' He gulped. Well, he just had to hope that that was true.

Simon sighted Ulundi just before nightfall and he rode through the Zulus who now milled around him without hesitation, fearing that to slow down or stop would lead to him being pulled from the saddle. At the entrance to the vast stockade, however, he was forced to halt as two giant Zulus left their posts and barred his way, their assegais pointed up at him.

He stood in his stirrups and said clearly, 'Mapitha. Mapitha.' He gestured. 'Bring Mapitha here.'

One of the Zulus frowned and spoke to him quickly in his own tongue. It was clearly a question. Simon shook his head and repeated, 'Mapitha.'

The two guards exchanged words and then, with a puzzled backward look, one of them loped away. Simon sighed with relief and sat his horse expressionlessly, attempting to disregard the crowd of natives who now pressed in on him, causing his horse to paw the ground nervously and to shake her head, scattering some of the Zulus who put tentative hands on her flanks. The remaining guard gave a guttural order and, with a wave of his assegai, dismissed those who came too close. Simon swallowed nervously. God, this was a gamble! Would he emerge alive from it – and what if Mapitha was not in the kraal? How could he explain his uninvited intrusion on the King? The smell that engulfed him from the people, perhaps a hundred or more, who surrounded him was alien and disturbing. It was a mixture of oil, sweat, spices and goodness knows what, and it added to his nervousness, bringing a dryness to his mouth.

Then, a buzz in the crowd signalled the arrival of a dignified, elderly Zulu, the isiCoco waxed into grey, tightly curled hair and a shawl thrown across his shoulders. He walked through the crowd and stood looking impassively at Simon, leaning on a staff as tall as himself.

Simon inclined his head. 'Are you Mapitha?' he asked, furious inwardly that the dryness of his mouth made the words emerge like a croak.

'I am Mapitha,' said the inDuna, in low, clear tones. 'What do you want of me?'

'I was given your name at Jantoni's kraal.' Simon tried to keep any emotion from his voice. It seemed the Zulu way. 'I am a trader who has been living with Jantoni for two months now, doing business with him. I heard today of the demands being made on the King by the British and I have come to talk with him, because I think I may be of service to him.'

'You have come to talk to the King?' There was a hint of surprise now in the Zulu's tone. 'Why has Jantoni not come with you?'

'He is in Natal. I have come alone because the matter is urgent. But I do not speak the Zulu tongue and I need you to interpret for me, if you will do so.'

Mapitha looked at him steadily. 'What is it that you have to say to the King?'

'I am sorry, but that should wait until I see him.'

The Zulu stood in silence, holding his gaze. 'Very well. I will see if the King will receive you. Get down from your horse, do not touch your gun, and follow me.' He gave an order to the guard who had fetched him, and the latter waited for Simon to dismount and then walked closely behind him as they followed the old man.

They made their way towards the great hut that stood by the central cattle kraal. The last time Simon had trod this path there had been a feeling of indolence about the place: children playing, men lying lazily, taking snuff and smoking, only the women working. There had been no hurry. Now, warriors were striding purposefully in the lanes between the beehive huts, the children had been tucked away and there was a general air of bustle. Was it, Simon wondered, preparation for battle? They came to the unpainted door and Mapitha gestured to him to wait, while the old man went inside. He was back within a minute and courteously held open the door, European-style, for Simon to enter.

The thick smoke fumes hit Simon like a wall again and he halted in confusion. It was a moment before he could focus on the group of men – no women this time – who were lying on mats at the far end of the room. Seven inDunas of varying ages, but mostly with grey-flecked hair, were ranged at Cetswayo's side, all facing the door. Simon bowed and then, with slight pressure on his arm from Mapitha, walked towards the group, halted and bowed to the King again. He looked carefully into Cetswayo's face. The mild eyes were regarding him without any obvious sign of interest, although one eyebrow was cocked – interrogatively? There was no invitation to sit and the King waved a finger, presumably an invitation to speak.

Simon turned to Mapitha. 'Please tell His Majesty that I bring him greetings and that I am grateful that he has allowed me to live in his country for so long.'

On translation, the King gave the slightest of nods but made no reply. Simon licked his lips. This was not going to be easy.

'The King will wonder why I have asked to see him. I do not wish to trade, for I have made my trade with Jantoni and am waiting at his kraal only until my associate returns before going back to Natal, perhaps with more cattle, perhaps not.'

At the reference to Jenkins, the King smiled and turned to his inDunas, who all nodded. He spoke a few words.

'The King says he has heard of your friend,' translated Mapitha. 'They call him One Who Fights With His Hands. He seems to the King as though he is a warrior, perhaps a soldier?'

Simon shook his head. He was anxious to tell as few lies as possible. 'His Majesty is gracious, but no British soldier is taught to fight with his hands. They have guns and cannon to do the fighting for them – although,' he gulped, 'I have been forced to fight with the King's subjects this very day.'

Mapitha gave him a quick glance. As Simon's words were put to the King, his attitude and that of his inDunas changed immediately. The lounging ceased, the King sat up, picked up an assegai from his side and pointed it at the young man before him. He spoke one word.

'Explain,' said Mapitha.

Taking a deep breath and speaking as clearly as he could, Simon told the story of the morning's ambush, emphasising that he had attempted to ride away from the patrol and had not fired until the spears had been thrown.

'Did you kill any of the King's warriors?' asked Mapitha, putting the question himself. Simon did not like the way the question was posed.

'I do not know if my bullets killed,' he said. 'But I hit three men who were leading the attack, perhaps one more. I did not have a choice. If I had not fired my rifle, I would be dead now.' He turned to the King now and spoke to him directly. 'Your Majesty, I was making my journey to see you. I was coming in peace. I did not expect to be attacked. I am sorry if I killed but I had no alternative. The young men were angry and wished to wash their spears in my blood. I did not antagonise them. I did not even speak to them before they attacked.'

Mapitha took his time to explain this and so gave Simon the opportunity to note the reactions carefully. Immediately, the King swung to the man on his right and asked a question, then repeated it to his left. A hum of conversation broke out in the group. Clearly, the King was angry, but at whom Simon could not be sure. Eventually Cetswayo addressed him again.

'If what you say is true,' translated Mapitha, 'then those who attacked you will be punished. We are not at war with the British people and it is not right that friendly travellers should be attacked. But if you do not speak the truth, then it will not go well for you.'

The King interrupted the old man almost before he had finished his sentence and Mapitha turned to Simon again. 'The King wishes to know,' he said, 'if you have come to Ulundi only to make this complaint or if you have some message for him from your people.'

'I speak only for myself, sir,' said Simon. 'I have lived in your country for several months now and I have grown to like and respect the Zulu people and particularly Jantoni and his family. I know that problems have arisen between your country and mine and I know that Jantoni is at this moment in Durban trying to understand what it is that the British want.'

After translation, one of the inDunas spoke angrily but the King gestured him to be silent and spoke quickly himself.

'Do you know what the British want, then?'

'No, Your Majesty. I am not a general or a politician. But I am sure that no one wants war.' He took another deep breath. 'Our leaders can sometimes be slow to understand other races. There is a feeling in Natal, I believe, that Your Majesty is anxious that his warriors shall wash their spears, and this is causing these harsh words to be spoken. I hope that the Zulu nation does not want to go to war with the British.'

The King now lumbered to his feet, looking huge in the light from the fire, and began talking in a low and earnest voice, keeping his eyes on Simon's but being careful to pause so that Mapitha could interpret.

'The King says that he does not know what power you have in the white man's land, for you seem very young, but he will talk to you as though you were Somtseu himself. For many years the white Englishman and the Zulu have lived happily

216

side by side. There have been many problems with the Boer Afrikaaner men but very little – except, he says, fly bites – with the English. Now the Redcoats are hitting their shields with their spears and stamping their feet. They are making it difficult for him over this Sihayo business.

'His people do not want war. It is true that there has been no washing of the spears for many years, but Zulus do not wish to wash their spears in English blood. If the spears are to be washed – and the King will judge that – then it can be done elsewhere. The King says that he has done everything to accommodate his English neighbours. The long dispute in the north over territory that is rightfully his – this dispute he has agreed can be settled by the English Commission that has been meeting for so long. He does not argue. He will accept the ruling when it comes.'

Mapitha was now having difficulty keeping up with the King's flow of words. 'However, this King has power in his land just as the Great White English Queen has power in hers. He does not tell the English Queen how to rule her people. So the English should not tell him how to rule his. If the English put their Redcoats into his land, he will eat them up. He has many warriors eager to prove that they are men. There will be great wailing by the women in the English kraals.'

Cetswayo had not raised his voice in delivering this peroration, but his manner had become more agitated towards the end. The assegai was used to emphasise his points, and as he concluded, he stabbed the air with it. The inDunas grunted their approval.

Simon cleared his throat. He had one more card to play.

'I understand all that His Majesty says and I will do all that I can to represent his point of view when I return to Natal and the Cape. But I beg him to restrain his young warriors. The British Army has modern weapons that give its soldiers far more power than their numbers. I have worked with this army and I have seen what it can do. In building their empire, these soldiers have defeated great nations all over the world. The Zulus—'

He got no further. Mapitha had been translating a phrase or two behind, of course, as Simon spoke, and as he began the warning, the King's demeanour changed again. His features contorted with anger, he pointed at Simon's face with the blade of his assegai and shouted a command. Immediately, two warriors seized Simon's arms and dragged him backwards to the door of the hut. Outside, he was turned and, assegais pricking his ribs, marched down several lanes and eventually pushed down into the interior of one of the beehive huts. No one followed him in, but the hide flap to the entrance was thrown down dismissively, and as he turned, he saw that the gut strings of the flap were being wound round the door post and tied. He was a prisoner.

Simon looked around him. There was little in the interior of the hut: a low, roughly hewn table on which rested two drinking gourds and a plate, an eating knife – short, blunt and useless as a weapon – and a stub of a candle. A couple of sleeping mats hung from the central pole, as did a long shawl made of dyed wool, obviously to be used as a night blanket. He draped it around him. It covered him almost completely and in the dark, maybe, he could be taken for a Zulu. Except for the boots. In darkness or not, they betrayed him as a European – and he could not walk a mile without them.

Throwing the shawl from him, Simon sat on the floor and tried to concentrate. Would Cetswayo kill him? His mouth dried again as he considered the possibilities. Surely he would have been taken away then and there and speared for offending the King, if death was an option. Or were they waiting for that patrol to return to check his story about the fight in the donga? Or would they keep him as some sort of hostage or bargaining tool if Dunn's intervention in Durban failed? He put his head in his hands. Either way, his gamble had clearly failed – and yet what else could he have done?

He beat the ground slowly in frustration. Then, on hands and knees, he crawled to the wall of the hut at the point furthest away from the entrance and tested its resilience. The young saplings had been interwoven with grass thatching and the wall yielded easily to a little pressure. With the knife, he experimented and found that, despite its lack of edge, it could be used perhaps to cut a low opening. But what then? Even if he escaped from Ulundi, his chances of walking across the country without being discovered were slim. His only viable option was to wait until John Dunn returned and intervened with the King. If he did not – and now Simon put his head back and clenched his fists – he would not go readily to the executioner. He would fight like hell!

Chapter 11

The days settled into a pattern of boredom and discomfort. He was not allowed to leave the hut except for visits to the sanitation pit nearby. There appeared to be a guard permanently stationed outside the entrance, even at night. There was no fire and the nights were cold, so that he was glad of the shawl as well as his own blanket. He had been allowed his saddle pack but not, of course, his rifle. The days crawled by and the monotony was hard to bear. Twice he unthreaded the tent flap and demanded, 'Jantoni,' and then, 'Mapitha,' of the guard outside, but the only response was to have an assegai put to his throat. Thinking through his conversation with the King, Simon realised that he had caused offence by seeming to threaten Cetswayo with talk of the efficiency of the British Army. Damn! He had overplayed his hand and committed an act of *lèse-majesté*, and been thrown into captivity as a result. But for how long?

Simon carefully husbanded the little dried meat and remnants of fruit that Nandi had provided. For the first two days they helped to vary the diet of bread, mealies and milk that was brought to him three times a day, but they were soon consumed. After the third day, he began marking the passage of the days on to the central pole with the old knife he had been given. As the days passed the threat of execution began to recede. The patrol with whom he had clashed must have reported back to the King or his council by now, so his story must have been believed, but his solitude remained unbroken. His thoughts, however, were free and they soared beyond the beehive hut. He recalled his home in Brecon and his parents with a tenderness that, hitherto, had been alien to him. He attempted once again to conjure up Alice's features, but the vision that danced before him was of dark skin, not fair, of black eyes, not grey. Questions about Jenkins pressed in on him: had he been kept in Cape Town by Lamb, or – terrible thought – had he attempted to make his way back to Dunn's kraal and met one of those spear-happy patrols?

In the days and weeks that followed he was completely ignored. He had decided that flight was better than this soul-numbing captivity when there came a life-saving break.

Simon was kneeling on his sleeping mat practising his Zulu clicks and clucks – it was a link, however remote, with Nandi – when he heard the distinctive tread of boots outside the hut. Then came a voice as welcome as it was unmistakable. 'What, in 'ere, then?' And crawling through the hole came a thick thatch of black hair followed by a moustache that was now badly in need of a trim.

'Jenkins!' he cried.

'Good God, is it you then, bach sir? Goodness, that beard don't suit you much.'

The two men embraced without reservation and then, somewhat shamefacedly, solemnly shook hands. They sat on the mat, grinning at each other.

'Who's goin' to start, then?'

'I think you should. You will have more to tell than I.'

'Well, I don't know about that, but I suppose you 'ave bin a bit anxious like.'

Simon nodded. Jenkins settled back on the second mat and began his story. He and the boys had driven the cattle to the Lower Drift at the Tugela without incident and had ferried the beasts across, with the help of the naval brigade who were stationed there. Then they moved the cattle on to Durban where, eventually, Jenkins found a provisioning captain who took them.

'Mind you,' he said, grinning at the memory, ' 'e wasn't anxious to. Oh, he wanted the best all right. They was good stock, I could tell that, an' this young captain, look you, was 'avin' trouble findin' meat for the army what was buildin' up out there – more about that in a minute. But 'e didn't 'ave no authority, see, to buy at that price. Oh, bach sir, 'e was a little man who was frightened of 'is own shadow.' Jenkins shook his head reflectively. 'Anyway, I waved the letter you gave me, throwin' in Colonel Lamb's name all the time, an' 'e agreed to 'old on to the cattle till I got to the Colonel in the Cape and 'e could telegraph authority, like.'

Jenkins's moustache twitched and he looked round the gloom of the hut. 'No beer in 'ere, then, is there, sir?'

'Sorry, no. We get a gourd of milk at midday – at least, I do. But do go on. Did you get to see Lamb?'

'All in good time, bach sir. Well, I catches the packet to the Cape from Durban.' Jenkins's eyes rolled. 'What a voyage that was! Them waves was as 'igh as—'

'Oh, I don't want to know about the damned weather. Get on.'

'Well, with respect, sir, you do, because I was so ill that they threw me off the boat at a little place called Port Elizabeth and I 'ad to wait another four days to pick up another boat.' Jenkins's face beamed. 'But you'll be glad to 'ear that the weather was much better for the second bit and I eventually reports to headquarters in Cape Town. I'm treated with a great deal of suspicion – me, dressed like this, see, askin' to see the Colonel Chief of Staff. An' I wouldn't tell 'em who I was, except that I 'ad come from Zululand and 'ad a special message for the Colonel. Anyway, I'm waitin' in a corridor, see, an' guess who walks up?'

'Not Colour Sergeant Cole again?'

'No. Not this time. It was our very own Colonel. Our CO, Mr Bloody Covington, excuse my disrespect, sir. Well, 'e's goin' to walk by me, but he stops, stares an' says, "Don't I know you?" Then, before I could say anythin', he says, "You're Fonthill's man." I reckoned 'e wasn't askin', he was tellin', so I didn't say anythin', see. So 'e glares at me and shouts, "Speak, man, speak." So I speaks and says, "The very same, sir." '

Jenkins rocked back and chuckled at the memory. 'So he asked me what I was doin' there, and I says waiting for the Colonel, and he says why and I says, it's very confidential, sir, so 'e gets very, very angry, so I 'ave to tell 'im that I've got a message, look you, from you to the Colonel, an' he says, let me 'ave it, and I says, no it's for the Colonel's eyes only, and 'e shouts, don't be impertinent, man, give it to me and that's an order, and I says no, so 'e 'as me arrested then and there.' The little Welshman beamed across at Simon, his great moustache spread across his face.

Simon waited for a moment and then said, 'You're not going to sit here and tell me that's as far as it went?'

'No, but I thought it was a good spot to take a breath, see.' Jenkins, thoroughly enjoying the tension he was creating, looked around the hut. 'I don't suppose you've still got that little flask thing, 'ave you, bach sir? My mouth's like the bottom of one of them dongler things.'

'No, I haven't. If you remember, I gave it to the King.'

'Ah, so you did. So you did.' He wiped his mouth sadly. 'Anyway, so I'm thrown into the guardhouse for three days, no less. An' I'm not brought up on a charge, mind you, durin' this time, which, accordin' to Queen's Regulations, is quite out of order.'

'Yes, yes. Do get on with it.'

'Right. All the time these orderly officers – obviously under instructions from the CO – are tryin' to wheedle your letter out of me, but I won't let 'em. Now,' Jenkins swayed forward in emphasis, 'it's obvious that they can't keep me in the jug and bottle for ever without chargin' me, so eventually I'm hauled up before Colonel Covington and charged with disobeying an order and bein' impertinent to an officer.'

'Oh no.' Simon put his hand to his head. 'Are you telling me that Colonel Lamb never received my message?'

'Now, bach sir, you're gettin' very impatient.' Jenkins leaned across and tapped his companion's boot reprovingly. 'It seems to me that we shall probably 'ave quite a bit of time on our 'ands 'ere, isn't it, so you can 'ear me out properly now.'

'Sorry, my lord. Do take your time.'

'Very good, then. So there I am, standin' in front of this firin' squad, so to speak, an' I'm gettin' a bit annoyed, see. I mean, I don't mind bein' busted for drinkin' an' fightin' an' all that, but 'ere I was doin' my duty, see. So I says, "I'm within my rights in demandin' to see the superior officer who I've got a confidential message for." An' I quote the proper passage from Queen's Regulations, see.' Jenkins chuckled again at the memory. 'Well, the Adjutant is sittin' next to the CO, an' 'e leans across an' whispers somethin' in 'is ear. The Colonel doesn't like it, look you, but 'e 'as to accept it because the old Adj knows the Queen's Regulations like I do, see. So that's 'ow I got to see Colonel Lamb,' Jenkins finished triumphantly, his button eyes glowing, his air that of a master raconteur waiting for applause.

Simon nodded his head slowly. 'Very good, Jenkins,' he said. 'Now, let's see. You manage to get thrown off the boat at Port Elizabeth and lose four days there, then you are insubordinate to our CO and get thrown into the guardhouse and lose another three or four days – all before you get to deliver the letter to Colonel Lamb.'

Jenkins's eyes widened in innocence. 'None of my doin', sir, was it?'

'All right. You gave Colonel Lamb the letter?'

'Oh yes, sir. 'E read it with great interest. You needn't 'ave worried about him not gettin' the code, like, 'cos 'e understood that right away. 'E asked me a lot of questions about what we'd done, where we'd been and so on – 'e was particularly impressed that we'd seen the King – and 'e made a lot of notes. Course, I 'ad to tell 'im why I'd been 'eld up gettin' to 'im, see, and I could tell 'e didn't like that one little bit. 'E made a note or two about that, too. There's one other thing 'e didn't think much of, I'm afraid, bach sir.'

'What was that?'

'The price old Dunn made 'im pay for the cattle.' Jenkins grinned. 'Gave 'im a bit of a shock, I'm thinkin'. Still, they was good meat an' I told 'im so. Anyway, the Colonel finished up as good as gold. 'E told me 'e was Welsh 'imself and that we'd done a good job. 'E allowed that the charges against me would be dropped and reminded me to say that if either of us got into what 'e called "further misunderstandings with the army" we was still seconded to his staff until further orders.'

Simon threw back his head in exasperation. 'Yes, but what about those further orders? Did he give you any?'

With mock annoyance, the Welshman clicked his fingers. 'Ah, I knew I'd forgotten somethin'.' He slipped off his jacket. 'They took my knife. 'Ave you got one?'

Impatiently, Simon threw him the kitchen knife and Jenkins hacked away at the lining of his jacket until, with a careful look at the hut entrance, he produced a letter and handed it to Simon. It was addressed to 'Simon Fonthill Esquire', and on uncrested paper, from an address in central Cape Town headed 'George Lamb & Son, Cattle Dealers', the letter ran:

Dear Mr Fonthill,

I have received your consignment of cattle purchased from Mr Dunn and have today forwarded to Durban a draft in his favour for the sum agreed, which, by the way, I felt was very high. The money has been deposited in Mr Dunn's bank there.

The information sent to me about the type of cattle available and the possibility of further purchases I have received with interest and gratitude. It will have a bearing on our further business plans. I doubt, however, whether we shall be making further purchases in the near future. Although any further news about availability and the vendor's inclinations towards selling would be valuable, I would suggest that your buying mission in Zululand is complete. I would further suggest that you return, with your associate, to Cape Town as soon as is convenient.

I am, sir,

Your obedient servant,

George Lamb

Simon passed the letter back to Jenkins, who shook his head and handed it back. 'I know what's in it,' he said. Wordlessly Simon tore the page and envelope into small pieces, divided them into four little piles and buried them in different parts of the floor of the hut, stamping down the soil with his heel. Then he sat again, opposite Jenkins.

'Right, 352. Tell me how you got here – but first, did the Colonel give any other message?'

Jenkins nodded. ' 'E told me to say to you congratulations and well done. It seems that we've got a new Commander-in-Chief in South Africa, a general called Thesiger, and all the information you supplied has been fed through to 'im and the General Staff, see.' He leaned forward conspiratorially. 'There's no doubt about it, bach sir. There's goin' to be a war. Everybody knows about it in the Cape and Natal. This new general – 'e's soon goin' to be called Duke Chelmsford, or somethin', because 'is da back 'ome is very sick and when 'e dies 'e'll get 'is title, like – well, he's preparin' the invasion of Zululand right now. I don't know if the information you sent back . . . by the way, where did you get all that stuff?'

Simon shook his head. 'Never mind that now.'

'Well, I don't know if it made any difference, but they all think that knockin' over the Zulus will be easy.'

Simon felt his heart sink. Had it been for nothing, his agonies over betraying Nandi, the risk they had all run? Perhaps he should have emphasised more strongly in his message the quality of the Zulu army. Perhaps . . . His line of thought was interrupted as the blade of an assegai pulled aside the hut flap and held it open and a Zulu woman crawled in, pulling behind her a crude tray. Simon was glad to see that food and drink for both of them had been provided, but Jenkins had gulped down his milk before she could turn. He gestured to her, beaming. 'Could I just 'ave a drop more, then, missus, do you think?' He held out his gourd. She took it expressionlessly and returned very quickly with it full.

As Jenkins took it, rewarding the woman with his face-splitting grin, Simon could not wait to get on. 'Tell me, how did you get here?'

'Everyone is bein' pushed into Natal, ready for the invasion, see. Our battalion, the 2nd, complete with old Covington – beggin' your pardon, sir – sailed out with me from the Cape to Durban, and I 'ear that our old lot, the 1st Battalion, has already been brought up from Kingbillystown to this Rorke's Drift place.'

Simon wiped the last of the mealies from the bowl with his bread. 'So, what about you?'

For the first time, Jenkins looked discomforted. 'Well, Colonel Lamb sent me back to you at Mr Dunn's place. Now, sir . . .' The Welshman looked as plaintive as his worldly-wise features would allow. 'You know that I'm just about the best officer's servant in the entire army?'

Solemnly, Simon nodded.

'You will also know that I am an extremely splendid 'orseman, a cognissuer of wine, look you, an' not a bad fighter?'

'For goodness' sake, get on with it.'

'Very good, sir. But what you don't know is that I couldn't

find me way from A to B if they was next door to each other. You remember that I was in Birmingham when old Coley recruited me? Well, I didn't mean to be there at all. I thought I was in Shrewsbury. As well as lookin' for work, I was lookin' for me brother-in-law, see. No wonder I couldn't find 'im.'

He fumbled in his pocket. 'Look, they gave me this compass thing in Durban. I was all right, see, ridin' from there to the Tugela at the Lower Drift thing where we crossed before, because there's more or less a proper road on the Natal side of the river. But once across in Zululand, I just got lost when the track ran out. They gave me a course to follow once I'd crossed.' His brow furrowed. 'I think it was north-north-west. Or was it north-north-east? I'm dashed if I know. They told me to keep the sun on my left shoulder. But do you know, sir, the bloody thing keeps buggerin' about all over the sky.' He sighed. 'In the end, look you, I didn't know my north-north-west from my elbow, so to speak. I'd been wanderin' around for about six days when this party of black lads surprised me.'

'You are lucky they didn't kill you out of hand. Did they treat you badly?'

'They wasn't exactly friendly at first, an' one lad would 'ave stuck me for nothing, there's certain. But I tried your trick of this "Jantoni" thing. I was tryin' to get 'em to take me to Mr Dunn's place, see. But this is where they brought me. An' bless me, 'ere you were. Now,' he leaned forward and slapped Simon's boot, 'I don't mind saying, bach sir, that I'm glad to see you. But not like this. What 'appened?'

Simon quickly related the events of the last weeks and the two men fell silent. The weather had turned and now the day was humid and hot. Jenkins looked around the unprepossessing interior. 'Why 'ave they stuck us together, d'you think?'

'I suppose it saves effort and manpower to have us under one guard.'

Jenkins wrinkled his nose. 'I don't fancy stayin' 'ere long. What are the odds on breakin' out, then?'

'Pretty short on getting out of the hut, I would say, but long on getting far without horses.' Simon gestured towards the back of the hut. 'It would be relatively easy to cut our way out over there at night, when the guard's asleep, but then the difficult bit starts. We should have to pick our way through the huts, get out of the stockade, then march across the plain about a hundred miles to the Buffalo – all without being spotted. How would a master batman, wine connoisseur and elite warrior handle all that, then?'

Jenkins wrinkled his nose. 'Not well at all. But can't Mr Dunn get us out of 'ere?'

'I've been hoping for nothing else for weeks. God knows where he is. I don't believe he would abandon us, but perhaps he has. Look, I think we must just get out of here and take our chances. At least we have two compasses now, and I can't stand being in this place any longer. We can cut a hole at the back there, tear this shawl into two, wrap it around us, carry our boots underneath it and just try and walk out when the place is asleep.'

Simon studied the back of his hands and his forearms, which had now lost their tan and looked white and fragile, like those of a scholar. 'We're out of condition for a hard march, we've no hard tack to take with us and no weapons to kill game or defend ourselves on the way. So we can't break out right away. We must save a little of our bread and milk each day to provision us for a while, at least.'

Jenkins sniffed. 'Won't keep long in this climate, bach.'

'I know. We'll give it three days and then go.'

The next day, however, John Dunn arrived. He pulled back the hut flap without ceremony and crawled through, his slouch hat in his hand and his brow covered in perspiration.

'My God, Mr Dunn, we're glad to see you,' said Simon with feeling.

Dunn regarded them without expression. 'No doubt,' he said dryly. 'You've got yourselves into a steaming pot of trouble this time, right enough.' He lowered himself to the ground. 'And I suppose you're looking to me to get you out of it?'

Simon decided that it would be a mistake to be supplicatory. 'We are, and you must, Mr Dunn. I have spoken to the King and it is important that we reach the British lines to give them the information that I have gathered.'

Dunn smiled wearily, his eyelids drooping and his body betraying tiredness and resignation. 'Mr Fonthill,' he said, 'if I wasn't so damned tired and indignant with you British I would find your air of self-importance just a touch amusing.'

Simon stirred uncomfortably but it was Jenkins who spoke. 'Now, now, Mr Dunn. That's a bit unfair, isn't it? Look you, Mr Fonthill 'as been stuck 'ere for weeks, existin' on milk and mush and without even the sniff of a gourd o' beer. We've got work to do and we've got to get out of 'ere to do it.'

'And if you won't help us,' added Simon, 'then we must break out ourselves.'

Dunn regarded them both impassively. 'So far, I've chosen not to help you,' he said, 'although there was precious little I could have done anyway.'

Simon's jaw dropped. 'Do you mean that you knew I was here all this time?'

Dunn raised a placatory hand. 'Now, don't get excited. The King wouldn't let me see you because he wanted you to stew for a while.' For the first time a wry smile spread across his face. 'To be honest, he just didn't know what to do with you – and neither did I. You got into this mess by riding to the King, shooting up some of his warriors on the way, and then raising his expectations before giving him a lecture on how bloody marvellous your army was. Well, things have developed quite a bit while you've been here.'

'Please tell us.'

'Right. You remember those trumped-up border incidents?' Simon nodded.

'I got nowhere in Natal. It was clear to me that the Cape Governor, Frere, was determined to use them as an excuse to invade.' Dunn passed a hand across his mouth and jaw and looked suddenly older. 'Well, he has. I've just got back from a big meeting on the Lower Drift of the Tugela between Shepstone, representing Frere, and the King's senior inDunas.' He sighed. 'The results of the Boundary Commission are out and they are completely favourable to the Zulus, so we all attended expecting that the judgement would be handed down and that all would be sweetness and light again. But not on your life.'

Simon realised that Dunn was speaking as though drawing from a deep well of personal sadness. Here was a man who was facing the destruction of everything he had built: his farm, his possessions, his lifestyle. His world was collapsing, not on the whim of the savage neighbour with whom he had lived so long, but as a casualty of the latest twist in Britain's long saga of empire-building. Simon leaned across and put a hand on the big man's riding boot.

'I am so sorry, Mr Dunn. Please tell us what has happened.'

Dunn shrugged. 'Shepstone announced the results of the Boundary Commission all right. But he made much more of the Sihayo affair. He is demanding the impossible. He wants Sihayo's son and his three brothers delivered for trial in Natal and he's levied a fine of five hundred cattle for that business and a further one hundred head for the so-called offences committed on those two surveyors. All of this within twenty days. But there's more. Much more.'

Dunn looked at Simon and Jenkins in turn with his sad eyes. 'Frere is demanding the virtual dismantling of Cetswayo's authority in Zululand.' He slapped one thick finger after another into the palm of his hand. 'He is ordering the disbandment of the whole Zulu army, with the men returned to their homes; every Zulu is to be free to marry on reaching maturity; all missionaries banished by the King – and what a troublemaking lot *they* were – are to be allowed to return and preach without asking permission of anyone; a British resident is to be established in Zululand to watch over the King . . . and so it goes on. There is plenty more. He is demanding the complete humiliation of the King – and he wants agreement to all of this within thirty days. If he doesn't get it, he will invade.'

A silence fell on the hut. Simon cleared his throat. 'How much time is left?'

Dunn gave a mirthless smile. 'This was all ten days ago,' he said. 'Even if the King bent the knee completely, he couldn't collect the cattle fine alone within the time limit. There is nothing to stop the invasion. Your redcoats are massing at three points to invade: in the north, in the south across the Tugela's Lower Drift, and in the centre across the Buffalo at Rorke's Drift. Lord Chelmsford himself will lead this central column and they'll probably all head for Ulundi.' Dunn leaned across to his listeners. 'So you will see that I haven't had much time to worry about you two.'

'What is the King going to do?' asked Jenkins.

'Do? What can he do? He still can't believe that the British would do this to him and he can't understand why they should. He is offering to pay the fines – although he needs more time to gather the cattle because the rivers are in flood – but he cannot give in to the other demands. That would mean the end of his reign. So he's playing for time.'

'Will he get it?' asked Simon.

Dunn pulled a lugubrious face. 'Wouldn't think so. Frere is determined to annex Zululand and that's the end of it.'

The sadness came back into Dunn's eyes. 'I must help the King as long as I can, but when the invasion starts, I'll just have to round up as many of my cattle as I can and then ride for the border with my family.' The Natalian looked round the hut. 'But that's not the point. You are the problem now.'

Jenkins nodded his head earnestly. 'Kind of you it is to think of us now, in all this bother.'

Simon got to his feet. 'Will the King have us killed?'

Dunn stretched and rose. 'No, I don't think so. But he is still undecided about you.' The Natalian smiled ruefully. 'He's no fool, of course, and he has a pretty fair idea that I've got to clear out because he knows I won't fight against my own kind, although I haven't said as much. That means that you could be useful to him in doing my old job of maybe interceding with the soldiers or writing letters for him.' He shot a sharp glance at Simon. 'I hope your Zulu has improved.'

Simon ignored the shaft. 'No. We can't do that. We've got to get out.'

'All right, but it's a hell of a risk, with the country literally up in arms. But yes, I will help you.'

Simon and Jenkins went to express their thanks, but Dunn held up a hand. 'Look, you will have to be patient,' he said. 'I can't do much until I get home and organise my affairs and that could take up to a week. Then I will send someone, probably James, to get you out of here. It will have to be at night, so sleep lightly. Here . . .' He reached into a game pocket in his jacket and pulled out a Navy Colt revolver. 'Keep this hidden. Don't use it unless you really have to, but it could prove useful.' Then, before they could argue or agree, he was gone.

Chapter 12

On New Year's Day 1879, Alice Griffith rode into Helpmakaar. The tiny settlement stood at the intersection of the main north road in Natal, leading from Pietermaritzburg and Durban in the south, and, to the east, the track that led down to Rorke's Drift and the border crossing of the Buffalo to Zululand, twelve miles away. Lord Chelmsford had chosen Helpmakaar to be the assembly point and main supply depot for his central column, and this had transformed the sleepy hamlet, with its three houses, into a bustling military camp of store sheds, cattle and horse pens and temporary cantonments of bell tents covering acres of scrubland.

Alice had camped that night some twelve miles south of the settlement and it was mid-morning as she entered the camp. Now she looked about her with fascination as she let the reins fall on to the horse's neck and allowed the beast to pick its way along the dusty track, long worn into corrugations by hundreds of wagon wheels. The place was a strange mixture of seeming indolence and great activity. Along the camp lines Europeans in a bewildering variety of dress – some in serge trousers held up by braces showing over green cotton vests, with cap comforters askew on their heads; others in long john drawers and little else – sat smoking, cleaning equipment or simply lounging. Soldiers on duty, in white helmets and red jackets or blue drill uniforms, bustled about their business. Civilian wranglers, rangy men with full beards and slouch hats, led strings of horses, and wagoners unloaded boxes of stores into tin-roofed shacks under the eyes of commissariat staff. Outnumbering the white men, however, were hundreds of natives, who milled between the tent lines, the paddocks and the huts like worker ants. Alice's inexperienced eye could not distinguish between them but she noted that many who carried spears, and some of them even rifles, wore a red rag round their heads. These, she presumed, must be some of the Natal Native Levies, whom Colonel Anthony Durnford, an experienced native fighter, had raised to supplement the white troops.

As Alice gazed about her, fascinated by the scene, so she, in turn, attracted many eyes. With her Kaffir servant, who now rode behind her leading a lightly laden packhorse, she had journeyed from Durban, stopping once at Pietermaritzburg but otherwise camping in her small tent at the roadside. Despite the days on the trail, however, Alice betrayed no signs of disarray. She wore a fresh cream cotton shirt, open at the throat and tucked into whipcord jodhpurs. Her riding boots, while no longer highly polished, gleamed dully under the dust and she sat loosely erect, astride the horse like a man. Her white pith helmet only partly concealed her long fair hair, that had been gathered together at the back with a scarf the colour of English spring grass. As she wound her way between the horse strings and bullock carts towards the centre of the camp, Alice cut a bizarre and even disturbing figure in that male environment.

Nor was she unaware of it. On landing in South Africa some three months ago, Alice had quickly realised that she was destined to turn heads. Her appearance in itself, with her cool white skin and confident bearing, was enough to set her apart from the mousy memsahibs and leather-cheeked locals of the Cape. But her role as the *Morning Post*'s accredited correspondent usually added, in sequence, disbelief, consternation and then cynical amusement to the studied courtesy with which she was first greeted by the officials and senior army officers with whom she had to mix professionally. Alice had long since decided that she would not let these reactions either daunt her or change her personality in any way. Accordingly, she neither dressed down nor up to go about her business and she displayed an air of careful politeness to all she met.

As she now led her modest cavalcade down the main street of Helpmakaar, then, she smiled and nodded a cheerful 'good morning' to whoever had the courage to hold her eye. A young captain of infantry, wearing a dark blue patrol jacket and the bright brass numerals of the 24th on his jaunty cap, caught it longer than most and saluted gallantly. She approved of him and nodded.

'Can I be of assistance, ma'am?' he enquired, reining in his horse.

'Good morning, Captain. Yes you can. I am looking for somewhere to pitch my tent. I must enquire of the camp commandant or senior officer. Where will I find him, pray?'

The young man's jaw sagged. 'Camp, ma'am? Camp? I, ah, don't think that will be in order. This is a military establishment, you see.'

'Yes, I know that. That is why I am here. But you are quite wrong. Even if I were not accredited to General Chelmsford's army – which I am – Helpmakaar remains a civilian settlement, despite the presence of the army. And so I should have every right to stay here.' Alice smiled again. 'Now, who should I see about pitching my tent? I know the General is not here because I saw him the other day at 'Maritzburg.'

The cool, assured tone as much as the reference to Chelmsford daunted the captain. He saluted again. 'Continue about two hundred yards down the road, ma'am, and on the right you will see the battalion headquarters of Lieutenant Colonel Covington. It is a large tent with a standard outside. He is the senior officer in the absence of the General and Colonel Glynn and Colonel Lamb. Good day, ma'am.'

'Thank you so much. Good morning.'

Alice smiled to herself. What luck! Covington was one of the officers to whom her father had written when she had finally overcome her parents' objections to her appointment. Those objections had proved to be stronger than she had anticipated but, as she had hoped, her father's underlying admiration for her guts in applying for and getting the post had finally tipped the scales, and, with pen and paper, he had settled down to call in his old contacts to help her. Brigadier Griffith hardly knew Covington, he had grumpily explained, but their paths had briefly crossed some years ago when Griffith had rejoined the regiment after a brief spell as an observer with Lee in the American Civil War. He had heard that the man had taken his battalion to Zululand and, therefore, could certainly be of use to his daughter. Alice rummaged in her saddlebag for a copy of the letter, as well as her accreditation from the *Post*.

She found the tent easily enough, dismounted, left her horse in her servant's care and presented her card to the sentry at the entrance.

'Please ask the Colonel if he can spare me a moment,' she said, smiling into the young soldier's flushed face.

Alice was kept waiting for perhaps two minutes and she sighed as she pictured the scene within the tent: the frown as the card was studied, the 'what-the-hell-can-she-want-here' and then the hunt in the files to find any reference to her. She felt sure that her father's letter would be forgotten. But she was wrong.

Covington rose from behind a trestle table and ushered her to a folding camp chair facing the table. He sat again and gave her a welcoming smile that, she noted, did not quite reach as far as his icy-blue eyes, which remained watchful. For a moment, her memory stirred. Wasn't this the man with whom Simon had had trouble? But she could not remember the details, even if she had known them in the first place. Simon had never been very communicative, either in speech or letters.

'I am so glad to meet you, Miss Griffith,' said Covington. 'Your father wrote to me about you, and alas, I never did get around to replying to him, what with the move to Natal and so on. Tell me, how is the Colonel?'

'Brigadier,' corrected Alice sweetly. 'He is very well indeed, Colonel, and sends his regards to you. I did wish to call upon you at the Cape when I first came out but somehow this was not possible. I know that you were posted to Natal quite quickly.'

'Quite so, dear lady. Quite so. Now,' he gestured to an orderly who had entered, 'I don't think it is too early to offer you a glass of sherry, even though I fear it will not be cool.'

'I would like that very much, thank you. And may I beg a cigarette? I am afraid that my own supply is exhausted.'

Covington's eyebrows rose for a moment. 'What? Ah, yes. Of course. Of course.' He opened a silver box on the table, seized a box of matches, rose and walked round the table to Alice. As he bent to light her cigarette, he took in the elegance of her booted leg and the slight cleavage revealed by the cream shirt. He lingered for a moment with the match, bending over her. 'I am so sorry that we missed each other in Cape Town,' he murmured. 'Such a pity.'

'Yes indeed,' replied Alice, allowing a stream of blue smoke to drift up into the Colonel's face.

Covington took two glasses from the orderly and nodded for him to leave. He handed one glass to Alice, took the other and, perching himself on the edge of the trestle table, looked down at her. He brushed back the sweep of his moustaches with forefinger and thumb and said smoothly, 'Now, what exactly can I do for you in this godforsaken land?'

Alice smiled. 'You can find me somewhere to pitch my tent, if you would be so kind.'

Covington's eyebrows shot up again. 'I beg your pardon.'

'Colonel,' Alice leaned forward, 'as you know, I am here professionally as the *Morning Post*'s correspondent in South Africa, and as such, I am accredited to General Chelmsford's army. I am here to report on the coming war, beginning, of course, with your imminent crossing of the Buffalo into Zululand. You and I both know that King Cetswayo will not be able to meet the demands made upon him by Sir Bartle Frere. So you *will* invade, of course. And I must report upon the preparations for the invasion.'

Alice knocked her ash on to the earthen floor. 'There is no hotel here, nor do I need one, for I am perfectly happy to live under canvas. But I quite appreciate that I cannot pitch my tent just anywhere. So I would be grateful if you could allocate a site for me where my servant and I can camp and be out of the way, so to speak, without being too far away.' She gazed coolly into the Colonel's eyes.

He looked away for a moment and then smiled. 'May I ask if the General knows you are here?'

'Oh yes.' Alice smiled back. 'I have had several interviews with Lord Chelmsford, as I have with Sir Bartle. I cannot say that the General, ah, altogether approves of my presence here, but he has been so far extremely courteous. And, of course, he cannot stop the British press from reporting upon events here. They are of extreme public interest.'

Covington returned to his chair, leaned back and crossed one long leg over the other. He looked down on it approvingly and flicked up the end of one moustache.

'Oh come now, my dear young lady,' he said. 'The movements of the army in the field are matters of the utmost secrecy. We could not allow you to publish details which could be of assistance to the enemy.'

'Oh come now, my dear Colonel,' Alice mocked. 'Are you really saying that the Zulus have spies in London who will immediately relay back to the mud huts of Ulundi my stories in the *Morning Post*? You are not exactly about to fight another great European power, are you? And in any case, I would not dream of reporting prospective movements, even if I knew them, the revelation of which might in any way compromise the army.' She gestured with her cigarette in emphasis. 'Although I must remove the case of the imminent invasion across the Buffalo from that promise. All the world knows about that, so Cetshwayo must too.'

Covington's frown had gradually lightened into a smile as Alice made her case and it lingered on her face as he looked at her now. He uncrossed his legs and allowed his chair to fall

243

forward. 'Very well. I will find you a camp site on one condition.'

It was Alice's turn to frown. 'What is that?'

The Colonel stood up and straightened his back so that his chest pushed at the buttons on his tunic. To Alice, looking up at him, he seemed huge. 'That you have dinner with me tonight.' The arctic-blue eyes smiled down at her.

Alice regarded him while her mind raced. His intentions could well be dishonourable, but in a crowded camp she could not see how she could come to harm. She had received many advances since she had come of age and, despite her general air of assurance in most matters, in this area she remained less than comfortable, not least because – and she was quite aware of this – of a latent sexual appetite that existed behind her calm grey eyes. But the Colonel could well be useful as a source of information – better probably than Chelmsford himself, who kept her at arm's length and gave nothing away. The gamble was worth the risk – and Covington had an undoubted air. She felt that familiar tingle of sexual awareness. Alice stood and extended her hand. 'Very well, Colonel. But please let me establish my own quarters as soon as possible. I have much to do.'

A sergeant led Alice and her servant through the camp lines to a sheltered spot, behind a copse. He touched his glengarry cap to her and said, 'There you are, miss. Send your man across the way for water. We've got a well there. Be careful with the fire, because it's very dry around the camp. Shall I get a couple of men to put up your tent?'

Alice declined and the sergeant flicked his cap again and left. Alice looked across to where her Bantu servant was sitting impassively on her rolled tent.

'Well now, George,' she said. 'It's been a long morning. You make a fire while I sort out the tea. Then we shall have a cup together and you must put up my tent. Quickly now, there's a good chap.'

The big man gave her his broad grin – the friendliness of this strange white woman still surprised and delighted him – then lazily stretched himself and loped off into the thornwood.

Later, Alice crept into her low tent and lay on her bedroll. She found she was perspiring. Damn the army! It was always the same wherever she went: incredulity, arrogance and then obstruction. Sometimes she was amazed that the Empire could function at all, with such reactionary dunderheads at its centre. She groped within her valise to find the cable that had arrived for her in Durban five days ago. It was from Fenby, the *Post*'s foreign editor. She read it again, gloomily:

Last piece used despite need for editg stop you are nt writg leaders stop reduce opinions and stay wi facts stop cable soonest 1,500 wrds on army's preparations for invasion ends

Alice washed herself as best she could in the little canvas folding basin and began making notes before her dinner with the Colonel. It was important she should decide on and then commit to memory the kind of 'facts' (damn Fenby!) she wished to extract from Covington. Then she lay in the stuffy little tent and tried to sleep. She would need her wits about her that evening.

She awoke, if not exactly refreshed, then at least determined. Facts, facts, facts, she kept repeating to herself. After careful consideration she decided to dress down for dinner. She therefore retained her riding boots, merely dusting away the detritus of the journey, and exchanged her jodhpurs for a long, anonymous cotton skirt, pressing out the creases as best she could. She replaced her shirt with a slightly more feminine blouse and the green scarf with a band of black velvet. She wore neither cosmetics nor jewellery. The Colonel must accept that she was a working professional.

The preparations for dinner, however, implied otherwise. On reporting to the battalion HQ, Alice was escorted by a corporal to a small marquee. She noted that flysheets had been fitted all round (to prevent shadows being seen through the canvas?), and inside a table had been set for two, and it was obvious that the officers' mess had been raided. The table glittered with silver plate and crystal glass and two candles guttered intimately from a handsome candelabra set on the starched white cloth. The neck of a champagne bottle protruded from an ice bucket balanced on a cane tripod and two folding chairs had been opened and set either side of it. The only element of incongruity within the careful setting was a distinctly moth-eaten red-plush chaise-longue placed at the rear of the marquee.

If Alice had dressed as simply as possible, then Lieutenant Colonel Covington had done his best to compensate. His white and scarlet mess jacket was cut to show his broad shoulders to best advantage and to reduce the slight paunch that now filled out his tall figure. The blue trousers, looped under his highly polished boots, could not have been tighter and he had affected a red cummerbund, giving him a jaunty and slightly oriental appearance. His cheeks, burnished by the South African sun, glowed behind the great moustaches and he bowed low over Alice's hand as she entered.

'Forgive the spartan nature of all this,' he gestured with his left hand, while retaining Alice's fingers in his other, 'but we are on campaign, of course, and I fear that we must rough it as best we can.'

Alice withdrew her hand and walked to one of the chairs. 'Not exactly spartan, surely, Colonel. Champagne? And goodness, even ice. On campaign?'

Covington withdrew the bottle and immediately began to remove the wrapper and twist the cork. 'Ah, my dear Miss Griffith, the army – or, at least, my battalion of the 24th – always gets its priorities right, although I am afraid you are wrong about the ice. The bucket is full of water, cool water from the well we have bored, but not as cold as ice. The label on the bottle will shortly float away, I fear. As I say, we must rough it.'

He carefully poured two glasses, handed Alice one, sat on the other chair and raised his glass. 'To the forthcoming campaign,' he toasted.

Mutely, Alice raised her glass and sipped. For the first time, she set herself to examine the Colonel. There was no doubt about it, he was handsome. Not yet forty, the only sign of approaching middle age was that slight paunch which, because of his height, his bearing and good tailoring, he could carry well. His hair remained full and was only slightly flecked with grey above the ears. Beneath the moustaches – they seemed to span the whole width of his face and slightly beyond – his mouth was firm, and the strong jaw had a slight cleft in the centre. She looked at the hand holding the glass but could see no ring.

Coolly, but not offensively, Covington let his eye take in Alice also. They sat silently for a moment, each regarding the other with a slight smile.

'Miss Griffith,' said the Colonel, 'I make no apology for inviting you to dinner tonight, even though our acquaintance is so short. You see,' he took a sip of the champagne and gently dabbed the bottom of his moustaches with the back of his forefinger, 'a soldier must take advantage of good company wherever he may find it. And, if I may say so, you undoubtedly seem to be good company. I like spirit.'

Alice inclined her head. 'Colonel, I could choose to regard that remark in two ways: as a compliment or as a mark of condescension. At the moment, I am inclined to give you the benefit of the doubt.'

Covington stretched out a long leg and threw back his head in a silent guffaw. 'Capital, capital,' he murmured. 'I shall endeavour to stay the right side of the mark, don't you know.'

The gentle sparring continued until the bottle was empty, and Alice realised that she was enjoying herself. The feeling was accompanied by a slight twinge of guilt, and for the first time for days, she thought of Simon. When she had arrived at the Cape she had enquired about him, off-handedly, for she did not wish to compromise her position, or his for that matter. No one seemed quite certain where he was – 'up-country on special duties' was the nearest she got – and she had not liked to push. She had written to him before leaving England but, of course, had received no reply. Perhaps Covington could help. Once they had sat to table and the first course was served, Alice broached the subject.

The soup spoon was touching Covington's whiskers when she mentioned Simon's name. It stayed there for a second, while the blue eyes flashed up at her in surprise. 'Fonthill?' He lowered his spoon. 'What is he to you? How do you know him?'

Alice waved a languid hand. 'Oh, he is more or less a childhood friend. Our fathers served together in the 24th and, as a result, we were rather thrown together years ago. But I have not seen him for some time. I heard he had been posted out here and I felt that I should pay my respects if he was nearby. But it is of no consequence.'

Somewhat mollified, Covington raised his napkin, wiped his lips and snorted. 'Man's a bounder. Worse than that. He's a coward.'

'What?' exclaimed Alice. Whatever she had expected to hear, it was not this.

'Complete coward. Feigned illness so that he would miss the draft out here with his battalion, the 1st. So he came under my command.' A cold smile stole across his face.'I made him jump for a few months, I can tell you. But to give him his due, he didn't crack. Then the damned Horse Guards got it into their heads that he was a linguist and could be of use out here. So they sent him on some sort of special mission into Zululand. As far as I know, nothing's been heard of him since. The damned man's probably deserted by now. I doubt if you'll ever see him again.'

Alice attempted to maintain an air of cool indifference as Covington's sentences shot across the table at her, like rifle volleys. But she could feel a flush mounting her cheeks and her heart sank. Simon a coward! Discredited! *And* lost in Zululand! She took a deep draught of the Moselle wine that had replaced the champagne and bent her head over the soup bowl.

'How extraordinary,' she said. 'Has nothing at all come back from him, then?'

'Oh, some sort of message, I understand, but I gather that it was garbled and virtually useless. If he does come back –

which I very much doubt – he will probably face a court martial.' He looked up. 'Oh, I say. I hope that this is not distressing to you?'

Alice gave a small smile. 'No, although I feel sorry for his parents. As I say, it is of no importance to me. Now, tell me. How long do you think that this campaign will last?'

She had expected reticence from the Colonel, but to her surprise and delight, he spoke freely of the task ahead. In Cape Town, Durban and Pietermaritzburg, every officer with whom she had discussed the Zulus had dismissed them as Kaffirs: braver, perhaps, than most but still likely to run away once they met British volley firing and the levelled bayonet. The biggest problem would be getting them to stand and fight. Covington, however, was more circumspect.

'Damned fine fighters, from what I've heard,' he said. 'Somehow I don't see them running all the time. More likely they will stand and fight on ground of their own choosing. We should be careful. Of course, we shall still knock 'em over, but they might just give us a bit of a shock. Can't quite get anyone to agree with me, so maybe I'm wrong. Confess I'm no great strategist but I have fought a few black fellers in me time and one or two have been quite handy.'

The Colonel, it seemed, had served with General Wolseley in the Ashanti campaign of '73, had received a spear wound there and had gained promotion in the field. The longer the meal progressed and her companion talked, the more Alice found herself warming to him. Beneath the studied elegance and the air of a veteran mountebank lay an obviously experienced and competent soldier and, it seemed, a man of courage. More importantly to Alice, he began speaking with commitment about the problems that lay behind the projected invasion.

Chelmsford, it seemed, had asked for but been refused reinforcements from England and had been told that he had to make do with what he had. The General was confident that his two battalions of experienced infantry, the 24th Regiment, plus an artillery battery, would provide the necessary hard core for the invasion force. But he was woefully short of cavalry and of transport in a country that demanded both. Civilian volunteers of a great variety of backgrounds had therefore been pressed into service and Durnford had been allowed to recruit friendly natives to make up the invading columns. The army would prevail, of course, but it was nothing like the finely honed force that the staff would have preferred.

As Alice listened, she pushed aside her wine glass. She had a good head for alcohol and was not afraid of becoming tipsy, but she was desperately trying to fix in her mind the facts and figures that Covington so freely laid before her. It would not do to take notes but here were the bones of the article she must send to London and she could not afford to let them escape. She concentrated hard, locked into the Colonel's pale blue eyes as he spoke and found it no hardship to do so.

'Enough of this war talk,' said the tall man eventually. He rose. 'Now I suppose some of this may turn up in the *Morning Post* but I don't see any harm in letting the public know what sort of mess the Horse Guards have put us in. In fact,' his eyes twinkled as he looked down at her, 'I don't give a damn. I've thoroughly enjoyed talking to you. Let's have a cognac and sit somewhere more comfortable.'

He grabbed a bottle and balloon glasses from the table and strode to the divan, where he indicated for her to sit beside him. Alice rose slowly to her feet. She was conscious that a slow, burning sensation of excitement was growing within her and that the time had come to make a decision. She moved to the divan and accepted the glass. The cognac was delicious.

She half smiled at him over the top of her glass. 'What comes now, Colonel – the seduction?'

The ends of the moustaches rose a fraction. 'You must excuse my language, Miss Griffith, but I damned well hope so. I haven't been seduced for ages.'

'You should know, Colonel, that I am a virgin.'

'Flattered, ma'am. Deeply flattered. A great honour indeed.'

She lifted her glass to him and then one foot. 'Very well. But pray do help me to get these off. I refuse to be deflowered whilst wearing riding boots.'

Alice awoke in her tent the next morning feeling that her head had been left out in the midday sun. Despite the pounding, however, there was a feeling of elation, a combination of both sexual and intellectual satisfaction. She luxuriated in it for a moment, stretching out on her camp bed and loosening her hair in a sensual movement so that it spread across the pillow. Her eyes stared at the canvas close above her but she heard nothing of the distant bustle of camp life. *She was no longer a virgin!* How delicious! How magnificent! How . . . how . . . *emancipating!* Good riddance to that girlish, awkward and overrated state. How her life had changed within the last six months. Here she was, living in a completely male-dominated world and making her way in it more than competently. So far she had made few mistakes and now, to top it all, she was a woman who had given and taken full sexual satisfaction.

Alice smiled and stretched her hands above her head and lay in the cot for one further, indulgent moment. Then, with a frown at her throbbing head, she reached across to her valise for a pencil and her notebook and began scribbling on to the lined pages as much as she could remember of what Covington (her *lover*, she smiled at the thought) had told her the previous night: the search for limbers, the pressing of a thousand civilian horsemen into a cavalry screen, the agonies about whether the black levies could be trusted. Slowly she sketched a factual story of an invasion force being created from bits and pieces around the hard centre of veteran colonial fighters. For once, her mind did not intrude with reminders about the injustice of their cause. In her notebook she painted a picture of the camp itself, with its colour, confusion and hustle, gradually moving towards order and determination. For the first time, she felt she had captured the smell and taste of Zululand and the tang of the danger it presented. By midday she had finished and she lay back with a sigh and closed her eyes again. The task of writing it clearly in cablese and of dispatching it safely back to Durban for onward transmission to London could wait until tomorrow.

Over the next few days, Alice maintained a low profile within the camp. She rode down to Rorke's Drift to see the little mission station, which was being converted into a temporary hospital and border post, and then further to the Buffalo River to gaze across its muddy waters into Zululand. The river was swollen and looked unpropitious for the crossing of the central column, which Chelmsford proposed to command himself. But engineers had already erected stanchions from which cables would be extended across the drift to take pontoons. Each day detachments of the column were moving down to the mission station to set up camp in preparation for the crossing.

Two days after her dinner with Covington she returned to her tent – she was now alone, her servant having been dispatched to Durban with her copy – to find, tucked discreetly within the opening flap, a small silver-plated hip flask. Tentatively, she sipped the contents. It was the delicious cognac she had tasted on the chaise-longue. Attached was a small sealed envelope containing a message scrawled in masculine, strongly sloped handwriting:

> Difficult to send flowers out here. Thought you might care to accept this instead. More practical, anyway. If you would like to taste a little more, you have only to say . . .
> RC

RC? Alice realised that she had no idea of the Christian name of the man who had removed her innocence. Robert? Robin? Randolph? Rodney? Rupert? Most likely Randolph. Yes, Randolph. It sat well on him. She felt no sense of shame or disappointment as she recalled the seduction. Covington had been gentle, considerate and then grandly passionate. She was glad she had acquiesced, glad that she had lost her maidenhood; glad that it was over and out of the way for ever. And also glad that it had happened with some style, with a man of some experience and authority. Now, Simon . . .

Ah, Simon! She blushed to think of how little she had thought of him since the Colonel's dinner, despite the shock of hearing of his alleged disgrace. Somehow, however, she could not accept the story. Simon, with his awkward honesty and natural diffidence, could never be a bounder. But could he be a coward? No. Anyway, it was most unlikely that the Horse

Guards would send a coward on a special mission into Zululand.

She turned her head and looked towards the east, to Cetswayo's kingdom. Was Simon somewhere out there? She longed to look for herself.

On 6 January, Lord Chelmsford returned with his staff to Helpmakaar and Alice immediately penned him a formal request to accompany the invading force into Zululand. She could travel anywhere within Natal and attach herself to the army there but she knew it would be impossible to enter enemy territory with the central column without permission from and the support of the C-in-C. Almost by return came a polite refusal, giving no reason but enclosing a formal invitation to dine with the General and his staff and senior officers the following evening.

Later that day, a message came to her from Pietermaritzburg. It had been forwarded from Durban and it lifted her heart. The cable was from her editor and read:

> Congrats on recent articles partic 1st one stop am payg into yr bnk acc cost of passage Cape stop reprt upn comg campaign best you can fm Natal stop do nt repeat nt enter Zululand ends

Alice dressed for dinner with the General and his staff with more care than she had lavished on Covington. Carefully uncreasing, as best she could, her only formal dress, she struggled into it and then added pearls, face powder and a little rouge. She permitted herself a flush of excitement at seeing Covington again.

The evening, however, was an anticlimax. She was placed at

table in the seat of honour between Chelmsford and his Chief of Staff, an excitable little old India hand named Lamb. The General spoke little to her, although he was impeccably polite, and on her right, Colonel Lamb declined to say anything about the coming campaign and was rather boring about India. Alice did consider asking him about Simon but was doubtful if he even knew about his existence so thought better of it. Covington had held her hand a little longer than was necessary on greeting her but, with a twinkle in his eye, had allowed himself to give way to the young staff officers who clustered round her over the pre-prandial sherry. In fact, with some chagrin and realising that, as the only woman present, she was restricting the after-dinner conversation, she retired before ten p.m. and allowed a young subaltern to escort her to her tent.

Three days later, on instinct, Alice moved her tent to Rorke's Drift. This time she asked no one's permission but camped in the lee of the little hospital there and rose when she heard the reveille bugles sound early in the darkness. Dressing hurriedly and nibbling a biscuit, she crawled out into a thick fog and light rain and hurried down to the Buffalo. She was in time to observe the first companies of the 24th Regiment embark on punts and cross the river. The invasion of Zululand had begun.

Chapter 13

For Simon and Jenkins, the days that followed Dunn's departure were the worst of their captivity. After a week, they expected every night to be woken by their rescuer, so they stood watch, turn and turn about, to ensure that they would be ready when the call came, but the system failed because even the one who was off watch stayed awake to ensure that every sound, however faint, was heard. The excitement faded after ten days and the old mantle of depression and boredom descended upon them again, except that this time it was harder to bear, because it seemed as though their hopes had been raised only to be dashed again. Each began to fear that Dunn had somehow fallen foul of the King and would never return. He had given them a calendar torn from a pocket diary and they passed a joyless Christmas together, the day exactly the same as the many that had preceded it. They were seventeen days into the New Year of 1879 before, at last, relief came.

The captives were dozing uneasily, about to slip into that final portion of the night before morning that brought them about two hours of reasonably full sleep, when both men were instantly awake. Outside the hut, by the entrance, there was a faint whispering and then, soundlessly, the curtain was drawn aside and a slight, slim figure entered quickly.

'Nandi!' cried Simon.

'Blimey!' said Jenkins.

She raised a finger to her lips and beckoned them to her. They crawled to sit by her in the dim half-light. 'Don't say anything, just listen,' she whispered. 'The invasion has begun and you are in great danger. You must leave Ulundi tonight and try and reach the main British column that is advancing westwards from Rorke's Drift. It is difficult country, about sixty miles as the crow flies, but,' Nandi looked pityingly at their white faces, 'you are not crows. It would be best if you try and hide during the day and travel only by night. There is no moon tonight but it will rise tomorrow, so you must go now.

'Here.' She handed them identical buckskin satchels. 'There is food and water enough for four days, if you are very eumonical . . . er . . . ecomi . . .'

'Economical,' prompted Simon.

'Yes. You must eat and drink little and save it. Papa says that you must head due west and you will then strike the Buffalo, if you don't meet with the British column before then.' She opened a bundle she was carrying. 'You must wear these blankets when you leave the hut, and here are scissors, razor and soap. Zulus don't have long beards like that so you must shave them off.' They could see now that her face was sad and that she had been crying. 'You don't look like Zulus,' she went on, 'but in the darkness I think you will pass well enough. I could not bring rifles, of course, because I could not hide them, but here is another of the handguns with some cartridges. I know you have one already.'

'Nandi.' Simon laid a hand on her arm to stop the earnest flow of instructions. 'How did you get in here? There is always a guard outside.'

The girl's teeth flashed in the gloom. 'Ah, tonight it is Nkumo. This is why it has taken so long to come here – or, at least, one of the reasons. We had to wait until Nkumo could get this duty. He usually does what I want him to, but anyway he is grateful to Mr Jenkins because Mr Jenkins did not kill him when he could easily have done so.' Then the smile vanished and she turned to Jenkins. 'But he says that he has now repaid the debt and that the next time he sees you he will kill you.'

Jenkins turned an ingenuous face to Simon. 'That's nice of the lad, look you. You couldn't wish for anything fairer than that, could you?'

Nandi held a finger to her lips and Simon asked her, 'Will you come with us?'

Nandi shook her head. 'No. I must leave before they find that you have gone and ride south, back home. Papa and Catherine and most of the children have already left for the Tugela with as many cattle as Papa could round up.' She looked with a hint of embarrassment at the ground. 'James was supposed to come here and help you, but after Papa had left, he refused to come.' She looked up at Simon with her direct gaze. 'I don't think he likes you, so I came instead. Anyway, it was easier for me, er, because of Nkumo.'

She became intense again. 'Now, listen. Nkumo is outside but he will be killed if it looks as though he helped you. So you must cut a hole in the back of the hut so that everyone can see that you got out that way. Take off your boots and carry them under your blankets.' The girl gestured with both hands. 'You must walk directly down the lane between the huts that are ahead of you. Then you will come to a small paddock. Your horses are there.'

259

'Thank God for that,' said Jenkins.

'But I don't know where your saddles are. You must ride bareback.'

'Oh lord,' sighed Simon.

'Bach, you'll never stay on. Best to walk behind an' 'old 'is tail, like.'

'Oh, shut up, Jenkins.'

Nandi went on, still in her low, conspiratorial whisper. 'The horses are hobbled and I don't think there is a guard on them. It would be wise to mount them right away and ride out through the gate rather than lead them. The guards could take you for Basuthos, but, in any case, Zulus don't seem to question people on horseback.' She leaned forward now and looked at them in turn with her round eyes to give emphasis to her words. 'But be very careful. Ulundi is full of warriors at the moment because this is the time of umKhosi, the first fruits ceremony. The army has come to the King's kraal to be cleaned and strengthened for the year ahead. In one way, this will help you because there are many strange people in the capital now, but there are also many assegais out there.'

She put her fingers to her face in quick horror. 'They will come after you when they find you are gone. So you have little time. If you get into trouble, just ride hard.'

Nandi rose to her feet and the two men joined her.

Jenkins took her hand in his and with aristocratic solemnity raised it to his bedraggled moustache. 'You are a very nice and a very brave young lady, Miss Nandi. Thank you for 'elpin' us, and take great care, now, in ridin' back.'

Simon took the hand reluctantly relinquished by Jenkins. 'Yes, Nandi, please be careful. We will wait here for half an hour to give you time to get well clear – just in case something goes wrong. Although,' he added hastily, 'of course it won't.'

Nandi stepped very close and looked up into Simon's face. He could see two silver streams of tears running down her cheeks. 'Simon,' she whispered, 'I do not know whether you have betrayed the Zulus and me by what you have told the British, but I am very sad that your army is now invading my country.' She blinked. 'I do not think now that I want to make a baby with you.' Then she turned and slipped through the entrance, leaving the two soldiers standing in the semi-darkness, staring self-consciously at each other.

'I'll start on the 'ole, eh?' said Jenkins. 'You'd better get shavin'.'

After a busy half-hour, the two men wrapped the blankets around them and, shoving their boots before them, crawled awkwardly through the hole. The night outside seemed blacker than within the hut, whose contours had become so drearily familiar to them. Save for the barking of distant dogs, all was still, although they knew that they had only perhaps ninety minutes before the anthill that was Ulundi would come to life again. They had to move quickly. The lane between the huts lay before them and they stepped quietly in their bare feet between the walls. No one stirred in this tranquil suburb of the capital, and after about four minutes they came to the open paddock where, untended, their horses were grazing.

'Thank God they've still got bridles,' hissed Simon. 'But you'll have to help me up. I shall never get on without a stirrup.'

'Don't worry, bach sir. It's all part of the service provided by a good officer's servant, look you.'

Jenkins hacked away at the hobbles with the food knife while Simon held the bridles and spoke soothingly to the horses.

Simon fancied he could see the horizon lightening to the east but it still remained a blessedly dark night, low cloud and a cloying humidity signalling the promise of rain.

'We mustn't put our boots on until we are out of Ulundi,' whispered Simon. 'They will betray us straight away if we wear them. So it will have to be barefoot as well as bareback for a while. Here, give me a hand.'

The Welshman bent and cupped his hands, half throwing Simon astride his mount. Then, with a practised hop and a jump, Jenkins was on the back of his. 'Where to now then, sir?'

Simon squinted at the compass in the darkness. 'This way. We'll follow the line of the paddock until we hit the thorn fence and then follow that down to the entrance. I think that's safer than going down the centre. Wrap your blanket tightly around you and don't sit upright. Slouch, the way the Basuthos do. Make it look as though we're going out to tend cattle.'

Like ghostly sentinels, slumped in their saddles, the two picked their way between the beehives, slowly and quietly so as not to excite the dogs who came to sniff at their passing. They saw some shapeless forms outside hut entrances here and there, probably sleeping off the excesses of the first fruits ceremony, but little other signs of life as they met the thorn barrier and turned south, to Ulundi's only entrance.

Simon rode in the lead, his eyes darting from side to side from beneath the cowled blanket. He drew in a long, slow breath as dimly, from the darkness, a wide gap emerged in the fence and he began to make out the squatted figures of Zulu guards on duty at the entrance. He felt his heart racing and his tongue ran over parched lips but his main concern was what would happen if he had to kick his horse into a gallop. His seat in the saddle had improved considerably, but . . . in the saddle only. He felt perspiration seep through his breeches on to the bare back of his mare. Carefully he eased himself along the horse's vertebrae. There would be no question of drawing the Colt if trouble arose. He would need both hands just to stay on the horse, let alone control it. If the worst came to the worst, he would let go of the bridle and put his arms round the horse's neck.

They plodded on, turning slowly to ride out through the entrance of the stockade. As they did so, one of the guards rose from his haunches, lifted his spear and spoke gutturally. Whether it was a greeting or a challenge was unclear, but, hardly turning his head, Simon raised a languid hand and grunted unintelligibly in reply. For a moment it seemed as though they would be stopped as the Zulu pointed his assegai blade at them and followed their progress past him with it. Then with a grunt he squatted again.

Once beyond the gate they urged their horses into a gentle canter. 'Didn't know you spoke Zulu so well,' said Jenkins, pulling alongside Simon. 'Was it all those lessons, then?'

'Oh shut up,' said Simon. He was in no mood to joke about Nandi. Her words had penetrated deeply, reviving the self-doubt about his actions and making him feel ashamed. 'Keep your wits about you. We're not out of the wood yet.'

They rode as hard for the first hour as their precarious seats, the rough ground and the darkness allowed. Then, as the dawn sent long red tongues splitting the dark sky, Simon called a halt. They shifted uneasily in their seats and looked around as the sun burst over a distant hill. They seemed to be alone on the undulating plain. Covered with stunted grass, burned yellow and brown by the sun, it stretched to low dark hills in the west and seemed to be broken only by the occasional thorn bush and a few paper bark acacia and white pear trees. They knew from experience, however, that it was fissured by dongas that could hardly be seen until they were upon them. Behind them there was no trace of Ulundi, nor was there any sign of a trail. Overhead a goshawk circled, and nearby, a hidden trumpeter hornbill called.

'There's not much cover for 'idin' by day, now, is there?' ventured Jenkins, shading his eyes and looking around him.

Simon nodded agreement. 'I don't know how far we have come from Ulundi but it can't be more than, say, ten miles or so, at the pace we've been able to make.' He squinted into the rising sun behind them. 'A Zulu war party can cover that distance easily. I think we are too close to Ulundi to hole up for the day, anyway, so let's keep moving.'

He kicked with his heels and the pair set off again, the horses picking their way fastidiously over a rocky outcrop that ran down from a slight rise immediately to their right.

It was from over that rise that the Zulus materialised, spilling over the top in that effortless, loping run that seemed to take all kinds of terrain in its stride. There were about ten of them, stripped down for war and carrying large shields. Jenkins saw them first and, without a word, drew the Navy Colt from his waistband, extended his arm and coolly fired at the leading Zulu, at a range of about one hundred yards. The shot kicked up the earth at the man's feet.

'Bloody popgun,' cursed Jenkins.

The report, however, caused Simon's startled horse to rear. As he slid down the beast's back, Simon just had time to grab a handful of its mane to break the force of his fall. Nevertheless, he hit the rocky ground with a crash that momentarily winded him and sent his revolver, which had been loosely tucked into his breeches, spinning away across the rocks. As he rose to his knees, Simon saw his horse bolting away to the western horizon and a throwing spear clatter into the rocks at his feet. There was no sign of Jenkins and Simon realised with sudden despair that he was back to where he had been in that donga some four months ago. This time, however, he had no rifle and no horse. Grabbing the spear, he turned to face his assailants, who were now almost upon him and had fanned out to surround him.

Then, with a scream that seemed to rise in pitch as it bounced back from the low rocks around them, the Welshman suddenly appeared. His horse, too, had taken fright and bolted, but Jenkins had turned him in a declivity and now he thundered towards the centre of the Zulus like an apocalyptic horseman, his steed at full gallop, his right arm extended aiming the Colt. Simon heard the crack of the revolver but had no time to follow Jenkins's charge. Spear in hand, he ran to a small passage between two rocks and turned to face the first Zulu.

The warrior came at him at a run, his right hand holding the short stabbing spear, his left extending the war shield, top down, as an offensive weapon. It was the Zulu's speed that saved Simon. As the native lunged at him, Simon grabbed the tip of the shield and pulled it down so that the bottom of the central pole became entangled in the man's legs and he sprawled headlong. Quickly turning, Simon plunged the throwing spear between the prostrate man's shoulder blades, twisted it and withdrew it. For the second time in his life he heard the sound of the iklwa.

There was no feeling of disgust this time because two more Zulus now confronted him. These warriors were more cautious than their fellow. Chests heaving, they stood off at six paces, their black eyes regarding Simon intently as they split to edge around him. Simon noticed that they both had the fibre circlet waxed into their hair and that their shields were of black and white hides. He sprang to his right, where the rock formed a head-high escarpment, and there he stood at bay, his back to the rock. He had a moment to bless the fact that he had the longer, though lighter, throwing spear to fight with rather than the shorter assegai. At least he had a length advantage and he presented the weapon now to the Zulus, low and two-handed, as though it were rifle and bayonet.

The long incarceration at Ulundi, with poor food and little real exercise, had weakened Simon somewhat, but at least he was carrying no surplus weight and his build – a slim five foot nine, with narrow hips and a fair breadth of shoulder – gave him ideal balance. There was no time for fear. Wide-eyed, he stood and waited, every sense alive.

The stand-off continued for perhaps twenty seconds, as, close at hand, Simon heard more revolver shots. At least Jenkins was selling his life dearly. Then the attack began, skilfully, as befitted older, more experienced warriors. Both Zulus presented their shields to Simon, from his left and right quarter, and then thrust at him with their spears around the edge of the shields. The first thrust lightly penetrated his left shoulder and sent a sharp pain through his body. But the Zulu had been too cautious, too uncommitted to the stroke, and the blade had not sunk far beneath the skin. The other warrior's stab came low and Simon was able to parry it and momentarily spin the man round on to the other's shield, exposing him so that he was able to kick him quickly in the genitals with his riding boot. Then, with a series of desperate lunges around the shield, Simon drove the first man back. But this foray took him away from the rock and left his back unprotected. He turned to find two more Zulus dropping down from the top of the escarpment, their spears raised.

Suddenly, seemingly from nowhere, came the clatter of hooves on rock and, once again, that high-pitched yell, and Jenkins came charging down the gully. It was impossible for his shooting to be accurate while riding but his first shot hit a rock and sent a splinter into the eye of one of the Zulus who had dropped down behind Simon. The man screamed and fell to the ground, clutching his face. Another shot, this time at point-blank range, ripped through the second Zulu's shield and took him in the chest. The horse attempted to jump over the warrior whom Simon had kicked and who was now trying to climb to his feet, but a flying hoof caught his head and laid him low again. The gully between the rocks was little more than twelve feet wide and Jenkins's charge forced both Simon and his original opponent to flatten themselves against the rock as the Welshman galloped through. Simon was the first to recover. As the Zulu turned his face, wide-eyed from watching Jenkins wheel at the gully's end, Simon's spear took him just below the cheekbone and penetrated deeply. With a cry he dropped his shield to put his hand to his face and Simon struck again, this time in the breast.

For a moment Simon stood still, trembling. Then he was aware of a horse at his elbow.

'Well done, bach sir,' cried Jenkins. 'Couldn't 'ave done better meself. Now,' he reached down a hand, 'climb up behind me and 'ang on for dear life. There are some of 'em still left and we'll 'ave to ride through 'em to get out of 'ere.'

With one foot on the rock face, Simon scrambled up behind the Welshman, just managing to retain his spear as he did so. They turned to ride out of the gully but three warriors appeared, assegais raised. Jenkins turned the horse about, only to find two more Zulus barring their exit.

'Which way d'you fancy, then, sir?'

'Go for those two. Charge straight at 'em. The Zulus are supposed to be frightened of cavalry. I'll use the spear as a lance.'

Jenkins chortled. 'Very good, then. Excuse the noise. It's a bit Celtic like but it gees up the 'orse, an' me an' all.'

He kicked the horse's flanks savagely, let out that piercing shriek once again and the startled beast sprang towards the two Zulus, who were tentatively advancing. The spectre of the yelling black-visaged Welshman bent low over his mount and the lowered spear was too much for the warriors. They broke and fled and the horsemen were through and away on to the plain, pursued only by two thrown spears, which fell way behind them.

For four minutes they rode at the gallop, Jenkins skilfully guiding the horse between rocks, dongas and bushes while Simon clung to the sweaty back of the Welshman, both arms around his waist and the spear standing out awkwardly across them, like a tightrope walker's balancing pole, crashing through branches as they charged through the scrub. Eventually, the exhausted horse was allowed to drop to a walk and the riders studied the plain behind them. There was no sign of pursuit.

'I think they had had enough anyway,' panted Simon. 'We must have put down half a dozen between us.'

Jenkins grasped the hands clenched round his midriff for a moment. 'Easier for me with a pistol than for you with just a spear.' He spoke gruffly, unable to turn so that Simon could not see his face. 'Honestly, bach sir. You fought like a Welsh collier back there with that bit of spear, like. Old Coley with 'is bayonet couldn't 'ave done better. I'd like Mr Bloody Covington to 'ave seen you, so I would.'

The pair fell silent as the tired horse picked its way forward. Simon, strangely touched, now occasionally adjusted its course with the help of the compass.

'It's due west we want,' he said, 'and that's roughly the way my horse bolted. We might just find her. Once we have put some distance between us and the Zulus, we'd better look for a kopje where we might be able to find cover and yet command some sort of view of the plain. We don't want to be surprised again.'

So they made their way westward across the plain, finding cover by early afternoon and then rising very early to make as good progress as they could in the darkness. On the third day, tired and hungry, they were late rising and the sun was up before them. The fugitives had camped between two high rocks on a kopje that afforded them a good view all around. To the south-west they could see a distant high peak, not a mountain but bigger than a hill, that stood out on its own. It had a flat-topped appearance and from it Simon felt that they should be able to catch a glimpse, at least, of the Buffalo. They had decided to make for it in the morning. They had been unable to find Simon's horse and travel, therefore, had been slow. Taking it in turns to ride, their every step had been marked by the need for caution and vigilance. However, they had seen no living soul – until now.

As Simon fed their horse with a handful of yellow grass growing high above its reach, his eye caught a quick flash of reflected sunlight to the north. With infinite care, he climbed to the top of the rock and, slowly, raised his head above its edge. For a moment, he saw nothing. Then, less than a mile away, his eye picked out a column of what looked like black ants moving quickly across the plain, sometimes disappearing as it wound its way sinuously down into a donga, then coming into view again before vanishing once more behind a hill. The flashes of light came momentarily as the sun caught a steel spearhead. Thankfully, Simon realised that the course of the column was away from their kopje. It was moving from east to west – and at a fair speed.

He called Jenkins to join him. 'How many do you think?'

The Welshman whistled noiselessly. 'Difficult to tell, but there must be thousands. Look, they're still coming. Maybe fifteen . . . twenty thousand.'

Simon shielded his eyes from the sun. 'It must be the main Zulu army. They've clearly come from Ulundi. But where are they going?'

'Well,' said Jenkins, absent-mindedly picking at his ragged moustache, 'if they're after us, they're goin' the wrong way.'

'No. Cetswayo's not going to send twenty thousand warriors after us. They are going to attack the British central column, for sure. So we must be quite near the army.' Simon squinted to the west and then to the south. 'I wonder where the hell it is. I wish we had binoculars.'

He weighed the odds. The Zulus probably knew the exact position of the column. They were bound to be aware of the movement of so large a body of men within their own territory. Their capacity for making the most of natural cover meant that they could probably hide a couple of impis and take the British by surprise. But surprise or not, Chelmsford would be on his guard in enemy country and there would be a battle. The chances were that Simon and Jenkins would get caught up between the two forces like grain in a grinding mill. For a moment, he considered the chances of making directly for the Buffalo River and the comparative safety of Natal. With luck, and by keeping well away from the direction in which the Zulus were travelling, they could make it without being detected. Anyway, they were in a poor state to fight, and two men could make no difference to the outcome . . .

He shook his head and turned to Jenkins. 'We must try and find the column and warn it before the Zulus attack.'

Jenkins blew out his cheeks but said nothing, and the two men slithered down the rock and untethered their horse. With Jenkins mounted and Simon walking a few paces ahead, they set course for that flat-topped rock that stood out above the horizon to the south-west. From it, Simon reasoned, they should be able to see the British camp if it was within a ten-mile radius. With the Zulu force only a little to the north, both knew that it would have been infinitely wiser to have stayed under cover all day. Their horse was weary and underfed – they could not afford to let it stop and graze – and with two men on its back, it would be difficult to outrun a Zulu patrol, let alone a couple of impis. The need to find the British army, however, was imperative, and neither man questioned it.

Throughout the day they made their cautious way under the hot sun, both heads continuously twisting to scan the surrounding country, Jenkins, as the best shot, holding the Colt. Once they saw a black-backed jackal slip through the long yellow grass, and the occasional purple crested loerie looked down at them from a blue sky puffed with white cloud balls. The plain seemed devoid of human life. Yet both men knew that they were not alone in that place, that somewhere near, large numbers of their own kind were marching on a collision course

– encircling them, perhaps – out there in the low rolling hills and among the rocks and dried water courses.

That night they camped again without a fire, and even the man off watch lay half awake, with an ear cocked for a rustle in the grass or the crack of a broken twig.

They rose on the morning of 22 January 1879 to find that they were near the edge of a plateau, the detail of which had been obscured in the brief twilight of their encampment the night before. A half-hour's march after sun-up brought them to the tip of the escarpment, which, in fact, did not decline sharply but fell away in gentle billows to a new plain below them. To their right, the escarpment marched to the west-north-west, gradually getting higher before it fell away in the distance. It was the plain below, however, which caught their attention. To the south and a little to their right, not much more than a mile away, it was dominated by the hill whose summit they had first discerned a day and a half ago. A bare block of sandstone that glowed dully red in the morning sun, it ran away from them, stretching some 500 yards in length along a rocky outcrop and then rising to about 500 feet at the flat-topped peak. Below its east-facing side the British column had made its camp.

The white bell tents shone brightly on the dull plain. They had been pitched in a straggling line running NNE to SSW at the base of the rock, the line bulging at the centre to encompass a cluster of wagons. Faint blue spirals of smoke curled into the sky from a score of campfires and the sun glinted intermittently on cooking pots and the other accoutrements of an army in the field. Faintly, despite the distance, the two men heard the low grunts of bullocks and the clash of utensils.

To Simon's eye there was something wrong, something

indefinable. Then he got it. 'My God!' he exclaimed. 'They haven't laagered the camp.' True enough, there were no barriers – no rough thorn bush zariba, no trenches, no line of wagons erected on the periphery of the camp to halt a rush of attackers. The most elementary precaution to protect a column encamped deep in enemy territory had not been taken. What languid halfwit had neglected to protect the camp in the presence of the enemy? Covington? Surely it couldn't be an officer with the experience and seniority of Chelmsford?

Jenkins grunted and elbowed Simon. 'Look.' He pointed to the east. There, where the plain melted into a low line of foothills, a long column of soldiers – cavalry, wagons and marching infantry – could just be seen disappearing into the blue haze of the morning. As they watched, the last riders slipped from view.

'What on earth's going on?' murmured Simon. 'That's more than a patrol. Why has he split the command like that?'

'I don't know, bach sir, but we'd better get down there damned quick and tell them about them black fellers.'

The two men now both mounted the horse and urged the beast down the escarpment. There was no track and the descent was more difficult than it looked. It was some time, then, before they met the first British soldier on the plain, a mounted vedette who looked at them in amazement as the doubly burdened horse plodded towards him.

'Who the hell are you?' he demanded, his carbine at the ready.

'Lieutenant Fonthill and Private Jenkins of the 2nd 24th,' responded Simon briskly, doing his best to sit erect with one arm around Jenkins's midriff. 'We need to see the CO immediately. Who is in command here?'

The cavalryman, a volunteer member of the Newcastle Mounted Rifles, looked unimpressed. 'You don't look like soldiers to me, man,' he said, covering them with his carbine. 'Where have you come from?'

'It's none of your damned business,' snapped Simon. 'Put that bloody thing down. There are twenty thousand Zulus just behind us and I'm damned if I'm going to be held up by some part-time soldier. Now, who is the officer in command and is he in camp?'

The patrolman lowered his carbine. 'Lieutenant Colonel Henry Pulleine, er, sir. The General has moved out this morning, so Colonel Pulleine is left in charge of the camp.' ﹁

Nodding with a grin, Jenkins urged the tired horse on. About 300 yards from the camp they saw a second column of about 500 men, half of them mounted and most of them black, march out in good order towards the east. The black infantrymen wore red bandannas around their heads. Behind them, moving more slowly, rode a small contingent of white troops, pulling three strange box-like contraptions on wheels behind them.

'Rockets,' said Simon. 'Now where the hell are *they* going?'

'I suppose,' said Jenkins over his shoulder as they approached the edge of the tent line, 'I'll 'ave to stop callin' you bach, now that we're back in the army, like.'

'Quite right. Try and sit up straight and get a move on.'

Watched by dozens of curious eyes, the pair threaded their way through the lines of the camp. Looking about him, Simon felt a faint but growing unease. He could not define the reason. Pickets were out, guards were mounted, soldiers were relaxing but properly dressed and rifles were leaning in regulation pyramids, ready to be snatched at the call of a bugle. He could smell coffee and hear a farrier at work on a horseshoe. All very normal for a column in the field, normal for a base camp awaiting the return of its commander – but a normality more suited to Salisbury Plain than an isolated unit camped deep in enemy territory.

Yet there was something more. Simon pushed himself up on Jenkins's shoulders to gain a better view and so establish the source of his disquiet. Of course there was the absence of a protective barrier, and perhaps it was also the way that the camp seemed to peter out on the part of its periphery not protected by the huge rock at its back, with only a handful of sentries spread thinly along the line. But it did not fully explain the air of oppression that hung over the place, as though the barometer was falling and a storm about to break. Yet the sky above was clear blue. What was wrong? Was he experiencing some extra-sensory premonition of disaster? Simon felt the hairs begin to prickle on the back of his neck.

The pair reached the CO's tent and Simon awkwardly slid to the ground, under the puzzled eye of the red-coated sentry. 'Morning, Davies,' said Simon. 'Ask the Colonel if I can see him urgently. It's important.'

Private Ivor Davies, once a member of Simon's platoon when both were stationed at Brecon, regarded the dishevelled figure before him with astonishment. A diet of milk and mealies had done nothing to fill out Simon's frame and his shirt was torn at the side and bloodstained at the shoulder where the spear wound had been roughly bound by Jenkins. The cotton pile on his corduroy breeches had long since worn away, leaving a thin, gauze-like fabric through which his thighs could be glimpsed. Both riding boots were scuffed and down at heel. But the young man's eyes shone brightly as they looked at the soldier.

'Good lor',' exclaimed the sentry. 'It's Mr Fonthill. Where 'ave you come from, then, sir?'

'Never mind that. Get inside quickly and tell the Colonel I'm here. Move sharply now.' Simon turned to Jenkins. 'Hang on here. I might need you.'

Within seconds Simon was sitting before Pulleine and telling his story. When he had finished, the Colonel, a square man with a red face, frowned. What he had been told by this bright-eyed scarecrow seemed incredible: a spying mission, a visit to the Zulu king's camp, escape from Ulundi, a successful fight with a superior number of pursuing warriors, a report of the whole Zulu army on the march . . . It was all a bit much. Too damned much. And hadn't he heard something about this young subaltern . . . some sort of disgrace? On the other hand, what was he doing out here, looking like an Afrikaaner in the middle of Zululand? He couldn't exactly be a Zulu spy. He'd heard of disgraced men going native, but there was something about this fellow that didn't fit with that. Better be careful.

'A whole damned impi, eh? How many would you say?'

Simon sighed. 'Can't be sure, sir. Anything between fifteen and twenty-five thousand. They were moving fast, towards the north of your line here. They will know you are here and they're bound to attack. Can you re-call that column that's just gone off to the east? I think you will need them.'

The Colonel shrugged his shoulders. 'Umph! That's Durnford with his blacks and the rocket battery. We heard gunfire in the direction of Lord Chelmsford's column, so Durnford's gone off after him to help. Couldn't stop him. He's senior to me, you see. Wanted to take some of my men, too, but I wouldn't let him. Now he could be in a mess if the Zulus catch him on the plain. But we will be all right here. I've got seventeen hundred men, including six companies of the regiment. I've got plenty of vedettes and pickets out. We can't be taken by surprise. I hope Johnny Zulu does attack. I'll give him a bloody nose.'

Simon swallowed. How could he convince this bluff regular army officer that, just for once, a well-armed British column could be vulnerable to spear-carrying aboriginals? How could he shake the complacency and arrogance of privilege and order, the inbred superiority of class? He must try.

'But sir. The camp isn't laagered. The Zulus attack so quickly. Twenty thousand of them could be upon and through us in no time.'

Pulleine's eyebrows raised. 'None of my doing. The General didn't feel it necessary. Difficult to do with all the to-ing and fro-ing over the trail back to the frontier. What's more, the ground's too damned hard. Can't get a bloody shovel in. Anyway, that's none of your business, young man. I—'

He was interrupted by a subaltern. 'Sorry to break in, sir, but . . .' He looked askance at Simon. 'Good heavens! Fonthill?'

'Never mind that,' said the Colonel testily. 'What's up?'

'Firing to the north, sir. Must be Lieutenant Cavaye's company. We can't see anything, because they are over the brow of the hill. But another thing, sir. It looks as though Colonel Durnford has turned back on the plain and is trying to regain the camp.'

Pulleine nodded imperturbably. 'Very well. Have the Adjutant stand-to the camp.'

He turned to Simon. 'It could be a false alarm. We've had the whole camp on stand-to already once this morning. But in view of what you've told me, this could be the real thing.' He buckled on his belt and revolver. 'Sentry.' Davies doubled inside. 'Take this officer and his man to the quartermaster and have them issued with rifles and ammunition. Oh, and . . .' he gave Simon a half-apologetic smile, 'get them something to wear and something to eat. That's all, Fonthill. Well done.'

Outside the tent, Simon could now hear the gunfire to the north, although there was no other sign of trouble. The bugle sounded the stand-to, but even then there was no air of rush or obvious anxiety. Quietly and in orderly fashion, the men abandoned their camp tasks, put on their helmets, buttoned their jackets and took their rifles from the stacks before falling into line. If the bugle's tone had not been so peremptory, the atmosphere might well be described as soporific.

It was then that Simon was able at last to pinpoint the cause of his unease. It was not just the fact that the camp had not been laagered or trenched. It was this air of almost smug complacency that seemed to hang over the place like a witch's curse. He caught Jenkins's eye and saw a sharpness in it – as near as the Welshman ever came to showing disquiet.

'I've got a feeling, bach sir,' said Jenkins in a low voice, 'that we're goin' to be in a battle at last – an' a nasty one at that.'

Simon tried to smile but found that he could not.

Chapter 14

The sentry took them to the QM's tent, where the Colonel's orders were relayed to a rather sceptical quartermaster sergeant, new to Simon. 'Can't give you red jackets . . . sir,' he said, wiping his moustache. 'Blue patrols all right?'

'Bugger the jackets,' said Jenkins. 'Give us the rifles.'

'That'll be enough from you,' snapped the NCO. 'And say "Quartermaster" when you talk to me.'

'That will do, Q,' said Simon gently. 'There is some need for haste because the camp is about to be attacked.'

'Yes, sir. Very good, sir. Now please sign here. Two blue patrols, one officer's, one Other Ranks'. Two Martini-Henry rifles and seventy rounds of ammunition each. Just there, sir. That's where you sign. And underneath, on the duplicate, please. You keep one and I keep the other.'

Contemptuously, Jenkins ignored the quartermaster and spoke to Simon. 'We'll need lungers, look you.'

'Ah yes, Q. Two bayonets, please. Yes, yes, add them to the dockets and I will sign.'

Now equipped, Simon and Jenkins found a cook, who interrupted the dousing of his fires to give them cold sausages, bread and cheese and lukewarm tea. Munching and drinking, their rifles slung over their shoulders, the two men walked to the edge of the encampment. In front of them, Pulleine had positioned his troops in a long line, about 800 yards out from the camp and, thought Simon, much too far away. For the moment it was incomplete, with gaps here and there, mainly left by the company that was now moving up the hill to the north, presumably to reinforce the troops out on patrol over the spur, whence came the firing. Most of the line was taken by the regular troops of the 24th Regiment, all of them, Simon noticed, from the 1st Battalion. That meant that Covington and the 2nd Battalion must have gone off with Chelmsford. The men of the 1st Battalion, plus one company of the 2nd that had been on picket duty out on the plain, now stood in two ranks, the rear rank a yard or two behind the front, with the men in staggered positions so that they could fire between their comrades. There was about four yards between each man, and so the front line was stretched perilously thin, with fewer than 600 men to cover almost a mile.

At the north-western face there was a rise, and here cannon were being manhandled into place. Between the camp and the southern end of the line stood contingents of Natal Kaffirs and bunches of white mounted volunteers, seemingly uncertain of their roles. Behind Simon and Jenkins in the camp scores of men – orderlies, grooms, bandsmen and civilians from the Commissariat – were milling about, and there was a general air of confusion. The contrast with the two lines of men was obvious and disconcerting.

Simon grabbed the arm of a fresh-faced subaltern who was hurrying past and who was unknown to him. 'What's the name of this place?' he asked.

In tones redolent of the best public school – indeed, he looked as though he had only just left the sixth form – the young man replied: 'Difficult to get your tongue round it, actually, old boy. I think this rock thing is called Isandlwana.' He pronounced it – correctly, as Simon was to discover later – 'Ee-sant-klwaanah'.

Jenkins looked at the slim back of the boy as he strode away, and crammed the last crust into his mouth. 'I don't like the look of it, bach sir,' he muttered, wiping the crumbs away. Jenkins was a survivor, always had been – from dirty cradle, through the childhood beatings on the farm, a hundred fights on building sites and the abuse of the Glasshouse. He could look after himself and *rely* on himself. But this was different. If his fate was in the hands of la-di-da schoolboys and fat old colonels who didn't know how to defend a camp, then he felt uneasy. 'I'm not much of a general, see, but shouldn't we be in a square or somethin'?'

Simon nodded absently. His mind was now a mixture of apprehension, because he shared Jenkins's doubts, and excitement, because he had never been in a major action before. But he hated this waiting. He could see, up towards the foothills of the escarpment to the north-west, what seemed to be men of the rocket battery dismounting and deploying their strange weapons. To the south, horsemen – he presumed they were Durnford's troops – were riding back to camp. Closer at hand, in the centre of the plain, a company of the 24th who had obviously been on picket duty was marching quickly back to the lines.

Jenkins was right. The two files of infantrymen seemed pathetically insubstantial, lining up so far out on the plain, without cover and away from the tents and the limbers. Simon threw away the remains of his sandwich. His mouth was far too dry to make the bread and cheese edible. He thought of the speed of the Zulus and the ferocity of their attack in the gully. Would they be able to turn these fragile lines? And would the men of the 24th suspect this? He walked towards the rear rank, the better to see their faces.

These were the best soldiers in the world. Unlike the forces of the other great powers of Europe and America, the British Army was always fighting. At any one time, somewhere in the world, the British Tommy would be fixing his bayonet or squinting through his rifle sights to keep the Queen's Empire together. These men of the 1st Battalion were fresh from the Kaffir wars in the south, and even the youngest had seen battle, while the veterans had fought Pathans, Malays and Ashanti tribesmen over the last few years.

The word about the Zulu, however, had spread: about his bravery, savagery and skill in battle and of how he had conquered all of the tribes in southern Africa. So, as Simon looked down the line, he noted perspiration trickling down sun-browned cheeks and tongues licking lips as dry as his own. Now that they were in line, called by the bugle, the lacklustre air of complacency had disappeared. The distant firing signalled to these experienced men that this was a *real* call to arms, even though the Zulu could not yet be seen. The general air of oppression he had noted earlier now seemed to have localised and settled above each white helmet. He looked out across the plain. 'Why don't they come?' he murmured. 'Why don't they come?'

'Godstrewth!' The exclamation came from Jenkins, who was pointing to the lip of the plateau to the north. The skyline was alive with tiny black figures – it was difficult to avoid the ant analogy again. They swarmed over the edge of the escarpment, and at what seemed, even at that distance, to be remarkable speed began debouching on to the plain. The black mass stretched for about two miles along the rim and it continued to cascade over the edge. The watchers in the line saw a brief flash from the rocket battery, stranded out on the plain, before it was engulfed.

The pace of events now began to quicken as the two men watched. The solitary company that had been on picket duty reached the line and took up position either side of the cannon. As they did so, the guns began to boom, sending up eruptions of red dust and earth among the advancing mass in the distance. To the right, Durnford's mounted men suddenly disappeared into a large donga about a mile from the camp. They immediately re-emerged, dismounted, manning the edges of the donga, and began pouring rapid fire into the Zulus.

'That's our southern flank covered, anyhow,' breathed Simon.

To the watching pair's left, on the northern end of the line and much closer to them, a company of the Natal Native Contingent appeared over the skyline, running in disarray back to the camp. A moment or two later, three companies of the 24th came into view over the spur, retreating in impeccable order and firing in sequence as one company fell back on the other. Behind them came the Zulus, a black mass whose advance seemed only slightly retarded by the volleys poured into it. As they neared the camp, the companies deployed smoothly, joining up with the line and bending it round so that the northern edge met the high slope of the rock, the native troops falling in with them. The line, then, was now complete in the north, but not in the south. There it was manned by a contingent of black levies at the furthest point from the enemy, and between their position and that of Durnford's men out in the donga lay a wide gap.

'Look, bach,' said Jenkins, nodding towards the Zulus. He could have been watching a football match, except that he was frowning and his lower lip was doing its best to swallow his moustache. 'Look at 'em. They're comin' on in that buffalo 'orn shape you told me about. Lovely to see, isn't it? Except they're so fast . . .' His voice drained away almost to a whisper. 'An' there's so many of the buggers.'

To Simon, staring wide-eyed, there was nothing to admire in the tactics of the fast-moving mass before him. Never had he seen so many armed men before and the prospect was terrifying. The plain was full of black warriors, the sun glinting and flashing from their spearheads like a thousand heliographs. Out on the flat, away from the rocky outcrop of Isandlwana itself, recent rain had made the plain soft, but even so, the force of so many feet pounding on the surface was raising dust, and as the Zulu army drew nearer and began deploying across the face of the British line, the noise was like that of a dozen express steam trains thundering at once into a station. Simon realised that the palms of his hands were perspiring and he wiped them quickly on his trousers.

It was indeed easy to detect the pattern of the attack now. Instead of a shapeless sea of men pouring across the plain, it was clear that the Zulus – still moving at a fast lope – had split by regiments into Shaka's distinctive encircling movement. The left horn was swinging wide, attempting to get round Durnford in the south. To the north, the right horn could now be seen moving out of sight behind the great rock to take the camp in the rear and cut off any retreat. In the centre, the chest of the buffalo was massing in front of the main lines of the 24th, who were now shooting coolly into their midst. There, at least, the Zulu movement had been halted.

'Get into line, you two.'

They did not know from where the order came, but Simon and Jenkins immediately unswung their rifles and joined the rear rank below the guns. The line was marked by a continuous billow of blue smoke, pierced by yellow flame as the volleys thundered out. They had fallen in on either side of a small corporal of the 24th whose cheeks were already blackened by the discharge of his Martini-Henry.

'This is a real cow, this thing,' he said confidingly in the sing-song of the Welsh valleys. 'Pulls me shoulder off every time I fire it, see.' He glanced at Simon and noticed the pips on his shoulder. 'Oh, beggin' your pardon, sir.'

Simon felt his hand trembling as he tore off the paper wrappings from the cartridges in his pouch, but he thumbed down a bullet into the grooved block behind the back sight of the rifle and levelled it to fire when the smoke lifted. As it did so, it revealed, less than 200 yards away, the heads of the Zulus, who were now kneeling, lying and taking whatever cover they could from the cruel volleys. He sighted on one giant warrior who was standing, his spear raised in defiance, the corrugations of his stomach muscles gleaming with sweat and looking like an ebony washboard in the sunlight.

'Rear rank, FIRE!' For a moment Simon hesitated, the unaccustomed weight of his rifle causing the foresight to wander away from its target. 'I *said*, fire,' said a cool voice in his ear. He turned and met the angry but puzzled face of the young subaltern.

'Sorry,' muttered Simon. He levelled the rifle again and pulled the trigger. It had been months since last he had fired a Martini-Henry and the vicious kick-back took him by surprise, turning him half round and causing him to wince as a shaft of pain shot through the shoulder wounded by the Zulu spear. Through the smoke he saw the warrior still standing. 'Damn!'

'Aim lower, old boy,' murmured the subaltern. 'These things shoot a bit high.' And then, in his high-pitched barrack-square scream: 'Rear rank, LOAD!'

Within a minute, Simon was subsumed into the orderly rhythm of an infantry front line in battle; reloading, aiming and firing in a smooth sequence choreographed by two young lieutenants whose orders ensured that each rank took aim and fired as the other was reloading. As the volleys crashed out, Simon rammed in the cartridges and fired them, beginning, at last, to understand the excitement of battle and to exult in the sense of comradeship, if not joy, of fighting with disciplined troops in action. He caught Jenkins looking at him with a half-smile playing beneath the bedraggled moustache. The Welshman gave a nod and once again put his rifle to his cheek.

The fire had been intense and virtually unanswered. Volley after volley had crashed out and torn great holes in the mass of spearmen that faced the redcoats. No warriors, however brave, could continue to run into that terrible barrage of heavy bullets. Yet Simon's elation had begun to ebb. The Zulus were still there, the gaps in their ranks immediately filled by reinforcements from the rear. Admittedly, they were lying low, but they were creeping ever nearer. The cannon and the modern rifles had not swept them away, as was supposed to happen when aboriginals came face to face with European firepower. And what about the ends of the line? Had they been turned? Simon looked left and right. The smoke was thick but the line seemed to be holding.

Now that the massed attack had been stemmed, the synchronised British volleys had been replaced by individual firing. The crack of sporadic shooting sounded almost feeble after the disciplined thunder of the volleys. Simon's mind raced. The line was holding, but it was a thin line and how long could it stand? The firepower of white soldiers was supposed to dispel the charge of native warriors long before the defenders' line was reached. But here, the Zulus had approached within spear-throwing distance of the redcoats and were now calmly waiting and taunting. They remained in overwhelming numbers. He peered through the smoke and attempted to calculate the odds – perhaps twenty to one, perhaps more.

The corporal at Simon's left caught his eye. The man's cordite-blackened face now seemed less sanguine. 'We're goin' to be all right, aren't we, sir?' he asked, almost plaintively. He nodded towards the Zulus. 'Only there's so many of them black bastards and they don't seem to be goin' away, see.'

'Don't talk rot, Corporal. Look to your front and select your target. We're all right as long as the ammunition holds out.'

As he spoke, Simon's fingers were foraging in his pouches for cartridges. Two in one pouch, five in another. Seven rounds left. He couldn't have fired sixty-three bullets since the attack began! He glanced at Jenkins. Intuitively, the Welshman held up just a handful of cartridges. Simon looked along the line again. Was it his imagination, or was the fire slackening?

'Do you have plenty of ammunition, Corporal?' he asked.

'About fifteen or sixteen rounds left, sir.'

This was serious. Looking behind him, Simon saw a white-covered wagon about five hundred paces back, towards which men were doubling, carrying their helmets like empty pails before them. It was clearly an ammunition point. He turned to Jenkins. 'Come on.' Then to the subaltern at the rear, 'We are running out of ammunition. We'll go and get some for the line.'

They ran back to the wagon, whose open end faced away from the fighting, and as they came alongside they heard the familiar voice of the quartermaster sergeant raised in peevish complaint: 'You're from the Native 'Orse. You've got your own supply wagon. This is First Battalion ammo. Bugger off.' The voice was accompanied by the sound of heavy hammering.

At the front of the wagon, the red-faced QM was addressing a black cavalryman who held out several wide-brimmed hats in supplication. Behind the QM two soldiers were crouched probing with bayonets in an attempt to break the steel bands binding the ammunition boxes. The QM caught Simon's eye. 'Can't get the bleedin' screws out,' he said, in half anger, half apology. 'They've rusted. Can't get the boxes open.'

The black trooper turned to Simon. 'Colonel Durnford's men out in the donga ain't got no bullets left, baas. I don't know where our wagon is.'

'For God's sake, Q,' shouted Simon, 'give him cartridges. These men are protecting our southern flank. If that's turned, we're done for.'

The quartermaster puffed out his cheeks. 'Can't do that without a proper requisition, sir,' he said. 'The Commissariat Officer would kill me.'

Simon climbed into the wagon. 'I'll kill you if you don't,' he hissed. 'This is no time for dockets, man.' He plunged his hand into the only open box and began filling the trooper's hats with cartridges. Behind the cavalryman, a line of soldiers of various denominations was forming, all anxious for ammunition. '352,' called Simon. 'Get in here and see if you can open these blasted boxes.'

For ten minutes the men laboured to prise open the cases. The steel bands were held firmly in place by screws that had rusted in the heavy humidity of Zululand. They proved impervious to the one small screwdriver with which the wagon was equipped, as they did to the bayonets. Only by smashing in the wooden sides with rocks could entry be gained eventually. As they struggled, the queues lengthened outside the wagon.

Simon took a moment to look at the line. There was no doubt about it, shortage of ammunition was making itself felt and the rate of fire had undoubtedly slackened. In fact, there were now no white puffs of smoke lining the edge of the donga out on the plain, and as he watched, he saw Durnford's mounted men pour out of the depression and begin to gallop back to the camp. God! Was the unthinkable about to happen? Was the line going to break?

The thought seemed to have communicated itself to the men waiting outside the wagon. Looking over their shoulders, they gradually began to break out of their orderly queues to bunch around the wagon opening, stretching their helmets and hats forward beseechingly. The air of oppression had gone. Fear was now in its place and death was edging in, just over their shoulders.

Simon turned his gaze to the south of the line. The sight of the cavalry retreating from the Zulus was too much for the men of the Natal Native Contingent who manned that section. Desperately short of ammunition, not well armed anyway, they saw the most feared warriors in South Africa storming towards them. Suddenly they broke and began streaming back up towards the neck of Isandlwana, from which led the trail to the Buffalo River drift.

'Fix your lunger, boyo.' It was Jenkins's voice in his ear. 'We're goin' to be in trouble now, look you.'

Simon pushed a handful of cartridges into his pocket, twisted the 21-inch triangular ground bayonet on to the muzzle of his rifle and jumped from the wagon. As he did so, he heard the bugle of the 24th Regiment sound the retreat and saw the line in front of him begin to fall back. To the south, the Zulus were already pouring through the gap left by the native troops. It was the turning point of the battle.

The retreat of the 1st Battalion in the centre began in disciplined fashion, with the rear rank covering as the front rank doubled back through them. But the fire was inadequate. From the heart of the Zulus facing them a strong voice called out above the noise and was answered from ten thousand throats with the great war cry '*USUTHU!*' and the thunder of spears on shields. Immediately, the whole of the Zulu centre now rose and rushed forward. This time there were no withering volleys to stop the charge and the Zulus broke through the retreating line within seconds, leaving the men of the 24th reduced to small islands of red in a surging torrent of black. The unthinkable had happened. The line had broken.

'God almighty!' cried Jenkins. He seemed transfixed by the hacking, stabbing multitude before him.

Simon looked round desperately. The two men had gained precious seconds by falling back to the ammunition wagon. 'Make for the higher ground, by the neck below the rock,' he cried. 'We might be able to hold them back there.'

'All right. You first. I'll cover your back.'

The two ran uphill towards the southern end of Isandlwana, where, at the base of the rock, a high neck was intersected by the rough trail leading back to the Buffalo and the crossing to Natal. The noise engulfed them as they scrambled up the slope: the crack of rifles, the shouting of the Zulus, the cries of the wounded and the dying, and now the whinnying of horses, for the Zulus had penetrated to the horse and cattle compound. Then one, singular sound which rose from the general hubbub – more a close, deep sigh than a groan – made Simon whirl round. He was just in time to see Jenkins fall to the ground, a throwing spear protruding from his back.

'Jenkins!' Simon sprang astride the fallen Welshman and was about to stoop to withdraw the spear when two Zulus, one of whom had obviously thrown it, were upon him. He dropped the first with the bullet he had slipped into the breech as he ran up the hill and faced the second with his bayonet. The warrior's shield was presented to him, so Simon quickly estimated where the handgrip might be and plunged the bayonet through the cowhide. He felt the point of the lunger jar on bone, sharply withdrew it and, side-stepping the raised shield, jabbed the bayonet firmly into the man's ribs.

Simon looked quickly down. Jenkins had not moved. He lay prostrate, the spear firmly embedded beneath his right shoulder blade, a trickle of blood oozing through the thick fabric of his patrol jacket. Simon bent and pulled the spear out. This produced a quickening of the blood flow from the wound, and unthinkingly, he attempted to stifle it with the flat of his hand. Jenkins did not stir. He seemed to be quite dead. A great howl of anguish sprang from Simon's throat and he thrust his hand to his mouth in despair. The Welshman's blood tasted warm and salty. The horror of losing Jenkins, the indestructible, ever-reliable Jenkins, engulfed him. 'No, no. Don't die,' he cried. The words emerged as a croak, so dry was his throat, so full of dust was his mouth. He tried to spit but could dredge up no saliva.

Then a spear clanged into the rock at his foot and Simon rose and presented his bayonet once again as the mêlée swung back towards him and engulfed him. He tried to remain astride Jenkins, thrusting desperately with his long bayonet and, where he could, ramming cartridges into the breech of his rifle and firing into the black figures around him, but the surge of the fighting took him away, up the hill.

Nothing in Simon's short life – his childhood imaginings, his months of disciplined training, his adventures so far in Zululand – had prepared him for this battle. All around him leaped the black warriors, hacking and thrusting, their spearheads scarlet, their bodies glistening and their yellow eyeballs rolling and painting them, as though with a last distinguishing mark, as the devil's mercenaries. The acrid smell of cordite, the heat, the dust and the din of screams, battle cries and – less frequent now – rifle shots all merged into a barbaric assault on the senses, horrifying beyond any one man's imagination. It was a hell's kitchen of a blood bath that defied rationality, and now, a kind of hysterical exultation took possession of Simon, turning him into a hyperactive combatant, plunging repeatedly at his assailants until, once again, he somehow gained a moment's respite in the middle of the maelstrom.

Drawing in deep draughts of hot air, he looked desperately for Jenkins, even crouching in a desperate attempt to catch a glimpse of his body on the ground through the thicket of legs. By now he was completely disoriented and was only saved – for an undefended back in that free-for-all meant death sooner or later – by the arrival of about a dozen red-coated infantry-men, fighting coolly shoulder to shoulder in a circle and inching up the hill under the command of a bearded sergeant, whom Fonthill vaguely recognised.

'Come in 'ere quick, Mr Fonthill sir,' the veteran shouted. 'Got any ammo?'

Simon dug into his pockets and hurriedly handed round most of what remained of the cartridges. 'I must get back,' he gasped, gesturing downhill. 'My man's gone down there.'

The sergeant shook his head. 'No way you can do that, sir,' he said. 'You'd never get through, and anyway, these bastards disembowel the wounded and the dead as they go. I've seen 'em doing it.' He looked with approval at Simon's rifle. 'Lucky you've got a lunger. The Zulus don't like the bayonet. You wouldn't 'ave lasted five minutes with a sword. Now,' he shouted to the others, 'those with ammo pick off the buggers with the throwing spears. We'll take the rest with the bayonets. On the left there, keep edging up this bloody 'ill.'

Shoulder to shoulder, elbow to elbow, the little group slowly made its way up to the neck below the rock, while the tide of warriors ebbed and flowed all around them. Sometimes it appeared as though the Zulus seemed to ignore them and they were able to shuffle onwards without hindrance. But mostly the warriors were all around them, thrusting with their assegais or swinging their knobkerries in great loops. Simon occasionally caught glimpses of other knots of redcoats, standing back to back and presenting their bayonets to their assailants, but the multitude of Zulus pressing around them made it impossible to link up to form a more sophisticated defence.

A thrown spear caught the sergeant through the throat and he sank to the ground coughing, his beard turning bright red. Simon, brutalised and machine-like, stepped over him, his weary arms holding up the long rifle, presenting and thrusting, presenting and thrusting. It was true, the Zulus seemed to respect the bayonet – and with some reason. With lunger fitted, Simon's rifle had become a stabbing weapon just under six feet in length, compared to the assegai's four feet, and time after time, his adversary would fade away to find easier pickings elsewhere. But it was desperately tiring work and Simon's arms and shoulders were now aching with the effort of wielding his heavy weapon and he could hardly see for the perspiration that poured down into his eyes. As he fought, the words 'Jenkins is dead' echoed through his head. His friend, his only real friend, had gone. His own fate hardly seemed to matter.

Once he saw, rising above the crowd, a young red-coated drummer boy skewered on a spear and held up as some sort of trophy. The boy could not have been more than thirteen years old and his eyes were wide open, as if in astonishment. Then he was gone.

The little circle was reduced to eight now, they were out of ammunition and fighting only with bayonet and rifle butt. Nevertheless, they had reached the summit of the neck, and in another brief break in the fighting, Simon was able to look about him once more. To the west, down the hill, most of the defence had been completely eliminated and the warriors were racing through the tents and commissariat lines, looting and shouting. There was no sign of Jenkins, of course, and there was no way he could have survived. Up the ledges of the great rock, other small bands were still holding out, firing and bayoneting. To his right, Simon observed a middle-aged officer with drooping moustaches and an injured arm methodically directing fire on Zulus – the impi's right horn? – who had swept round the eastern side of the rock. He was doing so, Simon realised, in an attempt to keep clear an escape route to the south-east, the track to Rorke's Drift and the Buffalo crossing, along which a motley line of fugitives were riding, running and hobbling, including a battery of artillery which had somehow managed to limber up before the Zulus were upon them.

Riderless horses were now cutting small channels through the mêlée and they had the effect of breaking up the little groups of organised resistance that remained as they charged, eyes wide with fear, in different directions. The moustached officer had fallen and the organised firing ended. Simon stumbled over the red-coated bodies of two officers. He recognised Lieutenants Pope and Godwin-Austin, great friends who, inseparable in life, now lay side by side in death, their monocles still firmly clasped in their eye sockets. The carnage continued but the battle was over. It was every man for himself now.

His comrades gone and Jenkins dead, Simon faced his own end with a coolness that surprised him. He was amazed that he had lasted this long. He had fought and he would go on fighting until he was brought down. Fumbling in his pouch, he discovered three cartridges. He pressed one into the breech and walked down the trail, carrying the rifle at the point of balance. Calmly he aimed at and brought down a Zulu who was chasing a limping infantryman, then a second who appeared, spear raised, before him. Pressing the last round into the breech, he fired at a third warrior but missed. Only the bayonet now.

Then, close behind him, he heard a horse's shrill scream. He turned in time to see a riderless horse crash into a small knot of Zulus and scatter them, bringing one to the ground as a hoof caught his knee. This had the effect of halting the animal as well as dispersing the warriors and Simon was able to grab the trailing bridle and clumsily insert one foot into the stirrup. There was blood on the saddle but a tasselled cavalry sabre still in its scabbard. As Simon hauled himself astride, he felt for the first time a glimmer of hope. Drawing the sword, he dug in his heels and set the horse down the track to the south-east.

The original herdsman's track had been broadened by Chelmsford's wagons on the advance but Simon could see that it was now completely blocked by Zulus. The road to Rorke's Drift was no place to be. Most of the fugitives had peeled off and were trying to make for the Buffalo across country. The thin line stretched away: soldiers in various uniforms, although none in the scarlet of the 24th Regiment; some cavalry, their horses wide-eyed, their riders low on their necks; infantry, most of them black, some attempting to run, some plodding resignedly; horses, their saddles empty, resisting every attempt to catch them. Everywhere, however, were the Zulus, leaping from the rocks at the side, running in and out of the fugitives on the marshy ground, stabbing and hacking at the hurrying men.

The tragic tableau stretched ahead as far as Simon could see, the sorry remnants of Pulleine's command being harried and cut down as they ran the gauntlet along the four miles to the Buffalo River. Despite the advantage of being mounted, Simon realised he would be lucky to survive on that route. Pulling his steed's head round, he set the horse to gallop back the way he had come. It was a gamble, but he reasoned that by going against the flow of the fugitives, out on to the plain, he might have a chance of surviving and even, perhaps, of making Chelmsford's column that had marched off to the east.

It proved surprisingly easy. Flailing his sabre at the few Zulus who tried to spear him down, Simon was quickly away from the scene of the battle. Looking over his shoulder, he realised that those warriors who were not pursuing the fugitives were looting the tents and the wagons. Some had already been put to the torch and, judging by the whoops, he realised that the liquor store had been found and breached. He slowed the horse to a walk and rode towards the low hills he could see ahead of him.

Out on that plain, Simon felt strangely alone without Jenkins. He forced himself not to think of his dead friend but to consider what the Zulus might do now, after their great victory – and what a victory it must seem to them! Never before could such a body of trained European soldiers, armed with the latest weapons and with veteran infantrymen at its core, have been wiped away so completely by native spearmen. Simon shook his head sadly. The Zulus must have taken frightening casualties from those volleys of the 24th but they so outnumbered the British column that Cetswayo's army would still remain intact and would waste little time in wiping out those pathetic fugitives on the trail. What would it do now? Come across the plain behind him and attack Chelmsford, or . . . Simon suddenly stiffened in the saddle. Of course! That right horn of the buffalo that swept round behind Isandlwana – it would mop up the survivors of the battle and then go on to attack Natal. That great fear of Lamb's that the Zulus would pour across the frontiers of Zululand into the lush pastures of Natal had become a reality at last.

He looked behind him. He had ridden too far now to see the camp, or what was left of it, although the great finger of Isandlwana still pointed to the sky, but there was no sign of warriors following him, no black ants swarming across the plain to finish off Chelmsford. Simon reined in his horse to stop and think. Cetswayo had probably sent a separate force to decoy the British general into the hills ahead and ambush him there. He remembered Dunn's words, 'He's no fool, you know . . .' Not a fool – more a skilled general. He had divided the British force and eaten it up piecemeal. He would rest his warriors for a while and then let them loose on Natal. This offensive move was the best defence he could possibly make of his homeland, for both of the other columns were bound to turn back to protect the British province. Simon gave a grim smile. They had called Shaka 'the Black Napoleon' but it suited the shrewd Cetswayo better.

Simon looked up at the sun. He wondered how long the King and his generals would rest the victorious army before it crossed the Buffalo into Natal. Perhaps, if he could ford the river well east of the Rorke's Drift crossing, he would be able to ride to the mission station and give the alarm so that some sort of defence could be mounted at – what was the place further back there? Ah yes, Helpmakaar – in time to rebuff the Zulus and re-call the other columns. He glanced to his right, to the south. It looked easy riding to the Buffalo and his horse was still comparatively fresh. He pulled its head round.

As he did so, a flash of light to his left made him pause. He stood in the stirrups, shielded his eyes and focused hard. There it was again. Zulus? Possibly, but the light was not sharp or bright, as reflected off a spearhead. It was duller and – yes, it flickered again. More like sunlight bouncing back from a gun barrel or a horse's harness. He sat for a moment, undecided, then dug in his heels and rode towards it. If it was Chelmsford, he must warn him. If it was a Zulu patrol, they would not have horses and he could outride them.

In twenty minutes he could make out a small party of dismounted horsemen, and in another five he realised that he was approaching a British patrol which had stopped to take refreshment, for a small fire had been kindled. He rode up to them and, with some difficulty, slipped to the ground.

'Who are you?' he demanded of a sergeant who rose to greet him. 'And where are you from?'

Before the sergeant could answer, a familiar voice came from the back of the group: 'All right, Sergeant, I'm coming.' And thrusting from the back, where he had been adjusting a saddle cinch, strode Lieutenant Colonel Covington.

Recognition was not immediately mutual, for while Simon could not fail to know who stood before him, a puzzled frown puckering that handsome brow, Covington took a moment to take in the bedraggled sight that confronted him: the gaunt, sun-browned and somehow familiar face, the long, unkempt hair atop a dust-covered figure and boots that gaped at the soles. Who on earth . . . and then: 'Good God. Fonthill!'

'Colonel,' said Simon. 'Look. There's been a terrible disaster at Isandlwana. The Zulus have attacked and wiped out the whole column. Virtually everyone has been killed. You must tell the General. I am going to ride into Natal and warn the settlers there, for I fear that Cetswayo is planning to cross the Buffalo and attack them.'

The blue eyes stared at him unbelievingly. 'What's this you're saying? The whole column wiped out? That's impossible. The General left seventeen hundred well-armed men there.'

Simon sighed. 'I know, sir. They've been overwhelmed.' His voice began to break. 'The killing was awful.'

'Don't talk rot, man. Look, where the hell have you been, anyway? You're wearing a uniform jacket, civilian trousers, and what's left of your boots wouldn't grace a rubbish bin. You're an absolute disgrace.'

Simon was aware that the members of the patrol were gathering round, listening to the conversation. 'I've been held a prisoner by Cetswayo but I escaped and got to the camp just before the attack. There is no time to be lost.' He spoke with tired emphasis. 'You must tell the General that he is in great danger, because I believe he has been lured away by the Zulus, who will now attack him. I must go to Rorke's Drift and Helpmakaar to warn them.'

He half turned to mount his horse, but as Simon had been speaking, incredulity had been growing in Covington's face. That arrogant sneer that Simon remembered so well replaced the look of astonishment and the Colonel grasped Simon's shoulder roughly and swung him round. 'Oh no, Fonthill,' he said. 'You're not going anywhere. You've been up to your old tricks, haven't you? Running away again. I don't believe a word of this rubbish. Sergeant, place him under arrest. This time you will be court-martialled, young man. I'll see to that.'

As Covington spoke, a great anger began to well up inside Simon. The agonies of the day – Jenkins's death, the horror of the battle, the memories of brave men dying – all merged in his mind into a great hatred of the sneering figure before him, who was now gripping his shoulder so tightly that he could feel the pain start again from the spear wound. Simon knocked away Covington's arm, swivelled from the hip and punched the man as hard as he could. It was a perfect uppercut, taking the Colonel cleanly on the point of the jaw and knocking him prostrate on the ground, where he lay, momentarily stunned.

Simon turned coolly to the sergeant. 'Now, where is the General?'

The sergeant's mouth was hanging open. What he had heard and seen seemed to have stupefied him.

'For God's sake, man,' Simon shouted. 'Where is the General?'

'Ah, er ... he's about twelve miles or so back, up in the hills, er, sir.'

'Right.' Simon gathered the reins of his horse and put one foot in the stirrup. He gestured to Covington, who was beginning to stir. 'Tell that bloody man when he recovers that I've ridden to the border to give warning about the Zulus attacking. And tell him from me that if he doesn't ride back now and warn the General, I will make sure that he is the one who is court-martialled, not me.'

The sergeant suddenly seemed to remember that his commanding officer had been struck. 'Hey,' he said. 'You can't ride off. I don't know who you are but you've just struck a superior officer and I've got to place you under arrest.'

Simon swung into the saddle and looked down at the gaping faces below him. 'Balls,' he said. He dug in his heels and set off for Rorke's Drift.

Chapter 15

Simon pushed his horse as fast as he dared. There had been no attempt at pursuit by Covington's men but he knew that he had little time if he was to reach the mission station at Rorke's Drift before the Zulus and give warning so that some sort of defence could be mounted at Helpmakaar. He had no idea of how many men Chelmsford would have left at the river crossing, but it was highly unlikely that it would be enough to stem the horde of warriors who would cross the Buffalo, so his only realistic hope was that the invading impi would stop to take snuff and regroup before making the crossing. It was just possible that he could arrive in time to help the mission station garrison pull back to Helpmakaar. He took out the old timepiece that had somehow survived his many vicissitudes in Zululand. Two forty. God, it was only three hours or so since he and Jenkins had ridden into camp! A lurid, horror-filled lifetime had been packed into that time. Jenkins . . . Covington. What was the penalty for striking a senior officer? He forced himself to look ahead and not back.

He reached the Buffalo to find that it was in flood, with angry brown water bubbling between rocks. He turned his horse to the north and, after an anxious few minutes, found a track leading down to what, in normal times, would have been a drift. Now the crossing looked ugly but he put the reluctant horse into the strong current and found that by part swimming and part scrambling they could reach the safety of the Natal bank. Kicking in his heels, he forced the animal to climb the steep bank ahead, and at the top turned north again, following the riverbank for a while. Nandi had told him that the mission was set about 300 yards back from Rorke's Drift beneath a large hill known to the missionaries as Oskarberg, which was distinctive enough to be seen for some distance. Accordingly, he rode away from the river, in the hope of avoiding any parties of Zulus who might have crossed upstream and who would, he felt sure, follow the bank to the Rorke's Drift crossing.

After an hour of difficult riding, he crested a hill and there, about half a mile ahead of him, loomed the swelling that must be Oskarberg. But he had no eyes for that, for his vantage point also gave him a distant view of the Zulu side of the river and of the track that undoubtedly led down to Rorke's Drift. There, covering the gentle incline into Zululand, as far as his eye could see, sprawled hundreds – thousands? – of Zulus. He had arrived at the crossing at the same time as the Zulu horn. He was too far away to see the condition of the impis but the question now was: were the Zulus resting for a moment before making the crossing and launching the attack, or were they preparing to retreat back into Zululand? He protected his eyes with his hand and focused hard. No, clearly they were resting. If they had made an attack and been successful they would surely be on their way into Natal; if they had been repulsed, they would be limping back into their homeland. They were probably taking snuff and, as Simon had learned from Dunn, the light narcotics they often imbibed before a battle to prepare themselves for combat. Once more he dug his heels into the flanks of his tired horse and urged him on.

Twenty minutes later he was looking down at the mission station from the crest of the Oskarberg. To his amazement, the garrison of the little station had not left for Helpmakaar. On the contrary, they had clearly decided to stay and fight, for as he watched, he saw preparations being made to defend the station. The post consisted of two low thatched buildings about thirty yards apart, facing the river, with a square stone kraal at one end to act as a cattle pen. Soldiers were now manhandling wagons and what Simon recognised as large boxes of biscuits and mealie bags to form two defensive lines, linking the two buildings. Obviously this had been a supply base for Chelmsford's army and these supplies were now being pressed into service to defend the post. But – Simon's mind raced – hadn't Nandi mentioned that this was a forward hospital, too? Were the sick and wounded still inside or had they been sent back to Helpmakaar? He tried to count the able men working – less than a hundred, although there were some coloured horsemen milling around outside the barricade. The fools! How could they withstand an attack by four thousand Zulus? They would have had pickets out at the crossing and would know how many warriors they would have to face. Why hadn't they left? He urged his horse down the steep hillside, taking it at an angle, for the surface was made up of treacherous shingle and stone.

As he reached the bottom, a sad-faced officer with moustache and sideburns and wearing the uniform of a lieutenant of the 24th came forward to meet him. Simon recognised Gonville Bromhead, from the 2nd Battalion, and was not surprised to see him. Bromhead, considerably older than Simon, was regarded as a competent officer and came from a distinguished military family, but his promotion prospects had long been hampered by a chronic deafness which meant that he – and therefore his company – was often allocated tasks which would not impose heavy demands upon him. He had obviously been left behind to look after the hospital away from the difficulties and glory of the advance into Zululand. An invading column was no place for an ear trumpet.

Bromhead raised his heavy black brows. 'Fonthill! Didn't expect to see you here. Where did you come from?'

'Isandlwana. There's been a terrible massacre. Do you know about it?'

'The battle? Is that where you've come from? I hear there's been a terrible to-do.'

Simon raised his voice. 'There are a couple of Zulu impis who are about to cross the river to attack you. Why didn't you leave? Oh, never mind. Are you in command here?'

'Command? Me? No. Major Spalding. But he's gone to Helpmakaar. Chap called Chard, a lieutenant of engineers, is in command. He's senior to me, you see.' Bromhead looked over Simon's shoulder. 'Look here. You'd better come inside the perimeter. We've been told that a whole Zulu corps is coming this way. Did you see 'em?'

Simon nodded resignedly but led his horse behind Bromhead through the last gap in the defences. As they passed through, shirt-sleeved men of Bromhead's company pushed a couple of hundred-pound biscuit boxes into the gap and then threw equally heavy sacks full of mealies on top of them. The perimeter was now closed.

Lieutenant Chard, a big, black-bearded man, approached Simon and the formal introductions were made by Bromhead. 'God,' Chard said, 'you look all in. But I'm afraid you've fallen from the frying pan of one battle into the fire of another.'

Simon shook his head. 'Don't worry about that. But does Helpmakaar know about the defeat and have they been warned that the Zulus are on their way?'

'Oh yes.' His voice took on a sarcastic note. 'Plenty of gallant soldiers have left Isandlwana to ride by us and break the news in Natal.'

Simon sighed. 'I thought I would be the first,' he said. 'But look, I think you should get out right away and make for Helpmakaar.'

'No, we thought about leaving, but we have sick and wounded here and we could never have made it to Helpmakaar by wagon. The Zulus would have overrun us in the open and cut us to pieces. We decided to stay here and fight it out. We have plenty of ammunition and we can hold them up all right.'

Simon looked around him. The little post hardly presented the appearance of an impregnable fortress. A shelf ran round the base of the Oskarberg about four hundred yards away, high enough to command the interior of the post – and Simon had seen the Zulus at Isandlwana picking up Martini-Henry rifles. If they could shoot accurately, they could cause problems. Mealie bags had been thrust underneath the wagons, and the two lines of boxes and sacks looked substantial enough, but they stood less than five feet high. The two buildings formed the end of the redoubt and jutted out vulnerably. As Simon watched, he saw bayonets breaking through the plaster walls as rifle loopholes were made from within.

'How many men do you have?' asked Simon.

Chard pulled at his beard. 'I've got the eighty chaps of Bromhead's B Company, plus about thirty odds and sods of sick and wounded, some who can fight, some who can't.' He nodded to the building at the western end of the post. 'That's the hospital and the weakest of them are in there. Difficult to defend – lots of little rooms with doors and windows facing outwards but no interconnecting corridor – but I've put a handful of men in with the sick to cover 'em. They've got the worst job but we've just got to do the best we can.'

He gestured to where a string of Natal Native Horse were trotting round the base of the Oskarberg to ride towards the drift. 'These chaps are Durnford's men who rode in from the battle and I've sent them out as a cavalry screen to hold up the Zulu attack. They are a godsend. And, as you can see,' he pointed to where native troops armed with rifles outnumbered the infantrymen of the 24th at the barricades, 'we have also picked up a whole bunch of the Natal Native Contingent. In all I've got about three hundred and fifty men. Just about enough to line the walls and keep the Zulus out. Now,' he smiled at Simon, 'you can probably make it if you ride to Helpmakaar. Or you can stay and help us. But you'd better make your mind up fast.'

Simon sighed. 'Of course I'll stay.' He was tired, his shoulder throbbed and his mind was in turmoil. Jenkins had been killed and he had hit Covington. He might as well stay and die with the rest of them – there was certainly no hope of surviving in this ramshackle little fort. 'Put me where I can be of most use.'

Chard was about to reply when the horsemen who had trotted out to defend the crossing and the base of the Oskarberg were seen galloping back to the post. But instead of reining in at the barricades, they rode straight past – their faces creased in fear and their eyes wide. Their European officer pulled up and shouted across the barrier to Chard: 'There are thousands of the bastards coming, man, and my lot have had enough. They won't take orders.' And with that, he dug in his spurs and rode off towards Helpmakaar, following his men.

A patter of shots was heard as the last of the riders rounded the hill, and that was enough for the native infantrymen manning the barricades. They threw away their rifles, vaulted the barricades and followed the mounted troops up the track towards Helpmakaar and safety. An angry shout went up from the men of the 24th at the mealie bags and some of them fired their rifles after the running men.

Chard looked around in horror. His barricades were now stripped of more than half of their defenders and huge gaps had appeared in the line. 'My God!' he murmured, as much to himself as to Simon. 'I'm down to a hundred and ten men.'

He turned to Simon. 'I don't have enough bodies to man three hundred yards of barricades now,' he said. 'Take six men and stretch a line of biscuit boxes across the middle of the compound from the front of the storehouse here to the middle of the wall over there, to bisect the yard. We can fall back here when we can't hold the line any longer. We'll just have to leave the poor devils in the hospital to look after themselves. Quickly now, they'll be on us soon.'

Indeed they were. Simon had hardly begun to detail a handful of men from the wall when he heard a cry from a lookout: 'Here they come. Black as hell and thick as grass.' He looked up and saw the first impi swing into view around the flank of the Oskarberg, running in that flat, loose lope and aiming straight for the back walls of the post.

Bromhead's men opened fire at about 450 yards – the distance to the base of the hill had formed a good measuring point for the setting of the rifle sights – and the effect was immediate. Simon saw warriors leap high into the air as the heavy bullets hit them and then go somersaulting back into the ranks of the men running behind. The Zulus ran forward to within fifty or sixty yards of the storehouse, but the attack faltered as they were caught in the cruel crossfire from the wagons and the loopholes in the building. Many of them took whatever cover they could find in a ditch and behind a deserted little outhouse, but the remainder carried on running around to the little hospital, where they settled down and began a steady fire – Simon was right, many Martini-Henrys had been found to add to the muzzle-loaders – on the defenders within, and on the soldiers who manned the low biscuit and mealie bag wall that had been built to afford protection to the open veranda on that side.

The bisecting wall within the compound finished, Simon sent his men back to the wall on the north side, where the pressure seemed heaviest. The post was now surrounded, so he too ran to supplement the thin line of defenders at that north wall. Then he stopped. He realised he had no rifle, just the cavalry sabre that he had tucked awkwardly into his trouser belt. That, he knew, would be useless against the thrusting assegais, so he threw it away and hurried to Bromhead, who was just marshalling a small party to charge with bayonets to help the defenders at the wall by the hospital.

'Bromhead,' he screamed, 'where can I get a rifle and bayonet?'

The older man peered at him. 'Yes, of course,' he said. 'Do come. But you'll need a rifle and bayonet. Look.' He pointed to where a young soldier lay behind the mealie bags, his shoulder shattered from a musket slug, his rifle and bayonet lying by his side. 'Take that.'

Simon ran across to the infantryman, whom he recognised. 'Jones,' he asked, 'are you all right?'

The young man grimaced but nodded. 'Just 'urts me when I laugh, see, sir. Eh, where 'ave you come from, then?'

'Just over there,' said Simon, and he picked up the rifle, dug into Jones's pouch for cartridges and doubled away to join Bromhead, who was forming up his little platoon.

'Right,' shouted Bromhead, 'we're going to drive those chaps off the wall by the hospital with bayonets. At the double – now!' In the lead, carrying only a revolver, the deaf officer began to run, and Simon joined the charging group of some twenty men following him.

The box and sack wall at the northern face of the hospital bulged outwards where a little salient had been formed to protect the veranda. The defenders here had been driven back, and the Zulus, by sheer pressure of numbers, had mounted the barricade and were now stabbing and hacking at the little group of infantrymen, who had had no time to reload and were countering fiercely with bayonets. Bromhead's men jumped over the back line of bags with a whoop and the sheer force of their charge and the extra bayonets drove the Zulus back over the wall.

Simon found himself lagging behind the charge, not for want of courage but because he could hardly summon breath or energy. Nevertheless, he plunged into the fray with a recklessness born of desperation. He thrust his bayonet into a grey-haired warrior who was raising his assegai to strike down Bromhead, who was himself coolly taking aim with his revolver to his left, seemingly unaware of his vulnerability. The few yards of cordoned ground between the barricade and the hospital veranda were now a cauldron of violence, and for the second time that day, Simon inhaled the sour scent of battle – the dust, the sweat, the indefinable smell of fear – and heard again the screams of men in pain and dying. Panting with exertion, but still caught in the madness of the charge, he climbed on to the mealie bags and jabbed down with his bloodstained bayonet at the hedge of assegais below him, stabbing again and again.

He felt someone tug at his jacket, and Bromhead shouted above the din: 'We can't hold this place. Fall back into the compound.'

The little party, together with the original defenders of the salient, ran back and scrambled over the short wall of bags and boxes running from the outer barricade to the inner corner of the hospital which had been erected as a fall-back line of defence. From it, they could still command the veranda, with its vulnerable doors and windows, but they could do nothing, of course, to take the pressure off the defenders manning the western and southern sides of the hospital. Their retreat set up a great howl from the Zulus facing them, who now climbed the outer line and hurled themselves against the second barricade.

Simon stood at the wall firing as fast as he could at the black bodies in front of him. He pressed bullet after bullet into the breech, working the ejector lever rapidly until the rifle barrel began to burn his fingers with the heat of the firing. Still the Zulus came on, showing incredible bravery. However, the defenders at this shorter wall were now virtually elbow to elbow and, well supplied with ammunition, they were able to create a wall of gunfire that eventually daunted the warriors on this narrow front, forcing them to fall back and take cover behind the outer wall.

Behind him, Simon heard Chard's deep voice: 'Fonthill, take four men and support the wall behind you. Quickly, now.'

Tapping the shoulders of four men at intervals, Simon turned with them and ran to the north wall to fill ominous spaces there. The Zulus were massed in even greater density. Here they had to climb a ledge on which the barricade had been placed and they were dashing forward to clamber over their own dead and using the bodies to climb up the ledge, thrusting upwards with their assegais, trying to grab the rifles and bayonets that flashed above them, hacking and clawing until they were shot or bayoneted in their turn and fresh attackers pressed them down. Simon found now that there was little time to load his rifle, only time to jab with the long bayonet and often space enough only to swing the rifle butt up in a series of vicious uppercuts. He was cut in the thigh by a jabbing assegai but, in the frenzy and the desperate exhilaration of the fighting, he hardly noticed it.

The attackers fell away briefly and Simon became aware of a new danger. A group of warriors had scrambled up the lower slopes of the Oskarberg to a shelf high above the perimeter wall and now began a steady fire upon the defenders. The fire seemed to be coming mainly from old muzzle-loaders and the aim was inaccurate. It had little effect on the men manning the south wall, who presented only their heads for targets, but the hard-pressed defenders on the north wall could be seen more easily and several were now being hit in the back. Simon helped to carry a stricken man to the storehouse, where, on the inner veranda, a casualty station had been erected. He laid the man down, lifted his own head wearily and looked into the black eyes of Surgeon Major Reynolds, his face streaked with sweat, a bloody scalpel in his hand.

'Good to see you again, Fonthill,' said the surgeon with the faintest of smiles. 'If you feel a little unwell, boy, take a few deep breaths and touch your toes with your hands.'

'What?' gasped Simon. 'Oh no, sir. I'm quite all right now, thank you.'

'Glad to hear it. Get back to the wall.'

The light was now fading and the threat from the snipers on the hill diminished as darkness crept over the mission at Rorke's Drift. As it did so, however, a rosy glow began to light the compound. It came from the roof of the hospital, whose thatch began to crackle and roar as burning spears plunged into it, spreading the fire from end to end and turning the western end of the beleaguered post into a brightly lit amphitheatre. The flames illuminated the scarlet jackets of the defenders at the walls and gave a demonic aspect to the black faces of the attackers as they thrust and stabbed.

The ferocity of the attacks never faltered and now came without pause from every side. Wave after wave of Zulus flung themselves against the boxes and sacks of the barricades and the stone walls of the two buildings. As they were cut down by the fire and bayonets of the defenders, so their places were taken by equally fearless warriors who came surging forward under the direction of inDunas who were watching the mêlée from vantage points on the Oskarberg and from the gardens of the old mission.

Once, looking over the black faces confronting him at the wall, Simon caught a quick glimpse of a corpulent Zulu on a horse down on the track below and raised his rifle to bring him down, but the inDuna trotted away under cover before he could fire. Later, he was to learn that this was no inDuna, but the King's brother, Prince Dabulamanzi kaMpande, the commander of the three regiments who had disobeyed Cetswayo's orders by crossing into Natal and were now attacking Rorke's Drift. The only justification for such insubordination would be victory. The Prince had to keep urging his men forward, and in truth, there was every reason to do so. The mission post had never been built with defence in mind. It consisted merely of the two small buildings, set apart, and the line of boxes and bags that Chard had hurriedly thrown together to link them provided an insubstantial and artificial line of defence, too long at about 300 yards overall for the handful of men to defend adequately. The tiny post was an island, surrounded by a sea of black bodies stretching back twenty or thirty men deep, with further reserves waiting to take their turn in the next wave of attacks.

Simon could see as much as he ran quickly back from the wall to intercept a chaplain, his dog collar smudged with blood, who was walking behind the lines coolly dispensing cartridges from a large open haversack hung round his neck.

'Bullets please, Padre,' he said. 'God, this is damned warm work.'

'Do not take the Lord's name in vain, Lieutenant,' chided the chaplain. 'There is never, never any excuse for blasphemy. Help yourself and fill your pouches. Fire straight and true in the Lord's name.'

'Er, yes. Thank you, Padre.' As Simon took handfuls of

cartridges by the light of the burning thatch and filled his pouch he scanned the walls. It was obvious to him that the full length of the barricades could no longer be held by the number of men available. Would it be obvious to Chard? His question was answered immediately, as a sergeant ran to him. 'Mr Chard's compliments, sir,' he said, 'we are to instruct half the men manning the north and south walls to fall back behind the inner line of boxes on the first bugle and the rest on the second. You are to take the north wall and me the south. They will be covered in retreat. Understood, sir?'

'Very good, Sergeant.'

Simon ran to the north wall and, as best he could during the fighting, gave the instructions. He saw that Chard had lined the inner bisecting wall with a reserve of infantrymen, who, rifles at the aim, were poised to give covering fire to the retreating defenders from the walls. Then a bugle sounded and every other man on each wall ducked and ran back to the inner bastion. As they did so, the first volley rang out, sending bullets into the spaces they had vacated at the barricades. Then the second call was made and the process was repeated. The fire was too hot for the Zulus to pursue and they stayed behind the bag and box ramparts, howling in derision at the retreat.

The defenders were now concentrated into the eastern end of the post, where the storehouse formed part of the southern and eastern face – luckily the veranda here faced inward and the stone walls of the building, pierced with rifle slots, formed a solid bastion. The hospital, however, was now isolated, thirty yards away across the compound, and was even more vulnerable than before, in that crossfire could no longer be brought to bear along the veranda with its outward-facing doors, against which the Zulus were now hurling themselves. The roof of the hospital was completely ablaze, sending flames shooting skywards and greasy black smoke curling across the empty compound.

Simon seized Chard, whose face was now stained as black as his beard. 'What about the poor devils in there?' He gestured. 'Can't we make a bayonet charge and get them out?'

Chard gave him a cool look and Simon wondered how much experience the engineer could possibly have had in this sort of hand-to-hand fighting. What would he know about a bayonet charge?

'Don't talk rot, man,' said Chard. 'To do that we would have to leave the perimeters and get out there amongst them. With our backs exposed we wouldn't last five minutes. Even if we could last long enough to get to the doors and open them, it would take ages to drag out the sick and the wounded. We would be cut down in a flash. No.' He bared his teeth in a grimace as he looked at the burning building. 'We've just got to hope that they can cut their way through the walls inside from room to room and then get through that window there.' He gestured to an opening facing into the inner compound, about six feet from the ground. 'If they can get out, we might be able to cover them as they crawl across the ground to the wall. If not . . . no – look!'

He pointed to the window, and Simon saw the frame thrown back and an axe wielded from within, widening the opening. Bricks, stone and mortar crashed to the ground and a grim, smoke-blackened face peered out. 'God,' shouted Simon. 'They're alive!'

Immediately Chard sprang forward and gave instructions to the men lining the barricade facing inwards into the compound.

The ground was clear of Zulus, who were still crouching on the outward sides of the deserted north and south barricades, fearful of the power of the Martini-Henrys at such short range – although their own sharpshooters were now levelling a spasmodic fire from the top of the walls. Then Simon saw that one man had refused to leave the compound when the bugles sounded. Corporal William Allen – Simon remembered him from Brecon – emerged from the corner and stood underneath the enlarged window, shooting at any Zulu who put his head above the parapet.

Another red-coated figure familiar to Simon now appeared from the window and, with one arm hanging useless and blood-stained, Private Frederick Hitch dropped awkwardly down and gestured up above for others to follow him.

So began one of the most remarkable and heroic escapes in British military history. One by one, a broken procession of sick and wounded half fell, half lowered themselves from the window. Private Hitch, faint himself with loss of blood, took the weight of their fall with his body, while Corporal Allen fired repeatedly at Zulus who lunged around from the front of the hospital. The men at the line of boxes thirty yards away kept up a withering fire along the top of the deserted barricades to deter the Zulu marksmen and spear-men.

Watching, Simon marvelled at the courage of the men, many of them wounded or in high fever, who wriggled out of the window into the open compound and that flaring night. One by one, eleven patients dropped down, nine of them helped to safety across the dangerous no-man's-land of the enclosure by Allen and Hitch or the handful of fit men inside the hospital who had survived the room-to-room fighting and who now escaped through the window themselves. One trooper of the Natal Mounted Police was too crippled to walk and attempted to cross the compound by dragging himself along on his elbows. He had reached the centre when a Zulu vaulted the barricade, darted forward and sank his assegai into the small of the trooper's back before a bullet brought him down. Private Robert Jones was the last of the hospital defenders to drop down. As he did so, the roof collapsed behind him.

A small gap had been created in the biscuit box line so that the sick men could be dragged through, and Simon helped to pull the survivors to safety. One man, his face flushed with fever and still in his nightshirt, grabbed Simon's shirt and pulled his face close.

'Do you know what they did to Joseph Williams, then?' he muttered hoarsely, his eyes wide.

Simon shook his head. 'Don't talk about it,' he said. 'The doctor's here.'

'Bugger the doctor. Williams was holding the door, see, as we crawled through the hole in the wall that John Williams had made. Then the door fell in, and Joseph was left to keep the buggers out with his bayonet. I was lookin' back through the hole when I saw them pull his rifle and 'im with it, look you. Then,' the man's voice broke, 'they ripped off his jacket, see, an' they 'eld poor old Joseph while they stuck spears in his belly, openin' it up. Oh, it was terrible, terrible . . .' and his voice died away and he sank back. Simon held the man's hand tightly and beckoned an orderly.

Then, suddenly, the sick man's eyes opened again and he sat up. 'From room to room we went, see, with John Williams choppin' away with his axe to make holes so's we could crawl

319

through. We'd only just get through one hole when the Zulus would break into the room we'd just left. My mate Hookie was kneelin' at one hole with his bayonet keepin' 'em back while we crawled through the next. 'Orrible it was. 'Orrible. Did I tell you what they did to Joseph Williams, then?'

'Yes, you did,' said Simon. 'Don't think about it, bach, there's a good fellow. The doctor will give you something.' Then the orderly came and took the man to Surgeon Major Reynolds, who was working grimly on the veranda by the light of the flames.

The perimeter now had contracted to the enclosure in front of the storehouse and the stone-built cattle kraal at its rear. With the yard abandoned, the snipers on the Oskarberg had lost their flame-lit targets on the north wall and they streamed down to join their comrades. The collapse of the hospital freed several hundreds more, who circled the compound looking for a weakness.

They found it in the cattle kraal. It had been comparatively neglected, and the little garrison there had been able to hold its own, despite the fact that the stone walls were not high and were not surmounted by mealie bag embrasures. Now, however, the glare of the blazing hospital silhouetted the defenders, while the Zulus came out of the darkness. Reinforced, they now attacked in a series of savage rushes, boiling up from the blackness beyond to reach the wall unscathed. The defenders were unable to stem the tide and fell back to a secondary stone wall within the kraal where Simon and a handful of redcoats joined them in time to engage in another desperate hand-to-hand conflict, bayonet clashing with assegai and rifle butt swinging against knobkerrie. Chard ordered men to climb on to the roof of the storehouse and fire into the masses in the kraal. The fire proved effective and forced the Zulus to take cover behind the stone perimeters of the kraal, giving some respite to the defenders.

Chard took advantage of the momentary lessening of the pressure on the kraal to call back a handful of men to his command post position in front of the storehouse, between it and the bisecting line of biscuit boxes. The boxes had all been used on the barricades, but plenty of mealie bags remained and he set the men to build a circular redoubt there, seven or eight feet high, with a scooped-out summit that could give protection to the worst of the wounded and a vantage point to a dozen or so riflemen. It was the last retreat. There would be nowhere else to go.

Simon pulled out his watch. It was almost midnight, and the fighting had been raging without pause for nearly eight hours. His shoulder ached from the kick of his rifle, and as he looked around, he could see overheated gun barrels glowing in the dark, cooking off rounds before their owners could raise them to fire. The heat softened the thin rolled brass of the cartridge cases, which then stuck to the chamber, while the extractor handle tore the iron head off the case. He could see men digging at the open breeches with their knives to pick out the empties. Some of these men had fired several hundred rounds through their scorching barrels and had wrapped rags around their left hands to protect them from the heat, or were now simply just resting the barrels on the top of the barricades and trying to fire with one hand. How long could it all go on? How long could the little band hold out against the unrelenting, surging waves of attack?

But the Zulus were not pulling back and the defenders in their enclave in and around the storehouse were running short of water. Most of the men manning the barricades had parched mouths, blistered lips and tongues that tasted of cordite. Their canteens were long since empty and the wounded were now moaning for water.

Confronting them in the no-man's-land of the yard – taunting them all – stood the post's two-wheeled water cart that Chard had prudently filled before the attack was launched. There had been no time to wheel it behind the line of boxes when the perimeter was shortened and it stood tantalisingly near the north wall, which was now, of course, manned by Zulus, who kept up a steady, if inaccurate, fire from behind the mealie-bag embrasures.

'Right,' said Chard eventually, having carefully assessed the options. 'Let's go and get it.' He called for volunteers and Simon wearily raised his hand. The big man looked at Simon's gaunt face and smilingly shook his head. 'Sit this one out, Fonthill,' he said. 'The night's not over. We shall need you later.' He selected twenty of his fittest men – all strong men with bayonets – and they crouched for a moment behind the boxes. Then, with a shout and with Chard in the lead, they boiled over the barricade and stormed down the north wall, bayoneting, shooting and clubbing the Zulus behind the bags along the wall, while three men grabbed the cart and pushed it to the enclosure. It was all over in less than ninety seconds, and amazingly, not one life was lost in the sally. It was impossible to bring the water cart within the enclosure, of course, but it drained through a valve and leather hose and it was a simple matter to lead the hose through the line and fill the canteens.

Simon watched the exercise with anxiety, and then admiration. The anxiety centred on the risk of losing Chard rather than the failure of the sally, for he realised how vital this officer of engineers was to the defence of the post. If Chard had been brought down by a spear thrust, he doubted if anyone else could lead. Bromhead had skill and bravery all right, but his disability must disqualify him from leadership in these circumstances, although, Simon reflected wryly, his lack of hearing undoubtedly bequeathed him certain elements of calmness in this noisy cauldron. Chard could lead a bayonet charge all right. In fact Chard, it seemed, could do anything.

As for Simon, he was now nearly exhausted. He had lost count of the number of attacks that had been repulsed, of how many bullets he had fired, and of how many times he had lifted that heavy Martini-Henry and thrust away with its long bayonet. He existed in a flickering, fire-lit eternity of rifle shots, screams and shouted commands. He looked with deep admiration at the scarlet backs manning the walls: they were fewer now, but they were still erect, still fighting – about eighty-odd Jenkinses, all, it seemed, sharing the little man's priceless virtues of courage and loyalty; all amazed at the ferocity and bravery of the warriors lunging at them, but all dourly determined to withstand it. Simon ran the back of his hand across his face and found that it came away black with soot. His head was singing with the cacophony of battle, and despite filling his canteen at the hose, his mouth was dry again. His shoulder was aching and his thigh pricking from where the assegai had penetrated lightly. But if these former bricklayers, boot boys and farmhands of the 24th Regiment of Foot could carry on fighting, so could he. He sniffed, inserted another cartridge into the hot breech of his rifle and took aim again.

Later, in a brief lull at the kraal wall, he extracted his timepiece to see how far through the night they were. Two thirty a.m. In the last fourteen hours he had endured two battles, lost his best friend, killed he knew not how many men and knocked his erstwhile commanding officer to the ground. He could now barely keep his eyes open, nor summon up the strength to present his bayonet to fight off yet another charge.

Yet Simon was not the only exhausted warrior at Rorke's Drift. The Zulu corps still pressing around the walls of the mission station had left Ulundi on Monday morning, and it was now Thursday. Its warriors had consumed their field rations within the first two days and had had nothing to eat, therefore, for the following two days. Since leaving the Nqutu plateau to attack Isandlwana, they had covered twelve miles to Rorke's Drift, mostly on the trot, and one of their regiments – the inDluyenge – had also harassed the refugees from Isandlwana on their way to the Buffalo. They had attacked the mission station now continually for ten hours in the face of withering fire and a small body of British soldiers who knew how to wield their bayonets and who refused to be beaten. They had lost they knew not how many of their warriors.

The assault on the walls continued, however, through the semi-darkness, with the occasional resurgent flame throwing the attackers and the defenders on the walls into momentary demonic relief. Then, at last, the ferocity of the Zulu charges began to weaken against the unremitting fire of the Martini-Henrys, and as the smoke from the gutted hospital began to die away, so too did the attacks on the walls. By 4.30 a terrible quiet fell on Rorke's Drift. The defenders still stood at the walls of their tiny fortress, but many of them could do no more than nod over their rifle barrels and start guiltily awake for a moment as a blackened rafter crashed on to the floor of the burnt-out hospital.

Dawn when it came showed that the Zulus had gone, leaving a terrible litany of bodies behind them. Against the ledge of the fiercely disputed north wall, they lay four or five deep, limbs protruding from contorted bodies and from beneath hundreds of discarded shields; a forest of assegais pointing to the early sky as a testimony to the fierce firepower of the Martini-Henry rifle – and to the courage of brave men.

But Chard felt no sense of triumph. He called for a count of his casualties and found that fifteen of his men were dead, two more were dying and eight were severely wounded. With barely eighty men left on their feet, he was in no condition to withstand another onslaught of the kind with which the Zulus had begun the battle, and his ammunition was running low. He could not see how reinforcements could reach him from Helpmakaar, and for all he knew, the General's column out there somewhere in the hills across the Buffalo had gone the same way as Pulleine's men at Isandlwana. So it was with great care, then, that he sent out a scouting party to ascertain if the Zulus had retreated or were merely resting on their spears before making a fresh attack.

The patrol returned to report no sign of the Zulus, but a rough count of the bodies around the post showed that some 370 warriors had died there – more than a hundred more were later found in the Buffalo, where the Zulus had carried wounded men away on their shields. A huge sigh of relief ran round the defenders – to be replaced almost immediately by a thrill of horror as the Zulu impi suddenly appeared again, squatting just out of rifle range on the western bank of the Oskarberg. There were hundreds of them, quite enough to overwhelm the reduced garrison, with its denuded ammunition boxes. Simon was shaken awake, as he lay with his back to the stone kraal wall, and joined the weary men who once again picked up their rifles and manned the walls, watching the impi in silence.

The Zulus were taking snuff and resting. They had nothing to eat and empty stomachs. They were far from home and faced a long journey. They also faced an angry king and the wailing of the women in the kraals of those warriors left behind on the field. As the defenders of Rorke's Drift watched, the Zulus gradually stood and walked slowly away, around behind the Oskarberg, towards the drift and their homeland.

Simon was asleep again, drooped over the mealie bags, long before the last warrior had disappeared from sight.

He was gently shaken awake by a smoke-blackened Bromhead. 'Quite a do, eh, Fonthill?' he said kindly. 'Well, it looks as though we have survived and the news should give a lift back home, after the downer at Isandlwana.'

Simon blinked. 'Sorry, Bromhead,' he said. 'I must have dozed off.' He looked around. The barricades were still in place but were covered in spent cartridge cases and torn paper from the cartridge packets, some of it dancing and scurrying across the compound in the light breeze. Discarded, once-white helmets, some of them smashed, littered the ground, as did squashed and trodden spillings of mealies from the bags, many of which bore the bloodstains of both attackers and defenders. Stretching out before him everywhere beyond the walls were bodies of Zulus, stiffening into great heaps where the fighting had been hardest. Long battle shields lay in coloured profusion: the all white of the uThulwane regiment, the white splashed and black of the inDluyenge, the red and white of the uDloko – none of them proof against the bullets of the redcoats' rifles.

Here and there small patrols of the 24th picked their way between the bodies.

Simon felt guilty. 'Sorry,' he said again. 'Let me do something.'

Bromhead gave his sad smile. 'What? Oh, help. No. Chard said we are all tired because we have fought a long and hard battle. But you, he said, have fought two. He insists that you go and lie down. Come on, we've found a corner where you can rest for a while.'

He led Simon to one of the rooms of the storehouse, cleared a space among the spent cartridge cases with his boot, threw him a blanket and was gone. Without a word, Simon lay down and immediately went to sleep again. So it was that he missed the return of General Chelmsford's column.

It rode in at mid-morning to cheering from the defenders, standing on the barricades, and from the van of the column. It had seen no action but *had* seen the battlefield of Isandlwana. Lord Chelmsford was riding at the head of the column and his relief was apparent to all when he found the little mission station battered, partly burnt out but still undefeated. As he questioned Chard, Bromhead and the men who had fought in the hospital, the immensity of the struggle and the heroism of the defenders became apparent. No fool, he realised also that the story of the defence of Rorke's Drift was a victory that could ameliorate the defeat at Isandlwana when the news reached home.

It was not until late afternoon of the day before that Chelmsford had realised that not all was well at the camp he had left. Finding that the unit in the hills that he had come to relieve was not, after all, under attack, he had decided to press on to a new campsite, sending back a message to Pulleine to strike camp and follow him. Later, several messages had arrived from Isandlwana but they were imprecise. Covington's party, which was reconnoitring the southern part of the plain, had not returned, so the General decided to go back to see for himself. He had hardly set off when he met a civilian commandant who had returned to the camp for provisions and narrowly escaped with his life. Chelmsford's reaction had been the same as Covington's: 'But I left a thousand men there,' he whispered in disbelief.

With his weary force, Chelmsford arrived at the site of the battle after nightfall. The stench of death told them what they could not see in the darkness and the flickering red glow to the south-west made them fear the worst for Rorke's Drift. Cetswayo's impis were probably storming through into Natal at that moment. But Chelmsford could do nothing but camp for the night, among the bodies and the carnage of the battle, and make an early start for the border in the morning. On the way, the British met the Undi corps of Prince Dabulamanzi limping back from its attack on the border post. The two columns passed only just out of rifle shot but Chelmsford's men had only seventy bullets apiece – their main ammunition had been left with Pulleine – and the General felt that he could not risk action. For their part, the Zulus had had enough fighting at Rorke's Drift to last them for months and had no wish that morning to tackle a fresh column of well-armed British troops. So the two groups trailed warily past each other, like neighbours after a row, each refusing to acknowledge the other when they met in the street.

Simon became aware of all this only much later. Now, while the returning column was passing cigarettes to the weary defenders and the General was questioning Corporal Allen,

Privates Hitch, Hook, Williams and the other survivors of the hospital, Simon slept blissfully on. It was only after the General had departed for Pietermaritzburg and tents had been pitched round the post to house the returned column for the night that he was awakened by a foot kicking his. He opened one eye and met that of a sergeant bending over him.

'That's the man,' said the unmistakable voice of Lieutenant Colonel Covington. 'Arrest him, Sergeant, and put him under guard. Be careful. He can be violent.'

Chapter 16

Early the next morning, Simon was taken under armed guard to Helpmakaar. There he was marched through the rain to the smallest of the three original wooden shacks that were all that the hamlet had boasted before the army arrived to transform it into a tented settlement capable of housing more than a thousand men. Small as it was, the interior of the shack had been roughly partitioned, and Simon was put into the largest section. Through the gloom, he detected a palliasse in the corner and a small table and camp stool. On a further table stood a collapsible washing bowl and a pitcher of water. One window let in what little grey light there was, but strands of wire had been stretched across the glass on the outside. It was the nearest that Helpmakaar had to a prison cell.

Only a few curious faces had watched his departure from Rorke's Drift before dawn. There was no sign of Covington, nor for that matter of Chard and Bromhead. Simon hoped that the latter were sleeping the sleep of the (heroic) just. The sergeant in whose charge he was placed was uncommunicative on the miserable ride through the rain to the little township, but once there, he was handed over to a sergeant major of the Buffs who was kindly.

'There you are, Mr Fonthill sir,' he said as he ushered him

331

into the room. 'Not very comfortable, I'm afraid, but we're a bit pushed for comfort around here. By the look of it, not many of your things have come with you from the Drift, but I'll have them sent in to you. Williams here will be on guard on the other side of the partition.'

'Thank you, Sergeant Major.'

The warrant officer paused by the door. 'At Ishandwanee, I hear, sir. And at the Drift too, then?'

Simon nodded.

The sergeant major scratched his beard. 'Not many fought at both, from what I hear, sir. In fact, after the first battle, a lot rode by the Drift. It seems to me, sir, beggin' your pardon like, that you should get a medal, not a court martial.'

Simon smiled. 'Not much chance of that, I fear.'

'Ah well, sir. I should try and get as much sleep as you can now. You look a bit washed out.'

Simon slumped on to the mattress. As the escort made to leave, he sat up. 'Sar'nt Major?'

'Sir.'

'I don't suppose you have any definite news about the dead at Isandlwana, after the battle, have you? I'm fairly certain that my man went down there, but I'd like to know for sure. His name was – is – Jenkins, of the 24th; last three, 352.'

The sergeant major frowned. 'I wasn't with the column that found 'em all, sir, but from what I've heard from them that was, there was nothing left alive there. Even the dogs had been speared. And all our chaps had been disembowelled – horrible business. But I will put the word about, sir.'

'That's kind of you. Do let me know if you hear anything.'

The thin door was firmly shut and he heard a padlock snap into place. There was a scraping as the young sentry pulled up a chair and sat down on the other side of the partition. Simon lay back on the bed, put a hand behind his head and silently began to laugh. For God's sake! He had only been out of Cetswayo's prison for a couple of days and now the British – his own people – had put him in another one! Well, he had no regrets. Whatever was going to happen to him – and he had no idea what the punishment for striking a senior officer might be – it would be worth it for that one moment of sheer joy he had experienced after knocking Covington flat on his back. He rubbed his knuckles reminiscently and then, thoughtfully, brought them to his mouth, as the smile died away. Could the sentence be death? After all, they were on active service and Covington had just placed him under arrest. He would have to plead guilty to delivering the blow, for there were too many witnesses to evade the charge. Could he submit extenuating circumstances to justify his act – the long imprisonment, the fight with the Zulus in the gully, the horror of Isandlwana and then Jenkins's death? And Covington *had* grabbed him roughly. What the hell! He would not go down without a fight and the world would know what sort of bastard was commanding the 2nd Battalion of the 24th Regiment of Foot. Anyway, if he was to be shot, then it would be a kind of poetic justice after narrowly escaping death over the past three days, when so many good men had gone. Pity about his parents, though. He put a hand to his eyes and rolled over.

His reverie was interrupted by the sound of low voices on the other side of the partition, then the key in the padlock. 'A visitor, sir,' said the sentry. And in walked Alice.

She stood for a moment and looked in the half-light at the figure lying on the mattress. Simon was still wearing the ill-fitting blue patrol jacket issued to him by the QM at Isandlwana, and from underneath it peeped the grimy bandage put round his shoulder by Jenkins. His breeches were threadbare and soiled and the right leg was bloodstained from where the assegai had administered the flesh wound on the barricade at Rorke's Drift – Reynolds had promised to patch him up as soon as he had seen to the more severely wounded, but Simon's arrest had intervened. It was Simon's face, however, which caused Alice the most concern. His eyes, which she had remembered as clear and alive, were now sunken and stared out of a gaunt face that carried three days of beard stubble.

To Simon, looking up in amazement at his visitor, Alice appeared as a vision from another, forgotten world. Still framed in the open doorway, she slowly took off her riding cape and threw it into a corner. Her hair had been pulled severely back and tied with that grass-green scarf, but it had been bleached in the sun over the months so that it shone now in the dust-rays from the window like a golden helmet. Her crisp white shirt was tucked into tight riding breeches and her long boots were still polished, so that they glistened under the raindrops. She stood looking down at him, a half-smile playing on her face. The door shut behind her and the padlock clunked into place.

Simon struggled to his feet. 'Alice!' He gave a wan smile and wiped the back of his hand across his face. 'You were just about the last person I expected to see come through that door. I'm sorry . . . I must look rather a mess.'

The girl walked towards him and, without ceremony or embarrassment, put her arms around his neck and brought his head down to her cheek. 'My dear Simon,' she whispered. 'My dear boy. What on earth has happened?'

Simon broke free awkwardly and pulled up the little camp

stool. 'Sorry again,' he said. 'This is all I can offer you, but do sit down.'

She remained standing, looking steadily at him. 'Very well,' she said. She pushed the stool towards the wall so that she could lean back on it. 'They tell me that you knocked down Colonel Covington. That doesn't exactly sound like the Simon I remember, but I suppose tribulations change a man. Anyway: true or false?'

Simon sighed. 'True, I fear.'

Alice put a hand to her brow. 'My goodness, Simon. I presume that you had provocation?'

'Oh yes, Alice.' Simon smiled. 'Plenty of that.'

'But what about the desertion charge?'

'The what?' The smile dropped from Simon's face and he jumped to his feet. 'Desertion? What do you mean?'

'Simon, do sit down. I have been told that I am allowed only half an hour with you, so it won't do to get excited.' She waited until he was sitting once more on the edge of his bed before continuing. 'Now, do you mean to tell me that the charges have not been read to you?'

'No. Not yet.' He shook his head wearily. 'The hitting of Covington, of course I know about. I thought that was bad enough. But what is this about desertion?'

Alice's face now betrayed no emotion. 'In addition to the charge of violence, Colonel Covington is also accusing you of lying about your activities in Zululand and of deserting from the battlefield of Isandlwana.'

Simon gave a mirthless laugh. 'But the bloody man was not there. How would he know what happened, for God's sake?'

'I understand that he has witnesses whom he will bring against you at your court martial. Now, my dear,' she took out

335

a small spiral-bound notebook and a pencil, 'we have little time and I think you had better tell me *everything* that happened.'

For the next thirty minutes, the two sat together in the gloom while Simon recounted his experiences since his crossing into Zululand two – or was it three? – lifetimes ago. Alice occasionally interrupted with a question but mostly she sat silent, her face expressionless. When Simon began his account of the battle, she started scribbling quickly, overriding his objections with a wave of her hand.

'I have already sent my dispatch back to London,' she said. 'What you have told me confirms what I have already hinted at. No laager around the camp, you say? How far did the runners have to come for the ammunition?'

When they had finished, Alice sat quietly looking at her notes. 'Hmmm,' she mused, then: 'Simon, I fear that you are in trouble. The problem is, you see, that these charges are brought against you by your former commanding officer who, I happen to know, is regarded within the army as an up-and-coming man of honour and courage.' Simon thought he detected a quick flush come to her cheeks as she uttered these words. But she hurried on. 'The fact that he was your commanding officer means that people will presume that he knows you and your character well, and that could be influential.

'However,' she gave him a bright smile, 'things are by no means lost, my dear. You are not without friends and it sounds as though your Colonel Lamb could be helpful.' Then the smile disappeared and was quickly replaced by a frown. 'The trouble is that Chelmsford sent him back to the Cape before the invasion to handle the dispatches with the Horse Guards – the General was still hoping to wheedle reinforcements out of London, you see – so he will be unaware of all this.' She stood up, thrusting her notebook away.

Simon scrambled to his feet. Tenderly, Alice kissed him on the cheek. 'I must go now, for I have work to do. But I shall visit as often as I can.' She walked to the door and paused for a moment there. 'Simon, make sure that you understand what your rights are in these proceedings and don't let them rush things through. I have a feeling that Lord Chelmsford will not want this court martial to be prolonged. He's got enough bad news to handle as it is, so I believe that he will want this affair to be pushed through as quickly and as quietly as possible, without it causing too much fuss back home. Hold fast and make sure that you have the witnesses that you want.'

She smiled and then rapped on the door and was gone, leaving in that fusty room a faint odour of perfume. Simon lay back on his mattress and felt a strange mixture of hope and despair blend in his puzzled mind. The hope came from Alice's presence and her advice. Perhaps she could help him, although exactly how he had no idea. But desertion . . .? Why should Covington bring this accusation? Somehow it rang deeper warning bells than the charge of assault, for it smacked of cowardice, of running away in the face of the enemy. It was the worst charge the army could bring against one of its own. And Alice was right, his peers (would there be a jury?) would presume that his former CO knew his character very well. Oh hell!

The next day, Major Spalding came to see him. Clearly ill at ease – not certain whether to treat his prisoner as a suspected criminal or as a colleague in difficulty – he explained that, as the nominal commanding officer of the post at Rorke's Drift and Helpmakaar, it was his duty to read the charges to Simon and to explain the procedure that would follow. The first charge was straightforward and accused him of striking a senior officer while in the field and on active service. The second, to which Simon listened with even more attention than the first, alleged that he had deserted the firing line at Isandlwana *before* its collapse, and had rushed to the rear.

The Major shifted awkwardly on the little stool. 'The Deputy Judge Advocate wallah has been in touch with me,' he said. 'Didn't know we'd got one in Natal, but it seems we have, or, at least, we do now. He tells me that the court martial is to be held here in a week's time and that you must let him, through me, know what witnesses you want to call in your defence. What happens, it seems, is that the prosecution witnesses are called first and questioned, then your witnesses are heard. Then the court adjourns while you and the prosecution write your cases. These are then put to the court – I'm told it's called "mailing" them, which seems a bit strange to me – and then this Deputy Judge Advocate fellah sums up and the court comes to a decision. Fairly straightforward, eh, what?'

Simon blinked. 'Don't I have any legal advice? A defending lawyer, or something like that?'

'Good lord, no. This is a court martial, not a civilian trial. It's much more straight and to the point. You're a soldier, so you will be judged by soldiers. Quick but fair, eh?'

'What if I am found guilty?'

Again Spalding looked uncomfortable. 'Not quite sure, actually. 'Fraid it could be a firing squad, given that you've got two charges against you. Or, on the other hand, if there are special circumstances, you could just be cashiered. But I can't really help you there, Fonthill.' The discomfort vanished and he rose. 'Right then. Let me have your list of witnesses as soon as you can. Yes, well. Right then.'

Witnesses. Witnesses . . . Simon crouched by the little table with a stub of pencil and several sheets of writing paper and thought hard. On the assault charge, he could produce no one who could help him. He had struck Covington and that was that. He must simply explain his tiredness and his frustration at being prevented from warning Rorke's Drift. Desertion was another matter. Alice had said that Covington intended to throw doubt on Simon's work in Zululand. Nandi and Dunn perhaps could help, but where were they? He only had a week. How to find them? They might well have left the country by now and he had no one to search for them – no team of lawyers or detectives. Jenkins . . . Alas, Jenkins was dead. He believed that now, beyond doubt, and his best friend could help him no more. He chewed the end of the pencil and dredged through his tired mind. Colonel Lamb would surely testify about his task in Zululand, and for the rest, he would just have to rely on character references: Major Baxter, who had mentioned him in his dispatches could, *must*, provide one, and Chard, of course, the other. That would have to do. He scribbled a rough note for Spalding and called for the sentry.

Alice visited him just once more during his week of waiting. He told her of the date of the court martial and of the procedure and she made a note in her book. She had gained an interview with Lord Chelmsford but had found him predictably guarded about Isandlwana and claiming little knowledge of Simon's case. However, to Alice's gentle suggestion that there did not seem to be much of a case to answer, the General had snapped that any question of insubordination and desertion in the face of the enemy by a commissioned officer had to be thoroughly examined. If not nipped in the bud, he declared, this kind of thing could run through the army like cholera – particularly when the army faced a savage and efficient enemy.

Simon's heart sank at the news. It sounded as though they were going to make an example of him. Alice was reassuring but somehow distant and preoccupied. She could not stay long, she explained, because she was dining with the officers of the 2nd Battalion in the mess that evening and the next morning she had a journey to make. For the first time since their reunion, a little flame of jealousy flickered within Simon – but it was as much resentment of Covington, who would assuredly be her host, and envy of the sparkle and comfort of the occasion as any sexual emotion. Nevertheless, he reflected, as he threw breadcrumbs at a beetle scurrying across his floor, Alice did look gorgeous: like some houri from a glamorous former existence, serendipitously reappearing to taunt him. Life as a foreign correspondent was obviously suiting her. He stood up and squashed the beetle with his boot.

The day of the court martial arrived with one small boost to Simon's morale. His campaign trunks, left behind at Cape Town when he sailed for Natal, had now been forwarded and he was able to wear his dress uniform for the trial: tight (although not so tight now) red jacket with light green facing and polished brass buttons down the front; narrow dark blue trousers; gleaming black boots (buffed by himself, for he was not allowed a servant); the fore and aft glengarry on his head, with its black silk ribbons hanging down his back; and his sword. He felt that, at least, he now *looked* like a soldier.

The court martial had been set up in the largest of the wooden buildings in Helpmakaar. Even so, the room seemed small to Simon, who was marched in and told to sit on a folding camp chair set to one side. Two large benches stretched the width of the room and they faced a long table, behind which five chairs had been placed. At the side of, but set apart from, the top table a much smaller table had been set, with one chair behind it. A captain of engineers sat on the first bench, sifting through a pile of paper. Behind him sat two orderlies, with further files in cardboard folders. Two privates of the 2nd Battalion, with rifles and fixed bayonets, stood guard at the doors (why the bayonets, for God's sake – did they think he would attack the whole court?) and the company sergeant major who had taken him to his shack stood ramrod-straight, cane under arm, against the far wall. He gave a friendly nod to Simon and just the suspicion of a wink. The room was hot and humid and Simon hoped fervently that he would not perspire and give the impression of unease. He had decided to comport himself authoritatively, speak the truth and react intuitively to anything that Covington threw at him. In the absence of seeing any formal submission of the prosecution's case, that was all he could do.

Then, to his surprise, he saw Alice, sitting on a camp stool at the back of the room. To Simon's eyes she stood out again as some fragrant anomaly in the harsh military surroundings of the room – a visitor from another planet where there were no bloodstained spears, disembowelments or butchered drummer boys. She had braided her long hair and wore it Dutch style, wound round her head to frame her face. Her blouse was now complemented by a long riding skirt in soft green, revealing the familiar polished boots. She seemed to favour no cosmetics but her teeth gleamed whitely as she smiled at him across the room.

Simon made to get up to speak to Alice, but a small shake of the head from the sergeant major made him resume his seat.

Feeling as though he was waiting outside the headmaster's study for a caning, he sat still, staring ahead.

Suddenly, the far door opened and the sergeant major bawled, 'AttenSHUN!' Everyone sprang erect except Alice, who rose languidly to her feet and began fanning her face with her notebook. Into the room filed five officers, resplendent in their dress uniforms although somewhat hampered by their swords, which trailed low from their belts. They were followed by a tall, slim civilian, wearing a black gown and lawyer's wig. The latter sat at the small table at the side while the officers arranged themselves behind the long table.

'Please do sit down,' said the officer sitting in the centre. He wore the uniform of a full colonel and his voice was soft. Thick-set and rather red of face, he wore a full beard and adjusted a pair of spectacles as he looked at the papers before him. Then he removed them and adjusted his gaze to Simon.

'Please stand,' he said. 'You are . . .' The Colonel tailed away into silence as he noticed Alice sitting at the back of the court. 'Madam,' he said, 'this is a court martial. A very private procedure conducted by the army. I am afraid that we cannot allow you to stay.'

Alice rose and smiled. 'With the greatest of respect, Colonel, I have every right to be here, as a member of both the public and the press, as long as I don't make a nuisance of myself. This court martial is not private; it is an open court. I think that you will find that the Deputy Judge Advocate will agree.' Still smiling, she sat down.

Slowly, the arm of his spectacles hooked into his mouth, the Colonel leaned back and towards the lawyer. They whispered for a moment and then the Colonel addressed Alice. 'You are quite right, madam,' he said. 'I am grateful to you for pointing this out and preventing me from making a mistake. Please do stay.' He gave her a courteous seated bow, to which Alice responded similarly.

The Colonel now turned to Simon. Having ascertained his name and rank, he explained that he would introduce each member of the tribunal and that Simon would have the chance of objecting to the presence of any of them. Their names were read to him: a lieutenant colonel, one major and two captains. The chairman introduced himself as Colonel R.G. Glyn, Commander of the 1st Brigade. Simon remembered that he had been in nominal command of the central column, under Chelmsford, and had accompanied the General on the ill-fated reconnaissance to the east of Isandlwana. He had therefore missed the battle.

Simon objected to none of the members of the tribunal and then listened with care as the two charges were read out. 'How do you plead to each charge?' asked Glyn.

'Guilty to the first charge,' said Simon, 'but,' he hurried on, 'I wish to offer mitigating circumstances. To the second charge I plead not guilty.'

With a slight frown, Glyn looked across at the lawyer, who gave a small nod. 'Very well,' said Glyn. He then went on to explain that the prosecution would be presented by Captain Bradshaw, the officer sitting with a worried frown and his files on the front bench, who would call his witnesses. These could be cross-examined by Simon, as could Simon's witnesses by Bradshaw – or any member of the tribunal.

'Now,' said Glyn, adjusting his spectacles again and holding up a document before him. 'I understand that you have requested that Colonel Lamb, of the Commander-in-

Chief's staff, and Major Baxter, of the Royal Artillery, should appear to give evidence on your behalf. I am afraid that this will not be possible. Colonel Lamb has urgent business in Cape Town and cannot leave there at present and Major Baxter is besieged by the Zulu with Colonel Pearson's force at Eshowe and, obviously, cannot be here. I understand that you wished to present both as witnesses of character rather than of events, so we have been able to obtain statements from them – with some difficulty, I may say, in the case of Baxter – which the court will accept as evidence. Lieutenant Chard, of course, will attend.'

Glyn looked over the top of his spectacles at Simon, who, feeling that some response was called for, said, 'I am very grateful, sir,' but inwardly cursed at losing the chance of fielding Lamb.

Captain Bradshaw now rather nervously rose to his feet. 'I have three witnesses, sir,' he said, 'one of whom will give evidence on both counts.' (Covington, of course, thought Simon.) 'The second will speak only to the first charge' (the sergeant, naturally) 'and the third only to the second charge.' (Now, who the hell can that be? mused Simon.)

Glyn nodded and the first witness was ushered in by the sergeant major. It was, predictably, Sergeant Evan Jones, of the 2nd Battalion 24th Regiment, who Simon had last seen standing thunderstruck beside the fallen Covington, out on the plain after Isandlwana.

Bradshaw, who had obviously rehearsed everything with great care, extracted from Jones all that he wished: the vagabond stranger riding out of the plain, being questioned by the Colonel and then suddenly striking down the senior man, before riding away quickly towards the Buffalo River, shouting vague instructions after him as he went. Glyn made several notes before turning to Simon, his eyebrows raised interrogatively above the spectacles.

Simon stood and cleared his throat. He must be cool, unprovocative, but firm. 'Now, Sergeant,' he said. 'Tell us what condition I seemed to be in to you, when I rode up.'

'Well, with respect, sir, you seemed to be a bit of a mess.' Smiles appeared on the faces of several of the officers at the table.

'What do you mean by that?'

'Well, you were a bit wild, like. You was agitated, see, and very badly dressed for an officer, like. You 'adn't shaved properly and your coat didn't fit and you looked a bit thin an' wasted, though that didn't stop you punchin' the Colonel very 'ard indeed.'

Simon frowned. This was not going the way he wanted it. 'Did it look like I'd been in a battle, then?'

The sergeant shrugged. 'Don't know, sir. You wasn't in proper uniform, that is certain.'

Simon tried another tack. 'Did you hear Colonel Covington put me under arrest?'

'Oh yes, sir.'

'Did you hear me tell him that the General's column was in danger of being ambushed and ask him to hurry back to tell the General that, while I rode off to Rorke's Drift to warn the garrison there?'

For the first time the sergeant looked shifty. 'Well, I don't know about that, see. I couldn't quite 'ear what the two of you was sayin'.'

'Very well.' The little swine had obviously been got at by Covington. 'Did you see Colonel Covington grab me by the shoulder – my wounded shoulder – and swing me round when he tried to put me under arrest?'

'I saw the Colonel put 'is 'and on your shoulder but I don't know about any swingin'.'

Simon let the man go. He had obviously been well coached by Covington and was not going to let slip anything which might put his CO under pressure.

Covington was the next witness. Once again Bradshaw rather ponderously set the scene, eliciting that Covington had been given the task of finding a trail back to the Buffalo and a crossing downstream of Rorke's Drift, should the column have to retreat. His questioning was so laboured, in fact, that Glyn interrupted testily. 'Yes, yes,' he said, 'this is all irrelevant. Where and when it happened is not in dispute. Please get on with it.'

Damn, thought Simon. They *are* trying to rush this through. Where and when may not be in dispute, but how and why almost certainly are. So it proved when Simon began to question the Colonel.

The tall man's blue eyes hardened as Simon rose. 'Tell me, Colonel,' he asked, 'what did I look like when I rode up to you on that plain?'

'Humph!' Covington let the exclamation hang in the courtroom for a moment, as if to underline his contempt for the questioner. He was, as Simon knew he would be, arrogantly confident, in no way fazed by the ritual of the court martial. 'You looked scruffy in the extreme, as though you had been sleeping rough in the bush for some considerable time.'

'But Colonel, I had fought at the battle of Isandlwana. Did I not look as though I had been through a battle – had been engaged in hand-to-hand conflict and seen my comrades massacred?'

'No. You looked as though you had been sleeping rough in the bush.' Covington repeated each word with emphasis.

'Did you not see evidence of a spear wound in my shoulder?'

'Certainly not.'

Simon looked at the completely blank piece of paper in his hand to hide his mounting anger. He must not appear provocative. 'When I told you that there had been a battle and that the column at Isandlwana had been wiped out, what was your reaction?'

'I didn't believe you.' Covington turned to the tribunal. 'I knew that Pulleine had been left at the camp with some eighteen hundred men and I could not accept that he had been overrun. If I may say so, the Commander-in-Chief had exactly the same reaction when he first heard the news.'

'Quite so,' murmured Glyn sympathetically.

'But you were wrong, Colonel, weren't you?' Simon pressed. 'I was bringing you accurate news straight from the battlefield, was I not?'

Covington gave a cynical smile. 'Oh yes. You'd seen the battle all right, but you hadn't fought in it. You had run away from it and we intercepted you.'

'You know that's a damned lie.'

Glyn's voice cut through the exchange like a sabre swing. 'I will remind you, Mr Fonthill, that you are addressing a senior officer and you will treat him with respect. If I have any more behaviour from you of this nature, I shall stop the court martial and a verdict of guilty will be returned without any more ado. Do I make myself clear?'

Simon cursed inwardly. He must *not* lose control. 'Yes, sir. I apologise.'

'Very well. Continue, but in a respectful manner.'

Simon turned and looked once more into Covington's icy gaze. 'But I was right about the battle and I urged you to tell the General immediately, while I rode on to Rorke's Drift to warn the defenders there. Why did you not do so?'

'Because,' Covington pushed up the end of one moustache and turned to address the tribunal again, 'I am not in the habit of accepting orders from junior officers – particularly those I believe to be deserters.'

Ah, thought Simon, a chance at last. 'But,' he said, 'you had no evidence *then* that I was a deserter, even if you have now – and I shall contend, of course, that you do not.'

Covington was quite unperturbed. 'You are forgetting that I know you, Fonthill, and, from my previous experience when you served under my command, regard you as a malingerer.' He addressed the tribunal again. 'I was attempting to detain the accused for further questioning when he suddenly assaulted me, without, I may say, giving me any chance to defend myself.'

Simon turned to Glyn in appeal. Surely the court would not let that charge of malingering lie unanswered? It did not. The Deputy Judge Advocate leaned back in his chair and, behind the backs of two of the tribunal, engaged in a whispered conversation with the chairman. Glyn nodded and addressed his colleagues. 'I am advised,' he said, 'that we should ignore Colonel Covington's accusation of malingering until some evidence is presented to substantiate that charge.'

'Ah, with respect, sir,' said Covington smoothly, 'I think that you will hear something more to that effect later in this hearing.'

So that old charge *was* to be resurrected! Simon's mind raced. Best ignore it for the moment and face it when it came. He returned to his questioning. 'Let us get back to the facts concerning my alleged attack on you, Colonel,' he said. 'Did you not seize my shoulder – my wounded shoulder – and swing me round quite sharply?'

'Can't say I did, actually. I merely put a hand on your arm to detain you from running away once again.'

Simon pressed on. 'And did I not say to you that it was imperative to tell the General about Isandlwana and that I must complete my task of riding to the Border to warn the garrison that the Zulus were on their way to invade Natal?'

'You were gabbling away somewhat incoherently as though you were in a blue funk, and I can't remember what you said.'

'And wasn't it clear to everyone that by detaining me you were preventing me from giving that warning – and that that was the reason I hit you?'

Covington smiled. 'Certainly not. You hit me to avoid arrest for desertion.'

Simon shook his head but turned to Glyn. 'I have no further questions for the Colonel, sir,' he said.

Captain Bradshaw also stood. 'I have no further witnesses to call on this first charge, that of assault, sir,' he said.

'Very well,' intoned Glyn, adjusting his spectacles and studying a paper in his hand. 'As I see that Mr Fonthill has no witnesses to be called, then I suggest that we now consider the case against him on the second charge, that of desertion from the field of battle at Isandlwana. Captain Bradshaw, please present your case . . . oh, and, ah . . .' He looked across at Covington, who was about to leave. 'I see no reason, Colonel Covington, why you need to leave the court and hang about outside, so to speak, until you are called as a witness on this charge. You will be needed in just a few moments, I expect.'

Simon jumped to his feet. 'With respect, sir, I do feel that it would be unfair for the Colonel, who I understand is the main protagonist in this case against me, to remain to hear what the other prosecution witnesses may have to say. It could have a bearing on the evidence he will give.'

Glyn's eyebrows rose. 'I don't agree, young man. This is a court martial, not some civilian court of law where, I understand, such frivolous objections may be heard. I shall conduct these hearings in the way *I* think fit, not you. I do not believe for one moment that someone of Lieutenant Colonel Covington's rank or stature would give prejudiced evidence and it does not reflect well on you that you should suggest it.' He nodded to Covington. 'Please stay, Colonel, if you wish.'

'Very kind of you, sir, I'm sure,' murmured Covington, taking a seat on the bench behind Bradshaw.

Simon turned his head to commune with Alice in his misery but she had left the court. He felt suddenly very alone and vulnerable.

Bradshaw now began his presentation of the second charge. He made no reference to the circumstances in which Simon had arrived at Isandlwana; they, he said, were a matter for conjecture and had no place in a court martial whose task was to ascertain the facts and to balance them. (The prosecutor, perhaps gaining in confidence from the performance of his two previous witnesses, was undoubtedly beginning to enjoy himself. As he gestured to Simon with one hand, he hooked the thumb of the other in his tunic, rather as a barrister would clutch the lapel of his gown. If he had a wig, reflected Simon, he would surely tilt it over his ear.) What mattered, emphasised Bradshaw, was that Simon Fonthill had been seen to leave the firing line and, via the ammunition wagon, double back up the neck of the mountain. Many others had done so, he conceded, but no officer had left the line *before* it broke. Such an act was tantamount to desertion in the face of the enemy and could well have contributed to the panic that ensued amongst the native levies and to the general collapse of the organised defence on the day.

It was, admitted Simon to himself, a competent and potentially damning indictment. But who could be produced as a witness to support it? – and Bradshaw (or rather Covington) had *two* witnesses to call on this charge. Who the hell could they be?

The first question was answered when Quartermaster Sergeant Morgan of the 1st Battalion of the 24th Regiment was called. Simon immediately recognised the smug features of the man he had last seen in a wagon at Isandlwana, refusing to provide ammunition for Durnford's native cavalry.

The questioning began. Morgan, it seemed, had escaped in his shirtsleeves from the battlefield by cutting across country and crossing the Buffalo further south of Fugitive's Drift, the name poignantly given to the main crossing point of the men who had escaped from the battle and been pursued to it by the Zulus. He had ended up, more dead than alive, at Umsinger on the road to Pietermaritzburg. He described how he had seen Simon and Jenkins ordered into the line by an officer and then, later, how they had both doubled back from the line and appeared at his wagon demanding cartridges.

'Then what happened?'

'Well,' said Morgan, 'the private soldier this officer was with, see, tells 'im to fix 'is bayonet, and they jumps down from the wagon and legs it up towards the road back to the crossin' place.'

Bradshaw's eyebrows shot up in surprise, making the most,

351

Simon surmised, of this little *coup de théâtre*. 'What?' asked Bradshaw, turning to the tribunal. 'This private soldier ordered the officer to fix his bayonet?'

'Yes, sir. Then they jumped out of the wagon and left me to it. Soon after, the Zulus were all around me and I 'ad to fight for me life. I think I got away because I wasn't wearin' me tunic, see.' He turned to Colonel Glyn. 'I'd stripped down to me braces, see, sir, because it was so damned 'ot in that wagon. That's what saved me life, I think, because the Kaffirs seemed to be only after our chaps in the red regimentals.'

Glyn nodded sympathetically.

'Now, Quartermaster Sergeant,' said Bradshaw, 'let me get this right. You first observed Lieutenant Fonthill watching the fighting, without taking part. Then he is ordered into the line to fight. Shortly afterwards, he runs from the line and appears in your wagon, and then – on the instruction of a private soldier, it appears – he runs back up to the neck of Isandlwana. Is that correct?'

'Yessir. That's about the size of it.'

Simon, aware that the eyes of the tribunal officers were fixed upon him, stared at Morgan while his mind worked fast. It could be said that the QMS had told the fundamental truth. But oh, what a pejorative slant he had put on it. If only Jenkins had survived – but he had not, and Simon knew that he would have to fight this battle alone. He must redress the balance somehow. Clutching his blank sheet of paper, he rose to question the witness.

'Q, do you remember how we first met?'

The question was met with an unmistakable 'Pshew!' from Covington.

'Pay no attention,' ordered Simon. 'Please answer the question.'

'Yessir. You and that private soldier came to me just before the battle with a requisition for me to issue you with jackets an' rifles an' lungers.'

'When you issued us with jackets, did you notice any wound on my body?'

'Don't think so.'

'Not on my shoulder? A spear wound?'

'Can't rightly remember, sir.'

Bastard, thought Simon. He tried once more. 'When I came into the wagon, wasn't it perfectly clear that I had run out of ammunition and had come to take cartridges back to the line?'

'Dunno, sir.'

'When Private Jenkins suggested that I should fix my bayonet because the Zulus had broken through the line, it wasn't an order, was it? He was advising me to do so for my own safety, wasn't he?'

'Dunno, sir. Wasn't time to consider all that, what with the trouble gettin' the boxes open an' all.'

Simon sighed. 'When we left the wagon, you say you saw no more of me or of Private Jenkins?'

'That's right, sir. I just saw you runnin' up the 'ill, like.'

'You did not see a spear take Jenkins in the back so that he fell? And you did not see me stand over him and try and protect him with my bayonet as the Zulus swarmed about us?'

A heavy, histrionic sigh came from the bench behind Bradshaw.

'No, sir.'

Simon let the witness go and Covington strode forward to give evidence again. This time, Bradshaw merely asked the big man a preliminary question and then let him address the tribunal without interruption.

'Colonel Covington,' said the prosecutor, 'you have brought these two grave charges against this young officer. You know that a guilty verdict on either of them can mean death for him' – Simon flinched at this, for it was the first time that punishment had been mentioned – 'so you must have a very good reason for doing so?'

'Indeed I have.' Covington thrust out his moustaches and addressed the officers sitting before him. 'The first charge needs little explanation. Without warning, this young man hit me and in so doing escaped arrest. He does not deny it and will not – he cannot – offer extenuating circumstances for his act. It is an open and shut case.

'However, on the second charge, you, sir, and your colleagues may wonder why I, who was not present at the battle, should bring it. The facts of the matter are these. When Fonthill was arrested at Rorke's Drift on the first charge I was naturally interested to know what he had been up to at Isandlwana.' A shrug of the shoulders and the tone of Covington's voice invited the tribunal to agree that this was a perfectly normal thing for him to speculate upon – and, indeed, the expression on the officers' faces showed that they agreed.

'So,' he went on, 'I made enquiries and heard the QM's story. Now, I was not at all surprised by this because, as I have touched upon earlier, I have long believed Fonthill to be a malingerer and, indeed, a coward. You see, he came under my command some three years or more ago when he was transferred to the 2nd Battalion from the 1st under rather unusual circumstances. It seems that when the 1st was ordered abroad to take part in the Kaffir War in the Cape, Fonthill collapsed immediately and missed the draft. He lay in some sort of coma for a couple of days or so and then, conveniently, recovered just after his comrades in the battalion had shipped out.'

Covington raised his eyebrows in mock surprise. 'You may wonder, gentlemen, what was the complaint that laid low this young officer just when the call came to go to war. I certainly did. But, as you will hear' (Simon pricked up his ears at this) 'the doctors were not able to find anything wrong with him at all. I have to tell you that the general verdict among his contemporaries was that he had deliberately feigned illness to avoid being posted into danger.

'Fonthill was transferred to my command and, to be frank, I told him of my feelings about him and gave him the chance of resigning then and there or staying with the 2nd Battalion, where I would test him to the extreme. Now,' Covington gave his idiosyncratic flick of the moustaches, for he was undoubtedly enjoying the telling of the story, 'in fairness the man did not crack, but he was damned clever. Somehow – I know not how – he convinced the Horse Guards that he had a good knowledge of Zulu and other Bantu languages and that he could ride well – which he could not – and scraped a strange posting in Zululand to be away from me and arduous line duty. I do not know what he was up to in Zululand but I am perfectly certain that this story of his about bearding Cetswayo in his den, being imprisoned by him and then escaping from Ulundi in time to join poor Pulleine's column just before the battle is poppycock. It is typical Fonthill make-believe, and as I understand it, he has no evidence of any sort to substantiate it.'

Covington now addressed Glyn directly. 'You will see, then, sir, that knowing what I know about Fonthill, and having been a victim of his sudden attack on me, I had no alternative but to bring both these charges.'

As Covington concluded, a silence fell on the court. Bradshaw indicated that he was finished with the witness and once again Simon thought quickly. He stood. 'Gentlemen,' he addressed the tribunal, 'I have many questions to put to Colonel Covington, but in view of what he has said about events three or more years ago and,' he took a deep breath here and looked at Glyn, 'since this court has extended a minor concession to Colonel Covington in allowing him to stay to hear the QM's evidence, I wonder if a similar modest indulgence could be extended to me in hearing the third witness for the prosecution before I question both him and Colonel Covington.' He hurried on, his voice on edge: 'As, from what I have heard, a death sentence could be imposed upon me in the event of guilty verdicts, I do believe this request to be not unreasonable.'

Covington was about to speak, but Glyn held up a restraining hand and shot a quick glance at the lawyer, who, almost imperceptibly, gave a nod.

'Very well,' said Glyn. 'Captain Bradshaw, call your last witness.'

Through the door guarded by the sergeant major came the unprepossessing figure of Surgeon Major Reynolds. His appearance caused a slight frisson in the little courtroom, not least because a long cut above his eyebrow (a Zulu throwing spear, a slip with the scalpel?) gave his already gloomy visage an even more threatening aspect. The doctor looked tired, irritable and ill at ease. With several men still on the danger list and demanding his care, attending a court martial obviously did not figure high on his list of priorities. To Simon he represented the joker in the pack – a witness who could either condemn or clear him. Which Simon would he portray to the tribunal: the suspected malingerer of three years ago, or the man who took his share in the defence of Rorke's Drift?

Bradshaw was soon on the attack.

'When Lieutenant Fonthill collapsed all those months ago in Brecon, how long was he unconscious?'

'About two and a half days.'

'Just long enough for his battalion to leave, travel to Southampton and board the steamer for the Cape, then?'

'I can't remember the exact timing, but something like that, I suppose, yes.' The Surgeon Major spoke without expression, neither his heavily bearded face nor his voice betraying emotion. But to Simon he evinced a weariness quite unlike his memory of the brusque little doctor with his staccato questions and sharp eyes. Working through the night sewing up assegai slashes and extracting bullets from torn flesh by the light of the burning hospital must have taken its toll, even on a constitution as iron-bound as Reynolds's.

'Could you find anything wrong with your patient?' Bradshaw, on sure ground, was pressing for the kill.

'No. Throughout the time he was in my care, I could find nothing organically wrong with him. There was no evidence of a wound, as with a bump on the head, nor trace of malaria, typhoid, typhus, diabetes or poisoning. Yet he seemed to be in a light coma, stirring and even taking spoonfuls of liquid nourishment occasionally, but not really conscious.'

Bradshaw leaned forward. The room was quite silent. 'Could he have been malingering?'

'Yes, it is quite possible.'

For a moment the prosecutor looked uncertain, as though a co-actor on stage had departed from the rehearsed script. 'With respect, Major, all things are possible. Did you *believe* him to be malingering?'

Reynolds nodded his head slowly. 'Yes, I did.'

'Ah. And did you give that opinion to Lieutenant Colonel Covington?'

'In the end, yes.' Reynolds lifted weary eyes to Simon and then to Glyn. 'The Colonel was pressing me on the point, y'see.'

'Thank you, Surgeon Major. That will be all.'

Reynolds looked about him in surprise. 'Is that it?'

Glyn intervened quickly. 'If the accused officer wishes to question you, Major, he may do so. But I feel that we have all heard enough for one day and I intend now to adjourn the court martial until eight a.m. tomorrow. I regret, then, that I must keep you from your patients a little longer and ask you to reappear at that time in the morning.'

Reynolds nodded gloomily, the sergeant major roared his stentorian 'AttenSHUN!' and within three minutes Simon was back in his makeshift cell, pondering the twists and turns of the day. In fact, his analysis did nothing to lighten the gloom of the shack. It was clear that the case was going against him and that he would need to break Covington somehow under questioning – an improbable concept – or to extract some sort of indulgence from Reynolds about his breakdown at Brecon. Either that or he must produce strong testimonies from his three witnesses – two of whom could only submit written references. He had no means of knowing how pertinently Baxter and Lamb had responded to the court's request, or whether they knew the extent of his plight. Alice had offered to help, but where was she? Simon sighed, thought again of Jenkins and, fleetingly, of his parents, and slipped eventually into a light sleep.

If Colonel Glyn had seemed unhelpful on the first day, he was positively surly at the beginning of the second, as though he saw no reason for continuing to waste precious army time on a legal ritual that ought to be terminated immediately with a guilty verdict on both counts.

'Now,' he addressed Simon over the top of his spectacles, 'you have the right to question the two witnesses brought by the prosecution on the second charge, namely Colonel Covington and Surgeon Major Reynolds. We do not have all the time in the world, since the witnesses and the members of the tribunal here are all serving officers engaged in a savage war. Do you still wish to do so?'

Simon stood. 'I do, sir,' he said, without a thought in his head of the best course to take with his questioning.

Glyn sighed. 'Very well. But Surgeon Major Reynolds has patients depending upon his attention and I insist that you question him first.'

'Of course, sir.' Simon eyed Reynolds as the surgeon re-entered the room, his face set in iron. The man had glimpsed Simon fighting at the drift so perhaps some concession might be wrung from him there . . . and yet a return to Brecon could be productive, if he took great care with the questions. He had nothing to lose, anyhow.

'Doctor,' he began.

'I'm a Surgeon Major, not a doctor,' rasped Reynolds.

'I beg your pardon, sir. May I take you back to Brecon and the evidence you gave earlier? Were you *certain* that I was malingering, that I was fooling everyone? After all, you told me when I came out of my coma that you had been sticking needles in me.'

The hard blue eyes regarded Simon expressionlessly. 'Oh yes, I was convinced all right,' he said. 'I thought I should give you the benefit of the doubt so I called a specialist in diabetes down from London, since this seemed the likeliest cause of your coma. But he could find no trace. So I put it down to blue funk and good play-acting. I didn't think much of that, of course, so I allowed you to return to general duties in the 2nd Battalion.'

Reynolds now turned to the tribunal and began addressing them as though Simon was not present. 'But I am glad that I have been asked this question because I was not allowed to develop my response on the same point yesterday.' He shot a quick, hard glance at Bradshaw. 'The case bothered me, you see. I knew that the boy was of good stock – his father was a distinguished officer – and he seemed to behave himself well during the remainder of his time at Brecon. I had been told that he had been a sensitive child, and certainly he did not seem to display the normal characteristics of a coward – no bluster, nor the other extreme, undue diffidence. Anyway, he went out to the Cape. But I could not get the case out of my mind.'

For the first time his face softened a little as he looked along the seated line of officers. 'I'm only an army doctor, not a mind doctor, y'know. So I consulted an old colleague in Geneva who had been working in the field of unconsciousness for some time. He outlined a possible source of the coma and directed me to see if the patient had suffered a blow to the head in the recent past before this so-called coma had materialised. The boy had not recalled any such blow, but I made some enquiries and found a groom in the battalion who told me that, a few weeks before his collapse, Fonthill had taken a fall from his horse while riding in the hills. He had hit his head and lost consciousness. It was only for a minute or so, I understand, and he had not reported sick. Nevertheless, it is quite likely that he had sustained concussion.

'Now, gentlemen,' Reynolds continued as though he was addressing a theatre full of students, 'my man in Geneva told me that it was not unlikely that Fonthill, a sensitive young man with a strong imagination, had experienced what was to him a severe shock when the news of the battalion's posting had been suddenly broken to him. This could well have produced what I understand is becoming known as hysterical fugue, whereby the patient suddenly reverts to a concussed state, a coma, for a while. He would have retained no lasting ill effects from it, but it remains a puzzling condition about which little is known.'

The blue eyes turned on Simon. 'So my advice to this young man is to control his imagination if he wishes to stay in the army.' He swung back to the tribunal. 'I don't know about the situation in which Fonthill now finds himself, but to sum up, I do not now believe he was malingering back in Brecon, and having seen him in action at Rorke's Drift, I do not believe that he is a coward. Now, gentlemen, may I return to my patients?'

Once again there was complete silence in the little room. Most of the tribunal members, including the lawyer, had been busily making notes as the surgeon spoke, and Simon's eyes were wide as he stared at the little man before him – the rockhard veteran who was now saying that he was no coward.

Glyn coughed and cocked a quizzical eye at Simon.

'Eh . . . what?' Simon stuttered. 'Oh yes, indeed, sir. Do. And thank you very much, Doc— Surgeon Major.'

With a curt nod to the tribunal, Reynolds stumped out of the room, leaving it in silence and Simon lost in thought.

'Well come on then, Fonthill,' said Glyn. 'Do you wish to question Colonel Covington on his evidence or not? We can't wait all day.'

Simon thought quickly. What could he gain? Reynolds's

evidence had surely destroyed Covington's claim about malingering and it would be better to give the man no chance of casting doubt upon what the surgeon had said.

'Thank you, but no, sir,' he replied. 'I believe that the Surgeon Major's evidence has poured light on the charges made against me by Colonel Covington and I have no need to recall the Colonel.'

'Very well, then. We must now turn to the witnesses for the defence, and I shall begin by reading the affidavits we have received from Major Baxter and Colonel Lamb. Then we shall call Mr Chard.'

The affidavits were short, to the point and similar in tone. That from Baxter expressed surprise at Simon's predicament and told the story of the shipwreck and of Simon's part in it in a matter-of-fact way, but commending the young man's initiative in lowering the boats and getting the troops away from the foundering ship. 'I find it most surprising that a young officer who I mentioned in my dispatches for cool leadership should have these charges levelled against him.'

Simon bit his knuckles and silently recorded a vote of thanks to the artillery major who was afraid of the sea but not afraid to admit it.

Lamb's submission was less eulogistic – not that Baxter's language had been anything but formal. It recounted the task that had been given to Simon and to Jenkins, and the receipt of Simon's coded message, and informed the court that the contents had been of assistance to the General Staff, although they had been received only after the decision to invade had been taken. Lamb then related how he had instructed both men to return to their base in Natal and that some concern had been felt at their continued absence. Fonthill, wrote Lamb, had appeared to be a good officer who had shown initiative in a difficult task, although the Colonel could not verify any account of his activities in Zululand.

It was clear to Simon, looking along the row of faces on the tribunal, that these officers were less than impressed by the two affidavits as strong bulwarks in his defence. And in all honesty, he had to agree with them. Lamb's statement, in particular, was objective but almost disinterested. He would have to do better with Chard.

The big lieutenant was announced by the sergeant major with a noise level several decibels higher than for any who had been introduced before. The bearded commander of Rorke's Drift had clearly become the Empire's hero, as was evident from the heartfelt tone in which Glyn congratulated him on his achievement and, it seemed to Simon, almost apologised for bothering him with attendance at something as unsavoury as a court martial when there were so many other calls on his time. God, thought Simon, this is becoming even more of a stacked deck as the trial goes on. Well, thank God for Reynolds and to hell with them all! He stood and began his questioning to a subdued and clearly rather puzzled Chard.

'When I rode up to the drift, what was the first thing I said to you?'

'You said that you had come from Isandlwana and that a large force of Zulus were on their way to attack us and then, presumably, to go on to invade Natal.'

'Did I believe myself to be the first man to convey the news to you of the imminent attack by the Zulu impi?'

'It seemed so. I had to explain to you that others had already brought the news of our defeat at Isandlwana and of our danger.'

'Did I urge you to pack up and leave?'

'Yes, but I explained that it was too late for us to do that because we would have been cut down on the road to Helpmakaar, and that we were staying to defend the mission and were prepared to fight.'

'Quite so.' Simon took a breath and decided to venture down a high-risk route. 'I was delayed on my ride to warn you. If I had arrived, say, twenty minutes earlier, might it have been possible for you to have packed up and gone to Helpmakaar and so defended that place with the help of the garrison there and with almost certainly fewer lives lost?'

Chard frowned for a moment. 'I suppose it would have been possible, but to be honest, I don't think another twenty minutes or so would have done us much good. We would never have got the wounded away in time. We had to stay.'

Damn! But it was worth the try. Simon reverted to his original line of questioning. 'When you explained the problem to me, did I then ride away as,' he shot a scornful gaze at Covington, 'a coward would surely have done?'

'No. I offered you the chance to do so.' Chard turned to the tribunal with a wry smile. 'Several others had previously ridden by, but Fonthill agreed to stay and help us defend the station. We had only two commissioned officers.'

'Indeed. During the defence, did I play a full part, manning the walls where ordered?'

Chard nodded vigorously. 'Very much so. Bromhead and I were glad to have you with us. You fought through the night with the rest of us.'

Thank goodness for that, thought Simon. An unequivocal tribute at last! He decided to leave it at that.

'I have no further questions,' he told Glyn.

The chairman nodded to Bradshaw, who rose slowly to his

feet. 'I won't keep you long, Mr Chard,' he said. 'But tell me. How long after Mr Fonthill's arrival at the drift did the Zulus begin their attack?'

Chard pulled at his beard. 'Oh, very soon afterwards, I would think. They seemed to be on his heels. Perhaps three minutes. Maybe even less.'

'Ah.' Bradshaw nodded sagely. 'So isn't it true that Mr Fonthill *really* had no choice in staying to fight? The Zulus were so closely on his heels – and he must surely have known this – that they would have cut him down in the open ground beyond the mission station, particularly with him riding a horse which must surely have been exhausted.'

Chard shrugged his shoulders and looked embarrassed. It was clear that he would rather have led a thousand bayonet charges against the Zulus than be forced to pin down a colleague from the witness box. 'I suppose so. But it didn't seem like that at the time.'

'You suppose so,' repeated Bradshaw. 'Yes. Quite. Just one further question. During the defence of the mission station, did Mr Fonthill play a *particularly* distinguished role? In other words, did you give him any task that demanded special standards of bravery and leadership – such as leading a sally against the attackers? After all, he was one of only three officers in the defending force and you must have been in need of senior soldiers who could take a leadership role. Or did he just take his place along the walls with the rest of the men?'

Once again Chard looked embarrassed. 'I . . . er . . . don't think so. He was very tired, you see, having been at Isandlwana. I let him play his part, with the men, on the walls.'

'Ah yes. Thank you, Mr Chard, I shall not bother you further.'

Simon had to admit that Bradshaw had done a good job.

Suddenly his role at Rorke's Drift had been cut down to size: not being able to run like a rabbit, he had been put on the mealie bag wall with the men, leaving the leadership to the hard-pressed subalterns Chard and Bromhead. Surely the young captain of artillery could earn a good living at the bar – particularly with Covington as his briefing solicitor! But Glyn was addressing the court.

'. . . will now adjourn this court martial. You, Mr Fonthill, and you, Captain Bradshaw, will now write your cases for the defence and the prosecution respectively and mail them to the court by eight a.m. tomorrow morning. The tribunal will read them and then the court will reconvene to hear the Deputy Judge Advocate's summing-up, after which we will adjourn again to consider our verdict. I estimate that we shall be able to reconvene for the last time to deliver our verdict by approximately four p.m. tomorrow afternoon.' He sounded pleased that the miserable business was being concluded so expeditiously.

'AttenSHUN!' once more, and then Simon was back in his cell, sitting at the small camp table, hearing again Reynolds's opinion of him as neither a malingerer nor a coward. It was the only good news he had received since first he and Jenkins had crossed the Tugela. Not a coward! Of course not. He had always known it – but how good to have it confirmed! What effect would Reynolds's evidence have on the court martial, though? Covington's case against him on the second charge was now circumstantial, although the QM's evidence remained potentially damaging. He must now write a reasoned defence, one that would save his life.

It fell, of course, into two parts. The justification of his knock-down of Covington must be that he felt that his arrest could delay the news of the Zulu attack so that the border post would be taken by surprise. Violence was the only route he could take to do his duty – and Covington *had* manhandled him . . . The second charge was more amorphous. Lamb had confirmed that his orders were to play an intelligence role behind the Zulu lines, but, dammit, he had no witnesses to show that he *had* played the role. That was the rub. Best simply to tell the truth and make it sound as plausible as possible. At least this time he had a serviceable pen and not a stub of pencil. He began scratching away.

The court was reconvened at eleven o'clock the next morning to hear the Deputy Judge Advocate give his summing-up, after he and the other members of the tribunal had read the written cases for the prosecution and the defence.

The tall man rose, arranged his notes on the small table in front of him, grabbed his gown with both hands at his breast and looked around him. His face was thin and clean-shaven and the years of studying briefs showed in his eyes, which, behind his spectacles, were pale and watery. He began by explaining that his role was to help the members of the tribunal by advising on points of law and, specifically, by summing up the written cases and the evidence that had been heard. The sentences on both charges could be challenged on appeal by Simon to the Commander-in-Chief in South Africa – if it was decided that he had grounds for doing so – and the C-in-C, if he wished, could pass the appeal on to the Commander-in-Chief of the British Army at the Horse Guards in London.

Simon looked to the back of the court. The camp stool had been untenanted after the first few minutes of the first day. Alice, it seemed, had better things to do. He tried to concentrate on the words that were being dropped into the quietness of the courtroom like dry pebbles plopping into a tranquil pond.

The prosecution case, as summarised by the lawyer, was pure Covington. Simon had hit him to resist arrest after fleeing from Isandlwana when the fighting became difficult before the line broke. He and Jenkins had been nowhere near Cetswayo's capital – how could any British officer who spoke no Zulu have survived there? – and had camped out in Zululand, sending back speculative information to the Cape, planning to rejoin the British column after it had successfully defeated the Zulus. However, they had got their timing wrong and had arrived at Isandlwana by mistake *before* the battle. The Surgeon Major's view on the accused's coma was, by his own admission, speculative, given the unknown nature of such a condition. Better to trust the judgement of Fonthill's CO, who had known him for three years. The judgement on both counts must be guilty.

The lawyer's summation of Simon's case was equally balanced and forensically presented. However, here the Deputy Judge Advocate began, almost imperceptibly, to interpose some doubts of his own: the blow *had* been struck, the defendant was not denying it, but was the justification for it warranted, even in time of stress and war? Also it might be felt that the accused's story of his four months in Zululand did seem perhaps to have been unusual, if not highly coloured. After all, he had been given an order by Colonel Lamb to return immediately to Natal and he had not done so. On the other hand . . .

The lawyer's dissertation continued, the cool, carefully balanced phrases dropping limpidly into the humid little room. Colonel Glyn hardly took his eyes off the tall man throughout his summing-up; and then Simon realised, with a start, that

Covington was sitting in the room, listening intently, one elegant leg crossed over the other, a finger stroking his moustaches.

Eventually the lawyer finished and, with a half-bow to Glyn, sat down. Simon felt that the delicate balance of the scales had been marginally tipped against him.

The Colonel took a gold watch from his pocket, consulted it and said, 'We will now break for luncheon and consider our verdict. We will reconvene as soon as possible afterwards.'

Once again Simon was led away to his room in the shack, but this time he had no appetite for the simple fare provided for him. Whatever euphoria had been created by Reynolds's evidence had now disappeared under the probe of the lawyer's analysis. It was clear which way the verdicts would go: he would either be cashiered or shot. Both ways would bring dishonour and, quite soberly, he decided that he would prefer the latter. He was well aware of how structured was the society in which he had been brought up and of how heavy were the penalties for those who broke the rules. It was quite acceptable to be a *privately* dishonourable man; many men were, and even flaunted it. It was the *public* disgrace that was unforgivable – and it would be shared, in that cruel fashion of the day, by his parents. He would rather join Jenkins, that inestimable man who had lived by his own clear and, to the sensible mind, quite moral set of rules.

And Alice? Betrayal? No, far too strong a word. She had obviously tried to help and failed, and anyway, what could she have done in this militaristic milieu? She had her own life to lead and her own career to follow. Clearly she had attended the first morning of court to see if it was worth reporting and, realising that it was not, she had returned to more important matters, like following the progress of the war. Yet he would miss her – and Nandi . . .

The call for the resumption of the court came quickly – too quickly. The judges must have made their decision with almost indecent speed. Simon felt the certainty of disaster. As the tribunal members filed in, not one of them caught his eye and the two young captains looked positively sad. A low, tuneless humming came from the back of the room: Covington was singing to himself.

The Deputy Judge Advocate was the last to appear, and as he flared out his gown to sit, so the door to the courtroom opened and in bustled Alice. Without a glance at Simon, she hurried to the lawyer, gave him an envelope and then returned to the stool at the back of the room, followed by an astonished glare from Covington. Colonel Glyn rose and addressed Simon, who was already standing and desperately trying to stop his legs from shaking.

'Lieutenant Simon Fonthill,' he began in low tones, 'this court martial has . . .' The lawyer was also now standing and leaning towards the Colonel, whispering to him. The two men stood together for some thirty seconds like conspirators, before the Advocate handed Glyn the letter and sat down. 'One moment, please,' said the Colonel, then he too sat, adjusted his spectacles and read the letter. After he had finished he leaned forward to the lawyer and began another whispered conversation with him. Simon strained hard but could pick up no discernible phrase. Eventually Glyn nodded and removed his spectacles.

'Please sit down,' he said to Simon and turned to address his colleagues ranged along the table. 'Gentlemen, although we have reached our verdict, there has been a development that I am advised we must take into account, and that, I fear, will mean a further adjournment after we have heard it.'

He held aloft the letter. 'This has just been delivered to the court. It is from Colonel Lamb, Lord Chelmsford's Chief of Staff in Cape Town, who has already submitted an affidavit to the court. The Colonel urges us to hear evidence from one more witness before we come to a decision – evidence that, he claims, is of some importance. I am advised that, as this letter has reached us before we have delivered our verdict, then we are still in session and that we should hear and, if necessary, question this witness, who is waiting outside. Do you all agree?'

Four heads nodded in agreement, but then Covington stood. 'Forgive me, sir, but I must protest. You have heard a great deal of evidence already and spent much time on this case. Isn't it time it was closed and justice done so that we can all return to the business of taking revenge for the awful reverse the army has sustained?'

Glyn looked enquiringly at the lawyer. The Advocate rose. 'The court martial was not closed when this new witness was presented by a senior officer of the General Staff,' he intoned. 'In my opinion, if you do not hear this evidence, then you give the accused clear grounds on which to enter an appeal against your verdict; an appeal which, in my opinion, would have every chance of being sustained.'

Simon looked at Alice with wide eyes. Covington, too, was now glaring at her. With a pretty gesture, she resumed fanning herself with her notebook and smiled sweetly at both of them in turn.

'I accept that,' said Glyn. 'Let us therefore hear the witness.' He held his spectacles to his nose and read, 'Miss Nandi Dunn.'

As the words echoed round the room, Nandi was ushered in by the sergeant major.

'My God!' exploded Covington. 'She's half Zulu. How can we give credence to what she says? She's a damned half-breed!'

The damned half-breed flinched as she heard Covington's words but gave a small smile to Simon and then a larger one to Alice, who nodded back encouragingly. Nandi was wearing the simple cotton shift that Simon remembered so well, and her glistening hair was pulled back demurely and tied with a scrap of orange silk. She was wearing shoes for the occasion, Simon noted: well-cut leather pumps with a high heel. She was clearly nervous but she looked ravishing.

Her appearance was not lost on Colonel Glyn. 'Please do sit down, young lady,' he said. 'Now,' he looked again at Lamb's letter, 'will you please tell us your full name, give us your address and tell us your occupation – if you have one, that is,' he added kindly.

'My name is Nandi Elizabeth Dunn. I live with my mother and father in Natal, near the Lower Drift of the Tugela. I have no formal occupation, although I assist my father.'

'And what does he do?'

'He is chief of intelligence to General Chelmsford for the column that is now being prepared to cross the Tugela and relieve Eshowe.'

Glyn looked up at Covington, and beneath his beard, his lips curved in the faintest of smiles. 'Is he now?' he murmured.

'Yes, sir.' Nandi now spoke with a little more confidence. 'He has just been appointed to this position by the Commander-in-Chief. My father is English, you know, or at least, Irish, although he has lived all of his life here.' She directed this last sentence, with a touch of hauteur, at Covington, who scowled at her. Simon was forced to put his hand to his face to hide a smile.

'Very good, Miss Dunn. Now please tell us in your own words as much as you know of what has happened to Mr Fonthill over the last four months, or since you met him. However, you must only tell us what you yourself observed at first hand. No hearsay. Please proceed.'

Nandi stole a quick glance at Simon and then, in her low voice, began to tell the story of his and Jenkins's sojourn in Zululand, taking in the dispatch of Jenkins to Cape Town, Simon's journey to Ulundi, his imprisonment and his escape with Jenkins. As she related her own nocturnal visit to the prison hut in the Zulu capital, her words seemed to echo in the courtroom, so profound was the silence.

'How do you know that they were able to make their escape?' asked the Deputy Judge Advocate in a rare intervention.

'I know,' said Nandi, 'because before I left Zululand, I talked to one of the Zulu warriors who had attacked Mr Fonthill and Mr Jenkins when they had gone about seven miles from Ulundi. He said that both men got away after fighting like wounded buffaloes – particularly the thin one.' She turned and nodded towards Simon.

'Hearsay, I'm afraid, and not allowable,' murmured the lawyer, half to himself. 'But interesting despite that.'

There was little more to be said. No further questions were directed at Nandi and the court was adjourned. Simon had no chance to exchange words with either Nandi or Alice before being escorted back to his quarters. There, he sat at his table staring unseeingly at the wall. His mind tried to grasp the significance of Nandi's evidence. Was it enough to show that he had not been lying about his imprisonment and escape, and more significantly, would the words of – what had Covington called her? Yes, a 'damned half-breed' – would they have weight with this tribunal of men who clearly regarded non-whites as inferior beings? Of course they had made up their minds to find him guilty before Nandi's arrival. Would they swallow their pride and change this verdict? The more he considered the question, the more he found it unlikely. Covington was such a strong presence in that group and he was clearly determined to pin his man down, like a butterfly to a dissecting table, and so complete the ritual of humiliation begun so long ago – and the force of this persecution had been redoubled after Simon had struck him. For Covington, the blow had been more than physically painful; it had been an affront to his dignity and his superiority. It must be avenged. Simon put his head in his hands. It all seemed so inevitable and so damned unfair! But he must prepare for all eventualities. He sat up and pulled pen and paper towards him and began writing a letter. It did not take long, for it contained only three sentences. He addressed the envelope, sealed it and waited for the call back to court.

It came within ten minutes, another disconcertingly short time. Simon rose as the tribunal members filed into the room and once again felt his knees trembling, so that he had to brace them against the chair to hide his weakness. There was no trace of either satisfaction or beneficence in the gaze of Colonel Glyn as he looked up from his papers and rose to his feet. The room was completely silent once more as the Colonel cleared his throat. Simon closed his eyes.

'Lieutenant Fonthill,' said the Colonel, 'on the charge of desertion in the face of the enemy, this court martial . . .' he paused as though for cruel effect, and Simon kept his eyes firmly closed, 'finds you not guilty.' Simon was conscious that the room behind him seemed to exhale in a gasp of both relief and surprise. He opened his eyes and realised that they were moist. His legs still trembled and he thrust them harder against the chair rim.

The Colonel continued: 'On the other charge, that of assaulting a senior officer, the court finds you guilty. However, it accepts that exceptional circumstances forced you to act as you did and the punishment levied on you will be one year's loss of seniority. That will be all. You may now leave this room and rejoin your regiment.'

Simon nodded abstractedly, put on his cap, saluted, turned and marched quickly from the room, robot-like, as though in a dream. Once outside, in the sunshine – the shimmering, liberating sunshine – he clenched his fist and raised it for a moment to the sky in unreal relief. Then he realised that he had not noticed if Alice or Nandi had been in the courtroom, so tense was he in waiting for the verdict. He re-entered the room. Alice was engaged in close conversation with Covington in one corner; he coldly erect, she talking animatedly to him, one hand on his arm in friendly intimacy. For a brief moment Simon felt that sharp pain of jealousy again. What was she saying to the bastard? What *could* she be saying to him that demanded she be so close and talk to him so earnestly? And then he saw Nandi, standing alone and uncertainly at the back of the room.

He beckoned to her and together they walked out into the sunlight. 'Nandi.' He took her hand and held it in both of his. 'How can I thank you enough? I think – no, I am sure – you saved my life.'

She gave him that wistful half-smile and he saw that there were tears in her eyes. 'Ah, Simon,' she said. 'You must thank

Miss Griffith, Alice. She saved you, not I. It was she who rode to Durban to telegraph the big Colonel at the Cape and she who found my father at the Tugela. He could not leave, so of course I was happy to come and give this evidence for you, but I would have known nothing of the trial had it not been for Alice.' She paused and looked down at the ground. 'She must love you very much.'

They both turned and regarded Alice, who was now standing in the doorway, laughing at Covington, whose icy demeanour had visibly melted. 'No, I am sure that is not so,' murmured Simon. 'But come.'

They walked a few steps. 'My dear Nandi,' he said. 'I am a very lucky man indeed to have two such fine people to help me when I needed them most. But, oh, I am so sorry that this war began. You must believe me when I tell you that I could do little to stop it. It is an evil war, brought about by politicians. I learned during the trial that the decision to invade Zululand was taken before the information you gave me reached Cape Town.'

He took her hand again. 'So, you see, you cannot be blamed for helping to bring the tragedy about. Nor can I – and I did try and persuade the King not to fight.'

Nandi nodded. 'I know, Simon, and I thank you for that. All of the British are talking about Isandlwana as a great loss for them. But even though the Zulus won that day, they also lost. Do you know how many men were killed by your rifles?'

Simon shook his head.

'More than two thousand. Some say it was nearer three thousand. Most of the inDunas hailed it as a great victory, but King Cetswayo says that Isandlwana was like a great assegai plunged into the bowels of the nation and there are not enough tears to mourn the dead.'

'Nandi, I am sorry. I really am.'

'Sorry. Sorry. What do you have to be sorry about? You have just won a great victory, so do cheer up.' It was Alice, fresh-faced and, of course, perfectly groomed, who had stolen up on them. She now looked with affection at Nandi and linked arms with her. Standing there smiling, they complemented each other perfectly: brown and white, black eyes and grey, the south and the north. Simon looked at them both with admiration and his old ambivalence returned. Was it possible – was it *honourable* – to love two women at once? They both smiled back at him.

'Wasn't she marvellous in there?' asked Alice. 'I think, Simon, that she saved the day, don't you?'

'I think, actually, that you both did.' He smiled ruefully at Alice. 'Do you know, I thought that you had deserted me. But all that time you were dashing around, working hard on my behalf. I don't know how you did it or how I shall ever repay you.'

'Oh tosh! The trouble was that there was so little time. When I read Lamb's affidavit—'

'What?' Simon interrupted her. 'You *read* Lamb's affidavit? You were not even in court when it was presented.'

For the first time Alice looked slightly embarrassed. 'Oh yes. I had to be well on the road by then. We journalists have our sources, you know, and they are not to be revealed. Anyway,' she hurried on, 'when I read what the Colonel had said, I thought that he could do better than that, so I rode to the nearest telegraph – which, unfortunately, happens to be in Durban – and requested his help urgently. He came back like a shot with the information about Dunn, so I took the letter and rode over to the Lower Drift to find him, and produced Nandi instead, which was probably better because—'

'Stop!' Simon put both his hands on Alice's shoulders and looked directly into her grey eyes. 'Alice. There is no way that that letter from Colonel Lamb to the court could have reached you in time. What exactly did you do?'

'Oh, for goodness' sake, Simon.' Alice waved her hand airily. 'Sometimes, you know, you can be a bit strait-laced. Of course I forged it. When I first came to the Cape I . . . er . . . purloined, I think is the word, a few sheets of the General Staff notepaper from HQ on my first visit there. They have been quite useful to me in the past in pushing open doors.' She turned to Nandi. 'As I am sure you know, my dear, we working women have to cut corners occasionally if we are to get anywhere. There was clearly no time for Lamb to write a letter and post it to the court. I doubted if I would have enough weight of my own to introduce Nandi as a witness at the last moment. So I put pen to paper. I am sure that the Colonel would have done so, had I been able to ask him. He seemed a sweet little man. I sat next to him at dinner once and he remembered.'

Simon cast his eyes towards the bright blue sky and grasped an elbow of each woman. 'I think it best that we get out of here quickly before they organise a second court martial,' he said, marching them away.

Chapter 17

That evening, Alice gave Simon and Nandi dinner, cooked by her servant, George, over an open fire blazing before her tent – she had repossessed her original campsite at Helpmakaar. At first the atmosphere was stilted. Alice overcompensated by being too jocular; Nandi was mainly silent, switching her black eyes between the others; and Simon behaved far too courteously to the ladies. However, as the champagne began to take its effect – once again Alice refused to divulge her sources – they all loosened and began to behave like old friends and young people.

After the fourth glass, Alice leaned across to Nandi and gestured towards Simon. 'I'm not going to marry him, you know. In fact, I'm not going to marry anyone. I am having far too much fun. But he does kiss rather nicely. Has he kissed you, Nandi?'

'For goodness' sake, Alice,' stormed Simon, 'stop behaving so shockingly.'

'Oh, I'm not shocked, Simon,' said Nandi, taking the question solemnly, as she so often did. 'Yes, Alice, he has kissed me. It was very nice. In fact we made ukuHlongonga together.'

'Nandi!' screamed Simon. 'How dare you! Alice, it's not what you think. It's not quite that. It's . . .' He halted in confusion.

'Well, my little wounded buffalo,' said Alice. 'You *did* it, so presumably you can remember what it was. I am dying to know. It could be useful to me – for purely professional reasons, you understand, Simon. Local colour and all that. Perhaps Nandi can tell me?'

'Nandi, if you continue this conversation, I shall leave.'

'Simon, don't make such a fuss. It is done quite a lot in Zululand, Alice, but as we are embarrassing Simon, perhaps we should change the subject.'

'Very well, my dear.' Alice sipped from her glass and her face grew serious. 'Now, Simon. What are you going to do? Apart from your loss of seniority – which, by the way, Covington regards as a slap in the face to him because he believes the sentence to be derisory, and he is quite right – the Colonel remains your enemy, I am afraid. There will be no future for you in his regiment and I presume that Lamb has finished with your services?'

Simon drained his glass. 'Oh yes. I know exactly what I have to do and I will do it first thing in the morning. But I would rather not discuss it further tonight, if you don't mind. I *am* enjoying this champagne. Where on earth did you get it? May I have another glass, do you think?'

'Of course. Nandi?'

The Zulu girl did not respond. She was now sitting with head bowed, and as both Alice and Simon looked at her with concern, a teardrop rolled down her cheek, on to her chin and dropped on to her bare knee. She fumbled for a handkerchief, blew her nose and looked up with starry eyes. 'I am sorry,' she said. 'I am so sorry.'

Alice rose immediately and kneeled by Nandi's side, putting her arm around her shoulder and drawing her towards her. 'My dear girl,' she said. 'Whatever is the matter?'

Nandi shook her head. 'It is nothing,' she said. 'Please do not be concerned.'

'No,' snorted Alice. 'It is certainly not nothing, for you are clearly upset. Is it Simon? Has he been beastly to you?'

Nandi smiled through her tears and gently pushed Alice away. 'Oh no. Of course not. I don't think Simon could be beastly to anyone.' Simon squirmed on his haunches and bit his lip. 'No. It is no one. It is just that . . .' The tears came again and quickly this time so that she was forced to open the folds of the shred of handkerchief in an attempt to stifle them. 'It is . . .' She frowned and now looked up at them both, almost accusingly. 'What is going to happen to my country? What are you white people going to do with us all when you invade again, as you are now preparing to do, with Papa's help? Will you kill all of the Zulus – my family, my friends? What have we done to harm you?' The words were now tumbling out. 'All we did was to defend ourselves when you invaded us. We killed a lot of white men in that big battle that day – but you killed more Zulus. You did that. The English. People like that big colonel in there who called me a damned half-breed.'

Nandi's face was tear-stained but her eyes burned with a fierce sincerity as she switched her gaze between them. Simon realised with a shock of guilt that inwardly he had always regarded Nandi as a European: a half-caste indeed, but one whose leanings were towards the white races and whose education and general upbringing had distanced her from the Zulu people with whom she lived. Now he perceived that he could not have been more wrong. Whatever her appearance and manners, her emotions and sympathies had been forged by her mother's family, not her father's – although his, too, now probably leaned that way.

He gulped and searched for words. But Alice, of course, was quicker. 'My dear Nandi,' she said, leaning forward and taking both dark hands in her own. 'We have been so insensitive and selfish, joking when you obviously had such deep concerns for your country. I . . . we . . . quite understand how you feel, and we both,' she shot a quick glance at Simon, who nodded vigorously, 'share your feelings. People like Colonel Covington have been raised in a narrow environment – English public school, the army, you know the sort of thing – which means that they do not understand or even consider the rights of less well-educated people whom they think stand in the way of what I suppose they would call the "onward march of civilisation", or something like that.'

Alice was now speaking earnestly and quickly and Simon dreaded that she was going to lapse into another of her lectures about the necessity for reform. Nandi needed something more than that at this stage.

But he need not have worried. With great solicitude, Alice produced a handkerchief of her own and began to wipe Nandi's cheeks. 'My dear girl,' she said, 'there will be no slaughter of the Zulu people, I can promise you that.' She held up her hands as Nandi made to interrupt. 'No. A general I am not, but I can promise you that. And there are several reasons why I can do so. Firstly, the British people would not tolerate it. We have a strong opposition to the Government in Parliament back home and there has already been much criticism of this invasion. Any gratuitous cruelty would not be countenanced.'

Simon sucked in his breath. That was all very well, but the British people, he surmised, would want revenge for what had already been described as a massacre at Isandlwana – and so would the army. He doubted if a dozen Gladstone speeches could prevent that revenge being taken. But he decided not to interrupt. Alice in full flood, anyhow, was not to be diverted.

'The second reason is that the British Government will want to rebuild Zululand: to recreate some sort of non-military government of your people *by* your people, for we do not have sufficient bureaucrats to put into this land to govern it directly ourselves. We will need the co-operation of your chieftains and tribal heads, as we do in India. For that reason alone, there could be no widespread killings.' Alice was now leaning forward, her face gleaming in the firelight, her hands gripping those of Nandi fiercely to drive home her argument. Nandi was listening wide-eyed, her tongue protruding slightly between her lips. Simon thought with a sigh that both women looked deliciously desirable.

'The third reason,' Alice continued, 'is me – or rather people like me. As a result of Isandlwana, a whole contingent of journalists, newspaper writers, are travelling here from England to cover this campaign. If the coming invasion is brutal, then, I promise you, we shall report it and tell the whole world. The General Staff here knows that and will be very careful.'

Simon cleared his throat, and Alice looked across at him and suddenly sat back and released Nandi's hands. 'Of course,' she said, lowering her eyes for a moment, 'there will have to be another battle, I am afraid, and this will inevitably mean more casualties.' Simon nodded his head as Nandi looked at him, following Alice's eyes.

'But,' and Alice shrugged her shoulders, 'this *is* a war and the Zulu are very warlike people, you must admit that.'

Nandi nodded slowly and looked into the fire. 'I hope you are right, Alice,' she said. She looked across at Simon again. 'I am so tired of all this killing, you know. So tired.'

Simon scrambled across to Nandi and seized her hand. 'Oh, so am I, Nandi,' he said. 'So am I.'

Alice took the girl's other hand and the three of them sat silently, hand in hand, as the flames of the firelight sent shadows flickering and dancing around the clearing. George crept silently in with another bottle of champagne but the spell of jocular friendship had been broken and the three sat, half-full glasses in hand, staring into the flames as the air grew colder. Simon's thoughts turned back to Jenkins and to the prospect of life without his brave and resourceful companion. It was a cheerless prospect and he made no objection when Nandi stood and gave her farewells. He kissed her still damp cheek, and that of Alice, and in sombre mood the little party broke up.

Simon rose early in the morning, having slept the night in his prison quarters, and penned a long letter to his parents. Then he carefully dressed in what was left of his civilian clothes: worn corduroy breeches, bloodstained still from the assegai thrust sustained at Rorke's Drift; torn shirt; scuffed, down-at-heel riding boots; and the blue patrol jacket issued to him at Isandlwana. He then reported to the tent that was the head-quarters of the 2nd Battalion and asked to see the commanding officer.

Covington looked up with interest when Simon was ushered in. His cynical smile turned to a scowl as he took in the young man's appearance. 'You're a damned mess,' he exploded. 'Why on earth aren't you in proper uniform?'

'Because I prefer to wear these clothes,' said Simon, his hands in his pockets. 'And there is no need to shout.'

'What?' Covington rose to his feet. 'How dare you talk to me like that? Consider yourself under arrest.'

'I asked you not to shout,' replied Simon evenly. 'I shall consider nothing of the kind.' He reached into his pocket, removed the letter he had written the day before and threw it on to the desk. 'I am no longer under your jurisdiction – or that of anyone else, for that matter. This letter is my resignation from the regiment, taking effect immediately.'

Slowly Covington's glare relaxed, a half-smile began to play beneath the whiskers and he sat back in his chair, languidly cocking one leg over the armrest. 'Ah, I see,' he drawled. 'Still running away, eh, Fonthill?'

'No, not running away. Running *to*. To freedom and to a life that does not include taking orders from mountebanks like you. If by some chance our paths do cross again, I suggest that you keep well out of my way. It seems that I am no coward after all and I should warn you that I have learned to handle an assegai quite well.'

Covington's eyebrows rose. 'Strong words from a man who usually lets a woman talk for him. Very well, Fonthill, creep away. I am sorry that I shall not have the opportunity of breaking you, but no doubt someone else will. Be off with you.'

'Oh no. Not quite yet. There are several things I want from you.'

'Damn you. You'll get nothing from me.'

'Indeed I will. First of all, I want a month's pay. I need to draw from the battalion's paymaster some cash against my salary banked in Cape Town. Secondly, I need fresh clothes – mufti hunting gear will do. I know that the stores have it. Then I need a Martini-Henry and a service revolver with ammunition, a bedroll and a horse, together with a saddle, bridle, and so on. I have noted these needs down here as an instruction to the

QM,' he threw the paper on to the table, 'and it only requires your signature. I will give you a receipt.'

Covington's eyes narrowed. 'You can go to hell.'

'No, not there. I shall go to Lord Chelmsford. I understand that he is already upset by the fuss you caused by calling this court martial on what turned out to be completely false charges, and he will not be amused to hear of the way in which you interfered with and delayed the delivery of my message back to Colonel Lamb. I shall call the Adjutant to give evidence that you threw my messenger into the guard-room for two days.'

Simon kept his eyes fixed on Covington's. 'If I don't get what I want, I shall relay to the C-in-C the full story of that interference and of your persecution of me. As it is, I doubt if His Lordship, with all of his other troubles at this time, is going to take kindly to the Horse Guards' reaction when they read the account of the court martial in the *Morning Post*. And the court martial, after all, *was* your idea, was it not?' He sighed, histrionically. 'Oh dear. I shall make an awful nuisance of myself . . .'

Slowly, Covington drew the note towards him and scrawled his signature on the bottom. He threw it back across the table. 'Take it and get out of my sight,' he said. 'By the time we next meet I too shall have mastered the ungentlemanly business of assegai fighting, I assure you.'

Simon had just saddled his horse and was lashing on the bedroll when he was approached by the sergeant major who had officiated at the court martial. The warrant officer saluted smartly and said, 'Could I have a word, sir?'

Simon took the man's hand and shook it. 'I'm glad I've seen

you, Sar'nt Major, because I wanted to thank you for being kind to me when I was down. I am grateful to you.'

The warrant officer looked embarrassed. 'Oh, that was nothing, sir. There was plenty who rode away from Ishandwanee who didn't get court-martialled and I just thought it was unfair, because I 'eard you fought like a good soldier at the Drift, if you don't mind me saying so, sir.'

'Well, that's very kind of you. There's no need to call me sir any more, by the way. I have resigned from the army.'

'Oh, that is bad news, sir.'

'Yes, but there it is. Now if you will excuse me, I have to get on the road to the Lower Drift at Tugela. There's a man there I have to thank.'

'Very good, sir. But there is one more thing . . . although it's probably of no use to you.' He fumbled in his jacket and took out a slip of creased paper. 'Ah, here it is. You asked me about that batman of yours, Jenkins I think it was. Do you remember?'

'What?' Simon grabbed the paper. 'What is this?'

'Well,' the sergeant major rubbed his nose dismissively, 'it may be nothing, but I did put the word out, like, and I understand that a Welshman has been brought in by a Boer farmer. He's in that place down the road towards 'Maritzburg called Umsinger or something. He's in a bad way but I gather he will live.' He raised his voice. 'Don't depend on it . . . it may well be someone else.'

But the last words were lost upon Simon, who was already galloping down the dusty track towards Pietermaritzburg.

Chapter 18

Most of the dust on the twenty miles of track that linked
Helpmakaar with Umsinga seemed to have transferred itself to
Simon by the time he rode into the little town. The passage
north of a ragbag assortment of hastily raised reinforcements
from Pietermaritzburg and Durban had deepened the wagon
ruts on the track, and fine weather for five days had let the dust
clouds gather. He had passed nothing that looked like a hospital
and he now seemed to be riding south, out of the town. Simon
wiped his dry lips and accosted a black man, clad in old khaki
overalls, who was squatting by the roadside.

'Where's the hospital here?' he asked.

The man spat. 'Ain't no hospital here, baas.'

'What's that building there, then?' Simon pointed to a long,
low shed, outside which were tethered several horses.

'Storehouse, baas.'

Simon dismounted stiffly and looped his reins over a
hitching rail. Inside, the atmosphere was gloomy, but he realised
he was in a vestibule. Opening a door to the left, he revealed
stacks of mealie bags. The distinctive smell sent a sudden shaft
of fear running through him as he recalled flames reflected
from spearheads, wild black faces, a burning roof and noise –
so much noise. Shaking his head, he opened a door to the right

that led into an open room, more brightly lit by two windows, and containing four beds. Three of them were empty, but the fourth, in the far corner, contained a sleeping figure, half hidden by a sheet pulled to the chin. With his heart in his mouth, Simon tiptoed to the bed. As he neared, he made out, first, spiky black hair sticking out like a broom bottom along the white pillow, and then, mercifully, the shape of that familiar moustache.

Treading softly, Simon stole to the other side of the bed and looked down at Jenkins. He now saw that the hair on his crown had been carefully arranged around a dressing on his scalp, and another bandage seemed to sweep around his shoulder. The face was drawn but Jenkins seemed to be breathing easily and, certainly, was fast asleep. If it wasn't for the dishevelled moustache, he would have resembled a cherub, swathed as he was in white.

Quietly Simon drew up a chair, sat down and began his wait.

He had no idea how long he had slept when he heard the familiar sing-song voice: 'Hello, bach sir. 'Ow long 'ave you been there, then? I thought you was dead. But then I thought I was, too. Perhaps we are, eh?'

The black button eyes were shining merrily, and slowly a hand disentangled itself from under the sheet and extended towards Simon.

Simon enfolded it in both his own and found that he was unable to speak.

'Ah, look you,' said Jenkins, 'we can't be dead. If we was, then I wouldn't be wearing this bandage and my 'ead wouldn't 'urt so.' He stirred to look around. 'On the other 'and, perhaps we're in the other place. No fires, though.' He smiled at Simon. 'So I think we've survived after all.'

Simon smiled back. '352, I am so glad that you made it. I had given you up for dead, I really had.'

Jenkins struggled in his bed and laboriously pushed himself higher on the pillow. As Simon bent to help him, the Welshman put out his good hand in restraint. 'No, no. I can manage and I'm feelin' quite a bit better, really. 'Ad a good sleep, look you. So glad to see you, though. They told me – as best I can remember – that very few 'ad got away from the battle, and I've bin lying 'ere, see, driftin' in and out of a kind of sleep, and thinkin' what a pity . . .' He smiled. 'All right now, though.'

'Who is looking after you?'

'Well, an army doctor first patched me up, see, an' then a nice enough little black woman 'as bin comin' in and out to feed me and change me dressings and that. But I bin sleepin' most of the time, I suppose. Tell me, bach, what 'appened? 'Ow did you get away?'

Simon related his story, omitting any reference to the court martial. He had almost finished when a small native woman appeared, gave a warm smile to Simon and, putting a thin arm under Jenkins's body, lifted him up surprisingly easily and fed him some gruel from a wooden bowl.

'It's just me 'ead and me right 'and, see,' said Jenkins apologetically. 'That spear in me back didn't do too much 'arm, but it knocked me down and it's still difficult to use me 'and, though it's gettin' better every day.' He sucked at the spoon. 'What did the most damage was crackin' me 'ead on a rock as I 'it the ground. I was out for quite a few seconds. Then I was dimly conscious of you standin' over me and fightin' with your rifle and lunger like . . . well, like a Welshman.' He looked across at Simon shyly. 'I was grateful for that, bach sir, so I was. If it 'adn't bin for you, they might 'ave put another spear in me as I lay, or torn me belly out, like.'

'Yes, I'm sorry. I was forced away by the Zulus all around. I tried to stay with you but couldn't. Then I tried to get back but it was impossible. But tell me, what happened to you?'

Jenkins took the bowl from the woman's hand, balanced it on the bedclothes and nodded cheerily to her. 'Thank you very much, missus, I can manage quite well now.' She smiled, stayed to wipe his mouth very quickly with a cloth and then padded away on shoeless feet. 'Very nice little woman. Looks after me well. Right, I'll tell you the story. It won't take long.'

He scraped the bowl with his spoon. 'Well, I was more or less coming to but I could see you 'ad to leave me, so I felt it was better to keep me 'ead down for a minute or two, see. Several of the black chaps just trod on me but they was a bit busy, like, and wasn't botherin' too much about me.

'I must 'ave passed out again at that stage because I came round and found I was lookin' at the biggest army boot you've ever seen in your life, plonked there, see, just by me face. I thought to myself, I know that boot. So cautiously I turned and looks at the other one, just there on the other side of me 'ead. Very carefully, in case it was a Zulu who 'ad captured them boots, I looks up – and I was right! There's old Coley, Colour Sergeant Cole, standin' over me with 'is rifle and bayonet at the ready just like England's Old Glory. 'E's a big man, is old Coley, and he looked a fine sight then. 'E'd lost 'is 'elmet and 'is 'air is quite grey, long and straight, and 'is white teeth were a-flashin'. Seein' me move, 'e looks down and says, "Malingering again, 352 Jenkins? Get up or I'll put you on a charge as sure as God made little apples." So 'e gives me a little kick, like, and, some'ow I struggles to me feet, me 'ead singin' like a lark in a field.'

As though his appetite was revived by the memory, Jenkins took a piece of bread and awkwardly wiped it round the bowl. 'Now, when I'm up, look you,' he resumed, 'I find I'm in a little circle of the lads from the 1st Battalion who were standin' shoulder to shoulder and slowly – with Coley in charge – movin' up the 'ill to that neck place on the top. They'd run out of ammunition but they was presentin' their lungers to the Zulus real proud, I can tell you. Anyway, Coley gives me a rifle an' bayonet from one of the dead chaps and I joins 'em, though I'm still very weak. In fact, if I 'adn't bin rammed into the circle, like, I would probably 'ave fallen down.'

He sniffed at the memory. 'Somehow we clung together, although there was 'ardly enough blokes left to keep a circle goin'. Then, suddenly, a lot of free 'orses – probably from those Natal Mounted fellers, remember? – galloped through the crowd an' broke us all up. Old Coley grabs one by the reins as it goes by – it takes a big man to do that – and I thought, Well now, 'e's off, an' good luck to 'im. But no. 'E 'alf 'elps, 'alf throws me into the saddle, looks me in the eye and says, "Jenkins, I got you into this bloody mess in the first place back there in Birmingham. Now I'm givin' you the chance to get out of it. Off you go!" An' he slaps the 'orse's arse and off we go, 'ell for leather, with me clingin' on like . . . well, no disrespect, sir, but like you.'

Simon smiled. 'What happened to Cole?'

Jenkins looked down his nose and paused for a moment before answering. 'Well,' he said at last, 'I looked back once and caught a quick glimpse of 'im. There he was, standin' as tall as Nelson in Trafalgar Square, presentin' an' lungin', presentin' an' lungin' as though 'e was showin' recruits 'ow to do it. 'E was on 'is own an' completely surrounded. It was as if the Zulus were afraid of 'im.' Jenkins sniffed. 'But 'e couldn't 'ave lasted five minutes like that, with 'is back unprotected, like. Silly bugger. 'E could 'ave got away, see, on the 'orse 'e gave me.'

The two men were silent for a moment. Outside they could hear the rattle of harness and the creak of an axle as a wagon went by. Inside, in the cool of the room, everything was quiet.

'He was a very brave man,' said Simon.

'Aye, he was. You know, bach sir,' Jenkins lowered his bowl to the floor and, with his elbow, pushed himself up higher on the pillow, 'I've bin thinkin' a bit about this bravery business. In particular,' he shot a quick, slightly embarrassed glance at Simon, 'I was thinkin' about you an' all that.'

'Ah yes,' said Simon, looking away. 'Well, you know very well that I'm not brave.'

'That's just the point, see. We're *all* not particularly brave. The bloke who struts about when the spears are flyin' is usually just a show-off, isn't he? But most of us can do our bit when we 'ave to. You did that on that bloody ship – and then in that gully when all you 'ad was a bit of a spear. But you are not and never was a coward, see. Although, perhaps you thought you was goin' to be . . .' He tailed off.

'You mean when I collapsed in the mess?'

Jenkins nodded his head vigorously, glad to have avoided having to spell it out. 'Yes, well, see, I knew what they was sayin' about you at the time . . .'

'That I'd faked the collapse?'

'Yes.'

'Did you think I was faking, back there in the hospital?'

'Course I did. You were, weren't you?'

Simon shook his head. 'No. I have been told recently that it was something to do with concussion that I received before – that and what has been called my high imagination. I think it's known as hysterical fugue, or something like that.'

Jenkins blew out his cheeks. 'Well, I'll be blowed.'

'But look,' said Simon. 'If you thought I was a fake, why did you want to be my servant, and then why stay with me?'

Jenkins wrinkled his nose. 'Well, at first I just wanted to get out of that 'ospital, and as I told you, I didn't fancy just goin' back to servin' in the ranks again and bein' told what to do by every Tom, Dick an' 'Arry. An' you seemed a nice young feller, with respect. The blokes in your platoon said that you was a good officer, though they said you couldn't ride for toffee.'

'Well, they were right about that. Though I'm much better now.'

'Glad to 'ear it. About time. Anyway . . .' Jenkins looked slyly up at Simon, 'I felt that you could do with a bit of lookin' after, until you found your feet, that is. An' then, on that blasted boat, I realised that you'd got good stuff in you, and once we were off that pleasure cruise, I began to enjoy myself.'

The effort of talking and of putting usually unspoken thoughts into words was making perspiration run down Jenkins's face, but he went on, leaning forward. 'That collapsin' business, look you. That was not really physical, see. You can be as physically brave as the next bloke. It's the brain stuff, p'raps, as did for you then – you got frightened about bein' frightened, see, and then you passed out. It's the imagination, see. But you've been there now, with a spear an' rifle an' bayonet, an' you've done it all. You know now that you can 'andle it, see.'

The force of the argument exhausted Jenkins and he fell back on to the pillow, his black hair plastered to his forehead. Simon smiled slowly at him.

'Frightened of being frightened, eh?' he said, his brain trying and failing to drag up once again his emotions on hearing the Adjutant's voice as he announced the regiment's posting abroad. 'Frightened of fear itself. Hmmm.' He leaned forward and took Jenkins's hand again. 'Jenkins, you are not only a splendid sommelier, a horseman nonpareil, a fighter par excellence and the worst boot cleaner in the world – you are also a master philosopher. I shall think about what you have said.'

Jenkins's eyes brightened. 'Very nice of you to say so, sir, although I 'aven't understood 'alf of those words. But now, what's next for us, then?'

Simon shook his head. 'No, first complete your story. How did you ride to this place? It's a bit off the beaten track and most of the refugees from the battle crossed the Buffalo further north and ended up in Helpmakaar, like me.'

'There's not much to tell, really. If I'd been a bit fitter, look you, I would probably 'ave followed the crowd to that Fugitive's Drift place they've been telling me about. An' I'd never 'ave got through there because I was as weak as a ninny and couldn't 'ave defended meself. I was so weak that I just gave the 'orse its 'ead and it must 'ave meandered off the trail and gone further south, or do I mean west? You know I can't find me way around on me own. We wandered off into the bush, and because the Zulus were a bit busy with you lot, we weren't followed. We crossed the river somewhere and that made me pretty exhausted, so I fell off the 'orse on the other side after a bit. A farmer bloke eventually found me and brought me 'ere. I've bin in a bit of a fever but I'm getting better by the hour.'

He touched his head dressing. 'They'll 'ave this off soon and then I can report for duty again. So – what do we do next? I'm still your servant, look you.'

Simon looked sadly round the room and then back at the little Welshman. 'I'm sorry, 352,' he said. 'I think it's the end of the partnership. You see, I have resigned my commission. I'll tell you about it when you're fitter.'

Jenkins's eyebrows rose comically. 'Well I'll be blowed again. But it doesn't matter. I'll come out with you.'

'How can you? How many years' service have you left to do?'

'Another three, I think. But don't worry about that, bach. I'll just desert.'

Simon laughed. 'They'd catch you and shoot you.'

'No. No.' The Welshman levered himself off the pillow again. 'I can't stay in the army without you. I was just beginnin' to enjoy myself. Besides,' his voice took on a plaintive tone, 'who's goin' to look after you?'

Simon looked at his friend for a moment. 'Do you really want to come with me?' he asked.

'Yes please. A gentleman needs a servant. An' besides – without me you'll keep fallin' off your 'orse.'

'Very well. I have money. I will buy you out.'

'I'll pay you back.'

'No you won't. Not on the wages I shall pay you.'

The two men grinned at each other for a moment. Then Jenkins said, 'Right. I'm grateful. Where are you goin' now?'

'I shall ride to the Lower Drift, where we first crossed the Tugela into Zululand. I want to see John Dunn to thank him. And . . .' He mused for a moment. 'He has a new job and it could be that we could be useful to him. Or maybe we will go to India, or even Burma. The Empire is alive with opportunity. But more of that when I get back. Now don't leave this place and go wandering off. Do you think you could be out of here in five days?'

Jenkins nodded. 'Quicker'n that, I reckon.'

'Good. I'll be back for you then.' A sudden thought struck Simon. 'Look,' he said, 'I can't keep calling you 352 if you're not in the army. What's your first name?'

'Oh, don't worry about that. 352 is fine.'

'No. I ought to know.'

'Don't bother yourself about it, bach sir.'

'Don't be stupid. I will need it to get your discharge papers. What is your first name?'

Jenkins looked round the room in despair. He cleared his throat and muttered something inaudible.

'What? I can't hear.'

'Cyril.'

'*Cyril!*'

The Welshman nodded, his eyes averted.

Simon thought for a moment, his face very straight, then said, 'Would you mind if I continued to call you 352?'

Jenkins closed his eyes. 'I would be very grateful, look you, if you would, sir.'

Simon clasped Jenkins's good hand and then walked out of the room. Outside, the sun sat complacently in a blue sky in which white puffball clouds gambolled – a sky that, improbably, reminded him of both Alice and Nandi. A slow column of volunteer cavalry, the riders dressed in an assortment of civilian clothes but all wearing slouch hats and bandoliers, trotted northwards, off to join the war and to avenge Isandlwana. The officer leading the column looked at Simon inquisitively but the ex-subaltern of the 24th Regiment of Foot paid no attention as he mounted his horse and set off to the south. As he left the storehouse hospital, he thought he heard the sound of singing coming from within.

Author's Note

Any author who mixes fact and fiction has a responsibility to inform the reader which is which. The background to *The Horns of the Buffalo* is true enough, or as true as I can make it. The history sketched by Colonel Lamb and the events leading up to the Anglo-Zulu war as told in the book by John Dunn and Nandi did occur as they related them, and I have based Simon and Jenkins's experiences at Isandlwana and Simon's at the mission station on several well-respected accounts of the battles.

The battles themselves, of course, were only the beginning of the war and not the end. King Cetswayo's hope that the white man would retire with his bloody nose beyond the boundaries of Zululand and not invade again proved futile. Sir Bartle Frere was stingingly rebuked by Disraeli's government for overreaching his powers in invading in the first place, but the British Empire, at the zenith of its pomp, could not be seen to allow the defeat of an army in the field to go unrevenged. Chelmsford therefore was sent reinforcements and re-invaded Zululand – this time displaying great caution – and defeated Cetswayo when the Zulus failed to break the British square at Ulundi. The assegai could not overcome the Martini-Henry a second time, not when it was reinforced by cannon and Gatling guns, firing from a secure defensive position.

There were quite a few unharmed fugitives from Isandlwana who took the road *past* Rorke's Drift, not staying to fight with the defenders, and it is possible that one of the fleeing officers was brought to court martial. Virtually all of the records of courts martial from the Zulu War, however, were destroyed when the Public Records Office was hit by a bomb in the Blitz on London, so there is uncertainty on this point. Only one official account of a court martial from that war has survived, and I have based the proceedings of Simon's trial on that record. Incidentally, the officer concerned was, like Simon, shipwrecked on the voyage out to South Africa and was also mentioned in dispatches for his cool thinking on that occasion.

John Dunn and his wife Catherine were real figures, and it is true that he became a Zulu inDuna, had a lavish lifestyle and numerous wives and progeny, and that he was reluctantly forced to become head of intelligence for the Eshowe relief force, although I have brought forward his appointment by a month or two. Simon, Alice, Nandi and Jenkins, of course, are fictitious characters, and the sardonic Covington bears no resemblance to the gallant officer who commanded the 2nd Battalion of the 24ths at the time. Colonel Lamb is another creation, but not Colonel Glyn (who was the chairman of the court martial referred to above), nor Lieutenant Colonel Pulleine and the other senior officers I have mentioned. Lieutenants Chard and Bromhead, of course, have gone down in history as the leaders of the famous defence of Rorke's Drift, although it is less well known that Bromhead was, in fact, very deaf at the time. He, Chard and nine others at the Drift were awarded the Victoria Cross after the battle – the most awarded for any action in British history.

To those who would say that imagination has run riot in allowing a young woman to be accepted, in Victorian times, as a war correspondent for a daily newspaper, I would point to Frances, Viscountess de Peyronnet (born in Suffolk plain Frances Whitfield), who reported the siege of Paris for *The Times* of London. The resourceful Frances used a balloon to float her dispatches over the lines of the besieging Germans in 1871, seven years before Alice arrived at the Cape. Then, in 1881 – only two years after the events recorded in this novel – the grand *Morning Post*, Alice's own paper, commissioned the young and spirited Florence Dixie to travel to the Transvaal to cover the first Anglo-Boer War.

If appetites have been whetted for more information about the Zulu War, then there are many books about this most fascinating and tragic of conflicts, but I would particularly commend the definitive *The Washing of the Spears*, by Donald R. Morris, or any of the many well-researched accounts written by Ian Wright.

Finally, records show a bewildering multiplicity of spellings for Zulu names. For sanity's sake, I have chosen the simplest form.

When the Eagle Hunts

Simon Scarrow

Is the unflinching courage of the Roman army a match for the ruthless barbarity of the British tribes?

In the bitter winter of AD 44 the Roman troops in Britain are impatiently awaiting the arrival of spring so that the campaign to conquer the island can be renewed. But the Britons are growing more cunning in their resistance, and are constantly snapping at the heels of the mighty Roman army.

When the most brutal of the native tribesmen, the Druids of the Dark Moon, capture the shipwrecked wife and children of General Plautius, quick action is called for. Two volunteers from the crack Second Legion must venture deep into hostile territory in a desperate attempt to rescue the prisoners. But will Centurion Macro and his optio, Cato, reach the General's family before they are sacrificed to the Druids' dark gods?

Praise for UNDER THE EAGLE and THE EAGLE'S CONQUEST:

'Thoroughly enjoyable read . . . full of teeth-clenching battles, political machinations, treachery, honour, love and death' Elizabeth Chadwick

'A rip-roaring read' *Mail on Sunday*

0 7472 6631 X

headline

Killigrew and the North-West Passage

Jonathan Lunn

1852: The most famous rescue mission ever attempted.

Joining the search for Sir John Franklin's ill-fated voyage has long been a dream for Lieutenant Kit Killigrew, R.N. However, a captain more interested in personal glory than the safety of his own crew soon turns the voyage into a reality more akin with Kit's wildest nightmares. And just when he thinks it can't get any worse, a creature of almost mythical proportions starts to pick the crew off one by one . . .

Killigrew and the North-West Passage evokes in terrifying detail the true horror of an Arctic winter – the mind-numbing cold and desolate landscapes – and a darkness which seems almost to permeate men's minds. It's Jonathan Lunn's most chilling and exciting novel yet.

Praise for the Killigrew series

'A hero to rival any Horatio Hornblower. Swashbuckling? You bet' *Belfast Telegraph*

'If you revel in the Hornblower and the Sharpe books, grab a copy of Jonathan Lunn's action-packed saga' *Bolton Evening News*

'On a par with Douglas Reeman or Bernard Cornwell' *South Wales Argus*

'A rollicking tale with plenty of punches' *Lancashire Evening Post*

0 7472 6525 9

headline